Kym Lloyd

Kym Lloyd was born and grew up in Swansea. As a schoolchild she won a WHSmith Young Writers Prize and, after gaining a degree in French and working for a publisher in Oxford, chose to concentrate on her writing. While supporting herself in a variety of jobs from cleaning to van driving, she succeeded in getting short stories and poems published in several magazines. She now lives in Hertfordshire with her husband and twin daughters, and is working on her second novel.

Kym Lloyd

Erskine's Box

SCEPTRE

First published in Great Britain in 2003 by Hodder and Stoughton
A division of Hodder Headline

A Sceptre Paperback

1 3 5 7 9 10 8 6 4 2

A CIP catalogue record for this title is
available from the British Library

ISBN 0 340 82430 1

Typeset in Sabon by Palimpsest Book Production Limited,
Polmont, Stirlingshire
Printed and bound in Great Britain by
Mackays of Chatham plc, Chatham, Kent

Hodder and Stoughton
A division of Hodder Headline
338 Euston Road
London NW1 3BH

To my father

One Moment Before

On the outside. A nothing. Forgotten by all but the guillemots. They enclose, watch as if I am one of their kind. I make the call of their young – plee-o, plee-o. Do they hear my aloneness?

Layer by layer, a wall of ice grew between us. Thick and impenetrable. I was frozen out. A mouth mouthing silence behind glass. An image burns until it blinds: the two of them, holding hands, joined as one; they have pushed me right to the edge of the picture, excluded me from all that was mine.

And could be mine again? For a crack appears. Hair-thin but enough. A thought, like a finger, prises, worms a way in.

I hear the pounding of the waves. I see, far below, the rocks like the black jagged teeth of a beast. I see my hand moving out and almost touching the crimson frill, beautifully fragile, like the fluted gill of an underwater creature, the wavy flap of some exotic ocean flora. And I am imagining now a pebble dropping from the cliff top down on to those rocks and the jaw stretching and the tongue licking and the waves curling and snatching it away.

Ah, but not a pebble. A black knot of anger, a tight green emerald inside me.

My hand reaches out. Now the moment begins. Now everything will change.

But wait! There. Did you see it? Quicksilver quick. Slither and twist. Snake in the grass. Someone behind me. Clunk of a shutter. The weighted final eye-blink of fate.

I

A Return – A Worm Turned –
A Case of Return to Sender

Coming down the lane, three years ago, my heart was a cage of fluttering birds as I realised that the last time I had seen the house was through the window of the taxi that had whisked me away to Mr Charles Gethsemane's Mansion House. Though I had no idea then, of course, that it would be another thirty or so years before I again set eyes on Boxwood, or indeed upon Mama. Now here I was. After all these years. Coming home. To be reunited with Mama, with Boxwood. But would Mama want to see me? Surely, in the years that had passed, the tragedy had become but a faint memory and we could recapture those early days of my childhood, when it was just the two of us. But as I turned into the driveway, the vast house set against the backdrop of sea and sky, which had remained in my memory as a grand old sailing ship anchored in the bay, appeared to me now somewhat skewed, and as I approached it saddened me to see how badly the place had worn.

The front door was half open. I set down my case and knocked with the cast-iron paw. Where was Mama? I had hardly imagined she would be poised tippy-toe on the platform, waving a white lace handkerchief, straining for the first sight of my train – but I had hoped she might have been there at the door to greet me. Had she not received my letter informing her of my return, of my intention to forget all that that had gone before – of my desire to begin again?

I knocked once more. I called. Hearing no answer, I went inside.

The place was in chaos – boxes, packing cases, tea chests, stacks of furniture. As if someone had just moved out, or had just moved in. Had Mama moved? Was Boxwood now, as it were, 'under new management'? Might that explain why Mama had not replied to my letter?

Just then, a shuffling of feet along the landing above. I looked up.

Mama. Mama? Could it really be? This bloated creature plodding down the stairs like a sulky child. Surely this was not my Mama? Such dislocating shock! A reverse metamorphosis – the butterfly returned to the grub, to the pale obscene maggot.

'Mama?'

She approached me, hesitant, as if bidden but dragging her feet, the heads of bunnies or kittens (surely not puppy-dogs?) attached to the top of her lime-green slippers nodding with each step, the irises of the plastic eyes rolling maniacally. She was wearing one of those mock-Victorian nightgowns, laced and ludicrously ruffled, grey and grubby. Just above the left breast, like a rose in full bloom, was a large dark red stain. Blood? Red wine? Had Mama taken to drink? She had a polythene bag wrapped around her head like a scarf and secured at her nape with a thick rubber band. Her hair appeared pink – pinkish – not the carroty orange I remembered. Beneath the plastic it resembled raw flesh, as though she had been recently scalped. She stood before me, looked up, the pale doughy face bringing to mind the post-performance faces of the male drag artists with whom I had often been forced to share a dressing room in the early days of my career. Make-up removed, hair netted or greased to the scalp, the faces appeared bereft, the eyes piggy and disappearing into the flesh. But not these eyes, for though almost lost they were, however, emeralds, still Mama's eyes.

'Mama,' I said, 'it's me, Erskine.'

The face contorted, the eyes moving rapidly from side to side as though searching the memory's inventory of names and faces – then suddenly they widened in alarm to reveal raw fear.

'What?' she whispered. 'Who?' Her arm snaked protectively over her belly, cradled it; swollen fingers, like grubs feeding, worried at the white cotton ruffle around her fat neck.

'It's Erskine, Mama,' I said again. Was I really such a stranger? (Of course, my friends, I am by now used to being regarded in a certain way – with suspicion, ridicule and, yes, occasional alarm. I am, after all, an albatross, an oddity, a freak. But this – this was my Mama.) The last time we had seen each other I was but a young boy. But surely, somewhere within my forty-year-old visage there lingered a vestige of my ten-year-old self? Surely she must have seen my pictures in the newspapers? Or was I still the son she turned her back on thirty years ago?

Then, the half-crescent of a smile. 'Erskine? Oh, yes,' she said, 'yes. Oh dear.'

'You knew I was coming home, Mama. You must have got my letter.'

'Letter? Oh, yes, yes,' she said. 'My Erskine, my boy, come home, come home to me. But oh dear, now have I put the flags out?' She chuckled, guiltily cupping a hand over her mouth. 'Your room's all ready and waiting, monsieur,' she said. 'Up the stairs, turn left, lavvy's along the landing. You do remember your old room, now, don't you?' She saw me eyeing a supermarket trolley stacked high with empty milk bottles in a corner of the hallway. 'I keep finding them,' she said, 'down in the village. They keep leaving them outside the front doors.' Then she went off to the kitchen, singing 'Land of Hope and Glory' at the top of her voice, covering her ears with her hands.

I was left reeling. What had I expected? A frailty, stiffness, stoop, dowager's hump, a polite distance perhaps, an initial thin-lipped froideur? But never this . . . this barely recognisable creature I did not want to believe was my Mama. I picked up my case and made my way up the stairs, through the gloom and shadows of the corridor to my old room. I hesitated, steeling myself before opening the door. Finding Mama so changed, my mind now cast itself away from our reunion, the anticipation of our shared future, back to all that had gone before. Would this revisiting of old ground unearth more than I cared to remember? I had decided to shut the lid once and for all on the memories. Yet, as I knew only too well, the past is a persistent creature. And so much suffering had taken place in this room I was about to enter. Enough, perhaps, to lure the young Erskine from the depths, so that I might find him now, poor boy, his face buried in the pillow, his whole body tight and shaking as though experiencing the most intense physical pain. I took a long deep breath and walked in.

Thankfully the bed (made up in gaudy pink flowered linen) was unoccupied. As I set down my bags and surveyed the room, it was as familiar as if I had returned to it after months instead of many years. I recognised a few items of furniture – the tallboy, a china cocker spaniel someone had unaccountably given me for a birthday, the mahogany desk where I had planned my revenge. On the dresser stood a vase of assorted cut flowers (which looked so perfect I had to pinch and thereby damage one of the lush leaves) and, curiously, a cut-glass jar containing balls of cotton wool beside a bottle of make-up removal lotion. On the bedside table I found an alarm clock, a glass of water (a small dead fly floating on the dusty surface) and a musty old book entitled *Manners and Etiquette for All Occasions – How to Be in Company*, all the pages having been removed. Also on the table was a small hand-mirror-and-brush set made of pink plastic, such as might belong to a little girl. I looked in the mirror. Part of a nose and an eye. A weary, deeply disappointed eye.

I felt utterly depressed. Boxwood had decayed, was no more the grand sailing lady but a storm-battered, salt-bitten vessel. An old sea dog sagging under its own weight, its tired visage expressing a heavy-lidded, unsmiling acceptance, a quiet renunciation. The garden was lost, running wild now with nettles, brambles and patches of mushrooms sprouting amok like warts. (It gratified me to see that the summer house must have been demolished, for that would have been the ugliest wart of all.) The box hedge that had once grown regimentally around the walls of the house (thanks to the vicious secateurs of Treacher – or was it Traytor? – the former gardener) now reached halfway up the ground-floor windows. Boxwood was a neglected beast.

And Mama. Look what the years had done to Mama. But it was not simply a matter of the ravages of time upon what I perceived. For the one who perceives is also altered by time. Ah, yes. Things had changed. And I had returned a different Erskine. Had I, then, done the right thing in coming back home? It had hardly been a spur-of-the-moment decision. It had been simmering in my mind for some long time, ever since I experienced that ultimate betrayal, the terrifying sense of negation, of annihilation, which left me reeling. But I was reeling yet again. Was Mama pretending not to know me? Was she still possessed by the demon that had driven her to send me away all those years ago? Just me and Mama, Mama loving me. Nothing and no-one to come between us. Would I ever find what I was seeking?

I opened the window. Fresh air. And there, the sea. My sea. True, dependable, always returning. I closed my eyes, breathed in deeply. Without the sea, how very different things would have been. Indeed, how impossible. I splashed cold water over my face, brushed my hair with the little pink brush and made my way downstairs.

More acclimatised, I began to take in the details of my surroundings. The house had always been dark, cluttered with large, unnecessary pieces of furniture, a cold, unfriendly, labyrinthine place. Never a show house. Fixtures, fittings, soft furnishing – all a mishmash. Nothing had ever matched. But as I descended the long, grand central staircase, I saw that Boxwood was in complete disorder. There was even more furniture than I remembered. Or had it all been arranged, as it appeared, outside the rooms? But if so, to what purpose? Piles of magazines and yellowed newspapers lined the walls. There were stacks of cardboard boxes, carrier bags and black bin liners, stuffed full, like pods. (These last making me think of the mermaid's purses Mama and I used to find in the line of weed and driftwood and shells that separated the wet sand from the dry.)

Then Mama appeared at the bottom of the stairs. Dear heavens! It seemed she had squeezed her fat self into a cream-coloured bathing costume that was preposterously too small and – my lordy! – entirely see-through. Her breasts were balloons, like giant pupae she was gestating, or the soft cylindrical sea squirt *Ciona intestinalis*, the protruding thick, stubby nipples and the patterned dark of the aureoles (like the test of a sea urchin) suggesting complexity beneath the apparent surface simplicity. Her shoulders were hunched and her head lowered. Her hands were clasped in front of her pubic area, as if to cover her modesty, but I could still discern the mound, the thatch of red hairs (a few stragglers escaping from the sides). Despite the pubic hair, there was a suggestion of fleshy, pouchy pre-pubescence, the cream gusset disappearing into, and thus emphasising, the crack. (I would here like to make it known that I have never made a habit of studying young bodies to any measurable degree and certainly not with lecherous intent. Not my bent at all.)

'I'm going swimming,' Mama said. She smiled hopefully. 'Would you like to come swimming, Erskine? But you must have taken my swim cap. I've looked all over but I cannot find it anywhere. You must have taken it. Oh, swimming! I've been longing for someone to take me swimming.'

Hence the polythene bag. A makeshift hat, of course. A smidgen of sense, then, at least. A sign of hope. Then a brainwave – we shall have a picnic! A picnic, indeed, just like we used to. Sausage sandwiches, hard-boiled eggs – with salt in foil twists, mini-balls of cheese, shiny black olives, sea-green grapes, bananas and fresh figs. I salivated at the thought. Not simply of the food, but the delicious scenes from childhood now flooding my mind. Just me and Mama. Just the two of us. As it used to be. Swimming, climbing the cliffs, picnics on the beach, fishing in the rock pools with home-made nets (Mama's old stockings and garden canes). And what treasure we found! Anemones like bubbles of dark blood on the greeny-black skin of the rocks. The tiny transparent scuttling pincered creatures. And then, our outings to the town for delicious lunches – fresh fish in creamy sauces, wild mushroom omelettes, those delectable puddings: pyramids of chocolate profiteroles, spotted dick. After lunch, there'd be shopping – books and toys for me, clothes for Mama. Ah, I remember Mama, so beautiful, svelte and perfect as a mannequin, twirling before the mirror, choosing her dresses. Oh, Mama!

Mama looked momentarily bewildered, then—

'Oh, yes, Erskine, a picnic, yippee-yay!' she cried, clapping her hands with such vigour the pupae threatened to bounce free.

Just then a gust of wind slammed shut the front door. A box, the last atop a six-foot-high higgledy tower, fell forward.

Magazines began to slide out and slip to the floor in a continu-
ous stream. A cuckoo called from one of the downstairs rooms
as water pipes belched and gurgled. Boxwood had stirred, was
shifting its old bones, stretching its limbs, peering through a
half-shut eye to spy Erskine, back with his Mama. As we once
were. But all as it used to be?

Mama went to look for towels while I foraged for provisions. Clearly, in terms of nourishment at least, Mama had
been taking care of herself. I located the hamper, packed a
sizeable feast, and the two of us, hand in hand, set off for
the beach, along those familiar lanes that led to the cliff path.
As we got nearer to the path, to the point where a right turn
took you down to the beach, a left to the main coast path, I
experienced momentary fear, a chilly wave freezing me head
to toe. I closed my eyes, mentally reaching for a ruler and
a thick black pen. I would write 'END', 'FINITO'. Yes, the
past was over.

Once down on the sands, after we had eaten, I sat at
the foot of the dunes couched in the marram, writing my
journal, while Mama had her swim. (Oh yes, after her dip,
she removed the bag and set free that wonderful cloud of red
hair I held in memory. Of course, it was the polythene bag
that was pink!) I was not tempted into the water. For one
thing, freezing water shrivels the equipment – think brass
monkeys! And what equipment I have is already shrivelled
enough. But *plaisanteries* (and realities) aside, intense cold
sets up such a fearful throbbing in the warps and convolutions
of the flesh about my nether regions. And for another, I am
exceedingly sensitive about my physique. And I started to
wonder, then, precisely how much Mama remembered (or
did not remember), knew (or did not know), about me.
In the few hours I had been back at Boxwood, she had
made not one mention of the tragedy that had led to our
separation. Neither did she enquire about what I had done

with my life in the thirty years we had been apart. Mama appeared to be living in a bubble, a bubble that I now was forced to inhabit.

Lying in bed that first night back at Boxwood, I listened to the sea, focusing on the rhythmical breaking of the waves upon the rocks, trying to brush away the misgivings creeping up on me again. The way Mama had looked at me as we ate our evening meal – now with such innocence, such absence, now with absolute knowing. I should never have come home. How could I possibly have imagined things could ever be as they once were? But I should at least give us a chance. Give us time to get over the shock of meeting again, to become reacquainted, to get used to each other's eccentricities.

In the days that followed, I came to the opinion that the most likely root of her apparent tenuous hold on reality was simply lack of purpose, of routine. (And the state of the house was enough to send anyone gaga.) Perhaps all that was required was a little organisation. I decided we should fill our days with activities – shopping trips, visits to the cinema, restaurants, walks on the cliff path, picnics on the beach, swimming when the weather permitted – all the things we had once loved and shared, that I longed for us to share again. Indeed, it seemed the very tonic Mama needed. She took to reading the local paper over breakfast, enjoyed chatting to me about village events. She smartened herself up a bit, liked me to help wash and set her hair. (Until she complained I had the hands of a lumberjack and insisted I book her into the most pricey salon in the town.) Even her interest in the garden was rekindled a little.

But as the weeks went on, I grew increasingly disconcerted by her behaviour. I sometimes wondered whether she might be playing a spiteful game. For her mood could change within minutes. (I was even considering the possibility of schizophrenia.) I shape-changed before her very eyes. Some days I was her little boy again, in short trousers and home-knit pullover (peep-toe sandals for the beach, velvet dicky bow for going to town). She'd take my hand and lead me out into the garden to look at the flowers. One morning, she even brought to my room a box of old toy motor cars – a fleet of battered vehicles, paint peeling and tyres missing, which I was certain had not been mine – another containing naked plastic dolls, like a mini mass grave, and a bundle of children's clothes (for both boys and girls). She didn't suppose anything would fit now, she said, but I might give one or two of the jerseys a try.

At times, Mama appeared confused, distressed, spending hours, sometimes all night, searching the house, disappearing like a burrowing creature into the mounds of boxes and bags and clutter. She would not tell me, at first, what she was looking for. A surprise not altogether unpleasant to discover she had kept scrapbooks of cuttings from newspapers and magazines, reviews, details of radio broadcasts, et cetera. There was a whole box of memorabilia. It did not immediately register, while I was flicking through the books one day, that in order to have obtained concert programmes and tickets, she must have attended my performances. Had Mama really been there? It disturbed me to think of her – a small goldfish within the dark seas of the audience. And I had never known! But whenever I asked her about the cuttings, about seeing me perform on stage, she'd look at me with such bewilderment, I wondered whether I was not myself turning doolally.

I was beginning to realise that life at Boxwood with Mama could never be 'as it used to be'. And the more I shied from the truth, the more I was forced to admit that Mama, dear Mama, was rapidly losing her marbles. She became increasingly suspicious of me – frequently running from me, shouting at me to go away, not to hurt her, a look of terror on her face as if I were about to do her some harm. And when I once suggested we might have a clear-out, tidy up the place, maybe paint a room or two, she started weeping like a child, sat crouched in a corner, rocking back and forth, arms wrapped round herself tightly. Sometimes, mid-sentence, she would peer at me, frowning.

'Why? Why have you come back? What do you want?'

And in her eyes, what did I see? A flaw in those emeralds. The insect in the resin. Fear. And something else – accusation. The way she used to look at me in the days that followed the tragedy. Was Mama really so afraid of me? Still? After all these years? I was beginning to fear that my return to Boxwood had opened up a can of worms. And something else I had not bargained for. Mama was not entirely on her own. There was Marcia, for one, who was to return some months after my arrival to the cottage where she lived when I was a boy. Then Mr Pergolesi, the bus driver, who obviously had a soft spot for Mama. And the social services had started poking their noses in, convinced I was not able to look after my own mother. It was a growing concern – how to ensure that Mama would keep her lips sealed on the past. Not that she ever knew the full story, of course. But then who would listen to the blabbing of a madwoman? I realised that the state of her mind – the lapses, the gaping holes, its unreliability – could be played to my advantage. If my return had opened the can, it was up to me to ensure the worms stayed inside. I would have to keep a short rein on Mama. Keep her safely in the present, from straying into the dangerous waters of the past. I planned, organised, ensured our days were full. I took care, however, that we kept to the more remote parts of the beach and cliff path, that we ventured farther afield rather than leaving ourselves at the mercy of the village, alive with ears a-pricked. For almost two years this was the pattern of our life – far from the idyll I had imagined, but we managed.

And then, my friends, I received your letter. Your letter, the catalyst. Omen and portent. By the way, should I call you two my friends? For you were to betray me too.

Here, in my workroom, recounting the story I did not want you two to know. How different it might have been. What tragedies might we have been spared.

Oh, my friends, my sleuths, if only you had not found me, if only you had not found the journal, if only you had not come searching so determinedly for your truth.

2

Visits – Visitations – Voices from the Past – Dicky Lids

Such a dislocating jolt coming into my workroom this morning to find the two of you, white winged, white robed, haloed, hovering above your boxes like angels, like revenants. Your eyes were pleading, but there was a disconcerting immovability about you, an intention in the tight set of your mouths, in your palms open before you, neither in offering, nor expectation, but in certainty of receipt. It seems you will not rest, my friends, not until you have had your truth.

The other night, after our last meal together, I heard you whisper, 'Why? Why?', as I closed the door and turned the key. Oh! Such a clean, golden, satisfyingly final click. But you must have realised I had no choice. Truth or lies, whichever I told you, I was trapped. Imagine, this hulking albatross that I am, beating my wings against the bars of a cage. Not the grand finale I had in mind. But how to convince you none of it was my fault? My voice still rings with the sweet purity of a child. With innocence. And it is innocence I maintain. Or is it the darkness in my soul you will hear, the sorry song of a man who could not become, could not be, all he should have been – the dirge of a hapless soul from whom everything was taken?

Imagine, can you, the terrible lie of the half-life, knowing you are not and can never be who you know you should have been. That limbo state when yearning adjusts to mourning and loss tucks itself into every crack and crevice of your being. Like twins parted at birth, perhaps, forever seeking completion, one edge forever raw, eternally bleeding. Or when a loved one dies and the body is never found. I think maybe you, my friends, had some inkling of what it was like. And there lies perhaps our common ground, the reason we were brought together. For we were, all three of us, adrift, searching for connections and answers, for completion. Although, as you will discover, the answers are not always those we hope to find.

But let us go back to almost a year ago, to that fateful day when your letter arrived. I was here in my workroom when Mama passed it under the door, heeding my strict instructions never to disturb me when I was with my wood. Though her unreliable mental state meant that I could depend only on lock and key for guaranteed privacy. Like my cliff top, my workroom is a sanctuary. I do not welcome interruptions. The work I do in here demands absolute concentration. And respect. It is a labour of devotion. A passion. More. I am compelled. You will understand, it is difficult to talk about the precise nature of my work, about the end result. For you *know*. I have been revealed. You have removed the monster mask of my face and are looking at a soul that writhes, like a salted slug, in shame. Forgive me, it is hard. The wood, then. Yes.

Did I ever mention that I first came to appreciate what was at that time the pure pleasure of working with wood during those years at the Mansion House, while serving my minor apprenticeship under the expert eye of Joe, the handyman? Which partly compensated for the loneliness I suffered having been separated from Mama. How I loved those happy hours in Joe's shed, ankle deep in dust and shavings, sawing and planing, savouring the fragrances of carpentry just as much as those of Mrs Bainlait's cooking. Curious, given my whetted appetite, that another thirty or so years would pass before I would engage once more in the craft. And with an altogether different level of commitment. I might mention that it took

me a while to resummon the technique. In view of my
natural gaucherie, tool dexterity was not easy to master. It
is a deceptively complicated orchestration of one's physical
self. For example, when carving, the balance of the body
is paramount. One must adopt a stance that will maintain
balance when pressure is put on the tool. The right arm, the
wrist and the hand – this is the power flow, this is how you
make the tool do what is intended. (I may mention that I
work mainly with hand tools. I have a number of power
tools and machines – namely, a table saw, thicknesser, router,
circular saw and, the pièce de résistance, my combination
machine. But nothing can beat the pleasure of working in a
quiet dust-free workroom, creating silky shavings, controlling
joints with razor-sharp hand tools.) And the wood. Ah—

Of course, I will work only with the product of managed
forests. I abhor the sight of deserts of razed woodland. It is,
I feel, almost an emasculation. No trees are the same, even
within the same species – those woods, say, reminiscent of
shimmering sun on foreign waters, the smooth sun-gilded sea
of *Eucalyptus delegatensis*, of Persian boxwood, red alder,
the early-evening picture-postcard seas of mahogany, emeri,
the twilight seas of rosewood, Indian laurel, meranti, the
sunset of Douglas fir. Ah. Then the ridged desert sands of
ash, plane, western hemlock, the animal markings of zebrano,
European elm, goncalo alves and tigerwood, wenge, bastard
mahogany. Indeed, the variations of colour, pattern, texture
are infinite. And the wood is a capricious creature, never
what it first seems; witness the trickery of knots that appear
from nowhere as you smooth with the plane, or those that
are superficial, fading and disappearing when you imagine
they go deep. The finished piece, I believe, is inherent in
the wood, just as Michelangelo believed of his marble. You
take the wood, hold it, receive, let it speak to you. And
how my wood spoke to me. It beguiled, seduced. I became

slave to its master. Though it was to become both passion and curse.

A matter of synchronicity. Two events: the discovery of a block of fine oak – English, I believe – in one of the upstairs loos, of all places; and later that day, the sight of a discounted toolbox in the window of Farquhar's the ironmongers. A case of one plus one equals a whole lot more than at first appears. Having purchased the tools, I set about making what I had initially intended to be a set of fruit – apples, oranges, a banana or two – upon completion of which I had in mind to craft, with the aid of my turning machine, a large bowl for the purpose of displaying the fruit. I had even drawn a few designs. But the wood, it seemed, had a will of its own. Or was it the wood? Was there not some desire, some compulsion, within me? My own tricking knot. But not the kind that could be erased, or untied.

Oh, my bird, you should not have trespassed. It was a violation. When I realised you had found your way into my private collection, knowing as you did the room was strictly out of bounds, it was as though your eyes had cut through to my very core. You must know that I could no more stop my hands from creating what you saw in that room than pluck the sun from the sky. And so I began the boxes. To contain that which I could not contain within myself. And that is as far as I am prepared to go for the moment. Already, almost too far. I can hardly breathe. I quiver like a frightened pup. Shame is a barrier to honesty, to confession.

But back to the matter of your letter. I recall, now, a similar attempt to invade my life. Some years ago, as I was approaching the peak of my career. A so-called 'acquaintance' of Leodora. Yet another of those aphids from that collection of crawlers hungry for a bite of second-hand fame. What was it all about? Some arts documentary, I think – *Freaks of the Century*, or some such dross. I declined, of course. Allow them to pick over living bones and who knows what they might feast on.

But your letter. Yes. Most disturbing. And such a brief communication, though it took a while to decipher. A practically illegible hand, may I say – tight-knotted chains, minute. I imagined the pressed-white fingers tight to the pen, the hunched bony shoulders, nose to the paper. A wonder it got here. How did it get here? And how did they know where to find me? Some list of qualifications, wasn't it? Something about research.

'Your cooperation in writing your biography . . .'

Biography! Even now, a hot heavy somersaulting in my nether regions. Then, something, something—

Working title: DEFIER OF DEFINITION: WHO IS (or was it 'was'?) THE GREAT CERCATORE?

Can you imagine how I felt? Hearing the key working the rusted lock, waiting for the click, the shunt and creak as the iron bars slid open? Fear. Oh, yes sirree.

I decided to reply immediately but for the life of me could not make out the signature. Turnham? Turnman? Turnman Franklin? Whatever. Whoever. I was incensed. I wrote:

Dear Mr F
Frankly, no.
NO cooperation.
NO biography.

Then, ERSKINE FLESCHING in black capitals, underlined several times. The satisfaction of expressing such unequivocal refusal, however, was short lived. I could not read the return address. I tore up both letters. No cooperation. No biography. Such naive logic, I realised, when it dawned that if this Franklin fellow should decide to write a book about me, who was I to stop him? And what if he decided to go ahead without my consent, take umbrage even, come up with a concocted warts-and-all story of my life? Is an unauthorised version really less credible? I found myself veering towards the idea that it might be more prudent to go along with such a venture. At least present the more palatable facts of my life. But no! I would not have strangers prying into my past. It was all I could do to keep them at bay in the present. (I would not let them take Mama from me. Not even if they tried to pull her from me limb by limb.)

The letter was an omen, and the day did not improve. Indeed, from then on I felt like a spider caught out at the edge of the plug hole by the running bath tap, helpless against the maelstrom. Up until then I had sat my hefty bulk firmly upon the lid and had managed to keep the hound under control. But the beast was rattling its chains, gnawing at the links. And so I came in here, trying not to dwell on the implications of your letter by focusing on the ebony. A simple design. Two halves of a spectacle case, the lid supposedly fitting snug without hinges or screws. But at forty centimetres by twenty-five by twenty, a handful of a box, indeed, a chunky chappy. I confess here to having got a little carried away with the dimensions of the artefact it was to contain. 'Big as a black man's ding-dong' was a phrase overheard while waiting for Mama in the hairdresser's once, and as I recall from my Soho days, the coloured gentleman's pendulum (yes, I will call it such) is superior in all ways. Fully extended, it is breathtakingly enviable. The lady in curlers was spot on. The completed artefact was vulgarly huge; indeed, appeared to have enlarged each time I entered the private collection room. The thing had a life of its own, despite my efforts to hide it; would be found centre stage, mid-shelf, to greet me. It possessed, dare I say, a spirit, a power. I began to fear it. I had waited an eternity for Hackthrew's, the wood supplier's, to get hold of the exact ebony for the container.

It eventually turned up a shade lighter than the monster it was to contain. My attempts to stain it had made it too dark. And now the lid was refusing to sit straight. I had an urge to dash it to the floor and smash it to matchsticks with my size fourteens but Hackthrew had warned me his source had dried up and he couldn't bank on getting more ebony elsewhere.

My mood was not helped by the thuds and crashes of Mama rooting about upstairs. Like some malcontent thunder god up there – 'Thor fancies a rearrangement of the three-piece!' Boxwood growled, grunted, like an old dog forced to shift from its bed. Couldn't she let the beast rest? What the devil did she do up there anyway? Looking for things, she said. But what things? Heaven help anyone who can find any damn 'thing' amongst all that junk. What did a rummage through the entrails fetch up for you, my friends, my sleuths? The bugger's banana. Zilch. Ah, but one thing. One small though deadly significant treasure. I speak of the journal, of course. *My* journal. 'THEY PURSUED HIM RELENTLESSLY' might be an apt epitaph on your stones. And fittingly describes the tone of the aforementioned doom-laden day. The ebony and I were coming to blows. I decided to break for coffee and was on my way to the kitchen (anticipating the aroma of a special import of Hawaiian bean) when I heard the car. I looked through the window and I froze.

There, the beast, shiny black, all stealth, creeping down the drive, like a hearse all set to take Mama away. And that face again, behind the steering wheel, the jaw jutting with poisonous intent, lips pressed white, eyes narrowed. The face that had pursued and haunted me for almost the entire two years I had been back with Mama – a reflection in a shop window, in the mirror of the village café, there across the street, in the alleyway, amidst the crowd, peering round a corner, another corner, across other streets, a face that flew

up from the shadows, from the depths. The bat. The hawk.
The owl that eyes and spies and flexes its claws then swoops.
The accusatory, vengeful, inescapable face of Nemesis.

I tiptoed to the recess under the stairs. The doorbell rang.
Again. And again. Then a sharp rap of the iron paw. I prayed
Mama wouldn't hear for she would surely let them in. And
that would be the end. In the red frosted glass beside the
door a shape, a suggestion of eyes and a nose. A tap on the
window. Then they went away. But no sound of the car. Had
they gone round to the back of the house? Was the kitchen
door locked? I waited.

And it was then that the other face floated up from the
depths, an unwelcome ghost. It hovered, the eyeballs rolled
white, the mouth, a black O, emitting a sound – nay a note
– so piercingly high it was not heard so much as felt. The
hands were closed, palms together, as if in prayer. A ghoulish
chorister. And the lips were stretching, stretching, and the face
coming nearer, the O cavernous. The hands had changed to
wings, birds' wings, fluttering apart. Then the eyes returned,
slipped back into place with the mechanical click of a doll's
eyes, and they narrowed to slits, the nostrils a-twitch, sifting
the air for the quick red traces of the hunted. Frankie Deuce.
Got the smell of me. Yes sirree. I have not yet told you about
Frankie Deuce, of course.

We had once spent an entire day engaged in a darkly comic
dance *à deux*. Like some furtive bird courtship ritual through
the town, continuing for hours, until it grew dark and cold
and we ended up in a bar, pretending not to watch each
other, locked in stalemate, refusing to move until they rang
the closing bell. We left by different doors, tight faced, like
boxers seething to win next time round. The challenge came
sooner than expected. The next day, on my way to the park,
my sinister opponent stepped out from an alleyway.

'I'm looking for Erskine Flesching.'

'You and me both,' I said, 'you and me both.'

Then the familiar reaction – the pause, body inching back, eyebrows raised, neck muscles engaged. A moment's surprise clutched in the throat, swallowed. I opened my mouth, and a child climbed out.

'I believe you are – were – acquainted with a Miss Ableyart? A Miss Leodora Ableyart.'

A saving bell! Footsteps crunching a retreat down the drive pulled me from the past. The hearse rolled away. I came out from my hiding place to find a note slipped under the front door:

Mr Flesching, I must meet with you urgently about your mother. She was seen yesterday wandering the lanes in her nightgown. Not the first time, Mr Flesching, as you are well aware. Your refusal to discuss the matter may force me to inform my superiors. Yours, in haste and urgency . . . (another illegible signature)

Damn the woman. And her superiors. No. No. I would not be lured. I would not have Mama taken from me again. Not by anyone. I could hear her upstairs, singing 'Three Blind Mice', over and over, in that thin, grating little girl's voice she sometimes slipped into which set my nerves on edge. She called down from the landing, wanting to know who was at the door. It was no one, I told her, she must have been imagining things. Good, she said, because she still couldn't find her dress and she needed it for the garden party.

What garden party? Was it me? Was I mad? Was she playing a game? The act was so convincing she could have you believe . . . There was, of course, no garden party.

I made lunch. A reluctantly prepared cheese on toast. As you know, I always took such pains with our meals, but I had no appetite. (The troubling events of that morning had formed a dark cloud in my mind. And something else, equally dark yet more disturbing, crawling up through me as I stood in the shadows under the stairs. I moved out into the pinkish warm of the light coming through the red porch windows, realising I was all hunched up, that I had wrapped my arms tight around me, that my throat was aching with trying to hold in the sobbing that had started in my chest, like the sobbing of a child who knows they have been forgotten but who does not want to be found.)

Mama was looking down at her plate, anxiously. 'Is there a war on?' she said. She had on that grubby tent of a nightgown again. (I had bought her several new nighties, and an extremely expensive lilac candlewick dressing gown which you appear to have appropriated after Mama left us, my bird.) She had wound clingfilm round and round her head. She looked ready for surgery, and vaguely repellent. (I had seen something like her once, in a horror film.) 'I can't find my dress for the party! Where's my dress?' I could not bear much more of it. After lunch I made her coffee, adding a large enough measure of Scotch to keep her quiet for an hour or two. She was in one of the back rooms, looking through her magazines. I waited until she'd finished her drink and had nodded off, then I went to the cliff top.

Given all that has happened, my cliff top is the last place you might think I would choose to go looking for peace to settle my thoughts. Yet I have been drawn to the cliffs ever since that day I found out that Mama was no longer mine, when the thick, safe line around me was suddenly erased, leaving me edgeless, an uncontained self without shape or definition. There, on the cliffs, the sky above me, the sea below, the solid rock against my back, only there could I feel some degree of containment, of definition. And with the guillemots for company, of course, I was not alone. It was there that I escaped from the threat of oblivion. I'd stay out all day, until dark sometimes, when the birds would cluster on the ledges to sleep, still as stones. Sometimes the sea whispered to me, other times it raged – *you cannot be forgotten, Erskine! You must not let them forget you!* And there were moments when the sea was still, breath held, complicit, silent as the grave – my ally. Oh, the sea is no avenger, my friends. No matter what it may witness, it forgives, returns, faithful as . . . as a trusty old hound, I might have said. But as you are aware, no hounds will settle beside Erskine. Not like the birds. My birds. It is their sense of community I love, and that musical, plaintive 'plee-o' of their young, never ignored. A fact which both delights and distresses is that the mother birds learn to recognise the call of their young before they have hatched. So they have identity, then, before they are even born.

Ah, fortunate, fortunate creatures. They make their nests close together. Safety in numbers, of course. Guillemots can have no secrets. I have always felt drawn to these creatures. Although I am no ornithologist. It is the movement I love, the music. I feel an affinity. It is the look of them, perhaps, the full round body, the small head, the spindly legs, that smooth, smooth underside, that plaintive 'plee-o, plee-o' call. I recall how they came down to her that day, like miniature angels, their wings thick feathered, luxuriously layered, Victorian archangels, *figlioli angiolini*, keeping vigil.

Yes, a troubled Erskine on the cliffs that day, my friends. That health visitor snooping around. What did they expect me to do? Keep Mama prisoner? And what if they should find her wandering in her nightdress again? I could picture the scene – the ambulance, the men in white coats, Mama kicking and screaming hysterically as they buckled the straitjacket. Or worse, a meek and silent Mama, taking the outstretched hand, her head bent in supplication. The little girl lured from her hiding place. No. They could not. I would not let them take her from me.

And then, your letter. Like a cold, curling tentacle.

Up on the cliff top, I closed my eyes and breathed in the

tang of the sea. My sea. Purifying, washing the mind clean. Tabula rasa. Foetal dreams. The note, yet unsung, lodged in the heart, in the throat, on the cusp of silence and voice. Then I heard a cry – a scream! Not a bird. Blade-sharp, slicing the air. I opened my eyes, looked down. There, on the rocks, as if the rock was bleeding. Fresh blood red. And the waves were coming over, fingers flexing, curling. But they couldn't take hold of the red, could not wash away the red. Another cry. Behind me this time. I turned. No one there. When I looked down at the rocks again, the red had vanished. Just the black rocks. My mind was playing tricks, I told myself.

The chilly breeze turned my attention to Mama. She would be awake by now. Time to go home. On the way back I planned a home-made pasta for dinner – Meatballs *à la* Flesching, with my speciality basil and tomato sauce, to make up for the uninspired lunch. And then some work on the ebony before writing my journal entry for the day – certainly, one of my more colourful accounts. Had I locked the door? I could not remember. I really ought not to have left Mama on her own, not with Dick Tracy on my case.

Coming down the lane towards the back entrance to Boxwood, I could see her in the garden – Mama, dancing round the willow tree, weaving in and out of the branches as if it were a maypole. And what in heaven's name had she got on? As I approached, I realised it was a dress I vaguely remembered from years ago – black velvet, obscenely tight now, which pushed up her large breasts so they spilled from the bodice. Melons, indeed, all set to tumble from the grocer's shelf. Grapefruit in a string bag. And she was all done up like the dog's banquet! Red hair lacquered high, a purple velvet bow, and lipstick, a fierce crimson gash, like lips drawn by a child.

Mama. Oh, Mama.

She waved. Then she called out.

'Ursula. Ur-su-la. Is that you?'

Ursula? Ursula? What did she mean, Ursula? Why now? A hobgoblin crawled from her mouth, jumped to the ground, scuttled towards me, black bead eyes, teeth like needles, the silvery glint of a blade poking from its crimson cloak. Shut my eyes. Oh – like a knife in me. Twisting, twisting. Ur-su-la. After all this time, why now?

She was singing. The little girl's voice – *chopped off their tails with a carving knife* . . . Oh, stop, stop it, Mama. But it wasn't Mama singing any more, because when I opened my eyes the clown mouth, the crimson gash, was fixed in a smile, and the voice was filling, clarifying, an echo returning to its source. And I knew then to whom it belonged.

I walked towards her. I smiled, waved back.

'Erskine, Mama. It's me, Erskine.'

'Erskine?' she said, as if it were an unacquired taste. 'Who's Erskine when he's at home?' Then she looked me up and down. 'And who, child,' she said, 'who may I ask are you?'

Who? Indeed. For almost the whole of my life I have been haunted by the question: Who is the real Erskine Flesching? Will the real Erskine Flesching please stand up?

Those first five years, I was anchored, rooted. Erskine Flesching intact, whole. And inside me, life, like a ball of thread, tight and neat, beginning to unwind, a story unravelling day by day. Erskine and Mama. Blissful and golden. Until, one day – slish-slash! Out comes a carving knife, cuts through the thread. And there goes Erskine, falling, falling. Stone into the ocean. Feather to the wind. Lost and forgotten.

Here, now, my face in the surface of the wood appears almost that of a stranger. Like a face you think you should know yet cannot, for the life of you, put a name to, or situate in memory. As I polish this wood (I chose oak, by the way, for these final boxes; in my opinion the king of woods – such a beautiful grain and richness after polishing), as I polish, the features become more defined, the image sharpens. Yet I become less clear. I am as thin as a reflection, as empty and unknowable. I am still left searching.

Ah, Erskine, it will not do to dwell.

—though dwell you will, Erskine. She stole your keys and got into your private collection, didn't she? What an excoriation that was! Erskine F. revealed in all his glory. Did you feel the shiver in your heart and lungs and liver? Yet you had often, admit it, imagined your Ulva in there fondling your messieurs. You'd hold one of the pieces in your hands, close your eyes and rub your fingers over the smooth and shiny wood, and imagine it entering her and gently, slowly, pushing it right up inside, right to the hilt, to those deliciously neat ellipsoids. All your guilt and shame were locked up in that room, Erskine. But you could not contain them for ever, and neither could you contain the truth. You must have known she would have found it in the end. Yet still you could not confess. But you must get a move on, Erskine. You have work to do and Marcia is on the prowl. Yesterday, remember, on your way home from the village. Did you really think she had not spotted you hiding from her in the bushes as she drove past? You must expect a a visit from her any day now. She will want to know how Mama is. And she will surely enquire after Ulva. Them two gals bein' so close 'n' all. But Ulva. Your Ulva. She was not really your Ulva at all. Was not the bird you thought you knew. Face it, Erskine, the past. Face it like a man! Tell them, hon, tell them how it *reely-reely* was. Now where are you? Yes, lady and gentleman, out in the garden with Mama. The scene where the mad old tart confronts the bemused stranger, the confused child. Erskine has a knife twisting in his soul. And Mama has memories like hooks. Shadows, Erskine, they inch, edge, darken. Now the past comes a-snakin', a-slimin' in—

3

In Which Erskine is Disturbed by a New Bird, an Ill Wind, an Old Name – And 'Oh, Those Halcyon Days'

Forgive my digression, but all that talk about the cliffs yesterday reminded me I have been so busy in here with these last boxes (a much larger project, in all senses, than I have been used to) I have not visited my sanctuary for over a week. So I have just spent a couple of hours there, on my cliff top, looking at the sea, with my birds. There is one guillemot in particular, a cheeky little fellow, with a curious tear-shaped white marking beneath the right eye, giving him a pierrot look. He seems intent on keeping this eye on me and moves in closer and closer in a curious sideways hopping motion but remaining a couple of feet or so away. I believe I have even spotted him in one of the trees just behind Boxwood. Anyway, I was coming back from my cliff top, along the lanes, past a row of cottages, when I heard the most beautiful piano-playing coming from an open window. I could not tell if it was a recording. It sounded so clear, pure. And I could not put a name to it but I knew it was music I had heard before. Within minutes, I was transported back to the Mansion House, to the drawing room where Sylvia was seated at the mirror-polished grand piano, her fingers quickening over the keys, accelerado, as if, before she can reach the final note, the jaws of the gleaming beast might clamp shut. Her legs were sheathed in the dark green of her skirt, her blouse was of pale pink and lilac silk. She was an orchid. Indeed, there was a brushstroke of the exotic about Sylvia, in the slant of her ultramarine eyes, each eyebrow a tilde, long and upturned, in the pouting fleshy lips, and the long glossy hair, the rich red-brown of padauk, or more precisely purpleheart, which tapered to a point at the small of her back. Beautiful Sylvia. Sylvia my saviour. Bone-thin fingers, her touch so delicate and light, and her body like a ballerina's – supple, fluid, but strong enough to lift a bleeding Erskine from the ground and carry him across four fields to safety. And then I saw Joe. Joe in his shed, working his hammer, his lips sprouting nails, like a seamstress with pins, keeping in the words he could never quite articulate. The music, and the beat of Joe's hammer, grew faint. And I was tiptoeing, then, up the long staircase. I could hear noises – cries. Like a squealing pig. There's the door. Now, bend. Eye tight to the keyhole. Ah, there – look! A porky limb, dimpled buttocks, jiggly-jiggling flesh, a reddish-blond tuft. And then I heard growls. Growls? But of course, I had lost myself, was back in the lane once more. Was that another vicious cur there, behind the hedgerow? Fear drew a finger of ice down my spine. And then a large swaying head appeared over the hedge. Thick, wet, mottled nostrils. It was a calf! A lovely stupid calf, that was all. The hairs resettled. Nothing to be frightened of.

And now I must resettle, my friends, and continue. I finally managed to convince Mama it was me, but not until I had passed her test, which involved me dancing with her around the willow-tree maypole, which I did as a child apparently, but of this I have no recollection. Not me, perhaps, but another. Ah. Yes. Anyway, Mama went to bed in a sulk, accusing me of ignoring her. I was, admittedly, preoccupied. The day had been a day to forget, but I could not. The next morning, I was woken by the magpies' reveille – bursts of laughter, mocking, chillingly human, as I surfaced from a troubled sleep to consciousness, my eyes opening on the steel-grey March morning sky. (I must break off here, my friends, to beg forgiveness for the somewhat gloomy scene-setting,

which is merely to highlight your vivid entrance, my bird –
we are almost there!).

Over breakfast, Mama appeared chipper and communi-
cative. She was talking about planting seed trays for the
summer and putting in red-hot pokers in the back beds.
She told me she wanted to go on a bus ride. As you know,
occasionally she did the round trip on the local bus – along
the coast, into the village, out to the lighthouse and back, Mr
Pergolesi entertaining his passengers with arias from *le grand
opéra*, one eye on the road and one on Mama. I agreed to her
request. She seemed 'compos mentis' enough; was sanely, and
not unattractively, dressed in lilac skirt and matching blouse
(the purple velvet piping on the skirt complementing the
blouse's purple necktie). I packed her a flask and provisions
(fish-roe paste sandwiches, German sausage, and a couple of
fresh figs), adding pennies for the Ladies. I made her promise
she would not go wandering off. Then I walked her down to
the bus stop. Just as I was putting her on the bus, Pergolesi
calls out:

'Mr Fleschink! A duet. You and me. I be man, you be
laydee. How about it, Mr Fleschink?' (Oh, Flesch-ING, dear
man, Flesch-ING. Would he never get it?)

But what had Mama told him? Had she been blabbing?

'Mama,' I said, 'Mama, I thought I told you not to talk
about me, not to Pergolesi, not to anyone.'

'Whyever not?' she said. 'Have you done something wrong?
You haven't been a bad boy, Erskine, have you?'

I said I'd meet her at five and waved her off. I would
ignore Pergolesi. I would not be led down any Italian garden
paths. I had done nothing wrong. And I would not sing for
my supper, let alone Signor Pergo-Nosi. Bah! I decided to
spend the day getting to grips with the ebony. I was not
optimistic. (Indeed, now I am almost at the end, I must
confess that the entire project, for want of a better word,

has proved frustrating and exhausting. I refer mainly, of course, to the nigh impossible task of matching the woods of the boxes and . . . the messieurs. So I could well have done without fiddling problems of construction.) The ebony lid simply refused to sit straight. I seemed to keep chiselling too much on one side. At this rate, I thought, the depth of the box would be seriously threatened, and what it was to contain would not fit inside. I was loathe to spend much more time on it because there was the pressing urge now to create yet another monsieur. A white monsieur this time. The purest white wood I could lay my hands on. A candle to light my way through the descending gloom. Anyway, I reached for the mill-file in the hope I might finally crack the closure once and for all, only to discover it was missing. My precious mill-file was not where it should be!

As you well know, each of my tools has its place. Small tools are kept in cases lined with purple velvet, the cases set within outer cases (all my handiwork) and ranged according to size. Larger tools are stored on shelves and hooks within the locked cupboard over there. My tools are good friends, precious instruments, are vital extensions of myself. Where could my mill-file have got to? Then I spotted the Tales of the Riverbank mug on my desk. (My desk of Honduras mahogany, no less – now marked, as I discovered, with a white ring.) Mama! She should not have come in here. She had been warned. The door is, as a rule, locked. I am like a gaoler, a sporran of keys hanging from my belt. But the disturbances of the previous day had left me less vigilant. A quick lunch, I decided, then a visit to Farquhar's for a replacement. Before leaving my workroom, I checked the door that opens on to my private collection. It was, thank the eternal skies, locked. Then I decided to do another tool inventory.

Tools

MEASURING AND MARKING TOOLS
Steel tape measure (1), bevelled straightedge (1), engineer's square (1), combination square (1), mitre square (1), rosewood mortise gauge (1), spirit level (2)

SAWS
Crosscut saw (1), ripsaw (1), panel saw (1), Gent's saw (2), tenon saw (1), multi-saw (1)

PLANING AND SHAPING
Smoothing plane (1), jointer plane (1), small shoulder plane (1), jointer (1), convex spokeshave (1)

SHARPENING AND EDGING
Bench grinder (1), diamond lapping stone (1), burnisher (1), saw files (10)

CHISELS AND GOUGES
Bevel-edged chisel (3), paring chisel (2), small firmer chisel (3)

DRILLING AND MORTISING
Wheel brace (1), cordless electric drill (1), mortising machine (1)

SANDING AND FINISHING
Bobbin sander (1), disc sander (1), belt sander (1)

HAMMERS AND SCREWDRIVERS
Pin hammer (2), claw hammer (2), club hammer (1), cabinet screwdriver (1), ratchet screwdriver (1)

VENEERING
Bench knife (12), V-tool (10), chisel (15), miniature rasps
and files (21)

Farquhar has always kept a list of my requirements –
replacement tools, sandpapers, polishes, substances for cleaning wood and varnishes (these last being checked off on
a separate inventory, some of them, being highly toxic,
a potential danger, and no doubt a temptation). I have
remained a faithful customer, although my relationship with
Mr Farquhar has never amounted to anything more than the
transaction of business, superficial, as are most of my dealings
with others, owing to my natural sense of exclusion. (Though
one could not imagine Farquhar having a relationship with
anyone – but someone oiled his joints, now, didn't they!
Perked up his pepperoni, no mistake!) But as I was saying, I
have always felt different, otherwise. As indeed, my bird, you
were to discover, I am. I have never liked the way Henry John
Farquhar peers at me over his spectacles as I browse among
the tools. As if I were going to pocket one! And while I would
never stoop so low as to thieve, tools are my weakness. I have
more tools than I could ever need. But only one mill-file.

I finally selected a pristine mill-file from the tray. Mama
would not get her hands on this one. It turned out that Mr
Farquhar had gone to a funeral and I was served by some
young chap – all shirt, hair like a shiny-spined hedgehog
– who did not know his gouge from his chisel. Patience
was required, but having made a successful purchase of
the said file and a tin of varnish from the toxic list, I
was done.

Then. Then, my bird, I was on my way out of the iron-
monger's, pausing for a quick fondle amongst a tray of parting
tools, when something outside caught my eye. Someone.
Young. A she. Blond. Blond with streaks of rainbow colour.

And what curious attire, my dear! I stepped out into the street, looked. But you had disappeared. All that remained, an image. Or rather, an impression. For you had touched me. Like an angel's fingertip, light but definite upon my mind. I saw colours – turquoise, yellow, parrot green, kingfisher blue. I saw plaits, thin blond plaits with threads of red, orange, violet, indigo. I saw dangling bits, itty-bittyness. And feathers. Yes, feathers! A small fluorescent pink chickadee feather attached to an earlobe. Ah. A new species within our midst, then.

I was about to pop into the Been for Coffee for a recuperative beverage, having been thrown out of kilter by my avian discovery, when a bear paw, still familiarly comforting, rested heavily on my shoulder. The Ourse. Of course. Mama Bear. Marcia.

What a tragedy hides within that seemingly invincible (yet ambiguously mother-earth-cum-manly frame) – such pain. Did Marcia ever reveal the source, my bird? I am reluctant. I fear I cannot. Such excavation might unearth more of my own truth than I care to reveal. Suffice it to say that if it had not been for Marcia, the boy Erskine might have fallen off the face of the world. Suffice to say that look closely into Marcia's eyes and you might perceive, like a fly in amber, a small lost child. It was, shall we say, a relationship of symbiosis. Was. But I ought to keep mum. Oh, but even now, especially now Mama has left me, I feel a pang, a yearning for that paw, for a cushiony bosom. You see, when I found you, my Ulva, with Marcia, it was not shock I experienced, not titillation, but envy. Ah – Mama Marcia. Mama Mia.

I confess, when I first returned to Boxwood after so many years, I was rather looking forward to seeing Marcia again and I was disappointed to discover she had left some years earlier to look after her sister. I had been back at Boxwood six months or so when, one day, Mama told me, in passing, Marcia was back home. I thought better of inviting her to tea for Mama would only have taken over the occasion. I wanted to be on my own with Marcia for I still nurtured a small hope that the brief though special relationship we had once shared might be resumed. So it was with some bewilderment and hurt, when at last we met, that I witnessed, not the usual aforementioned physical recoiling, but a distinct veiling of expression, an emotional withdrawal – though not before I had caught the boy, the child, in the iris of one of those brown, not unattractive but incongruously small eyes. (A large woman, is she not – a virtual parachute of flesh!) Greeting her for the first time, after so many years, at the familiar cottage (with a bag of crumpets and best butter for old times' sake), I feared she was going to shut the door in my face.

'Marcia,' I said, 'it's Erskine. You do remember me?'

Then came the whispered 'No, it cannot be'.

'Erskine,' she said, 'you are well?'

Marcia. Fleshy. Large mouthed but weeny eyed. A dusting of face powder and the carmine lipstick. A vestige of one-time frivolity, a homage to a self lost long before I was a child in her parlour. Had she been beautiful once? Marcia. Home-knit mud-brown cardigan, pockets baggy with tissues. Did she still cry? Did she still sip gin and weep? Black galoshes, striding like a man with the arms of a mother.

The years had not been unkind. A few lines more deeply entrenched. But – how can I explain? – a general hardening which I knew I would not penetrate. On the surface Marcia, and here the cosy, messily lived-in parlour, here the coal fire where I had toasted crumpets, here the three-legged stool where I sat while she shared memories of the child, there the jars and earthenware plates bearing her collection of beach glass, but I realised as soon as I entered the parlour, saw the tiny stool, the unlit fire, that our former connection was no more. That book had closed. I suggested a game of cards, or dominoes.

'Like we used to, Marcia, remember?'

'I do not play any more,' she told me, 'not for years. Not since . . . no.'

Had Mama not told her I was back home? Indeed, Marcia did not appear concerned about what I had done in the intervening years, only why I had come back.

'You came home to look after your mother, I expect. She needs looking after, Erskine. I was shocked to find her in such a state. But I'm afraid I can be of little help. What with the vegetable deliveries and my charities.'

'I have come back to Mama,' I said. 'Simply come back. A new chapter. I wanted to begin again.'

And it was at that point, my friends, sitting in Marcia's parlour, with the bag of unopened crumpets, that I realised my dilemma. For what I really meant was not 'to begin again', but to go back to the beginning.

I have said too much. Marcia was more successful in drawing a line under the past, perhaps. It was as if she had never known me. She made it quite clear. I had returned Erskine the man, not the boy. Apart from keeping Mama under control, we would have little to do with each other.

Now. Where was I?

Outside the Been for Coffee. With Marcia. An angel's fingerprint marking my thoughts.

'Erskine, Erskine, my dear boy,' she said – nay, boomed. 'Listen here. A request.'

'Marcia. How nice.'

'A favour, Erskine. Golden Years Rest Home. Funding for the kitchen refurbishment. I'm organising a benefit concert. May I count you in?'

'Count me in, Marcia? Forgive me, but I . . .'

'Sing, Erskine, sing for us. Your mother has informed me that you sing.'

Mama. Dear Mama. Dear me, no. Memory is most certainly not to be trusted.

'When did she tell you?'

'When? Does not matter when, dear boy, only that she did and you will. It's a damn good cause and this village is miserably lacking in talent.'

'I can't, Marcia. I am sorry. I don't,' I said. 'Not for years.'

'Of course you can. You will.' And here, a hearty slap on the back and a snifter of gin as she came close. 'Throw modesty to the dogs. I'll give you a nod re rehearsals. See you anon, dear boy. Give my regards to your mother.'

I sat in the cafe, pondering over a cafetière of Brazilian Strength Five. So. Mama still remembered the Great Cercatore, did she? Despite the concern that she had been discussing me, a thread of pleasure tweaked within as I realised I was still a dim light (or faint sound) in Mama's rapidly darkening world. But I decided I would have to have words with her about this. Cercatore had gone. And so too the Voice. I could think of no greater hell than a resurrection of this kind.

On the way back home from the village, I was troubled by a vague niggling which, for the life of me, I could not define, or put word or picture to. Then this irksome niggling receded as, coming into my field of vision, flying into my cloudy bubble was – you! Yes, you again! Unmistakably you, my bird. On a bicycle. Flying on a bicycle. (And did you really turn round to look at me?) All bits and pieces. Colours. Layers. Jewels. Your plumage. The wind and speed were forcing the thin layers of your garments to cling to your breasts. Then I noticed the bike – the wicker basket, black paintwork, red mudguards. Marcia's bike. When Mama had no time for me, and I was left to my own devices, I'd go to see Marcia and, if it was a nice day, she'd help me up on to the saddle and push me along the lanes. Had the bird stolen it, I wondered? Bought it? An unauthorised loan, perhaps? Ought I to inform Marcia? The stranger was becoming a little less strange.

(Oh yes, my bird, clinging to you so tight, I could discern the small mounds of your breasts. Ah. Indeed. A stirring in the woods. The lacuna began, ever so slightly, to tingle.)

Opening the front door, I could hear the telephone ringing. (It had been permanently out of order in the weeks prior to my arrival. Unpaid bills, I suspect.) A novelty for Mama but an irritation as far as I was concerned. You never knew who it might be. Before I could reach it, it stopped. No matter. I turned my thoughts to dinner. A cheese-and-potato pie – or bangers and mash, yes. Then I realised Mama was not in the house. Twenty past five. I had forgotten to meet her from the bus. Hoping Pergolesi had the sense to keep her with him, I was about to call the bus depot when the telephone rang again.

'Erskine? Marcia here. In the village. The launderette. I've got your mother.'

Thanks be to Marcia, I thought. But the launderette?

'Bring some clothes, Erskine. At least a coat. She's only gone and put her dress in for a wash.'

Heavens. Dear heavens. Was she wearing a decent slip, I wondered? Trying not to picture the possible horrors of her underwear, I told Marcia I would be there as soon as I could. I grabbed a plastic coverall rain cloak and set off.

Mama was sitting in front of a washing machine reading a magazine. She was wearing a petticoat – peach, bosom to

41

knee and, mercifully, clean. She did not look up. I thanked Marcia for her trouble.

'Not at all, dear boy, though rather worrying. The memory's been going for some time, hasn't it.' Marcia tutted, stroked Mama's head with a natural affection that I found both touching and disturbing.

'She has moments,' I said quietly, 'when she's not quite, you understand, entirely with us.'

Marcia nodded, then bent to Mama. 'Erskine is here. Erskine. Your son.'

Mama looked up at me blankly. 'Are you the taxi?'

The washing machine shuddered to a stop. Mama put on the mackintosh. As we were leaving, I thanked Marcia.

'Lucky it was you who found her,' I said, 'and not some undesirable who might have taken an advantage.'

'No. It wasn't me,' Marcia said. 'That woman was in here with her.'

'What woman?'

'That health visitor. She'd tried to phone you a few times, apparently. Had to go off and see a patient. I said I'd take over with your ma. You really ought to get some help, you know, Erskine.'

Troubles indeed, my friends. And Mama, singing her way merrily to bed afterwards, oblivious. I could not settle. Not chance, more than chance they should have found her. Had they been following Mama too? The hand of Nemesis was reaching for the sword. They would not take her. I would not let them take her from me. Vigilance, Erskine. Eyes of a watchman. Ears of a bat. Secure all entrances. Locks and keys.

I decided to sit in my workroom, allow the grey thought that refused to take centre stage hover for a while in the wings of my mind. What to make of the day, my friends, what to make of the day?

I shall read. A brief journal extract. Listen. March 31. Before we had become acquainted.

31 March. The unexpected warmth of this clear March morning sent dear Mama off on one of her excursions. She returned joyful and alert with a detailed physical description of various passengers on the bus – a lady wearing the most exquisite dress, Mama said, patterned with dusky pink roses. The woman was with her young daughter. The daughter was called Rosamund! You could tell they were mother and daughter, Mama said, the closeness was palpable. Pergolesi had brought Mama a box of red roses. The ebony advances beautifully. So much peace here, a wonder I did not return to Boxwood sooner. Yesterday Mama and I had a picnic on the beach then took our buckets and nets down to the rock pools. Two shrimps and one tiny transparent crab – like the detached scab of a small wound. Such a day of delights! Spring in the air, perhaps, but I feel rejuvenated – juice in my bones! And many more days like this ahead. Treated myself to a new mill-file at Farquhar's (the old one having had its day.) My ornithological study – Birds of the Cliff Tops – is progressing nicely. Spotted a species new to these parts – remarkable plumage, colouring. I shall keep a beady eye.

As I set down my pen, the vague niggling suddenly thrust itself centre stage, sang out fortissimo: Mama blabbing to Marcia. Was that how this Frankling fellow rooted me out? Were they connected in some way, this Francklen chap and Marcia? I could not help thinking it was a kind of betrayal on Mama's part. But poor Mama. What did she know of my need to separate from the past? How could I ever have explained it? Had I even properly explained it to myself?

My friends, my silent witnesses, since returning to Box-wood, the last year or so prior to our meeting (fateful meeting, yes), I realised I had never lived my proper life. I can admit now that even throughout the Leodora years I was never truly myself. Mine was a half-life, its very essence snatched in moments, before I was ever allowed to become. And I have often wondered, if it had not been for that moment when the claw of the vulture gripped, took hold of the rope of consequence – who might I have been? And what might I have become? For this Erskine is not *that* Erskine aching for his Leodora, not the Great Cercatore, or the one peeping through holes with dark fascination, or the Erskine in the Mansion House, the lost boy, far from his Mama, Erskine in Marcia's cottage upon the three-legged stool, licking butter from his fingers, listening to Marcia's memories, taking comfort where he could get it, not that Erskine alone and suffering in the starched ungiving sheets of the hospital bed, all the pain of hell in his loins, thinking he was dying and not knowing what had been taken from him, or what it meant. Consequences, my friends, like a line of dominoes, falling inevitably one upon the other.

I was too distressed to continue with my journal entry. To bed, Erskine, I said, set a seal upon the day. As I moved to switch off the lamp, a small silvery-winged moth fluttered out from the shade, across the room, alighted on the lid of a box on the table. The bird again. She hovered. A feather floated. I plucked another. I saw a perfect mound, small, pink tipped. I reached for the sporran, selected the key, unlocked the door to my private collection. I entered.

The next morning, two letters in the post. Franklin again. And more pressing than the last: '. . . only be to your advantage (something something) . . . imperative . . . your story must be told.'

Damn the fellow. Persuasive, indeed. But no. There would be no story.

The other letter was from my pursuer. Apparently, they intended to inform the health authorities. They required an urgent meeting the following day.

I tore up both letters. Why couldn't they leave us in peace? Why couldn't they all let me be? And no, of course I did not meet the damn woman. What would I have said? Yes, be my guest, put Mama in the madhouse, pull her from me limb by limb with pleasure.

What next? Ah, yes. A day and a night best forgotten. I was here in my workroom writing up my journal. The words scuttled like insects. My eyes were being sucked from their sockets. I ached for sleep. Just after dawn and I could have curled up right here, a beetle in a drawer, a worm in the wood. But I had a madwoman to watch over. The spectacle of Mama in the attic in the early hours would not go away. Mama – haunches spread, backside upturned, pink and sweaty. The intimate brown of the split. A mere embarrassment, you might say, a comic interlude – the sad buffoon. But the comedy was growing dark. There are moments best left unforaged in everyone's past.

The previous day had begun so promisingly. There was a tang of early spring in the air. Mama had set the table for breakfast, in her fashion – three forks and a fish knife. There was a vase of daffodils she had picked from the garden. She was wearing a dress patterned with wild roses. Over bacon and tomatoes, touchingly, she suggested a holiday. Her eyes shone.

'Just you and me, Erskine. We'll stay in a big hotel. We'll do lots of shopping and go to the cinema and have ices and popcorn. Like our holidays at the Halcyon, Erskine. Remember?'

'Yes, Mama, I remember.'

The Halcyon. Did I ever tell you? Allow me.

The Halcyon – such a grand affair. Vast, white, gold. A dazzling incongruity. A cruise liner anchored amidst the drab grey box-like buildings of the town. How many times did we stay at the Halcyon? Three, four? One year we went twice. Just Mama and I. I was very young. I was six the last time we stayed there. Even now I recall those days in vivid detail, as though I am entering the past through a wide-open door. How I adored those holidays! We might have been living in our own special world. Our own ship sailing on our very own sea. All we could possibly need. So much to do – swimming in the pool, shopping in the penny arcade. Sometimes we went to the cinema across the road to see comedies, or films that made Mama what she called 'happy-sad' because, although they made her cry, she said, everything was all right in the end. While she wept into her handkerchief, I would take Mama's hand, put a proprietorial arm – like the wing of a white dove – around her shoulder, proud to take care of her. We'd spend the evenings in the games room playing darts, cards or billiards. The billiard table came up to my shoulders and I'd have to hoist myself up on to the smooth wooden ledge of the table, feet in the air, to hit the balls. And what I loved about hitting the balls into the pocket was Mama's 'well done, my love' – *my love* – so soft and warm, dropping into the pocket of my heart . . .

Weekends, Mama let me stay up an extra hour. After our meal in the hotel restaurant, she would lead me to the half-moon of polished wood in front of the band and we'd dance, me concentrating on my feet, trying not to step on her evening shoes. She wore exquisite shoes – gold lace, silver satin jewelled with diamonds, a pair in purple velvet with tiny orange satin bows like goldfish. Quick, light butterflies.

The hotel staff made me feel special, too. Like the doorman at the main entrance. Arthur Shoke wore a white peaked cap

and navy coat with gold-fringed epaulettes. While waiting
for Mama, I would trace over the two-foot-high brass letters
that spelled out T-H-E-H-A-L-C-Y-O-N, my fingers leaving
a greasy snail trail along the loops and curls. Arthur Shoke
would turn a blind eye. Just as I pretended not to notice when
he spat in the corner by the railings. He used to take me round
the back sometimes, let me climb up on to the bins and look
into the kitchen windows. He liked to puff on a huge cigar –
thick, brown, tight in his hand when he drew on it. Like an
extra finger. He kept the cigar in a paper bag in his pocket.
Sometimes, when Mama was taking her afternoon rest, one
of the maids used to take me down to the tea room for a
knickerbocker glory, bright as a parrot, lasting as long as I
could make it, until Mama came down, much later.

'Remember, Erskine?'

Yes, Mama. I remembered. I said we might consider a
summer holiday. Although the Halcyon would probably no
longer be there, of course.

'But a picnic, Mama. On the beach. Would that suit?'

'Lovely, lovely,' she said, clapping her hands. She darted
off in search of the hamper. (She had two ways of locomo-
tion, you recall, depending on mood – a meandering slow
sashay, as though moving to some smoochy tune in her
head, and a weird darting, like a nervous fish. Thus visibly
expressed, the impact of rapid change in temperament on
innocent bystanders was doubly distressing.) I prepared us
a feast – hard-boiled eggs, ham-and-relish sandwiches, tight
green pears.

As we walked down to the beach, Mama, buoyant, chat-
tered once more about the Halcyon.

'Remember, Erskine, they used to say it was awful, taking
a child to a stuffy town in the heat of summer, when we
had the beach right on our doorstep. But that was the
point. We could go to the beach any day. And you loved

it, didn't you, the hotel and the shops and the cinema and everything.'

I reached for her hand, squeezed it, grateful for the remnants of sanity that still connected us. Shared memories. How it should be.

Once down on the beach, we walked along the sand, Mama filling the pocket of her cardigan with shells and smooth blue pieces of beach glass, chattering with childlike, spilling excitement about a summer holiday. We ate our picnic at the foot of the cliffs, leaning back against the cool rock. Our favourite spot. Mama was humming to herself. It was then that I mentioned Marcia's concert.

'What concert?'

'To raise funds for the Golden Days. Marcia wants me to sing. Though I shall not, of course. So you told her, then, did you, about Cercatore?'

She looked right at me, baffled.

'Cercatore who when he's at home?'

'The Great Cercatore, Mama.'

'Never 'eard of 'im, guv'nor.'

'The Great Cercatore, Mama. Me. Me, Erskine Cercatore.'

'No,' she said. She smiled. 'No, I don't know hide nor hair of him at all. I'm going for a paddle.'

I watched her at the water's edge, skirts pulled up, skipping in and out of the frill of waves. The blanks, her apparent inability to connect when I wanted her to connect, left me disheartened and frustrated. Was she playing some game? If only there had been a note of innocence, of apology. But she seemed almost gleeful about her inability to recall what I wished her to recall. Or rather, in the case of Cercatore, wished not. For that Erskine, the one with the voice of angels, was, I thought, best left buried.

By late afternoon, the clouds were gathering. We headed for home. Coming off the coastal path, we stopped in the lane for Mama to watch the lambs. She was cooing, calling for me to come and stroke them, when I saw 'it' prowling about. Just yards away. Within smelling distance. A most evil-looking hound, the jaw hanging open, displaying the fangs. It was kept by some artist woman new to the village. (I have always made a point of investigating newcomers, am constantly on the lookout for holidaymakers and their wolves.) The tail grew erect, the eyes narrowed, then Cronus, Cerebus, Charlie-boy – whatever it was called – cocked an ear, barked, then ran off. I was saved, at least until the next confrontation. But the sighting of the hound had effected a change in my mood. And as we continued on our way back home, the memory of our last holiday at the Halcyon cast a long shadow. For during that holiday I hardly saw Mama at all and was put in the care of two chambermaids (who largely ignored me) and Arthur Shoke. Mama was so often sick, sleeping in her room for much of the morning. She no longer looked pretty and wore only black. She did not kiss me, not once. She would not even look at me.

Back at Boxwood, I put a freezer casserole in to cook and set about preparing a special hors d'oeuvre to lift my spirits. In the pantry I found a jar of caviar, a tin of olives stuffed with anchovy and some savoury biscuits. I laid a proper table – silverware, linen napkins, crystal glasses. Then I called Mama. She came down wearing her dressing gown over her clothes, one hand tucked into the buttoned front. Her eyes were wide, goggling pathetically.

'Look!' she said. 'I have cake!'

For a brief moment I was touched by her vulnerability. She pulled a family-size fruitcake from under her gown. She had already devoured a large portion and now proceeded to take huge bites, crumbs falling into the painstakingly arranged caviar and olives. Her fingers flexed and curled in pleasure as she gorged.

'Where did you get the cake, Mama?'

'Yesterday,' she said, 'after the bus trip. I got it from the shop.'

'But you didn't have any money, Mama, did you?'

'No,' she said. 'That lady, you know, the health visitor lady, bought it for me. I told her I was hungry.'

So. I was starving her now. Wonderful.

I begged her to stop. But she would not. Not until all the cake had gone.

'I enjoyed that,' she said, 'thank you. Now, I really must go to bed.'

That damn woman. It did not bear thinking about. The authorities would have me now for abuse. To clear it from my mind, I decided to watch one of my *Natural World* recorded films, then retired to bed myself with a large brandy and my journal, in the hope that the task of writing up the day's events, and the alcohol, would engender sleep.

I must have dozed off. The most terrible dream. The blackest, foulest mare. I was on the Halcyon. It was a ship. A galleon. There was a storm. But no one was steering the ship! And I was thrown back and forth across the deck. The waves were as high as houses. There was someone in the sea. I couldn't see the face. They were trying to get to the boat. And I thought I had to save them. I managed to get to the side and I reached over but when I looked down the ship was no longer on the sea, but balanced on top of a cliff, and the person, this black figure I had been trying to save, was not in the water but behind me, on the ship, and though I dared not look them in the face, glancing behind, I could see a long bony finger pointing at me, and all it took was one little push and I was falling, falling over the edge of the ship and down towards the black rocks below.

At this point I was woken by a terrific crashing. I feared the walls would collapse. I couldn't move my arms or legs.

I was in some kind of container. Going over and over, as if it was hurtling down a staircase, a long, long staircase, or down the side of a cliff. Down, down. I couldn't move, couldn't breathe. I realised then that I was wrapped in the sheets like a mummy, that the noise was coming from one of the attic rooms. Mama.

At first I did not take in the mess. All I could see, directly in front of me, was the gross, bare, upturned rump. The skin between the splitting cheeks, brown, ruched, then the shrivelled flaps. These previously unseen (for me at least) details of her anatomy compelled me to look, though I was flooding with deep shame. It was an invasion into her most secret places – like you in my private collection, my bird. Then I heard the wet splutter as she broke wind. Her small grunt voiced satisfaction rather than effort. Then a rich oily whiff of flatus.

'Mama,' I said.

She straightened, turned. I saw the stretched breasts, the star of nipple and aureole like the gilled anus of a sea slug. The skin of the trunk was mottled and dimpled, like thumbed clay. A reddish tuft of seaweed sprouted from her groin. I was at once repulsed and riveted.

'My bathing costume,' she said. 'Have you seen it?'

The room was a jumble of old clothes, shoes, ornaments and Lord knows what else. We were knee deep. Almost every one of the boxes and packing cases had been emptied. I waded through the junk, fished out a shiny orange garment and handed it to her. It was three in the morning, I said; what on earth did she want with a swimming costume at this hour?

'But I must have it,' she insisted. 'I must. I need my bather. I am taking Ursula swimming.'

Oh, Mama. Not again. Not this again. The knife twisted. Was she out to torture me? Out of the corner of my eye,

51

amidst a pile of dark clothing – jackets, trousers, pullovers, men's suits – a twist of crimson, like the iris of a marble. A marble rolling now, slow and steady, towards me. I closed my eyes. When I looked again, it had disappeared.

'No, Mama,' I said. 'No swimming. It's the middle of the night.'

'But Ursula . . .' she started.

'There is no Ursula, Mama,' I said. 'Ursula has gone. Don't you remember?'

She put her hands to her face, started to whimper, like a lost child.

I should not have been so harsh. But I would not have this ghost creeping in between us. Not again. Never again. I reached out my hand.

'Come, Mama, I'll take you back to bed.'

She looked at me as if terrified. 'No! No!' she cried out, and ran past me, down the stairs, darting along the corridor, an escaping fish. I found her in bed, the sheet pulled over her head. Then, as I was tucking her in, she sat bolt upright and peered at me.

'Who are you? What are you doing in here? Now be off, or I'll call the police!'

Of course, I could not even think of going back to sleep. I made tea and came into the sanctuary of my workroom. All I desired was to go on, for Mama and me to go on, together. And here was Mama hot on the heels of a past I could not bear to recall. What hope was there, when for the most part she did not even know who I was? That terrible, terrible feeling of exclusion was creeping back. Rat from the sewers, lifting the lid, crawling out, its yellowed teeth tight on an old crimson rag. Erase it, Erskine, I told myself. Empty the mind. Think of each new day as simple and unsullied, each moment untarnished by what has gone before. I tried to focus on the black walnut but it sat on my work table – a hard old nut to crack, refusing to pull me from my darkness. Oh, but I could still hear Mama's voice – Ursula, Ursula – whispering through the crack. Shut the lid, Erskine. Shut it. Lock it up.

I opened my journal, took up my pen, continued.

1 April. Yesterday, the first signs of spring. Mama and I took a picnic to the beach. Warm enough to brave the water for the first dip of the year – just as we did when I was a boy. A grand day. We fished for shrimp in the rock pools. Mama found a monster of a crab lurking in the weed – orange and crimson coloured, its claws fresh blood red. One of its pincers was missing. She held it out, legs and claws flailing, its underside etched like a palm, as if it were her claw. Plans for a summer holiday at the Halcyon. On our return, hungry as hounds, we ate casserole, with fruitcake.

—Tell them, Erskine, tell them. The Halcyon, my boy. What was it really like? Tell it like it *reely-reely* was. Hours waiting for Mama sometimes. At night, the neon signs of the cinema lit your room a thin eerie red. Oh, you were scared. You'd knock on the connecting door, rattle the handle. Mama, Mama, why won't they switch off the cinema? Can't sleep, Mama. Mama, are you there? The door was locked. Where was Mama? One day, when you couldn't find Mama anywhere, you looked for Arthur Shoke. You thought he must have been round the back, smoking his cigar. He wasn't there, but you could see people through the kitchen window. You climbed up on to the bins, looked through the glass. There was a girl, one of the kitchen workers. She was stretched back on the steel table, knickers round her ankles, legs wide, a hand clutching the block where they stuck the knives. There was the chef, his trousers dropped down under his backside, and underneath the front of his white jacket a thick brown bobbing pole. Like the one Arthur Shoke kept in his bag. You were frightened. You wanted your Mama. But you couldn't stop looking. Oh, where was Mama? The last holiday at the Halcyon, you could hear Mama crying in the next room through the connecting door. You were too afraid to get out of your bed in the dark, but early in the morning, if the door was open, you'd tiptoe across her room and slip under the covers beside her. The crying always stopped just as you snuggled up, but you knew it was still going on inside her. She used to turn her face away. Oh, those pale arms like broken stems draped over her face. You'd inch your way down the bed, until you could rest your cheek against the pillow of her belly. And you could feel by the clutch and shudder that she was still crying inside. But there was something else there too. A presence. A small relentless growing. A pulse other than the sad fluttering of your Mama's heart. A nub. Tar black, blood sticky. The grit in your eye. The fly in your ointment. A fist. A stone. A boulder come rolling between you and your Mama. Inside Mama's head, there were dark thoughts. You knew by the way she'd look at you, her eyes cold and un-focused. She recoiled when you tried to hug her, and if you did the slightest thing wrong, if you did not thank the waiter when he poured you a glass of water, she would scold you like a snake, hissing and spitting. 'Erskine! You're a bad, bad boy! Such a bad boy!' Had your Mama already stopped loving you, Erskine. Had she? You had no sense of guilt. Your father had gone for ever this time. But it was not your fault. Was it? No wonder, Erskine, it was such a difficult time for your Mama, that last holiday at the Halcyon. For she was both mourning the sudden and unexpected death of your father, and expecting a child—

Three of us when the man in the dark suit came. The dark-suited man went away. But he always came back.

Thin, tall. Like a black line. Like a line you couldn't cross. A barrier between Mama and me. I hated him. I did not even know him. Last time he came back, they found him one day. Under the old wooden bridge where he used to walk to and from the village pub. Some of the slats had rotted and he must have fallen through. Mama wore black for weeks. Just like she did after Ursula went. Face pale and tight. As if somehow he'd got into her. As if he were still with us.

—Erskine. Oh, Erskine. Porky-pies. Not the bridge. The cliffs, Erskine. Found him down on the rocks. Gone over the cliffs, Erskine.

4

Connections and Shadows

9 April. Mama full of the joys. She is a Chinese princess – demure, neat, her movements precise. Such dainty feet. Exotic butterflies flutter with each step. She went to see Aunt Frieda today. Two-hour train journey including one change. I was concerned about her going such a distance, though she returned safe and sound. And full of plans to decorate Boxwood! Aunt F. owns a guest house. Mama thinking along similar lines, apparently. The attic would give us three bedrooms plus a bathroom. Food for thought. My ornithological study Birds of the Cliff Tops *progresses. A thought after catching an item on the radio this morning. Perhaps the Chinese have got it right – one child is very probably sufficient. Single offspring is best. We are not birds.*

A red balloon. Full of hot air. Fell into the sea. Like the sun had dropped. No survivors.

10 April. Aunt Frieda telephoned to say how much she enjoyed Ma's visit. Aunt F. is coming to stay – a flying visit en route to her son. I keep forgetting Nephew Chester is an amputee. Was it in a car crash that he lost an arm and both legs? Or was it an aeroplane? Aunt F. said I really ought to go down and see him. Chester, apparently, doesn't get around much these days. Still in a deal of pain and ignored by his siblings. (I also forget just how large is our extended family.) Aunt F. said it must have been nice to have been an only child, for I must have had Mama's undivided attention. Later, Mama and I played a game of boules on the back lawn. I won, of course. I have always had excellent ball sense.

11 April. Mama has purchased a charming nightie. Violet. It might even do as a party dress. But which party? Invitations come like Christmas cards. Mama has also acquired a new hat – flowers being the dominating theme. Bright orange. Her taste remains utterly faultless.

Birds. Wings and prayers. I have not set eyes on the new species since. Or have I?

Have you missed me, my friends – my Ulva, my feathered one, and your four-eyed beau? I have been down to the village this morning, shopping for treats. I am sleeping worse than ever. I fear we are not alone. It is not my imagination. I hear things. Malevolence.

I purchased quail's eggs, fresh figs, fresh rosemary (for my lamb chops) and a large avocado. You remember, I have a passion for this fruit. I adore its creamy yellow-green – surreal as a field of rape. And that bulbous stone! Such an intrusion into that lush flesh. (I had the fleeting notion, after the fruit and fruit bowl idea, before the messieurs – the project – took hold, of producing a range of fruit stones, beginning with the magnificent avocado and working in descending scale to the lychee, to the diminutive cherry.) Coming back home – it is always coming back that I seem to suffer these awful experiences (however delightful the excursion, the return is invariably unsettling) – anyhow, on the way back I spied the hound again. It was sitting in the porch of the artist woman's cottage, its ears pricked, eyes fixed, the taut front legs ready to bound through the open gate. I turned on my heels and came the long way round, walking with difficulty. The lacuna was tightening, like a fist. And the fist was holding a knife, and the knife was gouging out flesh and muscle, and there was blood pouring out of me, so much blood I feared I would drown in it.

But forgive me, friends, I forget myself. See how my hands clutch my groin for protection, as if to staunch the blood. But there is no blood, no muscle, no flesh. Yet the agony remains. Like the pain of an amputee's dismembered limb.

I managed to get home safely in one piece and, after a delicious lunch of avocado-and-walnut salad, I watched one of my wildlife films. Your remark, my bird, that my video habit seemed like rubbing salt into the wound, led me to question my fascination for nature's savagery. It is not masochism, but empathy. I know how these poor beasts are suffering. And their suffering relieves mine.

I selected *The Lady Killers*, in particular, the sequence of the gazelle and the hyena.

A young gazelle has strayed too far from the herd. Zoom to the hyena on the rock, eyes fixing. Hyena slips from the rock, moves to hide behind a tree, then another tree. Gazelle drinks from the pool. Close-up of muscles rippling beneath the flesh. All intact. Pause. Hold the breath. Now, silent, quick as the wind, hyena runs, runs, leaps. Dust. Limbs. Writhing and contortion. Bodies twist, roll. But the struggle is brief. The dust settles and reveals the gazelle, quite motionless, tranquil. A tableau. Gazelle is anaesthetised by fear, stands there while hyena tears at its flesh. Pink flesh. As the flesh is torn away, you see the colours of the viscera beneath – pinks, purples and indigo. Now the entrails come looping out – like Mr Punch's sausages! And hyena jumps back – oops! As if it's surprised, as if it's found the treasure. It begins to gorge. Still, gazelle does not move. Then, finally, the blood pours, and the animal reels, its legs buckle, it falls. And in goes hyena's head. Deep. No, nature is not kind. Ah.

Now. Where were we? Yes, remembering. A rump. A brown split. Lost marbles.

Although Mama made no mention of the previous night's fiasco in the attic, she presented herself for breakfast wielding a rubber truncheon. It was, she said, in case of intruders, and to be on the safe side she would eat her cereal in the downstairs loo (where she spent a good portion of the day, reading some Neighbourhood Watch pamphlet). I let her be. I had my own troubles. I could not settle, not even to my wood, and found myself wandering from room to room, which only depressed me further. Had I been able to bribe Mama from the loo with a soporific tot of brandy, I would have escaped to my cliff top. Boxwood was not the place in which to escape the past. It was an overfed beast. Stuffed to bursting. Within Boxwood, the past persists, insists, will not go away.

I found myself in the back room overlooking the garden. I was by the French windows, looking at the curtains, a tired blue, greying now at the edges where years of sun had aged them. I touched the velvet and, as though this had summoned them into the here and now, Mama, a youthful Mama, and a lady friend walked into the room. They did not notice me behind the sofa. (Just as I did not notice you at first, my Ulva. Ah, what a creeper you turned out to be.) I heard Mama say to her friend, 'So, Erskine will have to share me now.'

'Do you think he'll get used to it – sharing you, I mean?'

'Oh, he'll have to,' Mama said.

Such a scorpion of a remark! I still feel its sting now, as I felt it then. Did she not care that I may not have welcomed renouncing even a part of her?

'Thing is,' Mama went on, 'I feel the joy of it, and yet the tragedy.'

'Tragedy? You mean . . .'

'Yes, the child will never know the father, yet will always be a memory of him.'

I was rubbing the rich blue velvet between my fingers,

comforted by its soft thickness, listening to Mama and not wanting to hear.

'You know,' Mama said, 'I wanted to believe the fall was an accident.'

Ah! Did she mean Papa? When Papa fell off the bridge? Because that was exactly what happened. Papa fell.

'But I don't think he fell,' Mama continued, 'I don't think it was an accident. I think he jumped from that ledge intending to land right on top of me.'

No. Not Papa. Me. She was telling her friend how we had walked through the countryside, days ago, and Mama had needed a rest before the last stretch home. We'd had to walk so slowly, Mama waddling along, hands supporting her back like wings, puffing and panting and not attending when I spoke to her. She didn't want to play any more. She was always too tired, too tired even to walk, so she lay down in the grass and closed her eyes. She didn't move. I waited. I thought she might have fainted. Or worse. What if she was dead and it was all my fault for harbouring such evil thoughts about her? I stared hard at her swollen belly. She was still breathing, the mound rising and falling, rising and falling, like a vast pump, as if this thing inside her belly was now her powerhouse, the breathing machine, was keeping her alive, and only this and nothing else and no one else mattered. I hated it. I hated her. I ran up the grassy bank behind us and looked down. And I jumped. It was a game we used to play. Mama would lie on her back. I would go far away. And then I'd run and I'd take a long jump right over her. But this time I landed with my feet hard on her belly. Oh no, Mama. No. I did not mean to. It was an accident, Mama.

The swollen mound remained. It continued to swell. Whatever it contained had the Devil's will to survive.

And then Mama and her lady friend disappeared. And there I was, on my own, in the back room. The grey threads of the curtains had come away in my fingers, the ends tipped with a rich royal blue. A small bald patch on the cloth made me think of the head of a newborn bird.

There was a box of knitting patterns on the floor. Had I really not noticed it before? Patterns more than forty years old. Baby and toddler wear, matinée coats, booties, mittens, a christening gown (did Mama ever knit?), a navy-and-white sailor suit patterned with little red yachts, a child's first dress. A dress knitted in lemon, the short puffed sleeves capping the dimpled flesh of those arms – arms reaching out to me. Hands splaying stubby pink fingers. The arms were growing longer, stretching, white searching roots. The fingers long and thin and curling, flexing. I brought my foot down heavily on the box. And I gave it a hearty kick behind the curtains. But it was still there. It was like a sickness, all this hoarding of hers, this refusal to let anything go. It was pervasive, was creeping into my bones, into the cracks and crevices of my mind. Enough. Time for a major spring clean! Fresh April air. Space. Light. Bring out the bin bags! Revived, I went in search of rubber gloves and cleaning fluid. Mama had emerged from the toilet, informing me she would not be available for some while as she had to do a recce of outside security. I had rather hoped she would be out of the way. I knew she would refuse to part with anything.

Starting at the top and working down, I decided to brave the chaos of the attic room where I had found Mama in the night. The room had an air of tragic stillness. A terrible sense of finality. Like the aftermath of some disaster, a bomb-wrecked party, bodies strewn beside the derailed train. As I stepped over the mounds of clothes, they began to take form – a sleeve protectively round a waist, a hood pulled up, a trouser leg hooked over the skirt of a long pink chiffon evening dress, legs and arms clutched foetally. Each one Mama. Each one a victim. The pastel limbs of babies crawled from a weathered brown suitcase. I tucked them back in quickly and buckled up the straps. The air was thick and musty. I smelt the residue of Mama's fart and was faintly nauseous. Opening the window, I could see Mama walking the perimeter of the back garden.

But where to start? I began to fold and pack. The flower-printed frock Mama wore on those glorious summer days at the beach, armfuls of evening dresses – bouquets of purples, magentas, blues, in taffeta, velvet, silk. These last filling me with sudden profound sadness: a swish of taffeta through a closing door, a whispered goodbye, her hand fluttering kisses, on my own at night in a hotel room.

By late afternoon I had got most of the stuff back into the boxes and cases, save for a quantity of jam jars and swathes of tissue paper. There was a variety of containers and cartons that had once held the tubes and jars of Mama's cosmetics. Too pretty to simply discard, perhaps. Embossed white and pink, with gold lettering. One with a ribboned lace seal on the lid, another with a transparent section, a pouch of liquid, in which floated a number of tiny pearls. (If things had turned out differently, my bird, I might have offered them to you.) I could see them stacked in pyramids, in rows inside the glass front cabinets of Delderfield's the department store, where they used to sit me on a high stool while Mama sampled the various creams. One of the women would swoop me up, sit me on the stool and give me a catalogue to look through. Sometimes they gave me a boiled sweet. I used to think at first they were nurses with their crisp white coats, the way they listened to Mama, nodding sympathetically, tutting as she described her latest ailment – 'Very dry and tight at the moment', or 'It's rather greasy, these little pimples, you see, around the nose'. Then one of them would reach an immaculately taloned hand into the cabinet and select a remedy. I'd flick through my catalogue of

perfumes and skin preparations, fascinated by the pictures of
bare-shouldered women, those smooth swan necks – though
compelled to watch the real ladies from the corner of my eye,
hoping to catch another glimpse of the soft mounds like split
risen dough which threatened to spill as a nurse leant to lift
me, or the intimate musk of the nurse right beside me as she
mounted the stepladder to reach the shelves above my head.
Or was that the shoe-shop lady? Mama had a weakness for
shoes. In the attic I counted over fifty boxes. Not your plain
white functional cardboard. But as shiny as patent leather, in
maroon, black, ruby with gold criss-cross ribbon, a summery
cornflower blue striped with lemon.

When I had packed most of the clothes, I started filling up a
box of bric-a-brac – jam jars, a blackened silver-plated candelabra, a pile of old dance records. A photograph album caught
my eye. Flicking through, faces I did not recognise. No faces
of children. Most of the pages were empty, marked only with
blank squares defined by plastic corner mounts. Then, tucked
inside the back cover, more photographs in a dusty, crackling
polythene bag – ready to be fixed into the album perhaps, or
having already been removed? A smartly dressed man in some
doorway (a hint of brass lettering). Had it been taken outside
the Halcyon? Another – the same man again leaning against
the bonnet of a car. One of Mama laughing, svelte in a bathing
costume, the cliffs in the background. Our cliffs? I pulled out
another photograph. And then my whole body tingled. Ah,
Cercatore! Come winging back from those glory days.

Yes, it must have been one of my first concerts, some
years before I met Leodora, for across my upper lip was
the caterpillar of a moustache I had found in some theatrical
suppliers. (And later removed permanently on Leodora's
insistence. I had nothing to prove, she said. I was what
I was, she said, and no goatee or Father Christmas beard
would render me otherwise.) It was a profile shot, the body

poised balletically, as though I was ready to take flight, a pose that was to become my trademark. I was, I have to admit, a handsome youth.

In the photograph I am gazing as if to the heavens – 'my eyes seeing the glory'. You half expect the lashes to flutter in adoration. What a ham I look! The caterpillar curled into the self-contented smile of the pious. But I was far from content in those early days of my career. Not the life I could ever have imagined for myself. Thinking back now, from the beginning the Voice had a will of its own. It would have made itself heard whether I liked it or not. I was, of course, quite unaware of my gift, knew only that singing brought a deep sense of release, could dispel my anxieties at being abandoned.

It was the piano tuner who came to the Mansion House who first set me on my path. He had heard me singing with Joe as we worked in the shed. The long and the short was, within weeks I was dispatched to an exclusive music college in London. (Even then Mama did not come to say goodbye, although by that time, having received no communication from her from more than five years, I had renounced hopes of ever seeing her again.) I was not happy at the music college. I had my own room and, crucially, my own bathroom – Lord forbid I would have to suffer the indignities, the terrors, of communal showers. But I was accustomed to solitude. And I was not like the other students. I did not fit in. My voice, its potential, required me to follow a punishing schedule of training and my three-octave range, my high 'C', became a source of jealousy to the other students and made life even more miserable. I suffered at the hands of the bully boys. After a class, one day, they set upon me and dressed me up in a yellow satin crinoline and ringleted wig and I was forced to sing, under threat of being beaten with a conductor's baton, 'Yet I can hear that dulcet lay' from Handel's *The Choice of Hercules*. (Even now I fear that were I to hear that music again my bones would be reduced to jelly.) Just as one of them was about to remove my underwear 'to see what the girlie was made of', one of the teachers came in and saved my bacon. From then on, I dreamt only of leaving. Fortuitously, or so it seemed at the time, I was, soon after, spotted at one of the college concerts by a talent scout who, as I later realised, regarded my abilities more in terms of a party trick. A Mr Mukari, if I remember rightly, a red-eyed weasel of a man who appeared always to be dressed in someone else's clothes. He secured me lodgings and bookings and I began a tour of what must have been some of the seediest venues in the land – run down holiday resorts, amateur talent competitions, even provincial pantomime.

But the Voice began to attract more serious attention. Even in the early days of my career, before Leodora snapped me up (let's say, for old time's sake, took me under her wing), I caused quite a stir. Offers arrived in a steady flow, requests for me to appear at small but select music events. At first, they had no idea what to do with me, such a strange pigeon was I! There began a revival, a resurrection of certain roles which had since the eighteenth century been performed only by those who sang haute-contre and countertenor, roles such as Handel's Rinaldo, Bertarido in *Rodelinda*, Gluck's *Orfeo*, Mozart's *La Clemenza di Tito* (indeed, the role of Annio in this last, though initially for a castrato, was sung by a contralto at the very first performance). Handel's arias became my party piece for a time, so too those of Farinelli's brother, Riccardo, in particular 'Qual guerriero in campo armato', known as the concerto for larynx. What a devil of a piece – one felt 'all throat', in the same way, I imagine, a ripe young man feels 'all cock' – and one of my favourites. Another, Giovanni Pergolesi's *Salve Regina*, gave me the wings of an angel, and whenever I sang 'Generoso risuegliati a core' from Hasse's opera *Cleofide*, the range of the Voice, from heaven to hell not to mention all those hysterically rolled 'r's', astounded even me.

I was prevented from lingering in my Cercatore reverie by the sound of a vehicle coming down the drive. I feared it was the hearse. No. I looked down. Marcia with the vegetable delivery. She was chatting with Mama. Ah, my bird, and was there another with her? In the passenger seat. A shape. In shadow. Another spy? By the time I was downstairs, Marcia had gone. She had wanted to speak to me, Mama said. And when I unpacked the fruit and vegetables (a huge bag of kiwi – oh, those delicate hairs and, couched in one's palm, such satisfying weight and texture), I discovered a note:

The Golden Years concert beckons, Erskine. Counting on you. PS. Is it a bad day for your mother? She mentioned something about calling in the SAS, and said you were selling all her clothes. I could always have a word with the health centre.

I phoned Marcia later and told her I would deal with the appropriate authorities and bade goodbye before she could mention the concert. I would not be singing, of course. Perhaps I was reading too much into it, but I found it somewhat coincidental that Cercatore should decide to resurrect himself (when he had been buried for so long) just at the time of Mama blabbing to Marcia about my singing career.

I filled up half a dozen or so bin bags which I set outside, only to discover later, while I was preparing supper, that Mama had not only fetched them back in but had taken them to the attic and emptied the contents over the floor. The past was like a relocated cat, intent on finding its way back home.

Oh yes. While changing for supper, I discovered the photograph of Cercatore. I must have slipped it into my trouser pocket absent-mindedly. A persistent ghost. I could have put it away in a drawer. Torn it up, even. But I wanted to keep him. Now that he was here, how could I be rid of him? Yes, my friends, Cercatore had spread his angel wings, had taken flight and come to settle like Munin on my shoulder.

Despite Mama rabbiting on about some new alarm system, it was an unusually delicious meal – lamb chops with fresh rosemary. And a large helping of Cercatore.

5

Angels and Monsters

I am a man seared with negation.

Fully clothed, I compare myself to Angelo Maria Monticelli's painting of the castrato Casali. Is there a copy of it buried somewhere within Boxwood? Where have I seen this painting – reproduced in one of the books within the vast library of the Mansion House? Or was it in one of Leodora's coffee-table tomes? The image of Casali is imprinted in my memory, is one which continues to fascinate for the very way it eludes definition. I shall, however, attempt a description. The pose is affected: left arm on hip, the right hand holding a sheet of music as though it were a tissue (tiss-ue, pronounced with sibilance), and an inconsequential prop, a small-glassed hand mirror from which the face is turned away. Casali might be saying, a tad impatiently, 'Is this how you want me?', or maybe, a little vainly, 'However poor an artist you are, Angelo, you cannot but help portray me a handsome devil.' There is a certain haughtiness about the figure, and pride. But devil or angel, it is hard to say. More precisely, the eyes have an eastern slant and, the fair colouring aside, could well belong to the face of a Lebanese herdsman, or an Egyptian prince, or a lady from Japan. The nose is long and, in profile, more slope than hill, and is elongated at its tip. The septum is pronounced (as is mine), the lips most definitely bow shaped, the lower lip slightly pouting. (Leodora said I had the most kissable pair of lips she had ever seen!) The chin is nothing to speak of.

Others have likened me to the master, Carlo Broschi,

known professionally as Farinelli, of course, the most famous of all the angels of song. Indeed, favourable comparisons have been made with regard to both mien and voice. I refer to another painting – not the one by Bartolomeo Nazari in which the singer resembles, in my view, a white poodle-permed spinster, but Jacopo Amigoni's *Portrait Group: The Singer Farinelli and Friends*, a reproduction of which hung in Leodora's Angel House. (Her intention, I now believe, was to highlight her own resemblance – though there was none – to the beautiful lady in the group, the singer Teresa Castellini.) There is a certain raffishness about Farinelli, a manliness – open-necked garments provoking thoughts of dressing in haste, or undressing. Yet there is too much flesh about the face, the expression is rather too benign. And the nose. What a bouton! No. My features are harder edged, sharper. More of an eagle than a dove, than an angel, perhaps. More racing hound than St Bernard or pug. Masks remain masks, my friends. A codpiece is but a most unnatural bulge. Always, the truth lies in the face.

And in the face of Cercatore, what did I see? An angel. A white candle shining in Boxwood's dark. The Voice pure, virginal – starlight travelling the past's long night. I propped the photograph of Cercatore the Great on my work table and I heard his song begin once again.

I had decided to abandon the spring cleaning. Mama was anyway uncooperative. ('You'll have me in a bin bag next,' she said.) And I was beset with an urge to start work on my white-wood project, an urge I knew could not be put off for long. Thus motivated, or driven, after an arduous session in my workroom, by lunch-time I emerged victor from my battle with the ebony box. The lid sat straight, almost, and what it was to contain, the ebony monsieur, could finally be laid to rest. Had ebony not been such a devilish wood to work (so hard and brittle – I was sharpening tools in my sleep), I might have considered adding a lock mechanism – and throwing away the key! But now that the box was completed, as I polished the wood I could, to some degree, appreciate its beauty. It was a titillation of perception, the outer surface smooth, the interior chiselled gouge marks for texture. An inverted shell. Shell. Seashell. A vacated seashell. Emptied. The absolute expression of . . . un-containment. And containment? Containment's absolute expression? Why, of course, a Russian doll! Forget the white-wood baloney, Erskine, I thought, how about a box within a box within a box, and so on – oh, indeed – each box neatly fitting its container, and identical, apart from size. I could call it the Definitive Version, and it could occupy me for years, years if I started big enough (or small enough), and I would use the easiest of woods, say *Picea abies*, the European spruce, and soft pine, Californian redwood, European walnut, and *Castanea sativa*, commonly the sweet chestnut, which could be the smallest box which would contain the surprise – a chestnut handmade from chestnut! Yes! But no. The Devil only knows the fantastic schemes and projects I have dreamt up, but none have yet enabled me to resist the call of the next monsieur. Like Lorelei on her rock. Into temptation I go. Oh, then the shame. Hot cheeked, I hear the insults. My own voice in my own ears. 'Erskine, bad boy, what have you done, Erskine, dirty bad boy!' The secret pushed down inside me cools, chills, hardens to a cold stone of guilt. Yes. The white-wood monsieur had reached out a hand, and I could do nothing but take it.

Just then, Mama called through the door. It was way past lunch-time, almost two.

'If you think you can starve me, think again. I'm a survivor, Erskine. I could live off bugs and grass if pushed. I once attended an Outward Bound. I've opened a can of beans.'

She couldn't wait any longer, she said, or she'd miss the

train. What train? Apparently, she was going to see Aunt Frieda. I later found Mama dressed in a straw hat, a coat over her nightgown, sitting on a stool in the bathroom. The window she appeared to be looking through was the bathroom wall. She had been travelling for almost an hour, I said, perhaps she'd like to stop for a snack? But it appeared the train would only stop for emergencies.

'I'll make eggs, Mama, scrambled with olives and spring onion. Your favourite. And passion fruit sorbet for dessert.'

'Sit down, sir, please, you're causing a commotion. The driver can't see his rear window.'

I noticed there was a pink hair curler sticking out from under her hat. It looked like something surgical, or a valve, perhaps, which might deflate her if pulled, or some extraneous plastic bit when they broke her from the mould.

'And by the way,' she said, 'I have never liked sorbet. And I abhor passion fruit. You should know that.'

I despaired. The previous day, she had called me Treacher. A gardener we'd employed. I misheard it as 'traitor' at first and was rather on the defensive. We were having coffee on the front lawn, engaged in a lucid discussion about discouraging snails. They had been gorging on her geraniums in the outhouse. Then suddenly she pointed a finger outside.

'Treacher, time to tie up the daffs!'

Daffs? She was daffy. Daft as a brush. I looked at the wattle, thought of those smooth stretched swan necks of the Delderfield's catalogue women. Momentarily, and quite uncharacteristically, you understand, I had an urge to strangle her.

'Vinegar, Treacher,' she went on. 'Wipe over the pots with vinegar. That soon changes their track.'

I could not help flinching. My friends, one could all too easily imagine. The grey mucus-coated vulnerable foot. Salt on a wound. The racking. The agony. Other agony. The first.

Mama like a fat shell, her secret coiled up inside her. Came sliming out of her. Insides out. Along came a blackbird and gobbled up the worm. How relentlessly weaves the past. I wanted to forget. Forget! I imagined my hands around the tortoise wattle.

Aunt Frieda's, then. Mama was best left to her own devices. I ate lunch alone. Frustration was mounting. The constant toing and froing of her mind unnerved me. I was a ball bounced around her fictions. Now she knows me, now she don't. I did not know how much worse it could get, how much more I could take.

But I had no more time to ponder. Though I fancied fresh air, a stroll to the cliffs, the afternoon was spoken for. First, the ceremony of locking Mr Ebony (at last!) in his box in the private collection room, then sketches for the white-wood monsieur. But returning to my workroom, my eyes were drawn to Cercatore. Despite the gawky adolescence, a handsome devil. Fifteen, sixteen, almost a man. Almost. The face wide, yet angular, and highly photogenic, jet-black hair (before this distinguishing grey streak appeared) without fringe or parting, a mane (not unlike Leodora's) giving a romantic flourish. I was never short of admirers, although I never allowed them to get too close. The closer they came, the more of a fraud I felt. Fraud, not freak. For this was not Erskine – at least, not the Erskine who should have been. I was always more at ease with the older women, right back to my time at the Mansion House when I'd look forward to the last Friday of the month when the ladies of the village came to play bridge. I'd settle myself under the table, surrounded by a protective fence of too thin or too plump legs, a puppy waiting for a pat on the head, a titbit. Always the biddies. Except for Sylvia, of course. And you, my Ulva, you.

I did not feel inclined to show the photograph to Mama. For one thing, Marcia's Golden Years concert still niggled like a boil beneath the skin. For another, who knows down what dark avenues it might have led dear Mama, what old wounds might have been reopened. Mama needed no encouragement to return. And whether the photograph was to remain on my desk or not, Cercatore had reached me. Munin was nibbling at my earlobe, his tune-sharp beak an ink-dipped nib. The song had begun, of passion and soul, of light and dark, angel and monster.

The phone was ringing. Hackthrew, the wood supplier's. My wenge was in. My wenge what? They weren't able to get the panga panga but the wenge was very similar. For a long-standing family firm, Hackthrew's often fell short of the mark. I had ordered neither wenge nor panga panga, I said (in any case, I frowned upon the very notion of substitution), but I was after a very special white wood, along the lines of European holly, the Sitka spruce, Finnish whitewood. It was suggested I come in and browse. Yes. Mama and I would have an outing into the town. I would treat us to a slap-up meal.

Her reaction was troubling, pathetic to witness. She might almost have been institutionalised, such was the combination of excitement, bewilderment and fear when I mentioned a trip to town. Yet she sat like a queen on the bus, occasionally waving discreetly, nodding through the window at passers-by. Duty calls, she said, winking. Did she intend to drive me mad also?

At Hackthrew's – an olfactory wonderland of fresh and seasoning timbers! – I purchased a quantity of *Acer pseudo-platanus*, commonly sycamore, enough for the two 'objects' of my white-wood project. (Experience had taught me always to purchase enough for two.) A matter of settling for the common or garden, or waiting weeks for an order of something more exotic. And wait I could not. I wandered around the storage area, noting such delights as the very rare snakewood, also known as leopard wood, with its deep reddish-brown heartwood marked with darker stripes and spots. Now what a serpent of a monsieur that would produce! I also spotted the striking blood-red chanlanga-da, or padauk. (I would much prefer things to have one name, wouldn't you? The padauk, for example, has another sixteen. What is its true name? And is identity enhanced, or diluted, by such proliferation of nomenclature? Does it not confuse?) I was drawn from such reverie on hearing Mama telling a customer she was building a boat. She was convincing – keels, gunnels and rowlocks, no less, which she must have gleaned from a magazine or the television. Was she going to sail around the bay, the man wanted to know, or was she intending to navigate more distant waters? Oh, round the world, Mama replied, and for her next venture she was off to sail the seven seas.

On the way to the café, Mama popped into the chemist's, having spotted the window flora of shower caps and swim hats. She purchased an orange one blooming with petunia-pink flopping petals, put it on and would not remove it. I gave up. At least, I said, we would not lose her out on the seven seas. Oh, but this is not for swimming, she said, this is for the shower. Passing a framing shop, I thought of Cercatore. He deserved a decent border. I would have a rummage through the shed. I had some cocobolo somewhere, a beautiful wood used often for rosaries, and buttons. At the café we decided to sit at one of the pavement tables. Passers-by stared at or looked away from Mama in her hat. We were doing a turn, didn't they know? Performance artists. Making a point, or no point at all. I was the straight man, of course. I was feeling defensive. I wanted to shout, Why shouldn't she wear the damn hat? I also wanted to tell everyone that I had absolutely nothing to do with her. I was about to devour a scone when it caught me, open mouthed, scone midair. This time on foot. Wings folded. Walking right past. Within touching distance. In the flesh. You, Ulva, my bird.

You. And when you turned and stared at Mama, a smile played over your lips. And something in those eyes. What was it? Something I half recognised. Ah. And I could smell you, already taste you.

Back home, Mama fell asleep in her swimming hat, the petals quivering in the breeze of her exhalation. Her green dress and the exotic cockscomb gave her the look of a giant cactus in flower. I did not want to disturb her and escaped to my workroom. I apologised to Cercatore. No frame today. He looked unfinished. Not the full packet. All shirt and no tie. Shoes and no socks. All cock and no balls. I sat with the sycamore for a while. Leave it to settle, to find its bearings, like a newly acquired pet, I told myself. The usual little game I'd have with myself. It was a fear, and yet an urge, that taking of the first step. Rather, I imagine, like the weakened recovering alcoholic presented with a bottle of Scotch, the reformed smoker finding a pack of ciggies in a drawer. I knew that once I set the wood on my table and picked up a tool, I could only go on. This was no puppy-dog or fluffy puss. And I would be powerless to resist. Though Lordy knows, I have tried, how I have tried.

I was loath to wake Mama for bed. But I couldn't risk her waking up later in the night to find herself alone downstairs in the dark. When at last she removed her cap, I saw it had left a purplish line around her forehead, like a circular scar, a join. Lift the lid and heavens knows what you might find! Halfway up the stairs, she said she thought she'd be very comfortable here, thank you, and did we do room service?

The following morning, I woke to foul weather. I stayed in bed late, resisting the pull of the workroom. I thought about searching for the cocobolo but could not face the cold damp shed. Instead, I made a soup of lentil, carrot and coriander for lunch. Dusky orange, vibrant orange, sharp summer (or rather spring) green. Colour amidst a grey-wash morning. Mid-morning, I began to miss Mama. She had not come looking for her elevenses as usual. I went in search. On my way to the garden, someone called through the letterbox. A voice I recognised.

'Mr Flesching? Mr Flesching, I know you are in there. Please open the door, sir. It is imperative that I speak with you. It's your mother.'

Damn. Damn the woman. Health visitor and Mama both. I did not move. Mama, in heaven's name where have you got to?

'Mr Flesching, your mother was spotted in the village earlier this morning. In her nightdress, Mr Flesching. In the pouring rain. Has she come home? Is she with you now?'

If she had come home, then she would be with me now. No. No. Oh, Mama. Didn't she realise what she was risking? Us, Mama. Us. I waited. Just when I decided she must have gone came the parting shot:

'Mr Flesching, your mother is in need of professional care. You are not cooperating, Mr Flesching. I shall have to pass the matter on to my superiors.'

Well, I thought, just you pass it on, then, dear lady. And just let them try. They would not take Mama away from me. I would put up a fight. I would barricade us in.

When she'd finally left, I knew there was nothing for it. I would have to go and look for Mama myself. On the way out, I discovered a note stuck to the front door: April 12th. Mrs Flesching seen a.m. in village in nightdress. Please inform of her return.'

Halfway down the lane, I saw the hearse, and that woman inside hunched over her mobile phone. She looked round at me. I turned on my heels and came straight back. I locked the door. Shut my eyes. I was splitting open, my insides bursting out, my heart rolling across the floor. Mama, oh, Mama.

What was happening? The fear was returning. Nemesis. Here she comes again. The first one. Frankie Deuce. Hot on my heels.

'I have done nothing wrong, madam, I assure you. What is it exactly that you want from me?'

They had caught me in the park. I was spending as little time as possible in the flat for fear they would call. Somehow, a locked door did not offer adequate protection. I mistakenly believed that outside they could not so easily pin me down. I took care to vary my movements as much as possible, never lingering overlong. I had thus been 'on the move' since early that morning and had stopped in the park merely to rest my feet. They approached me from behind – enough to set my hackles up in itself. I did not attempt to run. For that would only have aroused suspicion. What then would I have been running from?

'You are difficult to get hold of, Mr Flesching. Forgive me, you are Mr Flesching, are you not?'

'I believe I am. Yes.'

'Then let me introduce myself. Deuce. Frankie Deuce. Private detective.'

Yes. I knew. She was wearing a hat, as usual, a feminine version of a trilby, a small feather of iridescent peacock greens and purples sticking from a thin black band, and a long over-sized cream mac, a scarf, knee-length boots, gloved hands plunged into pockets. Only the eyes, shrewish, calculating, and the voice were evidence of life inside.

'You were, I understand, acquainted with a Miss Ableyart, a Miss Leodora Ableyart?'

'Ah, yes. Yes. For a short time, I was. Briefly.'

'For a number of years, I think. Not so briefly, then. Am I right?'

'I was. We were. Yes. You are.'

I was watching a child over by the edge of the lake, feeding bread to the swans.

'Swans are ugly, don't you think?' I said. 'Out of water, that is. Their grace and beauty are spoiled by their greed. They are powerful. Vicious in the extreme. I find it hard to think of them as birds.'

Frankie Deuce hissed with impatience. 'Leodora Ableyart has disappeared, Mr Flesching. Would you have any idea where she might be?'

But surely this Frankie Deuce already knew? I turned to walk away.

'Are you going somewhere, Mr Flesching? You won't mind if I join you?'

Where could I go? Certainly not straight back to the flat. All it took was a foot in the door. And I could not remember how I had left the place. What might Leodora have taken with her? What might she have left? I made a note to check through the things, and to change the locks. For now, I would walk.

'I am simply out for fresh air. Yes, of course you may join me.'

'No idea, then, Mr Flesching, where she could have gone?'

I felt better walking. Freer.

'It is,' I said, 'as I am sure you will appreciate, rather a delicate situation for me. Yes, we were very close – living together, you would call it. Unfortunately, sadly, the relationship simply came to a natural end.'

'A natural end? Forgive me, Mr Flesching, but it is the emotional state of Miss Ableyart I am interested in. Were there disagreements, any bad feeling between you? Didn't Miss Ableyart tell you where she was going?'

'Not a word. And no rows. Nothing at all like that. As I said, a natural end.'

We were approaching the pond. The little girl had disappeared. A clear plastic bag bobbed on the surface, visceral.

Stomach of a deer. An unbroken birth sac. The swans had returned to the water, to their white china grace. I was feeling a little more composed. Perhaps I should have spoken to Frankie Deuce sooner. I was even feeling confident enough to embellish a little.

'I think I am over it now,' I said. 'You may imagine, it has not been easy.'

'Rather like a death, might you say, Mr Flesching?' She stopped, looked right into my eyes. 'However inevitable, it is never easy.'

'I really wouldn't know, Miss Deuce,' I said. 'I am, as yet, fortunate enough not to have lost anyone to death.'

We were approaching the park gates. Had Frankie Deuce finished with me?

'I have an appointment, Mr Flesching,' she said. 'But I would like to talk to you again, if I may. I shall be in touch. You are not planning to run away, I take it?' She laughed.

(Isn't that what the police said?)

'When?'

'Next week, perhaps. I shall ring you.'

I had stopped answering the phone. We were ex-directory. How did she know the number?

'Yes. No. I am not going anywhere.'

'Good. Adieu, then, Mr Flesching.'

She walked off. I stood for a moment, saw a trail, a thin red line drawn along the ground with her steps. A thought:

'Miss Deuce. Miss Deuce,' I called after her. 'Who did you say is looking for Leo . . . Miss Ableyart? Who wants to find her?'

I could not hear clearly, but I think what she said was: 'Don't you know, Mr Flesching?' Or was it: 'Don't you?'

As soon as I got back I disconnected the phone. Then I plugged it back in. I could not run. From what or whom would I be running? I cleared out the flat. Bagged it all up and set it out for the bin men. Not one thing of Leodora's remained. Disappeared off the face of the earth. My Leodora, I knew why you had to go.

Mama returned at twenty past six. She was wearing the shower cap so at least her hair had stayed dry. Her nightdress clung to her body. She appeared to have been vacuum packed. She had the look of a frozen turkey.

'Mama, where on earth have you been? You've been gone all day, Mama. I've been worried out of my mind. And you're soaked to the bone.'

'Oh, Erskine,' she said, 'I've had such a lovely time. Shopping and all sorts. Look, look what I've bought.'

She pulled balls of wool from a plastic carrier. Pink, fluorescent pink. Little-girl pink. And a pack of knitting needles.

'I'm going to knit you a sweater,' she said, 'just like the green one. You like the green one, don't you? Buttons on the shoulder like my little soldier boy. Soldier shoulder shoulder soldier.' She chuckled.

'Mama, you mustn't, you shouldn't go out on your own, not without telling me.'

'Yes,' she said, 'oh yes. Plain ones and purls. Daughters and girls.'

I ran her a hot, a very hot, bath. What was I going to do with her? 'Please inform of her return . . .' No, I would not. I would have absolutely nothing whatsoever to do with them. They did not exist as far as I was concerned. Mama was staring at me.

'I didn't go out on my own, you know,' she said. 'She came with me. She was holding my hand.'

Oh no, Mama, please, not again.

Later. The nightmares.

Behind me. Striding out behind me, ten foot tall. Thin violet lips. Slit eyes. Behind me with those high shiny black boots slapping the ground. Huge strides. Frightened they're going to catch up. How many? Five, six, sixty? Hundreds, an army, a black sea behind me, rolling in. I'm pushing myself faster and faster, but they're still going at the same pace. Witchy black cloaks lifting in the wind – mouths have turned to hooks, to beaks. Avatars. I'm running, running towards the Mansion House now and I am in the fields. We are in the fields. I am lying on the grass. There's a horse. Is it a horse? A horse's tail. Sylvia. Sylvia's shiny purpleheart hair covering my face. Caressing my face. It's all I feel. Rest of me's numb. Sylvia's calling to me. She's far away, up in the sky, lifted by wings. Erskine! Erskine! She's calling. But is it Sylvia? Or Mama? Mama's mouth is wide. Wider. Hairy. Prickly. A huge splitting thistle. Teeth inside. Pointed teeth. Jaws wide.

I woke in the early hours. I decided something would have to be done about Mama.

Flicking through the journal just now, my friends, and look what I found. This was it. My one false move.

25 April. So easy. Wonder it did not come to me before. An opportunity presented itself. Sky grey, ungiving, promising nothing. Not many people about. A few down on the beach with their hounds. Keep out of their way, that's for sure. A sudden and delightful image of the den of lions – a haunch, a torso, indeed the entire victim (already injured, of course), tossed into the pit and the scrum of beasts like the first day of the sale, the gnashing and gnawing and licking of lips. Every scrap devoured. Not a shred left. What a clean-up. No. Not many about. Conditions ripe, though it was not planned. A chance meeting. That was all. On the cliff top. I had no idea she'd be there. I watched her for some time, nibbling at a chocolate bar as though she wanted it to last for ever. Wished it had now! She was sitting right at the edge. No other soul around. But me. Was she humming to herself? The wind came up a little, eating up my footsteps. (As on previous occasions, the elements were on my side.) She did not even turn, not even when I was right up close behind her. Put out my hand. Just a gentle push. Almost a caress. Quick over the edge she went. She gave a kind of gurgle or gasp. Had she swallowed the chocolate bar whole perhaps? And half twisting as she went, I saw in her eyes; not shock or fear, but surprise. Yes, surprise! More a register of recognition, like when you find yourself standing in a queue, and the person in front of you is someone you know from way back. Just like that. It seemed to go on for ever, that tumble of hers. She was scrabbling with her arms and legs. Why do that, when there was nothing to hang on to? Ah no, there was the chocolate bar on the ledge, of course. A few greedy guillemots competed for it, pecking viciously.

So. The sea would have her. It was welcome. Problem solved.

—Fully clothed, an angel you may appear, Erskine. But look in the mirror. Unclothe yourself. Between your legs. That pathetic nub. An apology of itself. In the glass, now, a grotesque apparition. What do you see – angel, monster or freak? And Ulva and Leodora and Mama – what did they see? Ethereal, Leodora said. But did she not mock you? Did they not fear you? Where are your redeeming wings? Did Ulva take them? That day she caught you in the bathroom. (Ah, you are thinking of Ulva now, what you saw in the dressing-table mirror, pinky-brown beads, small mounds, like cherry-topped macaroons. See how the nub perks to attention! Something's astir, some little thing, goblin in the woods – it's all you've got.) Was it Ulva? Or Leodora, or Mama? Perhaps you shed your wings long ago, after the mauling. Two sighs, last breaths falling – swish-swish – into the silent dark of the hospital night. Or before then? Your life rewinds fast and clear and final, as though through the mind of a drowning man: Mama gone mad, the return to Boxwood, Leodora, the guilt, the betrayal, the brief fame, the exile at the Mansion House, the tragedy, right back to the moment on the cliff top when you reached out to push, a moment that was to reset the course of your life. Were your wings unclipped then, by your own hand? Did they drop like doves into the raging sea below? Or will you find them in the cupboard under the stairs, like shrouds in a burial chamber? You will tell them it wasn't your fault. All those who have loved you have left. All those you have loved have betrayed you. They were threatening to take Mama and you had to stop them. You had to find a way to stop them leaving. Then along came a bird, one whose wings could be clipped.

6

Something Found, Something Lost

So. This was where you flew in, my bird. You were a glint of hope, the jewel in the guano, the surprise of tinsel in the laboured weave of twig, mud and down of a bird's nest – one imagines the twinkle in the eye of the bird, the chirrup of glee. You set my eye a-twinkle, my Ulva. I did not realise that our meeting had little to do with chance, that there was more behind that greeny-blue wide-eyed double-take of yours. (Marcia had surely prepared you, had given you some idea of my oddity. Or perhaps Marcia, another who does not blend with the crowd, had not.)

I was on my way to the village for provisions when, you recall, Marcia pulled up alongside in the van and thrust through the window at me a bunch of leaflets on senile dementia, caring for the elderly, et cetera (which I later deposited in the nearest waste bin). As I feared, she was trying to pin me down about the concert again. 'A second wind, Erskine. A relaunch!' As I leant down to tell her that I had no intention of ever performing again, there you were! My bird on the bike! But what were you doing in Marcia's van?

'My lodger, Erskine,' Marcia said. 'Ulva will be staying at the cottage for a while. I shall welcome the company.'

I admit I experienced a twinge of envy. So my company was not good enough, then, Marcia? But Ulva. Ulva? Ah, you.

I will admit too that back at Boxwood I found myself repeating (as one does) your name to the mirror, U-L-V-A, U-L-V-A, pronouncing its power, calling you closer. Ulva.

Your plumage was blond, though I suspected not a natural shade, for a darker blond, reddish, was emerging at the roots. Four thin plaits, the ends secured in turquoise beads, and a small canary-yellow feather decorated the otherwise free mane. You leant forward slightly, pushed a hand across the crown, through your hair. A movement which provoked a curious image – two hands crawling towards each other, like shellfish responding to mother nature's mating call. I heard the light clatter of thin silver bracelets along your forearm. I saw pale blues, lilacs, turquoise, aquamarine, purples, pinks. Layers of coloured garments. Your nails were painted pearly white – like metamorphosing pupae, the talons, I imagined, soon to emerge wet and scarlet. You were a vision engendering vision.

You smiled briefly, then looked away – not, I thought, dismissively. Were you a little coy? You see, then, and for some time after, I neither felt threatened by your presence nor sensed any hint of dark motives. Such a sweet and airy being. An innocent angel-chick. Would we meet, I wondered? And when?

My questions were answered when Marcia told me you would be helping out for a while with the vegetable deliveries. Ah, a guarantee, then, that I would be seeing you on a regular, albeit temporary, basis. Although exactly how our relationship was to develop I could never have guessed in a million years.

I clean forgot about my shopping errands. Mama and I had a makeshift lunch of stale bread, rindy cheese and a pickled gherkin apiece. Mama had no appetite anyway, having been off colour all morning. But tomorrow was vegetable day! What should I do? Engage you in a little chit-chat on the door-step? Should I invite you in, entice you with a slice of walnut cake? So long since I'd had the pleasure of female company.

In the afternoon, Mama retired to her room with the pink wool and knitting needles. And though longing to continue the reverie of you, my bird, I was lured to my workroom by the sycamore. I attempted once again to confound my inner demon by first drawing the box, in the hope that reversing the process might render redundant that which the box was to contain. But I was clutching at straws. And not a straw, but a thick member! For what use, I thought, is an empty box? It demands to be filled. Then I had another brainwave – a box without a lid, that is, a lid that cannot be opened, a block of wood in the shape of a box – an illusion! Yes! But it was to remain an illusion. For I looked down and saw to my horror what I had sketched on the drawing pad. A monster! Two foot long. The spheres at its base the size of tennis balls. What is more, and I am even ashamed to recall it, the pencil had drawn the grotesque helmet entering an orifice. I screwed up the paper, turned Cercatore to the wall, and lay on the floor overwhelmed by guilt and shame. How could I even entertain the ridiculous notion that you would wish to be acquainted with such a hopeless freak as Erskine Flesching?

The next day, there you were, at the front door. I recall the look on your face, my bird. You were such a petite fledgling creature, barely reaching to my chest. You stepped back in shock, did you not? Hopped back on your spindly legs. Did I frighten you? Did you fear these long, impossibly long, arms of mine might scoop you up and never set you down? Then when I opened my mouth wide and you heard, not the sonorous boom of a Thor, but the song of a sparrow, the smallest ditty of a hummingbird, of an ant, a dust mite, the cry of an elf, pixie, sprite, soft as the flutter of a butterfly's wing, the otherworldy call of Oberon, the pure and silvered golden testimony of an angel – ah.

'Sorry to disturb you. I had to ring the bell. Marcia said the box would be in the porch but I don't seem able to find it.'

The voice of a lark, summer-happy. I feared mine was lost in the clouds.

'My apologies. I quite forgot to leave it out. Memory, you understand.' I laughed. (Remember the self-deprecating titter, how I touched my temple with my fingertips? I had been rehearsing this little display of self-mockery since I woke. But did you notice my hand, a leaf in breeze, shaking as I passed you the money? That was for real, my bird.)

'I've just filled the cafetière,' I said. 'Have you time for coffee?'

'Yes, please. I have a few more deliveries, but I think I'm allowed a tea break.'

So easy, I thought, and you so willing! An eagerness which I then interpreted as compensatory but now see in another light. You were imagining an altogether more sinister set-up, that Erskine was a hard old nut to crack, that it would be some time before you could get a foot inside my door. But there was something about you (or was I imagining it? Or is it only how it appears to me now, in hindsight?), a 'something' which I had seen as you peered from the shadows of Marcia's van. What was it? Intent, and conviction, for you had a purpose, a certain knowingness.

You sat at the table in the place I had already designated as yours, opposite me. As I finished preparing the coffee, I noted your flimsy jade top, the calf-length jeans and, around an ankle, a silver chain, as though you had been tagged. A tiny pink gemstone studded a nostril. Your plumage was caught in a ponytail. There were a few faint lines around your eyes. But hadn't I seen those greeny-blue eyes somewhere before, on another face?

I had made the cake the previous evening. (I had managed to pull myself from the workroom floor to make it to the village before the shops shut.) A walnut cake with a rich cream filling. I had arranged the walnut halves in the shape of the nut on top of the cake, but the design more resembled a heart. Pretty and apt, but impractical, for when I tried to cut you a slice, the blade would not slice through the nuts, of course. You offered to pick them off. Which you did, so delicately! Ah, I was imagining those fingers . . . I watched how you crumbled the cake, set each piece on the teaspoon, dipped it into your coffee, then put it to your mouth, your lips pursing as you sucked the cake from the spoon. I was imagining those fingers light and cool on my skin, tracing the feathery scar lines, running over the ridges and bumps, until, between thumb and forefinger, they would take the nub. My mouth watered. I was experiencing an adjustment of tissue, a distinct stirring in the lacuna, a faint but persistent buzz – like a bee long trapped but endeavouring still to escape. But no sting in my tail, my bird, not in mine.

I was talking too much, I feared, about Mama, about Boxwood (and shifting about in the chair – remember the creaks – like Pinocchio coming to life!). You nodded, said little. I worried you were bored, then I realised Marcia must have filled you in. When you'd finished your cake, you took a tin, matches and cigarette papers from a small beaded bag. Considerately, you asked whether I minded you smoking. Mama had been coughing for a couple of days, but she was out of the way upstairs somewhere. While you rolled your cigarette, it occurred to me I might make a small box for your equipment. Nothing too elaborate, with a simple design in straight-line carving on the lid, a guillemot perhaps. Then you looked at your watch. I groped for more questions.

'You must be very comfortable at Marcia's. It's a very cosy cottage.'

'You know Marcia well? She hasn't spoken of you.'

'Ah. At one time,' I said, somewhat deflated, 'but I have little time to socialise. Mama keeps me busy. She's becoming a full-time occupation. Like this house. I'm afraid Mama has let it go over the years. And she's too unwell now to do much.'

Again you looked at your watch.

'I really ought to go.' You hesitated.

'Yes?'

'Listen,' you said, 'there's not much else to do once I've done the boxes. I'm finished by lunch-time. If you think it's a good idea, I could help out with your mother. The house too. If you like. I mean, whenever you need a break.'

Oh yes. Indeed. An excellent idea. An extra eye on Mama. And your eye into the bargain! And all without having to tempt you in. No need for crumbs on the window ledge, then.

'Well, that is most kind of you. I shall bear it in mind. Thank you.'

I said I would let you know. I did not want to appear too eager. Softly, softly, Erskine, slippers of mink. But after you had gone, I immediately went in search of Mama to tell her about her new companion. I could not find her anywhere. For a horrible moment, I thought she had gone wandering again. Then I heard coughing coming from one of the back rooms. She was lying on the sofa, her face flushed, two clown-like medallions on her cheeks.

'I'm feeling rather poorly, Doctor,' she croaked.

I told her I had found someone to keep her company.

'A young girl,' I said.

But she was too weary from coughing even to respond.

Returning to the kitchen, as I was sealing the plastic bag containing the cigarette butt and used match, my words 'a young girl for you, Mama' came back to me like a sinister echo. Three of us, then, not two. But at least I would have you close by. You would quickly tire of Mama's demands and spend more and more time with me. A most delightful plan.

Mama seemed to brighten a little as the day wore on, but evening came and the coughing returned with a vengeance. The sooner you came to play nursemaid, I thought, the better. Anxious to record developments, I reached for my journal. It was not in its usual place on my desk. My journal appeared to have been mislaid.

An error, my friends, the worst. I was handing myself to you on a plate, on an eighteen-carat diamond-studded platter.

I spent the best part of the next day hunting. (Thoughts of you, my bird, having been stored in a soft velvet pouch in my mind, from which I imagined your greeny-blue eyes peeping as I searched for what was proving to be an impossibly fine needle.) Indeed, the search was a doomed task in the dense unyielding haystack of Boxwood. Mama was no help – was equally dense.

'Are you looking for the *Village Journal*, Erskine?' she said, trailing me like a woebegone hound dog. 'Is it the newspaper? I use it for loo paper usually. It's never any good.'

I did my utmost to remain patient. She was looking worryingly peaky. I helped her settle with some magazines and a sherry and continued rummaging through some piles of papers and exercise books stacked in one of the little-used sitting rooms. Flicking through the books, I saw they were mostly filled with lists, such as:

10 pairs rubber beach shoes
3 years' quarterly editions of *The Good Housekeeper* (12 in all)
National Geography May 1957–June 1963
dog leads (12 dozen)
5 boxes rubber insoles
3 boxes cotton insoles
4 packs exercise books (10 a pack)
earplugs (100 pack)
throat pastilles (1 box of 2 dozen packs)
plastic bags of seashells, washed (8 bags)

And so the lists went on, each list under the heading of a room. The books, I realised, were an inventory of Boxwood. Pondering the state of mind requiring such an inventory

(Mama's, that is), and their neatness, sense of order, the detail and so on, I was inspired to make a more thorough, systematic search for my journal. Start at the top, work down (as I had decided on a previous occasion). On my way up to the attic, I was beset with shame thinking what you would make of it all, my bird. I would simply have to brave another attempt at a clear-out. I did not want you to think this was how I chose to live.

I began in a small room adjacent to where I had discovered Mama naked that night and opened a large box in the far corner. The box had once contained, apparently, drums of 'Choc-o-Nuts', chocolate-coated peanuts, two of which remained, like the droppings of a small creature. Inside the box was a collection of tarnished silver frames, all rather too large for Cercatore. Beneath those I found a set of three framed pictures depicting a game of cricket, cartoon style, and obviously from a magazine (the captions having been curiously omitted). Under those, a set of snooker balls, pristine, the seal on the plastic container intact, and beneath the balls a set of small boxes, all fitting inside each other, which might have contained, or been intended for perhaps, small items of jewellery, rings, earrings and so forth. There was also a series of six pictures in neat black frames of Birds of the British Coastline – a gull, a tern, two guillemots, and a shag. Then I pulled out another picture and bristled, for staring at me, tongue lolling, was a four-legged creature, the sort used to lead the blind (praises be I had my sight, I thought). The oak frame, however, was exactly what I was looking for, more or less the right size, and anyway I could always make a mount. The irony did not go unmissed – Cercatore replaces the Hound. Ha!

Delving deeper into the box, I pulled out a bag of photographs, all with a portion cut off, like wedding photographs after a divorce. Photographs of me, young Erskine, a babe in arms, a toddler in home-knit sweater and woolly hat. But I was not smiling in any one! Had I been born sad? Then I found one which made my skin tighten, my mouth suddenly dry. Her. Yes, most definitely. But a plump child and not at all as I had stored her in my mind all those years – slight, spindle limbed, the little match girl, a flung rag doll. She was bending over a rock pool, the crimson bather now faded to a tired orange, and the sea behind a murky brownish green. Until Ursula was born, Mama used to have an old box camera. Later, when the child would not sit still for any length of time, Mama bought an Instamatic. I remember the photographs sliding from the machine with such a laboured sound, as if they were being painfully disgorged. The Instamatic later disappeared, was lost somewhere, over the edge of a cliff possibly. I could not see her face. What was it she was poking at in the rock pool? Such a cruel child. How many fragile crab shells were cracked by her poking stick? I wonder. But who was that in the distance leaning against a rock? Mama? Then who took the photograph? And where was I? And then I came across a photograph of Mama, taken in summer, that summer, a swollen Mama, a Mama I did not want to remember.

She told me it would be all right. She told me it would soon return to how it used to be. But it wasn't all right. And I knew we would never return to how it had been ever again. Our world, tight, complete. Picnics and rock pools, shopping and cakes. Me curled on Mama's lap while she read stories, feeling the gentle sea-rhythm of her breathing, drifting on my boat out to wide calm waters – in, out, in, out – slowing my breathing in time with hers. I could smell her scent, like garden roses, and, after she'd drunk tea, the stale suggestion of tannin, old wood. After a while, I'd forget all about the stories, the words losing their meaning, becoming mere sound, shapes, as I watched her lips, mesmerised by the small and subtle movements, the flexing, curling, stretching. All my senses were alert, honed, and yet, as I lay upon her, my edges seemed to disappear. No boundaries between us. I became part of her. As if I had climbed back inside her. We were the figures in the Christmas snow scene, high on the mantelpiece, safe within the glass ball that I believed no one could destroy. My Mama. Mine. I would not share her. Not with anyone.

Mama's illness had taken hold the first weeks of summer during that last holiday at the Halcyon. Throughout those long hot months, she did not once come down to the beach. She did not want to play with me. She stopped reading me stories. Even when I tried to climb on to her lap, she'd push me away. Her hair turned greasy and her breath soured. She stayed in her room. Some days she did not come downstairs until past lunch-time. Some days not at all. She swelled up like a grotesque balloon. When I could not sleep, I'd creep out on to the landing and, through the banisters, watch her wandering about the house, from room to room, along the corridors below, spectral in her billowy white cotton gowns, heavy and swaying, like some ghost ship gliding through a labyrinth of underground waters.

I had never known the days so long, waiting hours for Mama to pay me some attention, for her eyes at last to find me, her hand reach out and touch. I had become an insect, tight in a corner, scuttling from the light, the heavy tread of those who did not want you in their way, under their feet. Two women came to look after the house. A nurse, who looked like a toad, with a broad fat face and a fat neck and belly and thin, thin arms and legs. The other, a young girl, helped in the kitchen and with the housework. The young one, who picked her nose continually, tormented me by making faces and pinching my arms whenever I passed. I kept out of their way. I was not allowed to go to the beach on my own, so I'd curl up on the chaise longue in the library, keeping company with the books – *The Lives of the Great Composers, Greek Myths and Legends, The Complete Cordon Bleu, The Proficient Carpenter, A Guide to the Seashore* – anything to fill the emptiness inside me.

The house became a dark shell. Boxwood was a beast in mourning. The old hound had drawn down the shutters, made fast the doors, clamped shut its jaws. The beast had gone to ground. Even the music stopped. Mama had always loved to play the piano. After lunch, or in the evenings before I went up to bed, she would play – Mozart, Handel, Artemis Schluck, Languedoc Nopalis, Gluck, Benthamine Vagrant, Labelar. I would sit beside her, on the purple velvet piano stool, watching her hands like scuttling creatures, like the crabs at low tide. Once, one jumped from the keys and landed on my head, clutched my scalp, and I screamed and grabbed Mama and she laughed and rocked me back and forth, her body swaying in time to the music she played. But Mama stopped playing. So I'd sit on the piano stool alone and imagine her there beside me, the movement of her body, my fingers rubbing the plush nap of the velvet for comfort . . . out in the hallway I see Mama, now, her mouth wide open as she breathes in deep, deep, sucking up all the life, all the good things until the house becomes a vacuum, as if she's feeding that precious thing inside her. She's singing to it now, and whispering secrets, and laughing. She's laughing at me; it is laughing, I hear it, chuckling like an evil goblin. She's making the thing hate me. I can hear her. 'Shall I tell you what I caught that bad boy doing? Putting bleach in my poor budgie's water, that's what he was doing. My poor Archie. Who's a naughty boy, then? Bad boy, Erskine.

'Erskine needs a playmate, someone to stop him getting into mischief. Erskine's a bad boy. We'll have to punish him, won't we? You know what we'll have to do with him, don't you?'

Oh no, no, Mama, please. Not that. I didn't mean to. I

don't like it in there, Mama, please don't put me in there. And I don't want a playmate. I don't want anyone. Except my Mama. But she's growing so big I fear she's going to burst. I've seen her naked belly, the skin stretched so thin I can almost see what's in there. And now I can hear her crying again, and the screams . . .

. . . the way it appeared to me then, I thought she was dying. They sent me out to the garden but I could hear it, the screams. I went back to the house, crept right into the bedroom, stood there watching, scared, yet compelled to look. I could hear the whispers – blood, blood poisoning, blood gone bad. I could see the bloody gash. It was ripping her apart, this thing inside my Mama, and still she was screaming and gasping for air and thrashing about in the bed. And then suddenly she went silent, and started to moan – 'Help me, help me.' One of the women was holding her down while the other got in between her legs and tied Mama's feet into leather loops, like horses' stirrups. When the woman moved from Mama, I could see the hole, the visceral colours – muted purples, dusky, liver brown, as if she were being turned inside out, and would emerge raw and glistening, organs dangling. Then Mama saw me, lifted her head from the pillows. She screamed, 'Get him out of here!' And one of the women pushed me out and, before she locked the door, I glimpsed something purplish, convex, a ball, pushing through the hole. And Mama writhing and wet and crying out. A high-pitched screech. Like an animal in the woods at night. I run, I run away, fast as I can, out to the garden, along the lanes, to the cliff top. And I stand at the edge and I look down at the sea, but I still see Mama, that thing emerging from her, blue and grey and wet and roped to her. And I feel overwhelmed with repulsion, hatred and the terrible weight of unaccountable guilt.

I ripped up the photograph, right down the middle, tearing Mama in two.

A voice then, a weak cry of help, from the floor below. 'Mama?'

Looking down, I saw her slumped against the wall. A hand clutching her neck. She was deathly pale.

'I fear I am failing, Erskine, I can barely breathe. Erskine, can you help me into bed?'

I helped her to her room. She was soaked with sweat. When I attempted to take her temperature, she clamped her teeth shut, so I had to make her open her mouth by pinching her and nipping the thermometer in quick when she cried out in pain. (I had an urge, I now confess, to force the instrument in, to push it in hard, right down her throat.) Her temperature was 103 and rising. She was boiling up. I made her a hot lemon drink with aspirin. She refused my offer of a lightly poached egg. I caught myself wondering about your bedside manner, my bird. If Mama did not improve, both in health and behaviour, you would certainly have your work cut out.

I ate a solitary bland lunch of two poached eggs on toast. After checking on Mama, who was now sleeping deeply, I came to my workroom, momentarily enticed by thoughts of your cigarette box. But the pull of the sycamore was stronger. I drafted a few preliminary designs, nothing elaborate, and I was already envisaging the box, a long box, of course, one that might be suitable for dominoes, or pencils. Though it would only contain one pencil, of course. The work took longer than usual. I was continually beset by unwelcome images stimulated by my discovery of the photographs. A plague of imagery which was only extinguished by watching, after supper, my *Great White Sharks* video. (What fascinates most: those minutes – no, seconds – before attack, that swift, silent, sinister homing in. You are watching the fish, the prey, and you know it's coming and there is nothing you can do.

And you look then into the eyes of the killer, cold dead eyes, the split second before the jaws open, close. Apart from the violent disturbance of water, it is the utter absence of sound which intrigues. No cries, yelp or screams. Is there pain? Is there life left at all in the ungorged ragged-edge half still with its own eyes wide open as it sinks to the ocean floor?)

Mama moaned and coughed the whole night long. I could not rest, bothered by the whereabouts of my journal. It is not a happy state of affairs to have one's innermost thoughts at large. I gave up my search. Boxwood had evidently devoured it. I decided there was nothing for it, I would have to begin another journal.

A regret. For if I could return now, go back now, I would have looked a little harder, my friends. And how differently things would then have turned out for all of us.

29 April. Excellent, excellent day. Mama and I dressed up to the nines and had lunch out – oeufs Florentine. Delicious. Mama asked for a second helping! In the garden, I made the acquaintance of the rare and surprisingly tame (it almost hopped on to my crumb-filled palm) Vulvaris amores. A feathered friend, indeed. I fancy it may have nested close to the house. Mama popped in to see Dr Foster, who pronounced her 'one hundred per cent fighting fit'. She has, he said, 'many, many more years to look forward to'.

NB. Guilt is only a state of mind. One is not guilty – one can be considered guilty or even consider oneself guilty. Guilt can be redirected from a feeling to a thought. And thoughts can be more easily erased than feelings. I am not guilty. I am not my guilt.

There had been a tragedy in the village.

It was Henry John Farquhar who told me the news. I was in the shop, stocking up on sandpapers, polishes and varnishes and so on, when he told me what had happened. I very nearly smiled. Just very occasionally, life conspires *with* rather than against. From then on, I was careful to display the proper response, just the right amount of respectful curiosity.

'What a terrible waste of a life, Mr Farquhar. Only a young woman, you say. Tut, tut. Though it's a wonder those cliffs haven't claimed more lives – any other lives, I mean.'

Mr Farquhar said that apparently there was talk of erecting some barrier. (I did so hope not – I much prefer a natural edge, edges where edges are intended to be.)

Details of the tragedy were already circulating in the village. Conjecture twisted into fact, embellished and expanded. A case of macabre Chinese whispers. In the chemist's, while buying cough mixture for Mama, I learned there was a man involved. This man and the health visitor appeared to have known each other. They were arguing. A violent struggle was mentioned. I pictured the scene, like one of those silent movies Mama sometimes watched – the drama, the flailing limbs, distressed damsel, swarthy villain. But no, not Mama, Mrs Bainlait. We used to watch them in the Mansion House parlour on Saturday afternoons.

Apparently the police had begun their enquiries.

A strange day altogether. When I returned home, I found Mama in the hallway. She was sitting on one of the stools from the kitchen. She had her coat on and a hat and was reading a magazine.

'Good morning, Doctor,' she said as I came through the door. 'I'd like another prescription, if you please. I'm not feeling any better.'

A vicious cough was developing. I gave her the medicine and settled her down on the settee. I decided to take myself in hand, come up with a definitive version of the white monsieur, which might give me time off for good behaviour in order to sketch out a design for your cigarette box. Later, I would have a rout around for the collection so I could stash away my latest find.

Ah, I believe I have never mentioned this. A confession for you. Just a little one. When you came for coffee the previous day, you left something behind. A feather. No more than an inch long. Canary yellow. Some hair accessory, if I remember. If asked, I would have returned it, of course. Though I did not think it would be missed. Over the years, I have acquired many such trifles, all of little or no value, except what they meant to me. Curls from the hairdresser's floor, an empty bottle of scent (though scent still lingering), a red leather glove (the other of the pair already mislaid), the long-legged spider of an eyelash (false), a brown paper bag. And so on. A veritable sorcerer's cache indeed. When I first came home to Boxwood, I stored the collection away (the box must have since been buried during Mama's nocturnal shiftings), never imagining there would ever be anyone else in my life again. But then, my bird, you appeared, flitting down from a blue felicitous sky.

The collection is here somewhere. But I have still been unable to locate it within the labyrinths of this house. It was my link, you might say. I had intended to show you Leodora's lipsticked kiss (one of her last) on the handkerchief, her nail clippings. All those bits and pieces. You see, I have never been able to be free of the fear that those to whom I am attached will someday go away. It enables me to feel still connected. With this feather, I could recall you. For you, my bird, had brought something back into my life. Though I knew nothing then, of your story about the truth of your identity. But there was something familiar. A vague resemblance. The greeny-blue eyes, a turn of the head, a certain expression, a nuance an artist might catch in the flick of a brushstroke.

I was on my way to find the collection box when I heard

Mama calling out. For the time being, I put the feather into the drawer of my desk.

Apparently, while I was out that morning, Marcia had come round to ask again about the concert. Of course, Mama had no idea what she was talking about. I explained, leaving Mama in no doubt that I would not be taking part. And then, the strangest thing.

'Sing to me, Erskine,' Mama said. 'Erskine, will you sing?'

'Sing, Mama?' I was somewhat taken aback.

'From that opera,' Mama said, 'you know, *The Aggrieved Son*. It was one of my favourites. I used to listen, you know,' she said, 'whenever you were on the radio. The final aria. You remember, before they say goodbye in the garden.'

Yes. This was one of Leodora's favourites too. They are out in the garden and the mother believes her son's words are intended for her. The son sings:

> You and only you are in my eyes.
> My hand is outstretched to your heart.
> This love between us grows like heaven's garden.
> How can I live and know we are apart?

'Oh, please, Erskine,' Mama insisted. 'Sing to me, just like you used to.'

Sing, Erskine. Like you used to. I opened my mouth. But of course, nothing came out. In the mirror above the fireplace, I saw the mouth agape. The dark O of silence. The nightmare. The Voice lost.

The first occasion on which I experienced a weakening of the Voice fell around the time of Leodora's involvement with her theatre project for the Disadvantaged. (She had her fingers in so many artistic pies.) Feeling under the weather, I had taken myself to bed, having had to cancel rehearsals for a recording of Handel arias (from *Theodora*, *Judas Maccabaeus* and *Belshazzar*, I recall). Leodora was off touring the North – schools, local theatre groups, community halls. There had been a rather arresting picture in *The Times*. What a surprise to turn the page and find her smiling at me. She looked stunning. Blooming. An exquisite Spanish-looking outfit: white with huge camellias, the hem cut unevenly and coming to a point down one side, suggesting a certain raffishness, a devilishness – the dress torn in passion, perhaps? There was a crimson rose in her hair. My Carmen, then. She was with some young man. (Her Escamillo? I wondered.) According to the article, he was 'an up-and-coming young playwright, in his early twenties and already commissioned by the National'. Miss Ableyart's latest protégé. The blurb stated that the playwright had already won a number of prestigious awards for his plays, which were 'acute and penetrating investigations and insights into the human psyche'. (How Leodora had raved about his latest work – *The Peepshow*, loosely based on the life of the Dutch artist Samuel van Hoogstraten, the construction of his optical illusion box and the simultaneous breakdown of a relationship. It was, I understand, Leodora who had suggested the idea.)

Leodora had been away for almost a month. I was missing her deeply and seeing her in the paper only served to intensify my low, dark mood. And I was sinking lower. One evening, when Leodora telephoned, I was on my knees, begging her to return. The Voice was no more than a rasp, my throat a raw and hollow inflamed tube. She told me she'd catch the next train home.

The night she returned, I might as well have drunk acid. I was convinced I was dying, veered from brief consciousness to terrifying nightmares in which I was drowning in an ink-black sea of steaming water, blistering hot and searing my lungs as I struggled to breathe. Whenever I managed to surface, I could see above, on the cliff top, a pack of beasts staring at me, and they'd jump and come flying down towards me – black, red-veined wings outstretched. What was worse – the fear, the anticipation of the pain, or the pain itself? Again and again they'd leap and pounce, their fangs penetrating my flesh, tearing skin and muscle and tendon, scraping bone.

Leodora was late. Hours late. I was vaguely aware of messages recording on the answerphone, her voice full of concern and apology.

'Erskine, forgive me,' she said. 'I came as soon as I could.'

I mouthed 'Leodora'. The beasts had feasted, had finally left me, a pile of bones on the shore.

Was there a hint of remorse? A glassiness about the eyes, perhaps, a just perceptible downturn at the corners of the mouth? I did not want to believe she had grounds for remorse. She summoned the doctor immediately. He examined my throat and could find nothing untoward. No inflammation, no swelling or redness. But I was in agony, I told him, tried to tell him. Agony, I mouthed. He prescribed mouthwashes of vinegar and Dead Sea salts. Leodora was to apply a compress of hot wax and brown paper every two hours.

She put her plans on hold for a whole fortnight to look after me. She fussed over me like the proper nursemaid. The Handel recording had to be cancelled. After a few days, when I was able to get up from bed – the throat was still on fire.

At the end of two weeks, there was a call from the playwright. To be frank, he said, she was needed for the opening of a theatre (or was it some awards ceremony?). Leodora wanted to arrange for temporary help, a professional nurse or companion to care for me, but I managed to persuade her otherwise. I would be fine on my own, I said. Though I was not fine at all. As soon as Leodora had departed for the attractions of the North, the nightmares returned intensified, so that often I'd wake in torture, the core of the pain no longer in my throat, but in my loins and travelling up through me, like white-hot wires pushing up through my body.

Months later, when the Voice regained strength, it returned as a stranger, not a friend. For another Erskine had taken his place inside me. One without a soul, one whose blood flowed cold, who no longer had the passion to soar. For three years I continued. There were the concerts at Angel House, of course. But by that time it all meant little to me.

My friends, certain events reoccur, are leitmotifs weaving a dark thread through the otherwise innocent tapestry of one's life.

Not the final aria. The penultimate. They are in the garden and the mother believes her son is singing to her, but then she hears a voice and she turns and sees then the woman in the distance. And now the son sings:

> Without you, Isadore, I am nothing, my love.
> I renounce all that I have,
> reclaim all I have lost.
> only you and I
> and no one else, my love.

I turned away from the fireplace mirror, from the wide silent mouth. I told Mama I had forgotten the words. In other circumstances, I might have been somewhat fazed by her request for me to sing, but my mind was preoccupied by other matters.

'By the way, Mama,' I said. 'They found a body. Washed up on the beach. A terrible accident. A tragedy. The health visitor woman – you know, she was always coming round here.'

I spared her the details. I did not want to risk upsetting her, feared it might awaken the ghosts.

Right over the edge. Over and out, then. Nemesis took a tumble, indeed. No one was taking my Mama away.

7

I. An Intrusion – A Goosing

—Erskine, Erskine, you see the damage, don't you? One box opens, and inside, there's another already raising its lid. Within that box, there's another, and so it goes on. The past has its own agenda, Erskine. It is not what you choose to make it, it makes you. No matter what you may long to forget, the memories will come a-haunting. Like notes upon a never-ending stave, black crows perched upon a wire singing a never-ending song. Just as one note ends, another begins. Like a row of dominoes, Erskine, all it takes is a fingertip and down comes the first on to the next. Consequences, Erskine, consequences. Select a memory and another is already bubbling to the surface. Something that happened yesterday, an hour ago, a second, recalls a distant event as vividly as if it is being relived. I know what you are thinking, you are thinking of Ulva's greeny-blue eyes and what they lured from the murky depths of the past.

When you first saw Ulva, the connection was made, although you refused to admit to yourself what you still will not acknowledge. When was it precisely? As she peered at you that first time from the shadows of Marcia's van, when she sat in your kitchen eating cake, or later as she was leaving and turned to you and waved? You refused to acknowledge the connection you had already made. But the memory would not stay buried. At night, was it really Mama's coughing keeping you awake? Or was it the memory of that last day with Leodora?

Her birthday, was it not? How apt! In the morning, when

you woke, you could hardly bear to look her in the face. And when she turned to cup your face in her hands and kiss you, you almost decided you could not, could never, carry out the plan. It was only after she was dressed and ready for the day out that your resolve was strengthened. Fortunate, that you had suggested she might be more comfortable in casual wear. And Leodora – always dressed up to the nines! Dressed to kill, you might say. But without her customary glitter, and bereft of make-up, she did not look at all like herself. And this suited you. And when second thoughts crept in during the journey, all it took was the sight of her eating a banana for the horrific scene you witnessed to be replayed in all its gory detail. They were like animals – were they not? – devouring each other. Fuel for your courage. You would do what you had set out to do. But admit it, Erskine, you felt guilty. You still wonder, guiltily, whether the end was not as necessary, as inevitable, as you once believed. Admit that as she turned and you saw the look of disbelief in her greeny-blue eyes you reached out your hand as if to save her.

When Ulva arrived, you were desperate for her to see you as a good man. For the man you wanted to believe you really were. Ulva flew into your life and you wanted to forget, you wanted to start again, just as you tried to do with Mama. And things were on the up! Oh, but Erskine, it was all going to get much, much worse. You see, there was no way to avoid it. You see, Ulva came with a past too. Easier, my old chap, if you came clean, came right out with it: the tragedies, Leodora, her playwright, what happened to young Erskine, what he made happen – all the tragedies. Oh, and while you're at it, the journals, Erskine, you might as well come clean about those too.

But wait! Someone's knocking at the door. Now, who might that be? You had better open the door, Erskine. You had better open up.

Disgusting. Repulsive. They were devouring each other. You could not begin to imagine my pain. I was consumed. I was, however, compelled to watch. Spying through the lace inset, focusing my vision through the holes in the lace (or the crack in the velvet?), imagining, while they moved, the obscured parts, those details of their bodies. Concentrating so intensely, I could picture the entire scene – limbs, flesh, the folds, the contours, extensions. Ugly. They are ugly. Limp or engorged, they are ugly. And the sac, a peculiar pinky brown, a tired gone-off sort of pink. And the pole stretching tight, the skin so thinned and tight you imagine it will split. Ah, so proud. Cocksure. An unshamable thing. Accusatory, even. The pointing finger. And she was sucking it. As if having it in one orifice wasn't enough! Begin to imagine, can you, my shame. The greatest inadequacy for a man. Neither this, nor that. Incomplete. An in-betweeny. A teeny-weeny in-betweeny. Look at it. A pitiful titbit. A morsel. She told me she was satisfied. But she was not satisfied. She was gorging herself. Elsewhere. At someone else's table.

Betrayal. I was no longer her angel. You must understand, it was the only solution.

My friends, for one awful moment I thought she was going to invite herself in. Marcia, I mean. She called earlier this morning. I almost jumped out of my skin at the knocking. It could have been worse, I realised, recognising her large shape through the frosted glass. At least it was not someone in uniform. But a tricky situation all the same. As soon as I opened the door, a black galosh stepped over the threshold. I let the door close behind me, stepped out into the porch so she had to move back. She was peering into the hallway as the door closed, her nostrils working away like those of a bloodhound.

'Marcia,' I said. I smiled.

'We have seen neither hide nor hair of you, Erskine. Not for some time.'

'No,' I said.

'And what about your mother? Is she any better? And Ulva?' Her voice dropped pronouncing this last. You had been a disappointment to her, my bird, a concern. You had let her down, I sensed.

'Ulva's gone away for a bit,' I said. 'To visit a friend.'

'I see. When she returns, *if* she returns,' Marcia said, 'you will tell her I was asking, won't you? I believe she may have something of mine.'

A pause. She must have realised I was not going to invite her in, or offer information.

'But your mother . . .' she said.

'Yes?'

'Have the health people been in touch, Erskine? They assured me they would call.'

Call? I heard alarm bells. Call? When? And why? As soon as I could get rid of Marcia, I would ring the health centre. I collected myself.

'Mama is rather under par,' I said (I almost said ground!). 'Very out of sorts. But the doctor's keeping an eye. Not our usual doctor,' I added quickly, 'a specialist. I am sure Mama would welcome a visit from you, Marcia, as soon as she feels up to it. I'll let you know.'

As I was about to bid her goodbye, she moved forward again. She sniffed, wrinkled her nose.

'You are quite sure, Erskine, that everything is all right?'

And she touched my arm. Ah, the strangest thing – a lump in my throat, tears welling. A split-second desire to hug her, to be held. I pinched my thigh. Forget. I had work to do.

'Quite all right, Marcia, yes.'

Was I convincing? We shall have to see. A wholly unwelcome intrusion, at any rate. Why did she sniff at me? After she'd gone, I realised I have been holed up in here so long, so engrossed with you two and these last boxes, that everyday matters such as personal hygiene have flown out the window. Or not flown. For there are no windows here in the workroom, and the air is thick, cloying. A sickly sweet smell. Yet one is nevertheless tempted to breathe, to sniff, to savour.

A sudden memory after Marcia left, from my days at the Mansion House. I was wandering through the nearby woods, on my own as usual, when I came across a child. It, he, was relieving himself behind some bushes. Solids. From the angle at which I approached, I could see the dark shiny turd emerging between the milky white of the backside. I caught a glimpse of the parts. I felt the vicious searing inside me. The child wiped its rear with a dock leaf and ran off. Just then, a four-legged creature appeared from nowhere, sleek, short haired, the skin tight to its body clearly depicting the muscles, its power. I saw the gross bags swinging between its legs. The beast was drawn to the child's faeces, of course, though it approached the turd warily, as if it might be a coiled snake. It circled the pile, turned away, approached, stood sniffing, one front paw raised, pulled in slightly, an oddly dainty gesture (the discreet, precise, curled baby finger of a hand sipping tea). Eventually, the wet and agitated nose sniffed closer. The jaws opened. The beast began to eat.

Fresh air. Fresh sea-salted air! No wonder I have been so befuddled these last days. The house stinks. I stank. I took a long bath, dressed in fresh clothes – a green moleskin waistcoat and a red velvet dicky for you today, my friends. And now I feel revived and ready to move on. No worries, my sleuths, the windows are open, but the doors are locked. I do not have to answer the door to anyone. A thought, before I continue. Could something be done about Marcia? I wonder. Yes. But with difficulty, I fear. Marcia is such an ox of a woman. And while my muscles are strong, fond memories may prove stronger.

No. The door remains locked. Just the three of us. No one else. Is there?

Now let me see. Mama was deteriorating. Yes. And the mind.

The mind was on its last legs. The cough had abated. There was even a little colour in her cheeks and she had made it down to the shops, but the fever had addled her further. That, and the news of the tragedy. I had spared her the ins and outs, but the village was ripe with gossip and it troubled her. Understandably. Apropos nothing, in the middle of lunch, say, she would stare, fork raised,

'She fell, Erskine, didn't she? It was a fall. They said it was an accident. It was an accident, Erskine, wasn't it?'

'Yes, Mama.'

Oh yes. An accident, Mama. I took great pains to ensure she understood this, to let it sink right in. An accident, a few weeks ago, the health visitor. I did not want any confusion in her mind. Stay in the here and now, Mama. I had enough disturbances of my own. The Pergolesi farce for one. That day I found you on the cliff top with Mama for another.

You had slipped into our lives so easily, my bird. And I was on pins worrying what you should think of us – of Mama, of the house, of me.

You came by with the vegetable box, one day, you may recall. I was the engine driver, shovelling coal, making 'choo-choo' noises.

'Where are we off to, Erskine?' Mama said.

'The Americas, Mama, Crete and Genethlium, the Gallipoli and the Saronic gulfs, the far distant . . .'

And then I saw you pass by the window. You nodded, gave a friendly but querying look. What did you make of us? Me, shovelling coal behind a row of chairs, Mama, with sandwiches and flask, in sou'wester and flowery shower cap. You knocked the paw. I was so glad. I did so want to catch you.

'Veg for you.' Then, 'Having fun?'

I was aware of my reddening cheeks. You were staring at my head. You emitted a small, strange kind of squeak, a strangulated yelp, a polite clearing of the throat. I removed the cap, somewhat bashful.

'You must think we're quite mad. It's my mother, you understand.'

You handed me the box of vegetables. You were wearing rings, thin silver bands, two, three at least on each finger. Tiny charms dangled from two of the rings, one a row of hearts diminishing in size to your small knuckle. You appeared rather pale, your skin as if transparent, veins clearly discernible at the corners of your mouth giving you a macabre air, presenting me with a sudden picture of the maiden turned vampire, blood drooling, or at least the stains of drooled blood. The image was replaced by a post-mortem scene I had inadvertently caught out of the corner of an eye coming in on one of Mama's television crime dramas. Vampire turned victim; it pleased me the victim won through. Oh, but then, what was that on your wrists as you raised your arms, lifting the box, and the bracelets fell back? White flicks? Frost on the glass. Mineral in stone. Fossilised pain, my Ulva. Ah.

Mama was calling that the train was about to leave. I sighed.

'I meant what I said,' you said, 'about helping out. I can start now, if you like. The next lot cancelled so I'm free for the day.'

So, you had invited yourself in. Effortless. I could hardly believe my luck. As you stepped over the threshold, a physical response – hairs prickling, stirrings in the nether regions, a twinge in the lacuna. And your smell as you passed, the musk tantalisingly familiar. Yes, I was glad the post-mortem scene won through. But your apparent insubstantiality, your flimsiness, concerned me. There was nothing solid or permanent about you. I worried you would not last, like a cheap garment that wears out after a few washes, tatty jewellery that turns your skin green and falls apart. And I worried then that I should have prepared Mama, for when I led you in and introduced you, Mama cried out, 'Oh no, no, it cannot be!' Then buried her face in her hands.

'This is Ulva, Mama,' I said, with an apologetic smile to you, 'a friend of Marcia's. She's going to keep you company. I told you. Remember?'

Mama looked up then. Her face was beaming.

'A playmate,' she said. 'Oh yes, what fun!'

You took your seat beside her on the train. Clearly, you were not adverse to a little role playing yourself. As I made tea in the kitchen, I could hear the two of you chatting away, laughing. And I found myself laughing along with you, my spirits lifted high, until they were deflated again by a knocking on the front door. A policeman. Plain clothes. General enquiries had reached me, then. If I should notice anything unusual, blah-blah, any information at all, blah-blah . . .

'No, Officer, no. I did not know the woman.' (She was not wearing glasses in the photograph he showed me.) 'Oh, wait, yes, a health visitor, wasn't she? Yes. That's right. She had called once, to see my mother. Or was it twice?'

On cue, then, Mama.

'Where's our tea, Erskine?'

'I'm just explaining to the policeman, Mama—'

'I didn't do it,' Mama said, backing away, 'it wasn't me. You won't take me away, will you?'

'She's not well,' I said. I winked. 'You know.'

The policeman stared at me as if I were the mad one. If I

heard anything, anything at all, I was to let them know. He was returning to the car when Mama tried to push her way past me.

'Ossifer! Ossifer!' she cried. 'I know who did it. I know. I know.'

I waved and shook my head.

'Now we don't want to bother the nice busy policeman, do we, Mama?' I said. I grabbed her arm and pulled her back in. I shut the front door. Mama started weeping.

'They still don't know how it happened, then?'

You startled me, my Ulva. Tippy-toed into the hallway as light as a hummingbird.

'These things can go on for years,' I said. 'In many cases they never know.'

'But I know,' Mama piped up, 'I know. I do.'

I took you aside. I told you she was tired.

'She is fanciful, embellishes, makes things up. You know, one minute she's the Queen of Sheba. You must take what she says with a pinch of salt.'

And right on cue, once again, dear Mama.

'I had a letter from Papa in India today,' she said, meek faced now, coy, fluttering her eyelashes. 'His maid starched the linen like I never could. She salted the laundry. The final wash. That was the secret.'

'Mama has many secrets,' I said. 'But you will come and visit us again. I'm sure it would do her good. You will visit us again? I really would be so very grateful.'

'Of course I'll come,' you said. 'I've enjoyed it.'

I noticed then your habit of pulling your sleeves over your wrists. You were always cold, my bird. You didn't wear enough, eat enough. You needed looking after. But what else do I remember from that day? That you seemed in a hurry to leave, such a hurry that you did not say goodbye, not even to Mama. I had left you two with your tea and fairy cakes while I spent a half-hour on my wood. When I came back, Mama was on her own, colouring in a picture book. She did not know where you were, she said. Of course, you must have said goodbye, I was probably too engrossed in my work to hear. I would think only well of you. As you would of me.

My intentions were quite honourable. I wanted you to know that. Erskine Flesching would be on his best behaviour. You, my Ulva, would think only good of me.

The next afternoon, I was in one of the back sheds, searching for my honing stones to sharpen my tools, when a police car caught my eye. It was parked up the lane. There were two policemen in the car. The tragedy business again? I hoped not. Locating the flat oilstone and a wedge-shaped stone into the bargain (for removing gouge burrs), I decided to make the first move. I walked along the lane, waving as I approached the car. The window opened.

'Good day to you, Officer. Can I be of any assistance?'

The policewoman muttered to her partner at the wheel. She turned to me.

'Surveillance,' she said. (Almost with glee, I thought. Well, if it was a matter of surveillance, what then were they surveying?)

'We stopped here for lunch,' the male said.

'A late one, then,' I said. (It was just gone 2.30 by my watch.) 'I shall leave you in peace, then,' I said, 'to eat your lunch.'

Coming back into the garden, I turned. Were they embracing? Surveillance indeed. My feathers were ruffled. We had never been bothered by police in these parts. Not since. Yes. Not for years.

Having left the canoodling coppers to get on with it, I returned to the house with the intention of asking Mama whether she'd like a trip down to the village. (For provisions, but I also wanted to keep my eyes attuned to the latest details about the tragedy. If the people were still lurking about the lanes, business was still unfinished, but was evidently, nevertheless, 'work in progress'.) Mama told me Mr Pergolesi had just been on the telephone. He was on his way over for a cup of tea, apparently. He was expected any minute. I'd leave her to it, then, I said. I told her I would be an hour or so. I had the idea of taking a detour via Marcia's van. Perhaps catch a glimpse of you, my bird. When I went back out, the police car had gone. I set off at a good pace for the village. I bought liver, bacon, onions, carrots, cheese with walnuts, more medicine for Mama and a tonic to perk her up. (As if she needed perking, as I would soon find out!) I also bought a box of fresh cream cakes to take to Marcia's. (I had already invited myself in.) But coming out of the cake shop, I spotted Marcia's van at the traffic lights. And beside her in the passenger seat, you, my bird. Marcia stuck her head out of the window.

'Taking Ulva to the station, Erskine. Overnight stay with a friend. She's coming to help out with your mother, I understand. How is your mother, by the way?'

I noticed then Marcia's large paw on your black Lycra-clad thigh. Mother bird asleep on a small shiny rock. A sudden image of my hand inside Sylvia's lilac cardigan. Bird in the nest. Warm young bird in a lilac-tree nest. It was Sylvia who had told me to put my hand in there. 'Feel how warm it is, Erskine. Like toast.' I felt the nylon vest, felt too what lay beneath.

'Erskine! Erskine, are you with us?'

I could have kicked myself. For with that the lights changed and Marcia called out, but her words were lost to the wind as the van drove away.

Yes, you did wave. But an exaggerated movement, as though miming window-polishing. But I did not read it like that then, of course. On the way home, I could not stop thinking about where you might be going. Who you were staying with. And whose friend? Marcia's, or yours? Who? Who? Why hadn't you told me you were going to stay with a friend? Should I attach any importance to the fact that you had not so much as mentioned it? Still, it was only a night. And very soon I would have the pleasure of your company on a regular basis. Mama and Mr Pergolesi, if he was still there, could tuck into the cakes.

Oh yes, he was there all right. Right in there. Even now, I grow hot with shame at the thought.

Coming up the drive to Boxwood, I saw Pergolesi's moped in the porch. The front door was wide open. I entered, calling out to ask whether they wanted tea. Mama and Mr Pergolesi were not in the drawing room, nor in the kitchen, nor the back garden. Perhaps they had gone for a stroll? Not too far, I hoped, for the weather was taking a turn for the worse, and I could not have relied on Pergolesi to make sure Mama was suitably dressed. Indeed, no.

From upstairs came the muffled sounds – moans, creaks. I removed my shoes, went upstairs. They'd gone out without locking up and a burglar must have thought it was his lucky day. I wished I'd had the foresight to arm myself. I would have to rely on brute force. They were in Mama's room. I pushed open the door.

Mama and Mr Pergolesi. In bed! Mama astride Mr Pergolesi. Mama bouncing. His hands on her great jubbly bouncing breasts. And when she rolled off him – a cow seal rolling flop-plop into the water – I saw the pole. Mr Pergolesi's pole! Italian salami! Oh, the hugest, the thickest protrusion!

'Ah, Erskine, er, Signor Fleschink, you must forgive me. Please. Please.' He was really pleading! 'I do not know how it happened.' He leaped from the bed and in his panic got his knickers in a twist, then started putting his trousers on backwards.

I was too shocked to respond appropriately, whatever the appropriate response may have been.

'Have a brandy, Mr Pergolesi.'

'Lenora, Mr Fleschink, Mrs Fleschink, she—'

'Yes?'

'She told me she was lonely, Mr Fleschink. She said no one hugs her any more. She said that you beat her, Mr Fleschink.'

'Beat her? Of course I don't beat her.'

Pergolesi backed away as though I might strike him.

'My mother is really not very well. In her mind. Out of her mind, we might say. It would be terrible if people were to find out you were taking advantage of an innocent. Who, Mr Pergolesi, who would travel on your bus then? And Mrs Pergolesi, what would she have to say?'

'Santa Maria, Mr Fleschink, Maria Francesca, she would—' And here he made the gesture to indicate decapitation. I pictured a carving knife and could not help looking down at his trousers. I saw a flash of scarlet underwear.

'Flies, Mr Pergolesi.'

'Not on me, Mr Fleschink. And not on my mother's life will it ever happen again.' He crossed himself several times. I believe I had frightened the man. And rightly so. What liberties! My Mama, indeed!

Just as he was leaving, he stopped, turned.

'By the way, Mr Fleschink. That woman they found on the rocks, that health visitor lady. The police have been asking. But I told them nothing. Nothing.'

'What, Mr Pergolesi? What did you not tell them?'

'That I saw you on the cliff path with her, Mr Fleschink. Just a few days before she was found.'

Oh no, Pergolesi. You did not see that at all. Pergolesi

finally left, cap in hand, bowing – though not quite as meekly as one might expect. Then Mama came downstairs. She was wearing a dressing gown I had not seen. A glamorous wrap kind of affair in coral satin and white lace, the movement of its elaborate flounces as she descended like one of those incredible tropical fish, all gills and frills, exotic and vulnerable. I recalled then, a boy in the Aquarium Centre. There was a tank of angel fish. The boy was studying them. After a while, he stands on tiptoes, puts a hand into the water, then quick! – catches a fish. He throws it on the floor, hard, then stamps, hard, over and over, rubs his shoe in. Nothing left of the fish. Just bits of grey mush.

'Mama?'

'I want to go to the pictures,' she said, 'and I want popcorn. And a hot dog. A big dog.'

We had been to the cinema only once since my return to Boxwood. It was some dark, depressing story – patricide, terminally ill sister, mother dying, son brain-damaged at birth, et cetera, et cetera. Not my cup of tea. Mama passed wind throughout, I distinctly recall, leaning to one side and lifting a buttock as though forcing it. People were leaving before the end. The film, the smell, or a combination of both.

I checked the local paper. There was little on. Some sex thing – adultery, incest or whatever. I for one had had quite enough for one day. I improvised on the hot dogs – chipolatas from the freezer and granary rolls. Mama had evidently worked up an appetite. I could not bear to watch her jaws working over the sausages. Save for the smacking of her lips and piggy grunts of pleasure, it was a meal partaken in silence. But what could I have said? 'How was Mr Pergolesi?' I felt obliged to make some reference. But what?

'Mama, one thing,' I began. 'In the interests of security, I think we should make sure the front door is at least closed at all times if not locked. And for another, if you do intend to have company, you could at least—'

Here she interrupted by offering to wash the dishes. So I took the opportunity to watch one of my wildlife films, *The Cruellest Kind* – did I ever show you? There is a long sequence of shots, about a hundred or so, each one depicting the moment of contact, the first penetration of flesh. Fangs sinking into the skin, then the disruption of the hide, the disarrangement of stripes or spots. One after the other – quick, quick, quick – each one causing the lacuna to retract. Unpleasant, yet I watch. The pain of the past reducing the pain of the present. Mama and Mr Pergolesi – the Italian Job – ramrod stuck up her. Damned police on my case. What were they after, blood? I was watching in slow-motion replay, the jaws of a black panther stretching, the lips pulled back over the teeth. Inside the mouth, raw red, as if it had already tasted fresh meat. The teeth broke the hide cleanly. As if it were thin stretched plastic. Then Mama came in, knocking on the open door. She shuffled in, curtseying, head bowed.

'A gentleman for you, sir. On the phone. Says it's urgent.'

Did I detect a cockney twang? And sir? Sir? What next?

Rather a shock, I must admit. I had put the matter quite out of mind. So, seeing as I had not replied to your letters, you had decided to ring. A series of books on unusual people, blah-blah. And how would you define unusual? I wondered. And how the deuce did you get my number? We are ex-directory. It was all too upsetting. I gave you short shrift, my friends.

'No,' I said firmly, 'no. There will be no record of my life. How dare you! I will change the number. In the meantime, you dare to ring again and I shall be in touch with the police. This is harassment.'

I was more than a little agitated, you will recall. I had to applaud your persistence. Like a dog with a bone. But why were you so interested in me? More to the point, what did you already know? Or believed, or assumed, you knew? I could not begin to imagine. I decided I would simply forget you. Pretend you did not exist.

My attention was then directed to the waterfall in the kitchen. Mama had left the sink taps running. She was putting away dishes oblivious, squelching in her slippers, the nodding pussies long drowned. What a mess.

A mess, indeed. Far better, far better for us all to have let sleeping dogs lie, my friend, to have left the beasts in repose.

Unable to sleep, I poured myself a large brandy and settled in front of the fire with my unsettling thoughts and my journal. Events suggested some kind of conspiracy. A sense of foreboding. Déjà vu, even. Is it, I wondered, that key events replay throughout our lives in various guises, over and over, often forcing us to witness the same horrors, the same tragedies, until we learn from them – or is it that we must suffer interminably? But how do you learn?

> *15 May. Thinking of adding a small conservatory on to the kitchen – with mini-pool and fountain. Mama went to the opera with Mr Pergolesi* – Sweeney Todd, the Demon Barber, *I believe. Or was it* Confessions of a Casanova? *Ulva and I spent a very pleasant couple of hours alone together. A feeling she is growing fond of me. Mid-conversation, her hand, feather light, like a fledgling dove, came to rest upon my knee, then . . . ah, momentarily, my thigh. There could well be developments. But I will not push. After luncheon, I took her to my cliff top.*

II. A Kiss and a Killing

So, my bird. You joined us at Boxwood. Just a couple of mornings a week to begin with. Though it wasn't long before you seemed part of the family. Knock on the door, peep in, lift up the latch, creep in – and in so quick, my Ulva, I barely noticed.

I was all a-jitter before your first session. Even Mama was telling me to stop fussing. I had hand-washed all our best table linen and glassware, filled vases with roses and greenery from the garden, hidden as many of the piles of boxes and papers and so forth beneath a quantity of tapestry throws and velvet curtains I had unearthed in the attic. The place was beginning to take on a theatrical quality, me in the role of stagehand. And I was praying Mama would not let me down. At the very most, that she would keep to the script. I had given her precise instructions—

'You can talk about today, Mama, and yesterday, tomorrow and the day after, but that's as far as you go. It's not thirty years ago, Mama, it's now. Keep to now.'

I crossed my fingers that, at the very least, she would remain fully dressed at all times. On several occasions of late I had discovered her, sprawled on a settee, legs akimbo, *sans culottes*, as it were. A painful spectacle. One thinks of poultry (plucked), the gape of a new-born bird, a moustachioed, bearded yawn. I hoped you were of not too delicate a disposition, my Ulva. Had I known.

You had just returned from your trip away. The overnight stay had lengthened to several days. Marcia had phoned to inform me. In a way, I wished she had not. It gave me too much time to brood. Where had you been exactly? Was the extension due to you having such a good time with whoever it was? And who – who was it? Marcia did not say. 'Who, Marcia?' I said. But she had not heard me, or chose to ignore me. Neither would you tell when you phoned to say you would be coming the next day, if that was convenient.

'So pleased you're back,' I said. 'Who . . .'

Then 'Goodbye,' you said, and put down the phone.

Breakfast was a speedy affair – Mama still spreading marmalade on her toast as I took away the plate. There was something she wanted to watch on the television, so I came into my workroom. I wanted to get the session with my wood completed before you arrived. I would not have felt comfortable working on it with you but a breath away.

I had been up since dawn titivating, had even hoovered the first layer of dust from the downstairs carpets with some ancient machine that resembled a geriatric kangaroo (called 'The Kanga-Mate'). The place was ready – almost – for opening night. It fairly sparkled. In my heady excitement, I pictured a wind-up jewellery box, a little girl's box, lined with pink padded satin, and mirrors, with a little platform for the pink tutued ballerina to dance upon when you turned the key.

And I was turning the key, my bird. But would you dance, would you?

In the workroom, then, dancing before me – Monsieur Sycamore. He had a mind of his own, was developing into the oddest fellow. Not the monster which had first appeared on my sketch pad, neither the subsequent design of twenty centimetres with a diameter of four centimetres, but a squat fellow – the stem barely a stub, the helmet gross and oversized, with markings beginning to appear now, on the underside, small uniform pleats. A mushroom of a monsieur, then. A poisonous variety? I wondered.

Then you. You! At the front door! Caught in the act! How long had you been knocking?

I answered red faced.

'Yes?'

'I was about to give up. But I could hear the television.'

There was, I felt, an accusation hidden somewhere in

your voice. Not nice, my bird, you thinking we were hiding from you.

'I've come to help with Nora. Remember? I phoned last night.'

'Of course. Do forgive me. Please.'

I was mortified. I should have given you a better welcome. I should not have got so carried away in my workroom.

You asked whether I was all right. But were *you*, my bird? For you appeared altered in some way. The same itty-bittiness, a thin shirt or two on top of other layers. But somehow more substantial. Was there more of you? Surely you could not have gained weight in so short a time? Perhaps I had made you too aerial a being, because I was worried you might fly away, for in my mind you were winged and hovering, ready to flit.

'Please, do come in.'

When you removed your mac, I noticed you were wearing black leggings which defined your not unattractively thin legs. It struck me that I had seen legs like that somewhere before. And wasn't there something different about your hair? Extra colour? Or was that dark red at the roots your own colour coming through?

'Is Nora in there?' you said, pointing.

But horrors! You were pointing at my workroom and moving towards it now. In my haste I had left the door slightly ajar, but enough for me to spy Mr Mushroom growing in the shadows.

'No,' I said, steering you towards the living room. 'This way. Mama's in here.'

Mama was lying down. The chest infection had taken her strength, had left her irritable and weepy. I wondered whether it was the beginning of her physical decline. I had read of it – the body being cruel to be kind, accelerating its own degeneration in parallel with the brain, a kind of inverted survival. Well then, I thought, Mama's body had better get its skates on.

'How are you, Nora?' you said loudly, leaning over her.

'Not deaf,' Mama said.

Oh dear. You might have smiled at the retort – the standard old-lady joke, after all. But I noticed the little moue of your lips, that quick narrowing of those eyes, before you told Mama you had brought her some magazines. (As if we didn't have enough.)

'We can cut out pictures, Nora. Make a collage.'

Mama perked up at that, took you off in search of scissors. You were not aware, but I watched you two sitting on the floor. You were cutting from a newspaper, so engrossed you did not appear to hear Mama's questions. 'What are you making? Will you help me, Ulva?' You held out a row of skirted figures holding hands. And then you scrunched it up into a tight ball. Mama looked confused, muttered, 'Oh, oh dear, I must fetch someone, this won't do at all, not at all.' But you pulled her back. A little harshly, I felt.

I often observed you. Were you ever aware? On a number of occasions. One time, in the butcher's, standing at the back of the queue, I overheard you probing Marcia – about me. And I frequently spied on you, here, in the house, as you wandered through rooms, looking, touching things, picking up ornaments. What did you take, Ulva? How many little trinkets did you secrete away? I watched you from behind the curtains. Did you know I was there, tucked behind a curtain, rodent in the wainscot, hardly daring to breathe, watching? Such a quantity of exposed skin. Were you trying to titillate, I wonder, in those loose, diaphanous tops you wore? Did I imagine they were transparent, only imagine the suggestion of small, dark raised circles? In certain lights, when you were sitting in front of the window, in the afternoon sun, one could clearly see the thick lanugo-soft covering of blond hairs on your arms, legs, in whorls on your shoulders. Like a moth. Once – ah, too much – a flash of violet gusset, of gentian. You were squatting on your haunches, primitively, collecting up pieces of a jigsaw. My hand was down in the trousers, beginning to rub, and you went off balance. Oops-a-daisy! Legs akimbo. I could not stop the gasp of pleasure. I sensed you looking round, staring right at the velvet drapes, but you didn't seek me out. I recall one particularly rare and delicious moment. In your bedroom. You, naked to the waist. I was passing by on the landing. Did you have your radio on? You appeared quite oblivious of me. And in the heart-shaped mirror – your neck, breasts. The lacuna was an inferno. (My other name is Tom – Mr Peeper. That's me!)

Mid-morning, having cut out a number of rows of paper dolls, Mama took a nap.

I called you to join me in the kitchen. I had made you cream-floated coffee and set out a packet of chocolate wafers. I had also prepared a vichyssoise, hoping the smells of melted butter and fresh chopped veg might tempt you to linger for lunch. I was watching the way you broke your biscuits into little pieces, just as you had done with the walnut cake, dipping each bit into your coffee before popping it into your mouth, making a little grimace with each mouthful as if it were too hot, or tasted bad. I noticed your teeth, small, though perfectly formed, like a child's teeth – or those of one of the smaller species of shark.

Your question was a hand gripping my throat.

'Nora says you're a carpenter.'

My face reddened. I could not swallow.

'Yes,' I said, and tugged at my collar. 'I enjoy woodwork. Yes.' I laughed lightly. 'It gives me something to do. In my free time, I mean, when I'm not looking after my mother. But of course, now you're here, I have a little more freedom. To do my wood. To work the wood. My woodwork, I mean.'

I was digging myself a hole.

'She says you used to sing.'

Bloody Nora.

'You were good, weren't you? Famous, your mother said.'

Did you hear my sharp intake of breath? Did you see my hand trembling? What had Mama been telling you? What had she not told you! I realised I would have to play up the madness a little more.

'What a chatterbox she is! No,' I said, 'I do not sing, not any more.'

Too many questions, my Ulva. *I* was meant to be the interrogator.

You licked your spoon – flicks of a neat brownish-pink triangle. Ah – perfect for cleaning the most minute crevices. I imagined it hard, insistent. Your tongue disappeared into its box. Your rose lips pressed tight.

'Another biscuit?'

'I must go,' you said.

But wouldn't you stay for lunch? I had made soup. There'd be oven-warmed rolls. Spotted dick from the delicatessen. Quick-defrost gateau from the freezer. What was your fancy? But no. You had to go.

After you left, I went in to check on Mama. She was sleeping, a handful of paper girls peeping out between her fingers. She was cold, her forehead clammy. I covered her with a throw, but as I was tidying the debris of your paper, her eyes still closed, she whispered, 'I do love Ulva. I do. I've known her for years. Years. She's my very best friend.'

Oh, but I wanted a share in you too. You were not entirely Mama's. Part of you belonged to me.

For a time, a few weeks – ah, the most delightful interlude! You came to the house two mornings and two afternoons. You were most punctual, and I was just as ready. I did not impose, though was on hand for tempting refreshments – like the hag in the candy house was I! Any excuse to be near you. When I brought in a tray of goodies, I would spy from the corner of my eye, you plaiting Mama's hair, reading to her from her favourite *Book of Myths*. Sometimes you wore a pelmet of a skirt that rode to your lean thighs as you settled on the floor beside her. Stick-thin legs that surely could have snapped like pencils. Your apparent fragility sounding in the peanut-shell crack of your knee-cap as you leant to pick Mama's handkerchief from the floor.

A tonic for old Erskine, and for Mama! She was growing so fond of you. Too fond?

Yes, bliss. A few short weeks. Was I in love? For I lived in a state of anticipation, could think of nothing else but your visits. Not even my wood. Once or twice, I found myself with a hand on the door knob of my workroom, about to turn the key, but I could not bring myself to enter. Poor Cercatore must have been so lonely! And the mushroom left untouched on the table – as though sprouted there naturally in the dark, it seemed, when, eventually, I was lured in one day after certain events left me feeling somewhat unhinged.

I wanted so much to remember the kiss, not the killing of the bird, not the day I found you and Mama on the cliff top. I wanted to think only good of you. But there were things beneath the surface I did not wish to see. For there were not two of us any more – but three.

I believed you were growing genuinely fond of me. Remember the kiss? It was but a moment. Ah, but the closest you came.

We were walking Mama that day to the bus stop. She was off on another of her trips. She had wanted you to go but you had vegetables to deliver.

The day was heavy and the air thick. Mama had been

complaining all morning. I suggested she sat at the back
of Pergolesi's bus with the window open. To be honest,
I was glad to be free of her for I wanted a little of your
company for myself. On the way to the bus stop, she went
on and on—

'I don't want to go with Nora. I'm not going with Nora.'

'But, Mama, *you* are Nora, *you*.'

'Well I'm not going with her. That's an end to it.'

I gave up. She had been like it all morning. At breakfast
there had been another giddying regression. She was looking for the swimming cap again. She had been up at five
o'clock rummaging through jumble in one of the third-floor
bedrooms, all the while calling out the name, a name I cannot
bring myself to speak, even now. I wondered whether you
might be ready for a little house clearance. If we could get rid
of the triggers, it might halt the memories. And any excuse to
keep you with me.

As Pergolesi was helping Mama on to the bus, he asked
me whether I'd heard any more about *that* lady.

'And which lady might that be, Mr Pergolesi?'

'You know, Signor Fleschink, that one, she went – *oops*
– right over the cliff.' He winked. 'Don't worry, I shall look
after Mrs Fleschink. And no hanky-panky. You take care of
yourself.'

When he said this, I was sure he was looking at you, my
bird. I made a mental note. Pergolesi was to be avoided.

The bus drove away. We waved at Mama, but she only
stared blankly through the window, like a lost child.

Shall I tell you, Mr Frankly, how it was, how she – my
Ulva, not yours – was with me? How close she was?

We made our way back to Boxwood. Behind us, monstrous
yellow clouds stretched vertically. The sky appeared doom
laden. Suddenly, the oppressive heat lifted. The wind came
up. And then the lightning flash. You covered your head

with your arms, broke into a half-run, whimpering. When the thunder rolled, you ran back to me, my bird, lifted my arm and tucked yourself under my wing. I guided you along the lane to the bus shelter, where we sat for a while.

She was trembling, my friend. And so was I. I let my hand simply rest. I thought it more appropriate not to respond. Did she think of me as cold? I would not want her to think of me as cold. Frankly, did she ever tell you? Did she ever talk about me?

Only when the lightning had moved away and the thunder was far into the distance did you emerge. Your head in my lap. I feel now the pressure of your head, of your hand rubbing when you smoothed your hair. An innocent kiss, my friend, one from which you could draw little conclusion. I did not want to frighten her. Imagine, this great bulk that I am, and she was such a little thing in my lap, such a vulnerable creature.

'We used to have a dog,' you said. 'When there was a thunderstorm, it used to hide under my bed. If it was night, then I'd crawl under and hide with it too.'

Did you feel me stiffen? My entire body. You sat up. Yes. You had felt it.

'I am not exactly what you call a dog person myself,' I said.

Such brief tenderness, but enough for me to store away for later use. An exquisite moment, one that I could not possibly have dreamed of. My Ulva, in my arms! Yet a familiar moment, as if rehearsed, as if it had happened so many times before. And you, my bird, did you have strange feelings too? You did not expect it, but you were to grow rather fond of me. Though it pains me now to know how much I was being used. How much did I mean to you really? I still wonder.

The sky was clearing as we walked back. I was planning

something simple for lunch. Faggots and peas perhaps, or a Scotch egg salad, profiteroles from the freezer with a glass of dessert wine. I planned to go back via the village so I could pick up provisions. You told me you had to dash. You were meeting someone. After you said goodbye, you ran back, put your hand on my arm, pulled me nearer, reached and gave me a quick light kiss on my chin, just missing my lips.

'You're an angel,' you said.

Was that what you told her to say, Mr Frankly? Your words? Words you knew I had heard so many times before?

For lunch I ate two extremely hard-boiled eggs. Rock hard. I could not stop thinking about that butterfly kiss. The feel of your lips. Moist, cool, interior. The lacuna did not know what had hit it. I spent the rest of the afternoon with my private collection.

It was only the next day that I saw another Ulva. You were not due to come back to Boxwood until the following day. Mama was having an afternoon nap. I had gone out to collect mushrooms, and to buy medicine. The cough had returned.

I was ambling along, thinking of the scene in the storm, when I saw the white van parked down the lane. You in there, not Marcia. I called out but you appeared not to hear me. As I approached, I saw that the van was about to drive away, so I quickened my pace, called out after you. Then I saw it on the road. Huge, grotesque. Its spindly legs stretching and flexing, its feet clawing at the air. A great ruffian of a crow, a thug. Its beak was opening and closing, stretching wide in silent agony. One imagines the terror of the nightmare, the unvoiced scream, the fear intensified because you cannot communicate it. The absolute expression of pain, the patient regaining consciousness mid-surgery, anaesthetised, impotent, the body inert, the mouth closed, but inside – screaming agony. I had an urge to get down on the ground, put my ear close, as one does to catch the last words of the dying. I shouted, put up my arms, waved for you to stop. But the van moved forward, went right over the bird, jolted to a stop, then reversed back over the bird, stopped again, went forward, reversed. Back and forth, back and forth. Each time the bird appeared, beak still gaping, legs clawing. Then one leg clawing, and one side crushed by the wheel. I ran to the van, thumped the roof. What the devil did you think you were doing?

You were killing it, you told me. There was no saving it. We could have taken it to the vet's, I said. That wasn't the way to kill it. It was part crushed, still alive, in agony. I bent over the gutter, retched. Torture. I thought of those great black wheels coming at it, again and again. The crow's panic, then paralysis – there must have been terrible distress. You got out of the van, looked down at the bird. It was motionless now, legs stretched out in a last desperate reaching.

'It's dead,' you said. 'I have to go.'

I picked up the poor creature. Its feathers pitifully ruffled. Its eyes closed. As if it had resigned itself to death. I took out my handkerchief and wrapped the broken body. By the time I got back to the house the stiff bundle repulsed me. I dropped it on the front lawn. A macabre baby in a white shroud. Some clear fluid was seeping through. I found an old towel, covered it. At least it deserved a proper box. I put it in an old tin and went to look for wood. It did not take long. A simple hinged lid. Then I dug a small hole at the far end of the garden.

And it was not too much longer, of course, before I was digging an altogether bigger, deeper hole.

Boxes within boxes. Bones a-rattling. All the skeletons come dancing out.

The following day you told me you and Mama were going for a picnic. Though you had to get back by three o'clock.

'I've got to meet someone in the village,' you said.

But who?

You didn't say.

I checked Mama was well covered. The cough was still bad and she had a slight temperature but she was determined to go. Watching you two walking away hand in hand down the drive, a sudden unexpected clutching within, a concentration of pain. Like lemon juice on a wound. I waited for you to turn and wave.

Back at Boxwood, I was feeling uneasy. I walked about the garden, pausing at the little cross I had made for the crow, but closing my eyes to say a prayer, saw again in my mind the van going back and forth. I pulled the cross from the ground. A black cross beside your name. Too much of a reminder.

I made a coffee, peeled some vegetables for supper, then came in here, into the workroom. I did not have the heart, but there was work to do. The sycamore monsieur had assumed ambiguity – phallus or mushroom, mushroom or phallus? It struck me then, that perhaps I had finally beaten this whip-cracking beast on my back. If the monsieur proposed itself as a mushroom, then a mushroom it would be! Ha! A way out! But carefully does it, I thought. Let the thing think it was just another monsieur, but turn it into something else. Thus would guilt be assuaged. Au revoir, then, messieurs – let us have mushrooms! And no more need for the boxes. I would be free at last. Inspired, I selected the appropriate tools and set to work carving the lamellae. But I was all fingers and thumbs, and pricking my thoughts now, the questions – who were you going to meet in the village? And why didn't you tell me? And why did I not ask? After an hour or so, I finally called it a day. I would go for a walk. With no particular destination in mind, I found myself on the coast path, on the way to my cliff top.

And there you were in the distance, you and Mama sitting on the ledge. The exact spot. The flat stone ledge, just room enough for two. I closed my eyes. If you dared, you could dangle your feet over the edge . . .

Sometimes Mama let me, but only when she was sitting right next to me and holding my hand. After we'd finish our picnic, we'd leave the remains for the guillemots, empty the bags over the side of the cliff and watch the birds swoop and scavenge. When it stopped being just me and Mama, I used to come up and watch them, spy on them, her and Mama, both so near the edge. And the guillemots circling, crying out. One time, I imagined a great big one coming down and taking the dimply fat arm in its beak, carrying her back to where she'd come from, the black returning stork. And I'd run then, back to the space beside Mama. My space . . .

I opened my eyes. I was in the cow field, hidden behind the hedgerow, should they chance to look up. You were at the edge, you and Mama. You were lying on your back. Suddenly Mama stood up, her toes right at the edge. I made my way down the field towards you, I broke into a run. I could see Mama swaying, teetering. I saw her fall. And then I saw her down on the rocks, my Mama, tiny down there and battered. Like a doll.

Oh, Mama, *you* were never meant to fall.

'Mama!' I cried. 'Mama!'

I came running down the field shouting. Do you remember? You turned and looked so frightened. What a shock I must have given you. But Mama was waving and laughing.

'She was far too close to the edge,' I said harshly.

'But she's fine. I'm looking after her. Really.'

You gave me a querying look. Your shoulders and arms raised in a gesture of incomprehension. Wings raised, a bird about to take flight. No, please, I was thinking, stay.

I felt somewhat foolish. It wasn't the spot. Not the exact

spot. Not the ledge. No sheer drop. Below you and Mama, there was a gentle slope, and another, graduating gently down to the sea. You would not have been so irresponsible, of course. I apologised.

'Forgive me. There's another place, just like this. But sheer. I was confused.'

'Erskine,' Mama said, 'we are having such fun. We've been singing, Erskine.'

'I know,' I said.

You were looking at me, eyes narrowed. Did you suspect me of spying?

We walked back together. Three of us. Mama was chatting away, but you and I were silent. At the end of the lane, you said goodbye.

'Who are you going to meet?' I asked as you walked away. But you did not hear me. Did you?

As you turned into the road to the village, Mama called out, 'I love you. I love you, Ursula.'

—Erskine, listen. You believed you and Ulva were meant to meet. Your recompense for Leodora's transgression. The kind face of Fate. You had no idea Ulva was on a mission. But how could you know? How can we ever truly know anyone? How can we ever know what they are capable or incapable of, what they choose to reveal – or hide? Not every egg cracks a fresh yolk. The kernel of the most perfect-looking nut is often bad. Capable, or culpable? And who ever truly knew you? Leodora? But then she surely would not have done what she did. Mama? But look how Mama let you suffer. Will the real Erskine Flesching please stand up? Now see how you sit with your feet firmly glued. You saw Ulva and Mama holding hands, didn't you? A fleshed V as though their arms formed one limb. No room for Erskine. Like seeing those two all over again. You would not be pushed out again.

II. A Kiss and a Killing

And Mama was turning Ulva against you, poisoning her mind – telling her about the tragedy, about Ursula. All downhill, Erskine, from here on. A glacier ride.

8

I. Celebrations – An Invitation – A Cuckoo in the Nest

What did I know about you? What did I want to believe?

I see the moon of your face above the candles – witchy, the candlelight warping its contours, as if it were melting wax, the scallop splay of lines around your eyes. You looked tired, jaded, older. Though my mind's eye still insists on its own more innocent version – the nursery-book cherubic North Wind with cheeks puffed, the halo-capped angel gazing down upon a sleeping babe. But innocent, my bird?

Ah, truth is but what we perceive it to be.

I wanted to believe you when you told me it was a stranger at your table in the café. I wanted to believe you were fond of me. And the night of your birthday, when I invited you to come and stay at Boxwood, I could hardly believe you so readily agreed. But you led me there yourself, my Ulva, all the way down the garden path. And I was blindfolded.

I wish Mama had told me it was your birthday. Why hadn't you mentioned it? And Mama had invited you to tea without my knowing! I had so little time to prepare. Although one way or another, it turned out to be quite an occasion, did it not?

That morning, over breakfast, Mama informed me she wanted a new dress.

'A party dress, Erskine. I want to look nice.'

Recently, she had taken to wearing whatever she had fished from the attic. She was beginning to resemble a bag lady. Her appearance was a worry – all it would take was another pair of spiteful snooping eyes and a report back to headquarters. Besides, the attic rags of former glory days were rather more deeply troubling, were tags signalling unwelcome memories lurking at the perimeters of my conscious mind.

I decided a shopping trip was in order. Mama was so excited.

'Oooh, dresses!' she squealed. 'New dresses at last!' Then she put her hands together, eyes raised to the heavens, as if in prayer – a display of such pathetic gratitude I felt guilty of neglect.

'I want a bright blue party dress,' she said, 'and a swimming costume. I must have a swimming costume, Erskine.'

That old chestnut.

'But you already have a costume, Mama. Anyway, it's too cold to go swimming in April, and you're not in the best of health right now.'

She glared at me, the emeralds like rubies a-glow. She stamped her foot.

'I am going swimming,' she said. 'I am. I'm going swimming with—'

I cut her short.

'No, Mama! You are not!'

She began to cry. Crocodile tears.

'With Ulva,' she said, weeping, 'swimming with Ulva.'

Was there not a twinkle in her eye? A brief smirk playing on her lips? Oh, she knew, she knew what she was doing, all right.

On the bus to town, I remembered my dream of the previous night. A premonition, you might say. You were lying on a plinth, my bird, eyes closed. My imagination must have worked overtime for I had not, at that point, seen you unclothed. I circled you, as if you were an exhibit in a gallery. I had a pad in my hand. I was taking notes. I cannot recall what I wrote. Was it something to do with your skin? Your skin was shiny, appeared edible: like the surface of decorative fruits on flans and pâtés – glazed, preserved. Varnished. I touched your forearm. It was cold, hard, like china.

As it would be, my Ulva, if I were to touch you now. I reach. But I cannot. I can't help thinking of the crow. I feel its stiff, cold body. I shudder. Even to the most experienced, death is never pleasant.

In the department store (which Mama insisted on calling Delderfield's though I had explained our old haunt had long since been demolished), Mama chose a lemon shift dress, an apple-green blouse and a skirt in peach jersey. I put on a brave face, though I could hardly bear to watch her doing a stumbling cow-like turn in front of the mirror. The reflection was a Mama so unrecognisable from the mannequin-perfect creature I remembered.

'Don't I look beautiful, Erskine? I do look so pretty, don't I?'

'Yes, Mama.'

Her hair needed cutting, styling, something. It brought to mind a wig left behind in my dressing room after a disastrous – some would say jinxed – production of *Macbeth*. It hung on a hook – I imagined the face turned to the wall. I had it removed, loath to touch it myself for fear I might be cursed. I believe I was: I received my first and only bad review. Beneath the wig, on the carpet, were dark red stains, probably wine, which apparently wouldn't come out. In certain lights, in her rags, Mama would have made a convincing Hecate.

The new clothes were an improvement. But her shoes were shabby and very much down at heel. When she lifted a foot, I saw that the sole had worn right through.

'You need new shoes, Mama.'

'And another dress,' she said, 'a party dress. For Ulva's party.'

'Party?'

'It's her birthday. She's coming to tea this evening. At five o'clock. I've invited her.'

Invited you to tea? Why on earth hadn't she told me?

'Jelly and ice cream, sandwiches and cake,' Mama went on, 'a big iced cake with pink candles.'

I was cross with Mama, and hurt. You might have mentioned it was your birthday. We would have to get our skates on if we were to get everything by five. I paid for Mama's clothes, including the party dress in aquamarine taffeta, then realised with alarm I had not got you a present. Some jewellery, perhaps? While searching the display cases, Mama picked out a silver bangle for you and a filigree silver treble-clef for herself – though I drew the line at a pair of cuff links in the shape of truncheons (or were they rounders bats?) she wanted for Mr Pergolesi. But what could I give you? I had not even begun work on your box. Then Mama found a small pink plastic trinket case in the children's section. I did my best to dissuade her, but she was adamant.

'But it's meant for a little girl, Mama. I don't think Ulva—'

'That one,' she said, 'and I shall scream for Security if you don't buy it.'

The box would be from Mama. I bought you a mother-of-pearl lighter – you have it still in your bag, I note – and a packet of your favourite Nectary Fine tobacco. I would get to work on my own box, a belated gift, as soon as I could.

I told Mama we would have to make do with a quick sandwich but she complained that she felt faint and was in need of iron and led me to a steakhouse where she ordered her meat extremely rare, sucking on each piece as she slowly chewed and mopping up the blood with bread. I was getting anxious. She had left me so little time as it was for shopping and preparations. And I did not want to let you down. I bought an iced fruit cake, a box of fancy cakes and some rum truffles. I also purchased some champagne, and a bottle of lurid purple liquid – Devil's Advocate – a ready-made cocktail Mama said you liked. She had got to know you far quicker than I, it appeared. I was hoping to catch the next bus home, but Mama then planted herself outside Les Enfants du Paradis – a children's boutique – refusing to move until I bought the dress in the window. Our bus went past. It would be another hour before the next. My patience had expired. I gripped Mama's wrist as she was about to enter the shop. She yelped like a kicked puppy. Then she turned to me, eyes glaring, growled at me to let go. Passers-by tutted, asked whether she needed any help. I pleaded. We had plenty of dresses at home, I said. I'd treat her to cream cakes and tea at the café. I threatened to take her dresses back to the shop. That did the trick. We went to the café.

It was then that I saw you. You were sitting at the back. I was about to point you out to Mama when I noticed you were not alone. You two were deep in conversation. You two knew each other. The person sitting opposite you was no stranger. I told Mama the café was closing and promised her a magazine and some marshmallows when we got back to the village.

It was not a pleasant journey home. One does not realise how many details can be assimilated in a matter of seconds. The long lean fingers suggested an artistic type. One hand clutched a fountain pen. A student perhaps? There was a writing pad on the table. Shoulders hunched. Glasses. Shoulder-length lank dark hair. Forgive me, my friend, but you were no hunk. (Your father's son, Frankly, I see now.) Who was he? The 'he' you had been meeting? Would you tell? You were laughing, my bird. Under the harsh strip light of the café, your hair, my bird, was quite red.

I was waiting for you to tell me.

I should have known when I saw them that first time in the coffee shop. Her eyes, earnest, and the way she hugged herself as she leant towards him over the table. That shiver of . . . what – excitement, passion? I saw, but I did not want to believe. He was, I noted, so young.

There is a point when, always, the degree of intimacy reveals itself.

She thought I was performing. She assumed I would be going to the party afterwards. But one of the tenors collapsed and fell off the stage. A heart attack, I believe. (Later, I did not mention it. And she did not pick it up from the papers. Evidently, Leodora had her mind on other matters.) I arrived back at the flat early. She had told me they were working on a play. There was, I remember, a manuscript on the coffee table. I saw them. On the red leather sofa which rasped and farted as they cavorted, like some filthy old beast. Unlike the fingers squeezing and rubbing her rump, the penis was short, stubby and thick.

I waited for her to tell me.

In the dark, I waited for you to arrive. I had recovered sufficiently to have everything ready for your tea party. Mama had gone upstairs to bath and change. When we got in, she had thanked me for the dresses.

'A nice day out,' she said, 'but can Ursula come next time?'

I was rather past caring. I closed the curtains, poured myself a large Scotch. I needed something to calm my nerves. Five o'clock came, five thirty, quarter to six. Perhaps Mama had made the whole thing up. You were not coming to tea. It was not even your birthday. You were still with your lank-haired friend in the café.

A few minutes before six, you arrived.

'I'm late, I'm sorry.'

But you did not explain why.

'Happy birthday, Ulva.'

You were wearing a black velvet top with the black skirt. My bird had been plucked. There was an aura of darkness about you – an angel in negative. Or was it my imagination?

'I wasn't going to say anything,' you said, 'but Nora asked me about this.' You fiddled with the pendant of a necklace I had not seen before. A thin gold chain from which was suspended a gold heart engraved with a scrolled initial I could not distinguish. I was thinking how I might enquire who it was from when Mama floated in, an aquamarine cloud, bearing your gifts and singing 'Happy Birthday'. I suddenly found myself on the terrace overlooking Boxwood's back lawn. The place was bedecked with ribbons and balloons. I was standing amidst a clutch of little girls in varying shades of pink. The cake on the table had five thick pink candles. The little girls screamed as Mama came through the French windows with a carving knife.

Did you like your presents? You did not appear appreciative, although the plastic trinket box seemed to amuse you. I rather wished I had put a little something inside. For it seemed you thought the point of the present was what was in the box. Your disappointment was clear when you raised the lid. Nothing. Was an empty box as much a bringer of bad luck as an empty purse? Possibly. You cast the box aside. And you left the presents behind when you went. Perhaps it was only other people's things you coveted. Small things went missing. Not of any value. But not yours.

But what an evening of twists and turns, my friends!

First, there was the delicate matter of how many candles we should put on the cake. I had settled for three for luck. I had reminded Mama before you arrived that it was not etiquette to ask a lady her age. Which, of course, as soon as it was time to light the candles, she did. Twenty-eight. Eight and twenty years old, my bird. A shock. A serious miscalculation. My bird. My fledgling. Oh, I must have appeared to patronise you, to have condescended even. I shuddered to think of what faux pas I might have made. How old did I think you were? I realised I had not put an age on you. Well then, the gap between us had narrowed somewhat. Not that it should have mattered.

It took a few attempts to light the candles. You must have noticed that my hand was shaking. We sang 'Happy Birthday'. And then you leant over the flames. A witch. A Hecate.

We opened the champagne. That and the Scotch had given me the courage to ask you. But Mama got there first.

'We saw you in the café today, Ulva. You were with a friend. A young man.'

I had not realised she'd seen you. There was a long pause before you answered.

'No, it wasn't a friend,' you said. 'I didn't know him. Just someone sharing my table.'

It was not the truth, I knew. You were not a good liar, my Ulva. But why the need to lie? I wondered.

After two glasses of champagne (and a tantrum over not playing any party games – I was rather hoping for Postman's Knock), Mama fell asleep on the settee. Which left the two of us on our own. I wished Mama had gone to bed. The rattle in her chest and her rasping breath irritated, was a worry I did not want to be concerned with just then. I was on edge anyway. You. I wanted to focus on you and what you had not told me. Your man friend. I could not get the café scene out of my head. I tried to think of a reason why you should have lied. Though, for whatever reason, a white lie, surely? Perhaps I should try to loosen your tongue a little. I offered you a Scotch. Then you pulled a bottle of brandy from your bag. Courvoisier, no less. And surely a coincidence, for you could not have known that Leodora used to buy me brandy. A gift, you said, for all the hospitality you had received so far at Boxwood. So far? As you passed it to me, our fingers touched, the lacuna prodded to attention. And I noticed then the tiny white scar lines at your wrist. You were sitting perched on the edge of the chair. Upright, legs crossed, your hand clasped around your knee. You were looking down. Your hair falling over, covering your face.

'Marcia's going to be away for a while. She'll be going in a few days.'

'Oh?' I waited. I sensed there was more. Still you would not look at me. 'Oh dear.'

I was looking at your legs – more precisely, at the foot of the crossed-over leg which circled first one way, then the other. Its familiarity was comforting and disturbing. I had seen it before. Another foot. Someone else. Long before.

'I'm not looking forward to staying in the cottage. By myself, I mean.'

'No. I'm sure you're not.'

But of course! It was a cue. How could I have been so dense!

'Well, you know, if you feel lonely, Ulva, you can always stay here.'

'Yes.'

And? What more? Then you looked up. You were biting your lip.

Of course.

'Oh, but this is such a big house – all these empty rooms. Why don't you stay here? Just while Marcia's away. Mama would love it.'

And so, my bird, would I, I thought.

'I'd love to, Erskine.'

'Excuse me?'

'Yes, thank you. I'd love to.'

Even now, in recollection, I hear it as 'I love you, Erskine'.

Mr Frankly, I immediately forgot all about the friend. It was as if she came dancing into my palm. But it was the other way around. Like the fox and the chicken. Ah, but who was the fox, my bird? Who indeed.

After you had gone (an apology here for my ungallant behaviour for I should at least have offered to walk you home), I thought about opening the brandy – a toast to our new guest. I decided to wait. We would make it together, on your first night. I went up to bed, leaving Mama snoring. Already, in my mind, I was clearing out your room, had you tucked under the covers. I could not sleep; neither could the lacuna.

So, something in the box after all. But for whom, my Ulva, for whom?

II. First Night – More White Lies – Lights Out!

First-night nerves. Pre-first-night worries. Three major anxieties – my wood, the lacuna, Mama. And regarding Mama I did not fully appreciate the risk until the day you arrived with your suitcase. It seemed Mama had already spilled far more beans than I had realised. With regard to my wood, I needed to ensure my workroom door and, more importantly, the door to my private collection remained locked. Working hours might need to be rescheduled – late at night, after you had gone to bed, perhaps, or early morning. It required some planning. Then, there was the lacuna. I could not conceive of a situation where you would see me unclothed. And here, my dilemma. For part of me longed that you would, was even beginning to consider how we might overcome the details of intimacy.

I am recalling now that day when you caught me 'in the throes', as it were – you remember, in the bathroom. I was still distressed after Mama's departure and had forgotten to lock the door. My back was turned to you, but you must have seen something in the mirror. You were embarrassed, yes, understandably. But you did not laugh, nor mock. Just as she, Leodora, did not mock.

Mr Frankly, you have no idea of my suffering. A small digression now, while I talk man to man. I have not revealed the details of, shall we say, what I lack until now, for I did not believe you were after such spoils. (Though a full-page colour enlargement would certainly have been a coup for you. Think what that would have done for sales of your biography!)

But the lacuna, Mr Frankly. The surgeon had managed to salvage a remnant. Although, in my darker moments, I feel it may have been kinder to have removed the whole miserable mess and be done with it. (I understand it had to do with maintaining hormone levels.) But how could you understand the frustration of never experiencing complete relief – that fiery accumulation in one's loins, the building tension, the whole of one's being straining for release. And all one achieves is an ant's thimbleful of gnat's dribble, barely enough to drown a fly. The absolute anticlimax, my friend, every time. They made a limbo man of me, an in-between. Frankly, my friend, whatever, whoever, you have lost (I refer to your father, of course), I am quite certain you have not experienced a greater loss than mine.

The lacuna, then. In its full-blown, fully activated state, one might say, the lacuna, raised red, is the pit of the volcano. Otherwise, at rest, it resembles the surface of a cauliflower – something akin to those waxy-surfaced, shrink-wrapped supermarket caulis, or a museum-kitchen cauliflower – and in certain lights has a silvery, leathery smoothness, like fossilised

flora. The nub – the tag, toggle – aside, the lacuna is like . . .
looks like . . .

Here, a list for you:

a shrink-wrapped supermarket cauliflower
the head of the Elephant Man
creamy cumulus (and other varieties of cloud formation: stratus,
cumulonimbus)
cottage cheese
the brain (bottled in formaldehyde)
solidified lava
a moonscape
certain glacial surfaces
bubbling batter
the inner surface of the mouth of a Great White
scar tissue

Shall I digress further? Shall I reveal a little more and tell
you of the origins of my habit, which really took hold some
time during those years at the Mansion House, outside that
bedroom door, my eye tight to the keyhole, watching Mrs
Bainlait and Mr Gelert-Bones? Peeping and rubbing. Peeping,
rubbing. Never anything to pull or stroke. A habit that
remained, indeed developed, after I had moved to London
at the start of my career.

I was on my way home one night after a rehearsal of
Gluck's *Orpheus*, singing to myself the Recitative – 'Oh ye
happy shades'. You may know of it, just as Eurydice is led
by the Chorus of Heroines to Orpheus:

> Ah, could ye but feel
> The fire that doth devour me,
> The am'rous flame
> That doth consume my love-torn heart.

The fire that doth devour me always, Mr Frankly, the

am'rous flame that flickers, splutters, is out like a snuffed candle. I want infernos, Mr Frankly, forest fires, pyrotechnics!

I was so engrossed in the music I must have taken a wrong turning, for I found myself in a narrow street, somewhere in the vicinity of Soho. Then I noticed the pink neon sign – 'Peep Show'. I might have been buying groceries; the girl did not even look up from her magazine as I handed her the entrance fee – a reasonable price to pay, I remember thinking, for a half-hour's viewing. I had my own cubicle – about the size of a small boxroom – which contained nothing more than a plastic swivel seat (the sort you find in passport photo booths), which adjusted your eye level to a small circular cut-out in the opposite wall. On a shelf was a discreet box of tissues. Man-size, of course. The man and woman were on a platform. They performed a mechanical routine – there was an air of banging out the same old number. Then the man withdrew, and the woman knelt before him. What a Master John Henry it was! Indeed, a magnificent horn. I was mesmerised. Then the woman opened her jaws – and such big teeth she had! Oh, I could hardly bear to look – the ultimate torture for poor Erskine. (Before my next visit, I put in a request: oral sex to be taken off the menu, if you please.) I became a regular customer. Twice a week, sometimes more. Of course, my habit ceased the minute I took up with Leodora. It would have been a betrayal. Although it was some time before our relationship reached a level of intimacy. And she knew, I believe, what I lacked, and it did not appear to matter – at least, not then.

We first met at a benefit concert for retired winkle-pickers or some other equally bizarre gathering. (Leodora would attach herself to any cause, high or low, go to any lengths for publicity.) You are well aware, of course, of her involvement in the promotion of the arts – what she wouldn't do to secure any job or client she had her eye on! I was, as usual, the oddity of the evening, the freak, long before I opened my mouth. They skirted me as though I had something contagious, and always the eyes on the trousers, trying not to look, as though my flies were undone. Only the Voice could lift them from suspicion and distrust of the unfamiliar. They would be visibly stilled, the smirks and grimaces wiped clean. I knew I touched every one, saw their eyes widen in disbelief, then wonder. And in their eyes I saw Erskine, defined, a golden-winged creature. Only the Voice could complete me. It was my only means of achieving fulfilment.

Ah, imagine it, Frankly, imagine it beginning deep, deep in the belly – an awakening, an arousal, rising up through the body, the chest, lungs filling, feeding, imagine the feeling becoming sound, swelling and flowing up through the neck, the throat, like blood pulsing through the veins, pulsing up, up into the mouth and, at last, come singing out. Ah, what satisfaction, what release!

Leodora could feel it. 'Sing to me, Erskine, Rinaldo's "Caro Sposa", sing.' (Her favourite operas were always on the theme of betrayal.) She would stand behind me, place her hands around my throat. And I sang. *Messa di voce*. The note beginning pianissimo, then swelling out to its fullest sound before diminishing back to pianissimo. All the while her cool white fingers around my throat, like white roots seeking nourishment, her breathing coming faster, deeper, then the dark, earthy moan. We were both left reeling in the aftermath, the Voice still sounding in the air between us.

Ah, but listen, listen to me now. I am quite breathless at the memory.

That night we met, she invited me to have supper at a quiet restaurant she knew, away from the crowds. She was such a handsome woman – tall, big boned, with thick reddish-blond hair. A woman who looked after herself.

I was afraid, my friends. It was my first involvement with a woman, a relationship I was to guard fiercely. I would allow nothing to destroy us.

Her kisses healed my wounded flesh. Her tongue coated me with gold. I see now her white smooth-skinned hand upon my gnarled flesh. A beautiful shell. And the ugly lumpen mass of the lacuna like a grotesque sea slug. She told me it fascinated her. She said it was a beautiful fossil. It was a fossil she would reflesh and return to life.

'I see an empty glass, Mr Cercatore. May I get you another?'

My mouth was open but I could not find words. Her hand was on mine and the physical connection made me freeze.

'The nibbles here leave much to be desired, wouldn't you say? I fancy something rather more substantial and warming perhaps. You are cold, Mr Cercatore. There's a bistro I know, five minutes away. Would you care to join me?'

A saint to a leper. A strong figure, clearly defined. A most handsome face. Expensive clothes. One thinks of the face of the matriarch, the wife of the diplomat, the chairwoman of the board. Nothing sharp or pinched or shrunken, but composed and strong, generously moulded. But you must have seen the press, my friends, all those celebrity pictures, the charity functions, society weddings and so forth.

'It would be an honour, Miss Ableyart.'

'Oh, Leodora, please.'

Over our meal (a distinctly delicious coq au vin washed down with a crisp and well-rounded white grape), it quickly became apparent that Leodora had been following my career with interest.

'What fascinates me, Mr Cercatore, is the real Erskine

Cercatore, the face behind the mask, the man behind the Voice.'

Very little man, I almost said.

Our relationship developed at a rapid pace. We met regularly, once a week, sometimes twice. She was, I could sense, quite taken with me. Each time we met, I would greet her with a bow and she would giggle and link her arm in mine, turning on her heel away from me, coquettishly, as if we were about to go into some sort of jive manoeuvre. The expert manipulator, I later realised.

She attended every performance, and always had a front-row seat, so that gradually, my audiences melted into an indistinguishable mass and all I was conscious of was Leodora, at the centre, a rare and precious jewel in an otherwise unremarkable crown. She had me entranced, spell-bound. She was a lady of magic, a high priestess. Soon I was singing only for her.

Leodora was wonderfully adept at steering me away from the after-performance gatherings to secluded restaurants or the cinema. Later, she would take me back to her flat.

Did you ever go to the flat? (Shortly after the investigation, it was turned into an art gallery, I believe.) How appearances deceive! An unremarkable building from the outside, dingy and run down. But inside – what extravagance! It was a breathtaking, almost suffocating experience entering Leodora's apartment. A glut of materials, textures, colours – crystal, woods, velvet, leather, purples, crimsons, pink, gold, gilt, a veritable abundance of ormolu, chandeliers, chests, tallboys, chaises longues, Old Masters – all crammed into five smallish rooms. I was reminded of the children's illustrated medical reference – *A Journey through the Body* – in the library of the Mansion House.

Leodora did not merely take me under her wing, she wanted to devour me. I think she began to sense my unease, noting that I would take an age over dessert, prolonging our post-*repas* chat before finally giving in to her suggestions of moving to the leather sofa for coffee and Courvoisier. Once, she said, 'You're an enigma, Erskine. Now wouldn't I just love to know what goes on inside that head of yours!'

I was aware of her hand inching from my knee to the inside of my thigh, where it stopped, the fingers pressing lightly. Ah-ha, I thought, but it's not really this head upon my shoulders you want to explore. And then she bent towards me, her lips parting so that I could see the pink tip of tongue behind her teeth. In the nether regions, a stirring, such as I had not experienced for some considerable while, like a creature waking from hibernation. Later, on my own at home, I replayed the first kiss, imagined Leodora's breasts tipped with thick brown nipples in my hands. I had not seen her breasts entire (though the low *décolletage* she favoured displayed ample fleshy mounds). But here they were jiggling on my palms and floating up now level with my face, while my hands went down to unzip the trousers and in and over the lacuna, rubbing, rubbing, rubbing, until – ah – some watery dribbled relief.

Now this new element in our relationship threw me into a state of confusion, even fear. How should Erskine handle it? Apart from Mama (and once by Sylvia), I had never been kissed by anyone. Leodora knew there was something amiss. She had known even before we met. Society gossips have such cruel tongues! Though she did not attempt any further physical contact for some months, and we both seemed to avoid the option of going back to her flat. Until, as I walked her home from the restaurant one night, her arm linked in mine, she confronted me.

'It's a physical relationship you're frightened of, Erskine, isn't it? Erskine, none of us is perfect. And I don't have to remind you, I am a great deal older than you. My body is not as it used to be.'

'But mine,' I said, 'has never even had the chance to become.'

She turned to me then, put her palm to my cheek.

'Look at me, Erskine.'

I saw that the dark had softened her further, had toned down her regal, leonine beauty, had rendered her vulnerable.

'I know, Erskine,' she said. 'You do not have to say anything.'

And I trusted her. Yes.

That evening she pressed me to come in for coffee. When she asked me to put away her coat in the guest room, I noticed that the room had been redecorated in subtle creams and maroon. More manly, she said, with emphasis. On the newly made single bed was a robe with EC monogrammed on the breast pocket. Beside the bed was a pair of matching slippers. On the desk, a writing set complete with pad and pen and engraved with my initials. In the wardrobe (the door had been left open) hung a row of silk shirts in creams, pinks and lilacs, which, I later discovered, fitted like skins.

'I want you to feel at home, Erskine,' she said. 'You don't have to sleep here on your own.'

I had never felt so vulnerable. Mr Frankly, think of salt on an open wound, razor blades and new-born flesh, the mouse in the vulture's eye, the slug in the desert. If she had laughed at me, one twist of her lips, one stifled titter – an end would have come sooner rather than later. (I had an exceedingly large brandy.)

She made of it a thing of wonder and beauty. No mockery. No pity. As though she had discovered a rare flower. So little to give her, yet it might have been the most precious thing on earth. She ran her fingers over it as though to make sure it was real. And then the cool, wet tip of her tongue. Oh.

I was all flesh. All of me reduced to that one small part of my flesh. My entire being brought to a state of extreme sensuous delirium by the light, quick strokes of her tongue. I was liquid. She was lapping me up. Oh. The first time I had even been touched there, like that, by anyone.

And when you are given something so precious, you do not willingly surrender it.

Leodora made me who I am, my friends. Who I was. She gave me name, identity, dignity. She made sure I had all I needed. All I had to do was sing. I see now, of course, it is quite pathetic. The singing bird may still be a caged bird. And Leodora may as well have put a leash around my neck. But I did not, at the time, feel the tightness of the collar, the tugs and jerks. And had it not been for Leodora, I might have ended up in some freak show.

It was, at any rate, a gilded cage. One of ormolu. Having spent a great number of my early days within the gloom and shadows of the Mansion House, I was uncomfortable, at first, amidst the opulence of Leodora's decor. An albino set in the heat and glare of brilliant sunshine. But I gradually adapted. Scratch away the gilt, and underneath it's only wood, after all.

It was a peaceful, routine existence. We did not socialise apart from the obligatory post-performance gatherings. Although Leodora had a full business diary which often took her away for days. I did not pry. She had work to do.

The clothes, I have to confess, rendered me a handsome devil. (After we had visited those prestigious men's outfitters and my measurements had been recorded – the taking of the inside leg always, you understand, a difficult moment – I would return from rehearsals to find at least two dozen shirts on my bed, a rainbow of silk, like a fan of delicately hued skins.) I grew to accept rather than revile my reflection. The mirror became a generous friend. Often, while I dressed,

I would see Leodora's face in the glass, her lips softening into a small swung dash. As if I had grown an extra red head.

That first night. My becoming.

'Come. Come with me, Erskine,' she said. 'Come to my room, to my bed.'

I swallowed the brandy, took her outstretched hand, and she led me across the hallway into her boudoir.

As I went in, I knocked into a small high table displaying china bells, one of which, in my efforts to right the table, fell to the floor. The handle broke. As you know, I am a gauche creature, and in Leodora's flat it was hard not to be a bull, filled as it was with trinkets, clutter, every surface covered. She did not seem to mind too much about the bell. It worried me more, I think. I am disturbed by broken things, my own damage having induced an acute sensitivity. It took me many months before I felt at ease. To make it more of a trial, Leodora had a penchant for dim lighting. Red light bulbs, like exotic fruit, grew from garish, over-ornate shades. There was a particularly ugly gold candelabra, each 'flame' an electric bulb. The heavy velvet-and-brocade curtains at the small windows, rather like those over-large, elaborate frames around insignificant paintings, prevented most of the natural daylight from coming in. The curtains were always drawn at the first hint of dusk, and certainly never before eleven in the morning. 'Light destroys and reveals too much,' she once told me.

'Take off your shoes, Erskine, and lie down on the bed, won't you?'

It was not a command. The words were issued gently, almost purred.

There was a music machine by the bed. She put on a compilation tape. An odd selection: Mahler, Schubert, something choral, then a string of hits from, musicals – 'Oklahoma' from *Oklahoma*, *West Side Story*'s 'America',

The King and I's 'Whistle a Happy Tune', 'Mac the Knife', many of these last familiar, Mama having taken me to see the shows during our Halcyon holidays.

Leodora came to lie beside me on the bed. She began smoothing my forehead, then slowly, very gently, began removing my clothes.

She was wearing a long satin dressing gown of embroidered turquoise silk, belted tightly at the waist, which emphasised her waist. And she wore loose trousers in the same silk. She kept both gown and trousers on. During our entire time together, I never once saw Leodora naked.

The brandy was taking effect, had planed the edge of my nervousness. I soon stopped trembling.

I have to tell you, it was the most pleasurable experience. Utterly delicious. She was so careful. As though she were unwrapping my skin. Old skin. Peeling old layers. First my tie, a bottle-green silk dicky. She took the two end flaps between her forefingers and thumbs, pulled, her face close to my throat so I felt her breath. Then she sat astride me. I closed my eyes as she removed my cuff links, began to undo the buttons of my shirt, taking her time, working down my chest. As she neared the last, I felt the muscles tighten, grip. She did not pull the shirt out from my trousers, but put her hands to my belt. I drew my breath. As though I were about to jump into deep water.

'Ssh, ssh, Erskine,' she said, and cupped her hand over my mouth.

'You have nothing to be afraid of, Erskine. Close your eyes. Allow me. Close your eyes.'

I thought of a black space. I was in a black space and turning, arms and legs spread wide as though I were stretched on a wheel, turning faster, now spinning. I was impaled. I could not move. And then the wheel stopped.

Ah. Oh. Can see, feel, now, Leodora's fingers, working on the belt.

knock on the door, peep in, lift up the latch, creep in

She undid the buckle, then she took the buckle in her mouth, between her teeth, pulled the belt out through the loops, drawing her head back, though not as if tearing flesh from bone. I glanced down. Her eyes were closed, something touchingly primitive about her, like a mother beast, the lioness tearing at the caul of a newborn.

She had the belt in both hands, now, her mouth wide, lips curled back. She undid the metal clasp of my trousers, leant forward again and opened the zip with her teeth, the belt still in her hands and stretched over me, pressing now, tight, tight. She was cutting me in half. The lacuna hot. Her teeth were those of a small shark, one you could hold in both hands, one that seems a harmless creature, until the mouth opens and you see the saw-tooth-edged jaw. Oh, Leodora, do not eat me. But there was little for her to eat. As you have seen, my bird, though my cupboard is not entirely bare, it is a strange and small feast.

She pulled down my trousers, over my legs, feet. Then she lifted my shirt. And then, oh so very slowly, she peeled back my underpants. Was it a touch of anxiety, fear or anticipation that momentarily tightened her face? She gasped—

'Oh, but it is beautiful, Erskine. Not what I . . . but beautiful.'

Her tongue was thick, fleshy, though when her teeth touched the skin, I flinched.

'You must tell me,' she said, 'if I hurt you.'

'I am not a man,' I said, 'and I am ashamed. It is that which hurts me.'

'But a man for me, Erskine.'

As she began to lick me, she put her hand down between her legs, began to rub.

For both of us, a quiet, sweet climax – she moaned, the lacuna shed a tear. She called it sweet. It tasted sweet, she said. My honey, she said.

She lay beside me for a while. We held each other. I had never known such peace.

And then she bathed me.

I remained a passive lover. For one thing, Leodora naturally took charge. And it was always Leodora who initiated our lovemaking. As I have told you, she always remained clothed. I did not mind. That she wanted me, gave me pleasure, was enough. She asked for nothing more. I was hers.

You will forgive me, my friends, if I leave you temporarily. Time for Erskine to take a bath. The lacuna, you understand. Awakened. I am a man, of sorts, after all.

First night. You in Boxwood, with us. With me. Ah, now that I had you, my bird, how could I possibly let you go?

First night, indeed. What a performance it was (like a couple of old pros, treading well-worn boards, were we not?) – revelations, a few embellishments, a certain unease. And a technical hitch!

I was not in top form, having spent half the night and the best part of the morning working like fury on the sycamore box, determined I should have it completed before you moved in. I cannot explain why exactly. There is no logic to either compulsion or guilt. I did not want the unboxed monsieur, or mushroom, to cloud the event, knowing it would prey on my mind, would prevent me from being 'all present', as it were, for you. And uncontained, at loose, Mr Mushroom was too much of a liability. In the couple of hours' sleep I was granted, I had the strangest nightmare (later to revisit me as hallucination) – you, a choirboy angel, ruff-collared, robed, glittering, holding Mr Mushroom before you like a candle to light your way as you stepped from a Christmas card into the darkness between us. Then, all morning, Mama, a vicious thorn repeatedly piercing my flesh, knocking on my workroom door every ten minutes, calling, 'Nurse Ulva, Nurse Ulva.' (Or was it 'Ursula'?) She was quite delirious and, I'm afraid, I had to resort to adding half a sleeping pill to her elevenses cuppa, which I regretted for it left her still dopey when you came by mid-afternoon to drop off your bags. Sensing your concern at how poorly Mama appeared, I tried to reassure you that the doctor was keeping an eye. I had telephoned, I said, just before you arrived.

I spent half the afternoon recovering my energies and putting the finishing touches to your room – brand-new linen, a vase of twigs in spring blossom, fresh towels and soap. Though my spirits were somewhat dampened when I brought you and Mama a tray of tea and fairy cakes and found the pair of you huddled and whispering. I could tell you were talking about me – Mama's guilt-glazed eyes, the way you turned your face away. Later, our tongues slackened with brandy, I realised just how much you had gleaned.

After you left, Mama's temperature soared. I gave her aspirin and, I confess, the other half of the sleeping pill. I did not want anything to mar my anticipation. I wanted to count the hours in peace, mull over what we might talk about, focus on presenting myself as the perfect host – to continue my metaphor, to 'get into character', allowing room, of course, for spontaneity, the unexpected. Though I did not realise just how much space was required!

Then – half past eight – there, on the doorstep. What a satisfyingly resoundingly final clunk as the front door closed behind you! You had stepped over my threshold. You were inside.

Mr Frankly, I feel inclined to present the scene in detail,

for your benefit and, quite simply, to relive myself such a delicious occasion. (Yes, it is almost a taste, elusive, packed with subtlety – cumin, passion fruit (of course), sensuous as garlic, truffle and fig, fig, fresh fig.) To re-experience, yes, for it was not too long before sweet, exotic, the acquired, was to turn bitter.

It was like Christmas! I had set the table with a red velvet cloth, silver candelabra, best china and a small but most thoughtfully selected feast of wild mushroom tartlets, lychees, black olives, pickled quail's eggs, pâtés and savoury biscuits. The bottle of Courvoisier with two crystal glasses stood at the centre. Log fire, low lights, plumped cushions, pine and rosemary room scent completed the picture. Erskine had thought of everything.

I led you to your room – you appeared delighted with my efforts – and told you to come down as soon as you had settled and freshened up, to join me in a toast.

You rose to the occasion, my bird. Brushed your hair, added a small diamante slide, a touch of pink frosted lipstick, changed from your flimsy multi-coloured layers into a navy top and skirt. The skirt was short, like the black one. The top was sleeveless and cut away at the shoulders so that I saw, for the first time, your long, lean arms, more flesh than I could have dreamed of, and (or had I seen it before, or imagined it?) the minute tattoo on your left shoulder which might have been a heart, a small animal (a bird?) but which I recently discovered was a lion's head. You were not as I first saw you. Another Ulva. Less decorated. More intense, deeper. Was it, I wondered, that you had removed your camouflage, your disguise, because you felt able to reveal your true self to Erskine? In the way lovers, after the blinding rush of passion, allow the veneer to dull, the dents and scratches to be seen. Had we reached that level of trust? But I was wrong to flatter myself. I was on the wrong track, Mr Frankly, was I not?

I poured two large brandies.

'To you, Ulva. May you be happy at Boxwood. It really is a pleasure to have you here—'

Apologies, my bird. The toast became a lengthy speech during which you kicked off your shoes and settled into a chair, planting your black-stockinged feet into the cushions. Ah, at home, then.

Did I reveal my nervousness? You must have noticed how I gulped my brandy. You were most careful – tiny sips, pipette drops on to the tongue of an orphan newborn – and how skilfully you skirted the issues, the information you wished to extract. Yet again, you enquired about my singing. How did we get on to that? Oh yes, Marcia's sister was rather worse than was first realised, Marcia would be away for some time. (How wonderful!) So, the concert was to be cancelled, at least, put off indefinitely. A brief sigh of relief from me.

'Why did you stop singing, Erskine? Nora said you were destined for great things.'

Did she now? I thought.

'Perhaps not that great,' I said. 'It was a throat infection. It did untold damage.'

I was deciding whether or not to go into further detail – though how much, I wondered, could I leave out? – when you asked your next question. I see now your greeny-blue eyes a-flicker, the busy working of your mind, though at the time your polite manner of conversation had me fooled. I was rather more concerned that evidently I could not trust Mama. What had she been saying?

'Your mother told me you had a sister. She died. Ursula. She calls me Ursula sometimes.'

I could not look at you. Damn Mama. Damn her.

'Yes,' I said.

You were persistent.

'It was some accident, wasn't it? Nora gets confused, sometimes she—'

'Indeed she does,' I broke in, 'yes.'

'I'm sorry. I can see how it still hurts you to talk of it.'

But could you, my bird? Could you really?

'It was many years ago – the tragedy. But it is never easy.'

'I know.'

You knew? A pause. I poured myself another drink. Even then, I had a sense of being cross-questioned. Frankie Deuce made a brief appearance from the shadows. A similarity in tone – quiet, but firm. Teeth hard and fast on a bone you would not relinquish.

'It was a shame about your career.'

'Endings are inevitable,' I said, 'a huge disappointment. But one is forced to come to terms – betrayal on the grandest scale.'

'Betrayal?'

The brandy had taken over. I had thrown you a large, juicy chunk. Too much. Too much, Erskine.

'As though I was betrayed by my voice,' I said. 'But enough of me. What about you? What do you do, apart from delivering vegetables, that is?'

You had studied art, you said, only to discover it was what your aunt expected of you. You had done this and that. You had not yet found what it was you wanted to do with your life. You needed other answers first.

'Answers?'

'Yes,' you said. Your turn, now, for reticence.

'Your aunt? Do you have other family? What about your parents?'

'My parents are dead,' you said. 'At least—'

And then your lips pressed tight together.

You see, you could have told me then. Indeed, you should

have told me. The whole story. If you had only come clean, the rest would not have had to happen. The consequences, Mama, my journal, how I had to deal with you and your accomplice, Mr Frankly – none of it would have had to happen. If only, my bird. Ah, in such fleeting moments our fate is sealed.

'Your glass is empty, Erskine. Can I pour you another?'

I took a sip. There was something about your profile, its now suddenly disturbing familiarity. You were talking but I wasn't listening. 'You're a bit of a dark horse, Erskine, you keep a lot inside.' Was that what you said?

'Pardon me?'

'Married, Erskine. Have you never married?'

I felt my edges tighten. I was withdrawing. A touched anemone. Oh, it was dangerous, didn't you know? All this tugging at my raw nerve ends – like a child at loose wires.

'It must be lonely,' you said, 'to have to go through the whole of your life on your own.'

What do you think I said, Frankly? Did she tell you? I did not want her pity. So I told her.

Listen, Frankly, I had to tell her something. She wanted some titbit from me, that was clear. And better to have tried than never to have been in the running. I wanted her to consider me a possibility, a suitor. But who cares what I told her. What is the point of knowing what has gone before? What good does it do? Tell me. Isn't the person in front of you now, in this moment, isn't that what really matters – the pristine self, untouched by what has gone before? But she was demanding something. She was hungry for it.

I told you it was a car crash, my bird. Mother and child. It was instant. The baby was unborn. A little girl, they discovered. We were married but two years. We thought we had a lifetime. (I noticed you were biting your lips again, my bird. How uncomfortable you seemed. How my story had touched you.) You asked whether the baby survived. And I recall putting up my hand – 'Please, please, no more'. Truth was, I had not given the details much thought.

Another brandy. I offered you the canapés, watched as you nibbled at a tartlet. Then you asked the time. I did my best to keep you. I insisted you taste the figs. I asked whether you were a swimmer. Did you ever brave the brine? I said (I was feeling quite light headed by this time.) No, you said, but Nora was always asking you to go swimming. (Nora. Lenora. Mama again.) I was imagining you in the waves, the chill and the salt tightening your skin. I was imagining your toned thighs, your surprisingly muscular legs. Sinewy legs. Legs of a running creature. I found myself recalling photographs I had come across in Leodora's flat, of Leodora in her youth: some amateur production of a play, *Hiawatha*, the cast dressed as Indians, faces yellowed with gravy browning, feather headdresses, and Leodora's strikingly athletic limbs, the muscles clearly defined—

And then the lights went out!

A power cut, my bird – not quite on the stroke of midnight but close enough at a quarter to. What fumblings we might have enjoyed in the dark! I went in search of torches and the fuse box. When I returned – oh! – I cried out in shock: you, rising from the chair, the choirboy angel, and in your hands the Sycamore Monsieur, held out before you, and you were staring at me with such fierce accusation. The nightmare come true!

A hallucination, of course. And not the monsieur, but a candle you had taken from the candelabra.

'Are you all right, Erskine?'

'Quite all right. You startled me, that's all.'

I gave you a torch and escorted you upstairs. The experience had sobered me somewhat. I could not have slept anyway, thinking of you in your room. I went to fetch my journal, and by the light of the fire and my torch, I wrote.

May. Spring. It is guilt, of course, which I must live with. I am flooded with it. Suffused. When I wake in the morning, I can taste it. I cannot look myself in the mirror, and sleep is now the collapse of the body through exhaustion. So many if onlys. If only it had not been raining. If only we had not been in so much of a hurry. Why were we hurrying anyway? Some appointment? Mine, hers? I cannot remember now. If only the car had not been coming round the corner when it did. It was at us before I'd seen it and our car skidded and I shouted, 'Keep away from the edge! Keep away from the edge!' – as if that would have saved us. All the time she said nothing, so still and silent, as if she was already dead. I could see the blue of the sky in front of me, just as if we were in a plane taking off, or on the back of a great bird and flying into the blue. For a second we were suspended, level with the horizon, as if a hand had slipped underneath the car and was supporting us. And then the horizon came up over us, washed up over us like a wave, and we were dropping down towards the rocks, the sea. And the whole time there was no reaction from her, she was a dummy beside me, and as we hit the ground I knew I was the only one alive. When we hit the bottom, the rocks, somehow I managed to get out. She was hanging half out of the car, lying on the rocks, stiff as a shop-window mannequin. There was no blood. I could not believe I was unhurt, that I could walk. But climbing back up the cliff, I was aware of a terrible pain in my groin. When I got to the top, reality hit. I had lost her. I thought about jumping. I don't know what stopped me. It was a tragedy.

2 June. I remembered reading somewhere that lilac is

*the colour of death. Why? I do not go in for that sort
of mumbo anyway. And lilac is a delightful shade –
pure and gentle, understated, just like you. One of
the colours that nature portrays most successfully – a
butterfly's wings, a wild flower.*

One of Farquhar's lads offered to do the job at a
competitive rate – cleaned out the rooms and took
some of the junk off my hands. Paid me a few pounds
for the ottoman, an oak box (antique) and a couple
of bits and pieces. I sanded down and revarnished a
chest of drawers. It required a few coats (I could get
carried away with this varnishing, such a satisfying
task) – a superb finish. I had taken the velvet curtains
from downstairs for cleaning, but they fell apart and I
had to buy some white lacy ready-mades. I managed to
find two purple velvet bows in the discount walk-around
store which I used to adorn the tie-backs. I bought white
broderie anglaise bed linen. I decided to keep the old
double bed. You were most touched. You have been here
now only a few weeks – but it might have been years. We
are still observing a few boundaries – and beginning to
cross others. Yesterday, we walked along the cliff path,
stopped for a while to observe the light-play on the
water. You linked your arm in mine. Our bond was
forged. The walk back home was particularly enjoyable
– an amble. After all, we have all the time in the world.

*5 June. Summer. The beach, the sea, rock pools,
swimming – what delights! Boxwood is too vast for
us, of course. Though I cannot contemplate living
anywhere else. I know Boxwood, and the house knows
me, and you do seem very much at home here. The
ghost house idea is an attractive option – we would
offer, say, three, possibly four, rooms with breakfast*

and optional evening meal. I will have to bone up on my cordon bleu. The house is labyrinthine . . . (my mistake – I meant guest house!).

6 June. I have waited my whole life for this. Completion. This is love. This is how it should have been. I know the whole of you, and you the whole of me. We are in symbiosis. You told me, 'No one in the whole wide world could ever replace you, Erskine.' And no one shall come between us. No one. I keep seeing you that day as you unpacked your things. So few possessions – one scruffy black nylon suitcase, a bin bag, two cardboard boxes. You sat amidst the nest of your worldly goods. So vulnerable. I once found a fledgling – scrawny, all eyes and wings, the few new feathers wet. The fledgling kept moving to the edge of the nest, put its head back and opened its beak wide. At least the satisfaction of hunger could be guaranteed. I went off in search of a worm, found a long fat one. But when I got back to the nest, the fledgling was no longer there.

You told me you were used to travelling light. Yours had been a nomadic existence, you said, though you would not elaborate. Have you been forever searching? And had you finally found whatever, or whoever, it was you were looking for? When I asked, 'Oh yes,' you said. I gave you a little time and space in which to find your feet, to establish your own routines at Boxwood. The place is yours as much as it is mine, but you must make your own tracks. By the same token, I will not pry. (Though I am so desperate to know everything there is to know about you!) It is odd how, when someone you think you know well moves in to share the same roof, how much more of a stranger they become. It is as though physical proximity *threatens the self, the edges, the boundaries. Just how far you can go before you tread on someone's personal space is gleaned at a subliminal level. But what am I talking about! Love. Love transcends all. This is the paradox – love defines and confuses. No, not confuses. Blends (?).*

You do love me.

I have decided. Nothing and no one shall come between us.

Last night, I crept into your room. The moon was an eye watching you through the half-open curtains. I was the panther in the Night Stalkers *sequence – you have not seen this particular recording. I caught myself in the mirror – such a powerful beast! You were wearing some singlet, vest, which left your arms and shoulders bare. I saw the thick covering of fair downy hair – an abundance of it; it formed matted whorls, like lanugo, as though you were not long from the womb, a newborn.*

10 June. Little sleep though so much to do today. I had an urge to go furniture-rearranging in the night. Did I wake you? The full moon was fortuitous.

Finalised plans for the back garden – the area of rough ground near the old oak. I have begun digging. It should not take long. A matter of hours.

11 June. Not in my wildest dreams could I ever imagine we would be together like this. Just us two.

It is the contents. Not the container.

12 June. I. I am . . .

My bird is staring. Her mouth stretches wide. Pink and gaping. So very hungry and too weak to make a sound. What she'd like most is a fat, juicy worm.

The lacuna nods in approval. A titbit. A nibble. Oh sirree, yes.

Mama was poisoning your mind. She was luring you away from me. Hardly the silly games of a mad old woman. She knew what she was up to. But why? To punish me? But hadn't I been punished enough? Remember how she ignored me? But I had gone through all that before. Yes. Something had to be done about Mama.

My friends, I loved Leodora. I trusted her. She allowed me to become. Gave me a shape I could inhabit. Gave me wings.

After that first night, there was a profound change in the Voice. Up until then, I had been a quiet oddity, a freakish taster to the main course, a talent that, though notable, remained on the outskirts of the music world. I had none of the presence or finesse required to make of myself anything more. I sang because I loved to sing, because I could do little else.

Then, after that night with Leodora, I woke to discover the Voice had changed.

I was in my room the next morning, dressing, humming the 'Che puro ciel' aria from *Orfeo*, and recalling my lacklustre rendition of weeks ago, when I felt it, insistent in my throat, a creature struggling to break free. I stood before the mirror. I took a deep breath. I opened the mouth—

> *Che puro ciel! Che chiaro sol!*
> *Che nuova luce e questa mai!*
> *Che dolci lusinghieri suoni . . .*

> How pure the sky! How clear the sun!
> And what new light is this?
> What sweet and flatt'ring sounds
> From these fair, wing'd singers

> Resound here in the vale?
> The whisper of the breeze,
> The brook's sweet murmuring,
> All here invites
> To eternal rest . . .

I sang the entire passage. I sang it over again. And again. Such energy coming up through me. As though I were being lifted from the ground. And as I sang, I watched in the mirror and I could see myself, Erskine in the glass, become more clearly defined. How can I explain? As though the copy of an image were placed over the original, a tracing set exactly upon the copied shape.

I did not need to call her. Leodora was already there, in the open doorway, in the mirror.

When I came to the end of the song, there was complete silence. She did not wipe away the tear that rolled down her cheek. She was trembling, breathing heavily. Her face was flushed, as it had been the previous night after making love.

'Erskine, is this really you? Never have I heard you sing like this. Your voice has always touched me but never, Erskine, never so deeply as this – as if your song has filled every cell of my body. Erskine, what has happened?'

She came to me, reached out her hand and brought my head near, kissed me, her tongue probing, reaching down into me as though she was hungry for this new richness. As though she was trying to locate the source of this new sound, for in her eyes, now, was such a strange look – of determination, or greed perhaps? Yes, the Voice had touched her. But there was a sharp edge to Leodora which cut, which extracted what it needed.

She gripped my arm.

'They will hear you, Erskine, and they will clamour for

you. You must promise, promise me, whatever they offer, you must not be tempted. Do not talk to anyone, Erskine. Just leave it all to me.'

My Erskine. Did she really say that? That is what I heard. I see her now, with me in the bedroom, her eyes wide, feel her grip. But you must understand, to be so utterly united with another, you do understand how I was not prepared to lose that.

Maybe it was in that moment, or during the hectic period which followed, that Erskine Flesching slipped away. The Voice was born. A whole, complete child had floated up through me. This was Erskine now. My essence.

Leodora Ableyart was in her element. Within days she had found a rehearsal studio and a pianist. Suitable music was selected. Excerpts from the Handel operas – *Rinaldo*, *Orlando*, *Tolomeo*, *The Messiah*, Serse's 'Ombra Mai Fu', Mozart's *Idomeneo*, Purcell's *Dido and Aeneas*, Britten's *A Midsummer Night's Dream*—

Ill me-e-e-e-e-e-e-e-e-et by moonlight proud Titania.

I recall the absolute silence, almost a whole minute's silence, which stilled each and every one during the first rehearsal, the heartfelt round of applause that followed my performance as Oberon.

And, of course, Gluck's *Orfeo – Che faro senza, Leodora?* Indeed.

The music required research. Leodora had considered enlisting the help of some student from the Royal Academy, though eventually decided she would do it herself. The fewer people involved, the better. I was a phenomenon, she said, the world would not know what had hit it. (As it turned out, the world, the real world, was never given a chance.)

Aria di bravura, ornamentations, *messa di voce*, *passaggi*. I practised for hours. I painted elaborate pictures with the Voice, embroidered rich tapestries. I did not have a tutor.

Leodora said I needed no one. But yourself, Erskine, and your heart.

A concert was arranged. A small select affair. The audience was hand picked. We would start with a whisper, Leodora said, set the rumour going. 'Then there'll be such a hue and cry, my Erskine, just you wait!' I trusted her.

That first public performance – a sensation! (You remember, I gave you that box of reviews? Ah, but of course, you never had the chance to read them. It is here, somewhere, in my workroom.) Women wept openly. Many got to their feet during my performance, only to pass out. I can picture them now, in the dark of an auditorium, dressed in their finery, collapsing in a faint, like exotic birds shot from the sky.

All I can tell you is what I felt, the power from within. Can you imagine? This Voice rising, rising, up from the depths of my being, through muscle and sinew and skin, surging through each and every cell, up up through the chest and the heart and the throat to the mouth, to the longed for release. My mouth poured liquid gold, silver. I was a vessel of fine porcelain, of glass. I had never experienced such ecstasy.

Leodora had not expected such a reaction. She observed each audience from the wings, like a hawk. She witnessed the effect I had on the women. I could bring the women to tears. I had magic. The Voice was my spell. They loved me.

Listen, some reviews –

Erskine Flesching is a phenomenon. Where has he come from? The breadth of range and purity astound. His voice is a gift from the gods.

If there are angels, then Mr Cercatore is one. Close your eyes and you will hear a nightingale singing.

A mother's voice heard by her unborn child. Unforgettable.

Otherworldly, ethereal, spine-tingling—

An incredible, impossible three-and-a-half-octave range – Mr Cercatore has stepped from the ranks of the eighteenth century's great castrati.

Leodora was so sure, so proud that first night she introduced me to the public – 'Ladies and gentlemen, I give you Erskine Cercatore – the Voice of an Angel.'

But even Leodora had not expected such a reaction. She was sitting in the front row and I saw her turning round to watch the moaning, sighing women leaning forward in their seats, as though unable to contain their passion. In the second half, I saw her in the wings. She was wearing a gold satin dress, her hair waved, lacquered high. The lioness lurking behind the trees.

Yes, I was reborn. Born. But without Leodora, I was nothing.

And without Mama, I was nothing.

9

In the Beginning is the End

Had to be done. That night. Of that night – two images. Black and white. White moon, tumour in a pitch sky. Mama's body, fat white root in the dark earth.

I could not have involved you, my Ulva. For I believed you would try to stop me, might even have tried to take my Mama away. You were fond of old Nora, weren't you? 'Go for a walk, Erskine. Nora's safe with me.' 'I'll take Nora up to bed, Erskine.' 'I'll take Nora out for fresh air, Erskine.' 'I've got quite a soft spot for your mother, you know.' Yes. My mother. Not yours. Never yours. All mine.

Soft spot, indeed. Where was your soft spot exactly? I will remind you that I had to resort to locking Mama in her room those last few days. Not only to keep her in, my bird, but to keep you out. A safety measure, if you will. I did not want to believe what I saw. You, in her room. Was it that day Mama told you what you needed to hear? Was it that day she gave you the journal? And so, because you had some, if not all, of what you were looking for, you no longer needed her. No, my dear. I think now you forgot yourself. Not an aberration, but the true Ulva. We are not Russian dolls, my bird. We do not simply contain, we hide. You looked so guilty with the pillow in your hands.

Yes, my bird, your Nora had spilled a few beans, but my guess is you were hoping she would spill a few more. My guess is that she had not then told you the whereabouts of the journal. Oh, she might have hinted, but considering the state of her short-term memory she could only have come across it by accident. I overheard you asking questions on several occasions: 'Where, Nora, where. Tell me!' 'If you don't tell me, I'll . . .'

What? What would you have done to my mother, my bird, my cold stiff bird? The same as you wished to do to yours? You cannot come the innocent with me. You hated her, your mother, understandably so, for what she did.

Ha! How frustrating it must have been for you, I later realised, to have to spend your time with my Mama, being nice to Mama, all the while resisting those dark urges.

You complained of a headache. It was because you were so worried about her, you said. You shut yourself in your room. I made Mama one of my special tisanes, sat with her while she sipped it, until she had settled back to sleep. It was a bad night for all. You came down to breakfast the next morning jumpy and baggy eyed. Mama, as I told you, had been wandering in the night. I was so concerned she might fall down the stairs I had decided to keep her bedroom door locked. In fact, I added, it would probably be best if she stayed in her room. She was sleeping most of the day anyway.

I really needed you out of the way, but with Mama now safely behind locked doors you had little to occupy yourself except cleaning and sorting. I should have been a little more alert to the reason for your continuing persistence in offering to help. Then there was a phone call and you disappeared for a couple of days, returning late each night.

So I was able to work on the box. As an extra precaution, I worked in my private collection room. It was, I have to say, a most beautiful box. Live oak (also known as true white oak). One of my first purchases of wood on returning to Mama. I could not resist. I knew it had a most special purpose, as if the end were already there in the beginning. Though I could not in a million years have known what the finished article would be. It was a difficult task. A labour of love. I was doing it for us, my bird. For you and me. Mama was coming between us. So how fortuitous, then, that she was very, very sick. The end was but days away.

My bird, it would have been too distressing for you. Which is why I slipped the pills into your brandy, just two, but enough to ensure your temporary absence. You knew how sick she was. And she had woken in the morning writhing and screaming in agony. Like knives in her belly, she said.

I suggested it might be better if you went out for the day. I would take care of Mama. (I even hinted you might meet your friend. How magnanimous of me! I said it might take your mind off things.) You wanted me to call the doctor there and then, but Dr Foster, I said, had come in the night. Apparently, there was little he could do. All that remained was to make Mama as comfortable as possible. And did Ulva meet you, Mr Frankly? She did not tell me, of course. It was only when she had gone that I realised I had no idea when she would return. And the later it got, the more difficult, indeed impossible, my task. Task. Yes. I considered it a task. A job. A deed to perform.

If it had been a long night, it proved an even longer day. Mama was a textbook case. She complained of pains in her belly and back. She vomited until there was nothing left inside. Approaching lunch-time, she told me she could no longer see. I realised it was a matter of hours. Throughout the day, I kept a close eye. Then you returned at 10.30, my Ulva. I detected alcohol on your breath. I considered it an advantage.

'You will join me in a nightcap, Ulva. Please.'

I was rather too insistent, though you appeared not to notice. What was on your mind? Something that kept you on your guard, yet hovering at my window ledge. What were you so hungry for?

I prepared your cocktail of Scotch and sleepers in the kitchen, adding to the tray a dish of stuffed olives and mini-gherkins (for which I knew you had a weakness), in the hope they might disguise any bitterness. You were settled on the sofa when I returned, your legs tucked under, your dark jacket draped around your shoulders, like folded wings.

'Are you cold? I can quite easily make a fire.'

'No. Thank you. I'm fine.'

But you were not fine. And I think now you were rather afraid. Of me.

Listen, Frankly, was it you who put her up to it, persuaded her to find out the truth at all costs? Or was the determination yours, my Ulva? At the time, I thought you were worried about Mama. You had become possibly too attached.

'Is Nora any better, Erskine?'

'I'm afraid not. No.'

'She's going to die, isn't she?'

'I love my mother,' I said, 'very, very much.'

'And she loves you.'

'Yes,' I answered. For it was a question, not a statement, was it not? It repeats now, most definitely, as a question. What I said next filled your eyes with such unfathomable pain.

'Ah. No one loves us quite like our mothers.'

You see, my bird, you appeared so unattached, so plucked-from-the-sky. Indeed, motherless.

You could not keep your eyes open. By 11.45, you were unconscious. I carried you to your room, slipped you under the covers – without removing a stitch! (Though I was tempted.) You were rather heavier than I had expected. After I put you to bed, I waited ten minutes or so. Then I set up the shopping trolley at the bottom of the stairs, fetched the roll of plastic sheeting and went to Mama's room.

When I wrapped her up, securing the plastic with parcel tape, it – the bundle – looked like a giant pod which I fancied might split, allowing a new Mama to emerge, moist, bewinged. I dragged the pod along the landing, down the stairs. Three-quarters down, I lifted the feet end and guided the pod into the shopping trolley. (I had realised I would never have had the strength to have carried her body through the house then another forty feet or so across the back lawn.) I had the unwelcome picture of myself as some dark agent of death, extracting Mama, slowly, excruciatingly, out of life. Not with the swift intent of the Grim Reaper appearing with the ease of apparition, or the neophyte hangman, not even the experienced executioner beaten by the last straw of conscience. I was none of those. I was the dutiful son engaged in the ultimate expression of love. I was the good doctor. I was simply doing what had to be done.

I left the shopping trolley with Mama in the pantry, just in case. Then I went outside to dig. There were a few clouds, and though the moon was not full it was waxed enough, and the sky clear enough, for me to be able to dig without lamps. I had read that six feet was the maximum depth. Foxes were not common in the area, but the scent of fresh meat carries far. One whiff would draw the hounds of the world in packs. I managed to finish digging just after two, which left me sufficient time to complete the necessary, filling in and so forth, before dawn. I returned to the house, checked you were still unconscious, then wheeled Mama across the back garden.

I finished just as the eastern sky was softening to amber. A new day. A new face. I thought of it not as a rebirth exactly, more as a relocation of self, a stepping back into the original Erskine. An Erskine without stigma or stain. The Erskine I was meant to be. The job was done. As I patted the final layer of earth back into place, I was drawing a line, closing the lid. Mama buried. Secrets, truths, confessions buried with her. There was no stopping us now, my bird. I loaded the wheelbarrow with the tools methodically, unhurriedly. I was at peace. As the pink sky on the horizon deepened, I felt my body relax, resettle. I was, I realised, smiling. I would have to exercise a little caution. I could not allow the mask to slip. Pushing the wheelbarrow across the lawn, I happened to look up at the house.

What I saw in one of the upstairs windows froze my marrow. A trick of the light, or the cast of a shadow, gave the figure wings. And whether it was the hair, or the white gown – where you wearing one of her gowns? – for one terrible moment I believed I was looking at Mama. But not Mama. It could not be Mama. Who, then? Leodora? Then horrors! A grown-up Ursula! Briefly, all three ghouls made an appearance.

But it *was* you, my bird! You were looking down at me, your arms wide, your hands pressed against the glass as though you were a prisoner desperate for the feel of freedom. You were a statue in the window. As I raised my hand to wave, you moved away, looked round briefly, sharp and clever, just like a fox, before you moved fleet and silent out of view.

You knew. Mama was dead and I had just buried her.

When I returned to the house, Frankly, I found Ulva in the kitchen. She was shivering. In shock, I suspected. Although the previous night's brandy and pills could not have helped. She was shaking so much she could barely roll her cigarette. I made her a mug of tea and gave her the facts. It had all been carried out, I said, according to Mama's wishes. I had a letter somewhere from her solicitors with detailed instructions regarding location of plot. An isolated spot out of view of both house and lane. No blessings or prayers. No marking of the grave with cross, plaque or statue. (The merest hint of the Virgin Mary and Pergolesi would be round every Sunday with flowers.) Dr Foster was also fully aware. The reason for such swift execution, as it were, was that it would hardly have been appropriate to dig the grave while Mama was still with us. It could only have been done at the eleventh hour, I said. Which, of course, made it a lot easier to cope with such a distasteful task. And, I explained, to help me further, I thought of digging the grave as constructing a box, or rather the inverse, excavating an interior. Either way, you end up with edges containing a space. Either way, Mama was in the box. But I realised I was talking to myself, Mr Frankly, for when I turned away from the sink, Ulva had disappeared and the next thing I saw was an angel, golden haired, white robed, gliding across the lawn towards the house. And then I realised it was you, my Ulva, and yes, you were wearing one of Mama's nightgowns and it was the early morning mist which had dissolved your feet.

Oh, but your face when you returned to the kitchen! Such a stricken look! As if your features were trapped. It looked such a mess, you said. Like allotments. You were right. I said I would order some turf. But it was, I emphasised, what Mama wanted. Before going out of the kitchen, you stopped in the doorway and without looking round you said, 'You'll probably appreciate some company now, since it's all happened so quickly, since you're on your own.'

You spoke in such a calm, measured way. You sounded so sincere. As I scrubbed the earth from under my nails, I was hearing music. Ah! The sweetest I had ever heard. I believed you meant it. But as I was to discover, you had other reasons for wanting to remain at Boxwood.

I do not know what it was I was expecting exactly – a drum roll, the crashing of cymbals, a choir of angels, the flapping wings of a thousand doves. But not so much as a thud as she slid into the hole. A mere unsatisfying swish as the plastic slipped over the earth. It was not the end I had imagined. After the fall from the cliff top, one waits for the splash, the full stop. Into the ground, old rotting root. White-root

Mama. But with eyes, ears, mouth. My Mama there, in the ground. Deep in black earth. Oh! Hear her still, the rhythm of her breathing. Leafy whispers. Mama? Mama? Are you there? Oh. Through a hole in the black sky – an eye. Eye of ice. Yellowed with spite, with vicious intent. Eye of the Huntress. Oh, did you see? Did you see? . . . When Mama went, all of me was sucked out. And where were my edges? Where was Erskine? Who?

—Erskine, Erskine. You were not going to tell her that Mama had died, were you? What was it, now? Ah, yes. It's all in the journal, is it not? After Ulva had gone out the previous evening, Mama had worsened. You feared pneumonia had set in. Your Mama was suffering, Erskine, in such pain. At times, she lost consciousness. You telephoned the doctor and within half an hour she was in the ambulance. Overnight, she had stabilised in hospital enough to be relocated. You had originally envisaged a dramatic helicopter journey in the quest for state-of-the-art medical equipment or some world-renowned surgeon extraordinaire. But an anonymous benefactor (some patron of the arts, an opera buff, perhaps) was offering an extended all-expenses-paid convalescence in an exclusive sanatorium somewhere in Europe. It was a condition of her treatment that Mama should remain for a time in total isolation. When she was a little recovered, you and Ulva would visit. You could picture it clearly, Erskine, the two of you, on a boat, a ferry, crossing the fjord, water true as a mirror, air crisp and fresh. You had your arm around Ulva and suddenly Ulva gazes up at you. Your story, Erskine. Indeed, for Mama's death, one might well read: The Death of Erskine. But when Mama died, you believed you had found Erskine again. Now Erskine could be who he wanted to be, who he should have been. But your fate is one of misidentity. Of being 'other', wrong, a lie, even to yourself. Yet you kept trying to climb back into a self, into what should have been but never was or could be. Ulva with you, with the Erskine you wanted her to see. You and Ulva.

10

Bodies and Other Phantoms
(Or Ghosties, Ghosties, Everywhere and
not a Ghoulie in Sight)

Those first weeks post-Mama – what a strange time for both of us, my bird. And for you, I would venture, most unexpectedly so. How often do we keep ourselves so tightly wrapped up in fear of what we might reveal – not to others, but to ourselves? In the dark of a lonely night, we tremble for fear of what lies within. The point is, my Ulva, I saw many things you did not know I saw, you did not intend me to see. Passing by Mama's bedroom, I caught you staring down at Mama, the pillow in your hands. Your skin so pale against your black clothes, deathly. Looking at Mama the way you looked at the crow. Mama, soft as a baby. She was holding the sheet tight to her chin, as if she knew. And her eyes, Mama's eyes, pleading and begging. I startled you when I rapped on the door. I asked whether Mama was all right, whether the bed needed changing. But no, she was fine, you said. My rapping on the door must have woken Mama. I saw her eyes, pleading, fearful. You with the pillow. I wanted to believe you. Still cannot bear to think, now, you could have done that to my Mama – my Ulva, could you? How could you?

We were like a pair of pallbearers creeping about this mausoleum. Even prior to Mama's demise, you appeared to be in mourning, wore black almost permanently, which, incidentally, aged you. Your rainbow plumage held far more allure. How I longed to spy my exotic bird flitting about the dark forest of Boxwood!

At last, I had the occasion to make use of the quantities of

black ties and black silk shirts Leodora had once pounced upon
in a Jermyn Street sale. (Leodora always demanded a certain
standard of dress. Even her play-man – he of the shine-worn
donkey jacket, tartan lumberjack shirt and castaway's coiffure
– underwent sartorial transformation. I ought to have read the
signs sooner. But her penchant for image makeovers was more
in line with the dressing-up of a plain or disfigured child, or
a pet – the tutued poodle, for example, the floral-frocked
or waistcoated chimpanzee. It had undertones of mockery,
patronisation, of master and slave.) For nearly a week, I kept
the curtains closed, which retained a subdued atmosphere and
meant (the house being anyway naturally dark) visibility was
considerably reduced. A number of times, my bird, you believed
yourself to be alone in a room, did you not? At other times,
you wanted me to think you thought yourself alone. I recall
one particular occasion. You had offered to do Mama's room.
(Such willingness for such a morbid task!)

'If you like, Erskine, I will sort out Nora's room. It won't
be easy, but—'

(But? Bah! You were itching, my bird. You could hardly
hold yourself back!)

I brought you some refreshment, my syrupy Bolivian coffee
– the colour of wood varnish, a most revitalising beverage.
I was coming up the stairs when, through the banisters, I
caught you sitting on Mama's bed. You had Mama's bag of
hair ribbons, were twisting the coloured strips around your
fingers and weeping. As I entered the room, you looked up,
startled to see me, wiped tears from your eyes and cheeks.
What grand and deliberate sweeps – how you must have
wept! How the tears must have rolled!

'Oh, I'm sorry. I didn't see you there. It's just, you know,
she used to like me plaiting her hair.'

(Oh, what a sweet heart you had, my bird. Have you ever
seen a bird's heart? Cherry red, cherry sized, which neither

beat nor fluttered, but whirred and turned within you like a
miniature musical box.)

'Yes,' I said, 'I know. You may keep the ribbons if you
wish. Mama would have wanted you to have a memento.
Take whatever you like.'

Poor Ulva. I gave you a handkerchief, found another in my
waistcoat pocket and dabbed my own tears.

'It is a hard time for both of us,' I said. 'I appreciate you
were close to her.'

But were you, my bird? I rather think not. But before
we delve deeper into your feelings for Mama, I wish to
continue for now along the vein of duplicity vis-à-vis others,
as opposed to vis-à-vis the self. A duplicity which somehow,
and unaccountably, at the time, rendered you more familiar.
(Or was it something about you which called up another's
duplicity? Forgive me – after so many years, it is still difficult.)
You were sitting on the floor in one of the rooms downstairs,
studying a photograph, your legs tucked beneath you and
stuck out awkwardly to one side. (I remember thinking
how uncomfortable it looked, quite unnatural, and odd.
Yet hadn't I seen you in this position many times before?)
And then I experienced a subtle shift in my mind. A kind of
rearrangement. I can describe it no other way. As though one
has changed the furniture around, so the room looks larger,
fresher.

There were unaccountably vague but persistent memories
of you, do you see, to which I could never match you exactly.
Yet I was certain they were, indeed, memories of *you*. And yet
it was as though someone else had slipped into your place, in
my mind. And now I am thinking of a microscope slide, of a
specimen mounted between glass plates. Now I am peering
down into the microscope, seeing the specimen in absolute
detail. As if, indeed, you were suddenly magnified, my bird!
But! Something slipped over you: the pipette drop, glass slide,

lens; whatever it was, I was viewing through another medium. And none of this could I yet properly articulate to myself. Just as I have difficulty now. And still I can hardly bear to face up to it.

We will go to any lengths when we wish not to see the truth, to ensure it will not be seen.

I could not get Leodora out of my mind. Neither her, nor her betrayal. Just as she could never be separated from her badness, so she was inextricably linked with you. Everything pointed to it. Yet I would not see it.

Oh yes, Mr Frankly, the photograph she was studying was of Mama. Ulva's head tilting to one side expressing loss – you should have seen her. Ha! How hammy was that! Or was it? Oh, I came across various such tableaux about the house – 'Lonely Girl Mourning Lost Love', 'The Stoic Daughter Puts On a Brave Face', 'Little Orphan Annie Dries Her Tears'. Yet she never seemed to want to stay long in my company. There was an intensity and a wariness about her, Mr Frankly, I could neither fathom nor define.

As for me, I had planned most thoroughly. *I* was not going to let anything slip! My role was simple – the bereaved son. Thanks to my stage career, I knew enough about method acting to enter into character, and stepped into a pair of dull black leather shoes, such as those that might befit an undertaker, the soles discreetly muffled in order to maintain respectful silence as they trod the paths between the living and the dead. My physiognomy assumed additional heaviness, graveness. I was one of the recently bereaved beside a grave, my entire being drawn to the loved one below ground. I was convincing. In danger even of fooling myself.

But I must come clean. For a few days, within my sombre disguise, I was experiencing relief and release. I was the prisoner stepping over the threshold into bright fresh freedom. Boxwood was transformed overnight. I was the new owner anticipating the pleasures of strange surroundings becoming familiar. I could only think of Mama as one thinks of the departure of an irritating guest. And 'Alone at last!' I might have confessed to my dark-suited reflection while dressing for dinner. But I could not work up sufficient enthusiasm, was beset by a feeling of anticlimax as the memories of romantic dinners and more intimate occasions gathered, only to be dispersed by the image of Mama like a hungry she-wolf approaching a flock of lambs. Our evening meals – we saw little of each other during the day – were more endured than enjoyed.

My bird, you thought I was coping. You believed me. (I confess, I was in danger even of fooling myself.) But it was no mask, but skin and tissue and nerve. This was no act.

One evening . . . When was it? Some time towards the end of the second week, I think. I recall a disgusting, quite inedible flan of puréed carrot which you pretended to enjoy (but carrots are intended to be firm, not mush!) I filled up on red wine, got myself rather drunk and, after you had gone to bed (fortunately!), had a sing-song – 'Bye Bye Blackbird'. I remember laughing, that unstoppable hysterical laughter which brought me to my knees, forced tears to roll until I did not know whether I was laughing or crying. Until I knew I was crying. The following day, I stayed in bed until late afternoon. It was not the after-effects of indulgence – although my head thumped and I could not have faced food. It was terror. I had woken around ten and was on my way to the bathroom when I thought I heard her. No. I did not 'think'. I really did hear her. She was calling – 'Er-skine, Er-skine', a lilting yet sinister whisper I heard all around me. Desperate to relieve myself, I confess I had to use my bedroom sink as an urinal, then I went back to bed and pulled the covers over my head. I could not stop shaking. I believe a couple of times you knocked on my door, but I could not speak. Around teatime, I forced myself to get up – more through the dread of the falling light, the night to come and whatever, whoever, might be lurking in its shadows. Perhaps I could somehow persuade you to an all-night card-playing session, or to watch my complete set of *Natural World* films with me. I could not face being alone. I dressed, then decided a bath might help to wash away the fears. On the way to the bathroom, for courage more than anything, I called out to you, but there was no answer. I ran the water. And then I looked in the mirror. I could not see myself. There was no reflection. Nothing. I remember shouting for you, scrambling downstairs (I almost fell), running from room to room, crying out like a madman. I looked down, shielded my eyes. I would not look in the mirrors, I would not look at anything. It meant I kept bumping into furniture, sustaining a number of bruises and one or two knee cuts. Fortunately, my bird, you were not in the house, for you would have had me certified.

It was, I can only assume, delayed shock. The nightmare began and lasted several days. Temporary agoraphobia kept me inside the house. The mere thought of my cliff top – that dizzying height, that expanse of sea! – made me giddy. And a physical inertia rendered me unable to get up from bed until at least lunch-time, and often had me returning as soon as I had eaten whatever you, my Ulva, had prepared (you were no cook, my dear), or had me sitting downstairs before a dying fire, my eyes tight shut or fixed on a just-glowing coal, for fear of what, of whom, they might see. Mama, I mean, and the others.

It started with the dreams. Mama fleeing from me in terror. Sometimes just a sense of Mama – flurry of nightgown, flash of red hair. Sometimes her face was close to mine, green eyes wide in utter incomprehension and searching my own—

Oh, oh, Erskine. Why? But why?

Why what, Mama? Tell me. Please, Mama, stay with me.

But, always, she'd move away, float away from me like a balloon lifted by wind, and then, high above me, she'd turn and run, run through the air into the clouds. And I would be left aching and empty.

Then Mama stepped out of my dreams and I saw her during the day wandering Boxwood once more, at the end of a corridor, at the top of the stairs, disappearing around a corner, drifting through the garden. A Mama from years ago. Like the Mama in the photograph albums. But fleshed, whole, substantial. Did you see her? I wondered. Could you? Not just Mama. The others. I saw all three of them once, outside your bedroom door. Mama and Ursula and Leodora. I shouted, 'No, don't go in!' And they fled just before your door opened. I was afraid of what they might do to you. In death, you see, they had united against me.

Then even you, my Ulva, became a spectre. As if they were somewhere in the shadows sucking the life out of you. You in your dark clothes, in the dark of the house. You were but a ghost, a hovering face, thin, angular, eyeless – like the skull of a goat.

Oh, my Ulva, I only wanted to protect you, for us to be together. But nothing was as I had planned. I feared I was losing you. I believed myself to be the source of your apparent suffering. You remember when you left the house in tears that evening? I was trying so hard to please you. We were sitting at the kitchen table. I was sorry, I said, that I had not been up to much, that I had not been able to cook food, that I'd left everything to you. I promised I would go shopping the next day and ran through an off-the-cuff list of tempting dishes (fat-soaked crumbs on the snowy ledge): liver and bacon casserole, heart stew, guinea fowl, thick spicy salamis, bratwursts, sausage and mash. And puddings, puddings galore! Spotted dick, plum duff, banana split with dollops of clotted cream. You made no comment, smoked your cigarette with such force that each line of exhaled smoke seemed a litany of compressed anger. But why should you be angry with me? Was it anger? Something darker – rage? Some dark emotion born of conflict, loss, a desperation to be loved. It was to do with Mama, was it not? Though Nora was but a means to an end. Your attachment had awoken feelings buried deep. Ah, my bird, mothers have much to answer for.

'I'm sorry,' I said, 'for my behaviour. It's just that I miss Mama.'

'Yes,' you said. 'It's quiet without her.' There was a forced hardness about your mouth which suddenly somehow rendered you fragile. The foot of your crossed-over leg swung violently. Your eyes narrowed. Then you looked away, biting your lip.

'We're not exactly without her,' I said.

Through the open door, then, on cue, a cloud of white cotton floated like a parachute from the top of the stairs down over the side of the banisters. A jellyfish descending the deep. A perfect mushroom.

'You look like you've just seen a ghost,' you said.

'I have,' I said. 'Can't you see her?'

'See who?'

'Mama. I see her. I can see her now. She's right behind you.'

I had frightened you. You would not even turn around to look. You stubbed out your cigarette. You stood up.

'That's not funny. How could you?' You were shaking your head slowly. 'How could you?'

'I'm sorry, Ulva, I didn't mean . . . But where are you going?'

'Out. I don't know. To see my friend. Don't bother to wait up.'

Hard to say what was real and what was the nightmare. It

was jealousy, pure jealousy, which made me see what I saw. And the nightmare ended. As all nightmares do.

I closed my eyes. You, my bird, you and your friend in the café. The picture was crystal. The two of you were naked. Beneath the table, something dangling between the young man's knees, like a thick black hairy tail, meaty, devilish. Were you really such a devil, Mr Frankly? But this was no set tableau. You were climbing on to the table, the two of you. Such a curious movement you had, Mr Frankly. You crawled up, scampered up, on all fours, a grotesque monkey. And then you stood. You were both standing, swaying as you faced each other. Your eyes were closed. Ah, but his were glowing. And it wasn't a tail at all, of course. A python! What a member! Lordy-lord! Shiny black. With a ruby-red pulsing tip. All two feet of it stuck between the legs of my bird. And he was thrusting and you were moving – back and forth, back and forth.

I waited until nine o'clock. I grilled a pork chop but could not face it. You had told me not to wait up, which meant you would be late. Perhaps you would not come home at all. Perhaps you would never come back. You had not taken the van, and I was picturing you walking on your own in the dark along those lanes where all manner of beasts lurked in the hedgerows. I could not get the image out of my mind. You and your friend. His black python. I kidded myself it was your safety I was concerned about. But I can admit now it was imagining the pair of you, in the flesh. By now I had convinced myself this was exactly what you were doing. Perversely, I wanted to find you to ensure that this was not what you were up to, yet I had convinced myself it was, yet I pretended it was because I wanted to make sure you were safe. At 10.30, I decided to go in search. Halfway along the lanes, I realised I had no idea where I was going. You could be anywhere. Your place, Mr Frankly, perhaps? You had already begun to assume a more corporeal presence in my mind. No longer a shady figure, sir, but flesh and blood and dimensions. But where was your place? The guest house in the village, perhaps, or one of the two rooms in the Cock and Bull? Or were you now staying at Marcia's? Marcia was still away with her sister in London. Was Ulva keeping you tucked away there? Was that were she had been disappearing to since Mama had gone? But why was she staying at Boxwood? What was keeping her with me? By this time, I was almost at Marcia's cottage.

There were lights on in the house. I tugged four or five times at the rope attached to the brass bell hanging beside the back door. The clapper was missing. There was no apparent sound, but I thought perhaps it had to be attached to some interior sounding mechanism heard only inside the house. Then I realised it was possibly not working. I knocked with my knuckles on the door's red-glass window. As I did so, the door opened itself. I called out your name. In the kitchen, a half-empty bottle of red wine. A bowl of giant cashew nuts. I called out again. Noises, muffled. Moans? Someone crying? Laughing? As I tiptoed down the hallway, it crossed my mind, not without alarm, that the place might have been burgled, that perhaps the burglars were still on the premises. In such circumstances, I would not consider myself a man of particular courage, though my size is much in my favour – as long as I do not open my mouth. There were no signs of disturbance as far as I could see. And then I heard muffled voices coming from one of the rooms off the hallway. I could not find the light switch and groped my way through the darkness, pushing away the scene of you two swaying and thrusting atop the table – that thick black snake, the forked tongue flickering from its bulbous ruby head, you, my bird, swooning ecstatically. I stood outside the half-open door. My friends, I needed to see it all for real. The flesh-and-blood copulating pair of you. To have my suspicions confirmed. Better to be hurt once by the truth than to eternally suffer possibilities. I knocked. I pushed open the door and peered in.

Ah, my friends, what did I see? Could I believe my eyes? Not you and your man friend, my Ulva. You with another. But man or woman? Marcia! Even in the darkness, despite the large fleshy rump and (though relatively small) breasts – that familiar aura of masculinity suggested by a way of moving, and emphasised here, now, by the thick neck and square, firm-set shoulders. Yet how it cut through me when she moved the hair out of your eyes, and leant to kiss your forehead.

As my eyes grew accustomed to the dark, I saw that you were lying together on a bed settee, but at such an angle I did not have a satisfactory view of you beneath Marcia. Then, suddenly, Marcia's legs opened. I saw the thicket of black hair – a head of hair between her legs. Then the most extraordinary thing that I can only describe as a double exposure. Marcia, the head between her legs, but a grey-green slime-covered head emerging from her. Marcia was giving birth! I experienced such a constriction in my throat I could not breathe. I stepped back, leant against the wall, loosened my bow tie. I breathed deeply. When I looked again it was to see the creature sliding to the floor. Marcia bent then as if to retrieve it, but she came up with a box. She opened the lid, took out a black object which resembled a pistol. Surely she was not going to kill you? Or was this some kind of suicide pact? Marcia was belting something around her waist, then she turned so I could see this huge black monster protruding from her groin. I gasped and feared you had heard me. You were whispering. And I fled. My footsteps triggered the outside light and I kept tight to the hedge at the edge of the drive. I did not want to be caught out as a Peeping Tom. I spotted something shiny on the path. It was a small heart-shaped trinket. I put it in my pocket. I never returned it. Not even when you asked whether I had found it.

My friends, what was I to make of it all? For if you were with Marcia, odds were that you would not then be inclined to be with Mr Frankly. The possibility that you were, shall we say, a woman's woman had not occurred to me. But if you were, then you would not want me. For I am a man. But not a man. And Marcia was not all woman, at least not a womanly woman. So this ambiguity attracted you, then, so you would then be attracted to me. Of course!

Yes, yes. A spurious logic, I will now admit. But at the time I was desperate, I would have made myself believe anything. I wanted you, more than anything.

Back home, I poured a very large brandy which I downed in one. I considered a *Natural World* film but decided I had seen enough in the way of nature's beasts in action for one day. Falling asleep, my head was alive – a bestiary, a Bosch inventory of flailing limbs, grotesque appendages, mouths transforming into genitals. There was her play-man and all those I had spied through the walls of the peep show and through the kitchen windows of the Halcyon. And Marcia with the big black ding-dong sticking out from between her legs. Ha! The lacuna had a ball.

When I came down the next morning it was to find you drinking coffee in the kitchen. You merely nodded as I came in. Briefly, I thought you must have seen me spying on you at Marcia's. I felt my cheeks redden. I took a breath.

'I must apologise—' Then I remembered you had left yesterday, in tears. 'I must apologise. Yesterday. Talking about Mama. I upset you. You will forgive me?'

'Yes. I'm sorry too. I shouldn't have rushed off like that.'

You sounded harsh, abrupt. Like a child forced to apologise. You looked washed out. What a pair of tight-lipped strangers we were. You were not aware, I believe, that, as you leant to take another spoonful of sugar, your dressing gown opened to reveal a small pink-tipped bud, a secret

hiding beneath the dark leaves of green silk. I imagined how
it would taste. Of almond. How your breast would fit neatly
in my palm. I did not want to think of you with anyone but
me. I did not want to think of you with Marcia, like a babe
in her arms, your head nestled in the crook of her arm, her
fingertips drawing lightly across your forehead, smoothing
out your fears. Such sweet affection. Ah.

Apropos nothing – and everything. I have a sudden desire to
talk about seeing you with Marcia. What exactly did I see? For
it was, I admit now, wishful thinking. Marcia's arms about
you, wishing it was me, me in Marcia's arms. But no, no, not
that – a previous occasion, one that I have glossed over in the
telling (like the difference between varnishing and polishing
the wood – one embellishes, the other reveals). Was it yesterday I told you? Or the day before? Two days? Barely aware
of time now. I am outside all of it. Yes. Mama and Pergolesi –
Mama and . . . unmistakably Pergolesi and Mama's ugly rump
a-jiggle. But after I had sent Signor Pergolesi packing, tail
between his legs – ha! – afterwards, another picture, the past
sliding over the present, and there was the summer house. And
through the peephole, I watched them, him and my Mama –
his balls a-dangling, a-jangling, diddly-dandling—

August. Ulva and I made love. All day long. We made
love outside in that secluded part of the garden beneath
the willow tree. We made love in the summer house. Two
white shoots, entwining. We grew ourselves. We were
growing ourselves into one beautiful . . . the orchid
and the lily. Flowers, birds, my stamen, my beak – this
enormous pumping pricking pipe of mine.

—Erskine. Erskine? Come on, what happened next? No
getting out of it, me old rogerer. Own up. The fact is,
you wanted her to see you in the bathroom, didn't you? Deep

down, you feared you were losing her (as if you'd ever found her!) and you reckoned this would win the sympathy vote. But surely it must have crossed your innocent mind that your bird might have reacted otherwise? How could you be so sure of her? You had already glimpsed another, darker, spiteful Ulva. Remember? The crow that pulled Nora's hair, that pecked her hard, though not hard enough to give evidence of a bruise. And you haven't forgotten the times Nora was calling to Ulva that she was thirsty and Ulva pretended not to hear. How could you not even consider the possibility that you were to be ridiculed, that she may have laughed her vicious little head off at the sight of you in all your naked glory?

Aha! You knew, didn't you? Maybe you were not consciously aware but in your mind a connection was already being forged. Ulva and Leodora. A confusion, or rather a fusion. A link. You knew. But you could never admit to yourself. It's true, Erskine, isn't it?

—I loved her.

—Erskine, just tell them what happened next.

I . . . ahem.

You must understand, I was not myself. The whole business with Mama, then finding you and Marcia together. I did not know what to think. I could not think. All should have been hunky-dory. Mama gone. You and me. But nothing was as I had imagined it.

I was sitting at my desk, staring at the wood which had been delivered that morning courtesy of Hackthrew's – 'in honour,' so it was noted on the compliment slip, 'of your valued custom'. Two pieces of wood, approximately fifteen cubic centimetres each, one *Juniperus virginiana*, or pencil cedar (traditionally used for high-class pencils, by the way), and lignum vitae – 'wood of life', a near-black beauty of a wood, coveted for the medicinal properties of its resin (which also provides self-lubrication). Or, I wondered, was this last not *Guaiacum officinale*, the main species, but *Guaiacum sanctum*, often referred to as bastard lignum vitae? Perhaps I ought to telephone Hackthrew's to establish provenance. Whatever, the wood unsettled me – since when had Hackthrew's been given to offering freebies? And its presence was an intrusion, aroused my suspicions. At one point I even began to imagine it contained (though I could not conceive how) some kind of surveillance device. But the main concern was that the wood was bait for the monsieur business. With the drama of recent events, the need had abated somewhat, but the moment I took the pieces in my hands I sensed again the pull, the desire. But for the life of me, I could not decide which was monsieur and which was box – proof of my unsettled state of mind, for wasn't the rule that the container must be of the exact same material as what was to be contained? Perhaps the rules were relaxing themselves, then, offering me a little freedom of choice. I decided the monsieur (working title 'Mr Pencil') would be made from the cedar – but it would have to be a small monsieur, the smallest I had ever fashioned, and an equally small container, of course.

All this decision-making made me hungry, so I prepared myself an early lunch of fresh tongue sandwiches and pickled walnuts, setting aside your covered plate for your one o'clock break. (I had somehow summoned the enthusiasm to go down to the village, though only because it was early morning and still quiet, and I had had the brainwave of adopting the disguise of hat and dark glasses – I wanted to be recognised by no one. Mama would have been on the conversational menu and I wanted to avoid that. As it was, Pergolesi spotted me. Well, I am, in view of my size, obvious, but a handy alleyway meant I could escape. I'd had the presence of mind to take the cool box – (it was a particularly warm August morning)

– and purchased a large trout for supper and a bunch of cucumbers for a chilled soup.)

You were sorting and cleaning upstairs. You appeared to have taken on the role of domestic. You were not a natural, I might venture. You had little or no organisational skills and were rather slapdash, in my opinion. Your attempts usually left the place in more disarray than before you had started. You were, of course, driven by the spirit of the huntress rather than by a desire for order.

Mid-afternoon, agitated by the wood and having to deal now with the familiar inner tussle which would soon become a battle – the urge to make the monsieur, the urge not to, the desperate attempt to first produce the box – I went for further sustenance, lemon tea and seed cake, a tray of which I took upstairs for you. I should have called out to you. I should have announced myself.

The door was open. You were in your room. I opened my mouth to speak. I could not. You were sitting at the dressing table. You were naked. You had your back to me. You were putting your hair up. Ah, such a sensuous pose – your arms raised, that gentle arch of your back forcing your fleshy buttocks to spread. The dressing table was directly in front of the south-facing window and the August sun highlighted the down on your arms and back. Your skin was not as I had pictured, but rather blotchy, more reddish than creamy. Your shoulder blades were clearly defined, like wings about to break the surface. Somehow, naked, you appeared more substantial. And this body was disconcertingly familiar. A body, a shape, I recognised. I stepped behind the wall, set down the tray and went to the bathroom.

I removed my clothes, applied the lotion and closed my eyes. I began to rub.

You, in my head, you, in my arms, all of you – breasts,

belly, thighs – and I was licking your face, like a bitch cleaning her pup, licking down over the whole of your body with my thick wet tongue, over your neck, your breast, you belly, your thighs, the mound between, legs, ankles, toes, and then my tongue was travelling back up again – over your breasts, your neck, ears, face. But not your face. I returned to . . . hers, Leodora's face. And she was looking down at me so sweetly. Ah, I could not forget. I was rubbing and rubbing and then, just as the nub filled and thickened, threatening to burst, the bathroom door opened. You. You, my bird. You looked down, down at the lacuna, then your eyes met mine. Oh, quick, quick! What could I read in those eyes? Pity? Compassion? Please, let it be compassion. Then you put your hand to your mouth, and fled.

I closed the door. The whole time with Mama and I had never once slipped up. I had even remembered to plug the keyhole. How could I have been so remiss? What would you think of Erskine now?

We avoided each other until dinner-time. You had laid the table to keep out of the kitchen (the fish knives set, in ignorance, with the soup spoon). I brought in the food. I could not look at you for a while, but when I did I recognised your expression as hers. In your eyes acceptance, just as she had accepted me.

You see, Mr Frankly, I believed her. Or I saw what I wanted to believe. She loved me, just as Leodora had loved me. Ulva and I could be together. She had seen my incomplete and damaged soul and had not mocked me.

We remained at the dinner table – the formality somehow seemed appropriate. And I told her, Frankly, about the tragedy, my tragedy, about the mauling. Not for sympathy, you understand, merely by way of explanation.

It was the first time I had told anyone. Not even Leodora

knew the whole story of how Erskine Flesching died in the fields that day.

I trusted you, my bird.

I trusted you.

I I

In the Garden of Gethsemane – A Tragedy

'Mama, can we play on the beach?'

'No, Erskine, not today. Leave me, Erskine. Mama needs to rest.'

Those grey and empty days after the tragedy, before I was banished to the Mansion House, she'd stare at me with eyes like stones. She would weep for hours, tears snailing her cheeks, hands clutching at her hair, pushing me away whenever I tried to comfort her, shrinking, as if in fear. But what did my Mama have to fear from me? Can you imagine? Just the two of us, together again, no one to come between us, and she did not want me. I had been severed. I was without air or nourishment. I would wither, die. Perhaps if I had never known those blissful days, just me and Mama, I would not have felt the loss so acutely, would not have felt so abandoned and betrayed.

Did I ever forgive her for sending me away? For never coming to see me? How could I have forgiven her? When she finally went, after I had put her in the ground, I have to admit to a profound sense of peace.

Only weeks after Ursula died, and Mama in my bedroom telling me I was going away to the Mansion House. Just for a little while, she said. I was sitting on the floor with my jigsaw and I looked up to see her towering, a giantess, fists tight to her sides, clenching, unclenching, like two struggling creatures. Her mouth a dark red slit.

Someone came one day, a distant aunt, I believe, or some

friend of Mama's. A sharp, tight-lipped woman, all points and angles, a crow, a witch, cloak a-flying. She barely spoke to me, barely looked my way, packed my clothes into a suitcase, drove me to the station, put me on a train. Can you imagine what a journey it was? Me, ten years old, on a train to some strange place. Where was my Mama? She had not even kissed me goodbye. I remember straining to look back through the rear window and seeing Mama in one of the upstairs windows. The moon of her pale face. Face blank. She did not even wave.

Those first few days at the Mansion House, I ached for my Mama. At night, in bed, I imagined her goodnight kiss on my cheek, the memory not succour but depleting me, numbing my skin, rendering places where she used to hug me dead.

Oh, I felt I had been most terribly wronged!

If it had not been for Mrs Bainlait and Joe and Sylvia, I could not have survived, would have coiled myself into a tight ball like a matchboxed grub. Small displays of affection assumed huge importance, touched me deeply. I could hardly wait for the afternoons when Joe (who became a kind of older brother in my mind) allowed me into his workshop, greeting me with a nudge of his elbow – 'How are you doing, me old skinny mate!' And I longed for Sunday nights, bath night, Mrs Bainlait's bulky bosom pressing into my back as she scrubbed my scalp, scrubbing a little too vigorously if she'd caught me disturbing Sylvia again.

Mrs Bainlait was the housekeeper at the Mansion House where Sylvia, her exceedingly pretty daughter of sixteen, also lived. Sylvia received piano tuition. She had an extraordinary talent and was, apparently, destined for greatness. Mrs Bainlait had made it a rule that I was not to worry Sylvia while she practised her playing. I used to hide behind the curtains in the drawing room while Sylvia sat at the grand. I adored watching her play, not simply for the beauty of the music, but to witness the slow sway of her body, the intricate dance of her fingers over the keys.

One time, quite suddenly, she stopped and, without looking round, called softly: 'Erskine, I know you are there. But you must be very quiet now, and let me get on. I am to be a concert pianist when I grow up and I shall travel the world.'

And she played a little more, then, her hands just lifted from the keys, as if in afterthought, she said: 'And you, Erskine, what about you? What are you going to be?'

There was I, behind the curtains, peeping between the gap, fumbling for an answer.

'I don't know.'

She turned, and her face, oh, beautiful, incandescent and quite, quite serious when she said:

'But you must know, Erskine, or you will never be.'

It frightened me, my 'I don't know'. I did not know. How could I possibly consider the future when the present was not even mine? Oh yes, there was temporary brightness in the dark – those few hours with Joe and Sylvia – but even then it was as if I were pretending, playing a part because the real Erskine was not in the Mansion House but at Boxwood, with Mama. You might think that given such an almost unbearable present I would be focusing on the future – the jailbird dreaming of that patch of blue seen though the cell window growing into the vast sky above his head the day he steps into freedom – but I no longer knew where or what my freedom was. Some part of me knew, oh yes, that my life at Boxwood, with Mama, as it had been, was irretrievable.

It was a lonely existence.

In the whole time I was at the Mansion House, I only ever saw Mr Gethsemane, the owner, three or four times. He worked abroad for long periods. When he did return for brief visits, I was only aware of him working at his desk, his vacated chair at the breakfast table – apart from breakfast, I ate my meals in the kitchen with Mrs Bainlait. On those rare occasions we did meet, he appeared more nervous of me than I of him. I recall distinctly the time I went into the library and curled up in one of the leather armchairs to read. I had not noticed him in the far corner of the room. He hoped I would make much use of the library, he said. Was I comfortable? Did I have all I needed? If I required anything at all, I should ask Mrs Bainlait. I remember he stared at me for a long time. I felt he had other things to say, but did not, could not. I felt, oddly, close to him. Once I received a parcel from him, when he was away in the States. A box of books – boys' adventure stories – a few tourist trinkets – postcards of the Statue of Liberty, the White House, a guidebook to New York and so on – and a leather-bound journal and a fountain pen inscribed with my name. There was a small card on which was printed Shakespeare's – 'nothing's ever good or bad but thinking makes it so'. His parcel gave me much pleasure. I read the stories over and over, put the postcards on the wall of my room. One day I picked up the pen and, asking Mrs Bainlait if I might have a bottle of ink, began to write. I wrote, not about my suffering, but about how life might otherwise be.

There were few pleasures. I had been sent away to suffer. And I suffered. What happened to me one day in the fields beyond the Mansion House was meant to happen.

It was my fate. It was as if Mama had summoned the beast herself.

Though I had been at the Mansion House almost four months, I had neither seen nor heard from Mama, though she lived inside me, both in dreams and nightmare, a troubling presence. I longed for her touch, her smell, the sound of her voice, her sweet smile, yet I was aware of another Mama, a Mama of steel, cold and ungiving, a black witch tight with curses. Some nights I woke in terror – 'I didn't do it, Mama, it wasn't me,

I didn't do it!' And I'd will her to change, reimagine her soft and lovely, gathering me up in the velvet bow of her arms.

I was in the library that day, a room which comforted me, the French windows opening out on to the back lawns, reminding me of Boxwood. My retreat when Joe and Sylvia weren't around. There were no children's books, mostly reference – art, music, politics, history – which did not engage me, although some contained beautiful illustrations, and simply turning the pages soothed me in a hypnotic way. I was thus engrossed in a biography of Handel when I heard Sylvia calling from the garden. I went to the window. Her back was to me and she was looking out across the lawn. I went out to join her and she turned and half ran, tiptoeing towards me.

Sylvia always moved quickly, lightly, barely disturbing the air around her. She had a quality of transience, as though she was continually in passage. I never saw her still – at the piano, her body swaying, fingers dancing over the keys, she was never still.

She looked serious that day, dressed in a cream blouse and navy skirt.

'Ma says I can see you this morning while the piano's being tuned. Someone's coming this afternoon to hear me play. They want to see if I'm up to playing for some benefit concert. Royalty will be there, Ma says. Do you think I'm good enough, Erskine? We can play cards. Do you play cards?'

I could not speak. I had, of course, put her on a pedestal so far above me I had the sense she was always looking down at me, on me. My cheeks reddened.

'Or we could just walk around the grounds, Erskine, if you like.'

'Yes. OK.'

We walked on in silence for a bit. I think I had made her

feel awkward. Then she turned to me, inclining her head as if to see the whole of my face, which allowed her thick, heavy hair to fall over one shoulder.

'Do you know why you're here, Erskine?'

What could I say?

'It's because my Mama's not well. She can't look after me.'

'Do you know why she's not well? It's about your sister, isn't it?'

'Yes. I think so.'

'Don't you know so, Erskine? Do you miss your sister?'

'I think . . . yes,' I said. 'She was younger than me. I'm . . . I was six years older.' And the words rushed from my mouth then. 'I'm glad you're older.'

'Do you have a father, Erskine? My father is a famous musician. He travels all over the world.'

Then she went silent. She stared straight ahead, her eyes screwing up slightly, lips pressed tight. As if she had said too much.

'I think he is,' she went on. 'I mean, he probably is.'

'Don't you know?'

Then she did a funny little skip and twirled around.

'I'm a foundling. Ma found me. In a hedge. In a cardboard box. Ma's not my real ma, you see. They couldn't trace my real mother – my parents – so Ma ended up adopting me.'

'Do you mind?'

I felt it was a stupid question even as I asked, but Sylvia's confession regarding her unusual origins had left an uncomfortable gap between us. It *was* a confession. For she said then, in a low serious tone, 'Promise me, hand on heart, you won't say anything. I've never told before. Ma says it's best not to.'

Then we heard Mrs Bainlait calling. The piano was tuned. Sylvia had to practise.

I returned to the library, picked up the Handel biography and continued flicking through. Sylvia's shared confidence gave me something to ponder, and I had a warm sense of connection. She must like me, I thought, to have told me. I began to think that maybe life was going to improve – at least become more bearable.

I asked Mrs Bainlait if she'd prepare me a picnic for lunch. I wanted to explore the fields, and I think she was glad to see me out of the house as nothing was to disturb Sylvia when the man from the benefit concert came. So I took myself off for a walk. I had never been outside the grounds before. As I walked, I began thinking about what Sylvia had said. It had been niggling at the back of my mind. At the time I had been somewhat taken aback. Her question, did I miss Ursula, which I believed had been an innocent one, set up two trains of thought. In the first place, I felt intensely grateful to Sylvia. It was the first time anyone had considered my feelings – including Mama, particularly Mama. Second – and it came to me as a revelation, this – perhaps I should have behaved, acted, a little more as if I missed her. It occurred to me that, had I shown more distress, Mama might not have sent me away. It also occurred to me that perhaps it was not too late, and I had the notion of writing to Mama to express my feelings. These thoughts offered some relief, my mood brightened. This, I realised, might prove my return ticket back home. Feeling positive, even joyful, I ran. I ran the full length of the field to the barbed-wire fence. I crawled under the fence. Somewhere near the middle of the next field, I remember stopping to pick up two tiny bird's eggs, like sugared almonds, but they were cracked and empty.

It was then, as I collected the shells, that I became aware of its presence, sensed it was homing in, that I was already prey. I half turned to see the black shape rushing at me. I could see the eyes, the half-open white-edged jaw. Before I could even think of running, I was doubled under by the force of it as it jumped on to my back. I was aware of hair, rough hair, not human, of its intimate smell. Feral. I was down on the grass, on my back, kicking, fighting it. But it was far more powerful than me. And my attempts to break free only angered it more. It was lunging at me, jaws gripping, ripping my clothes. And then it turned, trampling me with its sharp-clawed paws. Its rear was right in my face, its head and jaws down in my loins. It sank its teeth into the top of my thigh. Then there – there – into the soft meat between my legs.

I do not remember pain. But I was aware of pain. White-hot, searing pain. But I was removed from it. Like the zebra standing passive, obedient, while the hyena tears at its guts. I was both wracked with pain and numbed. I remember its heavy balls, dangling grotesque and rude, bouncing against my face as the beast tugged. The hairless vulnerability of the scrotum. I closed my eyes. I grabbed the soft pouch and twisted, yanked at it. The beast yelped, screamed. It twisted round, its jaws stretched, its head thrust back in agony. It lunged at me. Somehow I managed to scramble to my feet. I ran. It was after me. Again it jumped. Again I went down. I was almost at the barbed-wire fence, but this time I threw myself over the wire into the next field. And then I ran. When I dared to look back, the beast had gone. Oh. Oh God. The pain, then, knives in me, as if my soul had been ripped out, and blood pouring from the gash. I kept running. Then I fell. Silence. Me in the field. Here was the grass, there the sky. Me in the field between ground and sky, on the edge of the world. The world was spinning, aware of the world spinning and knowing now my smallness on the vast curve. Lost myself. My self gone, taken up into the silence and space that surrounded me, that was part of me, of which now I was a part. Erskine had gone. Then I must have lost consciousness.

Cold when I opened my eyes. And raw, raw down below.

'Erskine? Erskine?'

Opened my mouth. No sound. Someone above me. She. A halo of purple heart. No! Not a halo, a waterfall of hair falling into my face. Her face, then, becoming clear. No avenging angel – Sylvia. See her now, removing her blouse, the tracery of veins over her breasts when she removed her blouse, stanching my wound. She helped me to my feet, put one arm around my waist, told me to lean on her. But I could not. She lifted me then, carried me across the fields.

In the hospital, falling in and out of consciousness. There was Mama's face wet with tears. (Mama *was* there, wasn't she? Only once. But she did come, didn't she?) Tears pouring down Mama's pale cheeks and the sheets wet, the whole bed wet, and Mama soaked through and her hair all wet too as if she'd just come out of the sea. What did she have in her arms? Some kind of bundle. Crimson bundle of rags. Mama's face. Dissolved by tears. Did not see her again. Not until half a lifetime later. I told myself she could not take any more – one child dead and another damaged. Oh, but a lifetime's suffering, Mama. On her deathbed, she sent me a poison-tipped arrow. Oh, but Mama, I paid. Mama, didn't you think I had paid enough? Oh, did she, did she come to see me in the hospital? Was it a dream?

An angel visited me one night. Small, so small and naked. Flew close to my face, hovering, arms crossed over her breast and pure white at first, then, as though bleeding through the whole of her skin, turning pink, then rose, then rich red, dark red. She was laughing at me, black eyes on me. She fluttered away over to the window. At the window, she kept banging into the glass like a moth at a light bulb. Ting! Ting! And faint cries of pain – 'Help me, oh, please help.' Someone else in the room, dressed in white, so dazzling I had to close my eyes. Heard them say 'bled to death'. The air was thick with whispers. Was I dead? Did I even exist? One time I was up on top of a cupboard looking down at myself in the bed, sheets pulled up, like a shroud. When I floated down and pulled back the sheet, there was nothing there. Even when Mrs Bainlait nursed me, wrapping her fleshy arms around me, pulling me into her cushiony bosom, I felt nothing.

It was, of course, the medication. They pumped me full. I cannot imagine the intensity of the pain without it. In rare moments of lucidity, I recall talk of reconstructive surgery, prosthetics. (Ha! Imagine that, my bird – Marcia's black member will not lie low in my mind!)

Joe and Sylvia came to see me. Joe had fashioned a walking stick of ash, the handle most inappropriately carved (though I'm sure Joe's intentions were only good) into a dragon's head. (When I eventually returned to the Mansion House, there was another present from Joe – my very own box of woodwork tools!) Sylvia had brought me a book of boys' adventure stories and a large box of chocolate-covered Brazils. (When the chocolates were eaten, I kept the empty box the whole time I was at the Mansion House, filled it with my collection of 'finds' – a curl of hair, a ribbon, a nail clipping, a cream kid leather glove.) Once, when she leant to pop one in my mouth, I could smell her, slightly sour, musky, as though she had just got out of bed in the morning. I whispered in her ear, 'Sylvia,' a thin, reedy whisper, for the anesthetic had taken my voice. What did I want to tell her? I did not know. Words eluded me. I realised, in that moment, I would never be able to give what I wanted to give. Ah – can smell her now. Musky Sylvia.

Or is it you I smell? A faint quickening below. The last echo, ghost breath, the pale, thin arm of a child reaching up through the water.

Stale, airless in here. I have sat here too long. Boxwood is suffocating me. My wood. The oak. I have work to do.

By the way, was it not me who suggested the major spring clean? I was looking for something for you to do, fearing that, with Mama gone, you would drift away.

Before I leave you (temporarily – I must eat, we are not done yet), thoughts for you to ponder. The journal. Listen—

6 August. Airless. Boxwood is suffocating. We are going to redecorate throughout. White white white. Crystal chandeliers. A palace.

The beach is full of holidaymakers and day-trippers (the worst!) – at least their hounds are banned from the beach for the summer. We have taken to swimming after breakfast and early evening when it's quiet. The surface of the sea shines, as if it's been varnished.

7 August. Rather a sad day. Mr Pergolesi died. The body's being flown back to Italy apparently, so there's to be no funeral. Perhaps a bunch of flowers at the bus shelter would be apt. It was a heart attack. In flagrante delicto. They thought he was practising for the Golden Years concert, but he had a maiden from the village in his bed. A bad habit of his, so the gossip goes. O sole mio! Here I come! (As it were.) Mrs Pergolesi was . . .

9 August. Three – two – one – question – when is a he not a he? Answer – when it's a she! Boom-boom! Question – what's big and black and goes in and out? Answer – a gorilla doing the hokey-cokey! Da-daa! One she plus one she equals touché – don't she?! Bum-bum!

No. People are not who they seem to be. No one is who they appear to be. So often the container belies that which it contains. You, my friends, understand this, surely. How many readjustments were needed before our true selves were revealed? And still you had not reached the core of me, my bird. My final act came, did it not, as a total surprise.

No, the wrapping does not always match the quality of the goods. The gift so often disappoints.

You were my gift. I loved you. But the gift was not all it appeared.

Neither was I, my sleuths. You should have left well alone. Sleeping dogs, my friends, sleeping dogs.

August. So smooth and perfect you might just have slipped from the mould. I knew the contours, the soft suggestion of curves, as if I had made you, shaped you from a block of wood. Pale ash, both strong and giving. Ash for rebirth, new life, the Moon Tree, Lightning Tree, Lady of the Woods, Yggdrasill – the branch of Nemesis. In the firelight, your skin pale and shining, as though varnished (but no puppet you), as though moist – like a creature emerging from a shell, an egg, a cocoon. Almost too beautiful to touch. Almost too frightened to touch you. I remember the gold in your hair. You were so silent. Though you gave a small cry, less through pain than fear, as I entered you. As I lay over you, so worried I might crush you. Break your bones. I imagined your bones as a trellis, a delicate support – wild roses, passion flower, honeysuckle rambling and entwining. One blood rose, your heart, petals tight packed. Your heartbeat frantic at first and then it quietened, stilled, until 'Ersk-ine, Ersk-ine, Ersk-ine,' it said. You tasted of peach, and cinnamon, the sea. You might have been birthed from the waves. Venus, mermaid, dryad. All yet none of these. The sea kept you for me.

NB! My worry over dimensions. Who said size does not matter? Would the key fit the lock? I wondered. The usual insecurities. It has cost me dear as far as relationships with the opposite sex go. And you were so slight, so small. But you were ready for me. You accommodated me like a hand slipping into a velvety glove, the foot fitting the slipper. Slip slip slipper. Eels, ah, eels. It was like slipping a tongue in your mouth. You have taught me that perfection does indeed exist. You, we, are proof.

And we are not Romeo and Juliet. Tragedy plays no part in our lives.

You said that when I hold you close, it is like stepping into a warm comfortable house. A home, you said. Large and warm. And soft. A great bear. Ursine. Yes.

I must not, I will not, allow guilt to spoil what I have now.

Forgive, for you wanted me to tell you about Leodora. What else shall I tell you? Without Leodora I was nothing. Without Mama I was nothing. What shall I tell you? That we should be careful about those to whom we give our hearts? I loved Leodora. I gave her my heart. I believed she loved me. But, with hindsight, the perspective shifts. You see what you did not see. Take a box, a gilded box, of ormolu, say, one that might catch your eye in a trinket-shop window, which you might open to find one or two glittering stones, but fake. Nothing, then, of any lasting value.

12

I. The Calm

*You and I, my bird, have reached that delightful level
of intimacy when silence over a meal or a drink in
front of the fire is comfortably appreciated. There
is no awkwardness between us. You have quickly
– almost too quickly? – slipped into the space that
Mama has left in Boxwood. Here I am, surrounded
by the accumulation of her life – and yet I could so
easily forget she has ever been here. You are, I notice,
diplomatic not to push and, despite our closeness, you
still observe a certain boundary. We are two lovebirds
perched upon the same branch . . .*

I had trusted you and I felt I had done the right thing in
telling you of the death of Erskine Flesching. I am not
over-dramatising, it *was* a death, for in the days that
followed (oh, too, too few!) I sensed a closeness between
us, my bird, as a result of my 'opening up'. (Why – I should
have told you sooner, then!)

You did not mock me. 'Poor thing,' you said, 'I'm really so
sorry' – didn't you? And, correct me if I'm wrong, I believe
you reached out and touched my hand. And there *was* a
softening in your eyes – was there not? – into another level
of understanding, and compassion. Ah, I did so want to see it.
In the mirror, I began to see a rather more acceptable Erskine,
an Erskine more clearly defined. Standing naked before the
full-length glass, I realised I was, in fact, rather protective,
indeed almost fond, of the lacuna. It was, after all, unique. It
had a beauty all its own. I began to imagine your touch, your

fingers probing its nooks and crannies, tracing its contours. Imagined your lips, your tongue. You would not find me lacking anything. You had a pen, a magic wand, and had drawn an indelible outline in the glass, a shape into which I fitted exactly.

But a cause for concern – I will tell you. The day after my recounting of the mauling, I thought you were upstairs still busy at the task of sorting and cleaning for which you had volunteered (I felt you required a little supervision, you were not born to it, though I did my best not to interfere). Then, taking a break from my labours in the workroom, I discovered your note by the telephone: 'Just popped out for a while. No need to keep supper. May be v late. Ulva.'

(The small squiggle following your name I deciphered as a cross – a kiss?)

Had you called out to me when you left? Had I nodded off or been too engrossed with Mr Pencil to catch your goodbye? (And more, far more, to the point – where had you gone? Another little rendezvous with Marcia? Or to see your friend?)

Had I been alert enough to hear you leave, I might have, diplomatically of course, managed to delay you enough to find out where you were off to. Would you, though, have told me? Would you have told me the truth? Again, more to the point, did you call out? Surely you did not slip out to avoid me?

I ripped up the note, retaining the piece with your name and the squiggle, made a beverage and returned to my workroom, cursing Mr Pencil. Cursing him, it and the dark force that compelled me. Damn the wood! Damn Mr Pencil! He had become an intrusion – a thin, fourteen-centimetre-long intrusion to be exact. A veritable thorn in my side! (No titters, please, but the image I have is of a plump bird straight from the roasting oven, a skewer piercing the thigh and the juices running clear. Now, was I the bird, or you, my bird?) You see, I was so afraid the bubble would burst – ping! That I might lose the joy of those precious days – you tra-la-ing upstairs, bird in the Boxwood forest, catching you watching me, just as I had once watched you. I told myself you were falling in love with me. Oh, but I did. Do not mock. Lord and lady of the manor. Picture the scene: Boxwood gabled, black and white, diamond-paned, wood-mullioned casements – a Tudor manor; us dressed, let me see, you in jewelled long dress, heart-shaped headdress, short veil, me Henry VIII and you Anne Boleyn; hand in hand, taking a turn – to the strains of Henry's composition 'Madame Helas' – in the carefully manicured gardens, there the herb garden, there the maze, there the garden of roses, the topiary. The dream as reality. And you also appeared inspired by us together in Boxwood. Briefly (but days!) your decoration returned, a pink feather here, some turquoise beads there. You had taken to wearing your myriad silver bracelets again, and one day I noticed (was shocked by) a small tattoo on your cheek – a blue-irised eye – which later, thankfully, washed off. (Two eyes on Erskine was quite enough, thank you.) I sensed too a lightness in your step, a coquettish air. (Or was that only as I saw it? Were you jumpy, perhaps, on edge – your dance more away from rather than towards me?) I believed you were dressed for courtship – though it signified something other, darker. Camouflage, then? (Did you not just now flinch, my Ulva? Have I hit the nail?) That brief interlude before the storm – oh, I could not then have believed you were afraid.

Ah, had it not been for Mr Pencil, I might have been more attuned. It – he – was taking hold, just like all the others. Though I fought hard against him. I told myself: Make Mr Pencil, make the box, put the bugger inside, shut the lid, job done, over and out. I ought to have realised it was not that simple. He lured me – the smell and taste of the wood so deliciously pencil that a couple of times I found myself, while ruminating on your absence, with him in my mouth, imagining my orifice was yours, that I was penetrating you. I was both excited and bitter – for what I had to offer you, as you had witnessed a couple of days before, could not even match a pencil. Had I length on my side it might be different. How could I make the best of it? (The pencil business, I mean?) A long shot, but it struck me that perhaps Mr Pencil was on my side – perhaps he was trying to tell me something. But what?

As I sucked on the wood, I imagined you. Was it a premonition? A taste of things to come, as it were? It was an appetising notion upon which I feasted for several hours through that afternoon, sending me upstairs to the bathroom to relieve the lacuna – three times! But as the hours passed I was less convinced, began to entertain the possibility that Mr Pencil was saying 'beware', was but a wagging finger, a warning wag – for you would laugh at the very idea, and there really was no hope of me ever being truly with you, in you. It was a joke. I even had the punch line. For I had no lead.

Around teatime, fortified by a Scotch-spiked Bolivian and a slice of gooseberry tart, I sharpened a couple of blades and began to whittle. I would whittle Mr Pencil out of existence, reduce him to nowt. But barely had the first shavings fallen to the floor when I found I was whittling another piece of wood, a branch I had broken off in anger on my way back from the summer house all those years ago. And I was no longer in my workroom, but in my bedroom, nine years old, my penknife slicing the wood as though to rid myself of what I had just witnessed through the peephole in the wood-plank wall of the summer house.

I cut my finger – see? A scar. You did not notice the

bandage when you eventually returned, preoccupied as you were with other matters.

Having at last, through sheer fatigue, extracted myself from the grip of the sycamore (and damn Hackthrew's this time), I set about preparing my solitary supper – *oeufs à la Florentine*, a meal over which I wept silently, thinking of that day with Mama, both of us dressed to the nines, and Mama asking for more! She had been to the doctor's, I recalled, and he had given her a clean bill of health. Then, having finished the tear-salted eggs – a result of my vulnerable frame of mind, no doubt: the troubles with the wood, the distressing whittling flashback, Mama – I began to agonise further, was beset by wild (or not so wild?) imaginings. Having seen me in the bathroom, you had gone to sell your story to some sleazy tabloid. I pictured reporters at the door, the police, the health authorities, a team of medical experts, a padlocked cage. When I could bear it no longer, when I believed I could actually hear them banging on the front door shouting 'Freak! Freak!', I drank two large brandies and went upstairs to bed. On my way to my room, I saw that you had been doing the room next to Mama's. Outside the door was a pile of old magazines and a nest of wicker baskets, the innermost one containing pebbles I remembered Mama and I had collected. I knelt and picked up one in each hand. They were egg shaped, the veins of minerals like cracks on the surface. But we had collected these years ago. I had been climbing the rocks at the base of the cliffs. When I saw them, I thought they really were eggs. Next to the baskets was an album, the black leather cover embossed with gold. I opened it to find it full of photographs of headless bodies, bodies I recognised, the faces scratched out with, perhaps, the tip of a knife. Who had done this? Mama? I had not removed the faces. Had I? I was aware then of the doorbell ringing. You.

'I didn't mean to disturb you. I forgot to take the key.'

I will tell you now, seeing you in the doorway, for a moment you could have been her. I even whispered her name – 'Leo-dora.' Did you hear me? You were wearing the long dark coat, midnight-blue silk. She'd had an evening coat just like it.

'I'm sorry,' you said, smiling a smile that was, I think, intended to endear and in the tilt of your head, your almost beseeching eyes, what did I see? *What* did I see? Willingness? Acceptance? Affection? Even love? Oh, I saw all of those. Perhaps a little awkwardness when you held out a small package.

'Here, for you. A present. I didn't want you to think I'm not grateful. For letting me stay at Boxwood.'

Fresh figs, a packet of cream cheese with walnuts.

The hour was late but I suggested a snack – a midnight snack. Would you join me? And a brandy nightcap perhaps?

So touched by your gifts – the first, the only, it meant a great deal – I gave no immediate thought as to your whereabouts that day. But what a strange evening it turned out to be, my bird, what questions you asked! And then came your request, so innocently put, that I . . . but wait, I am confusing the occasion, for it was the following evening that you popped the question. The calm was already passing. A rumble, in the distance, but coming closer.

I returned with the tray of figs and brandies only to find you had fallen asleep on the settee. I decided not to wake you. Then, as now, you looked so peaceful, so – what can I say? – contained.

II. The First Distant but Approaching Rumble – Omens – A (the) Request

Omens. The following day (you were up and dressed before me), a letter. From the health authorities. They required information about Mama. What medication was she currently taking? When had she last seen the doctor? And so on. 'After the recent tragedy', said the letter (for one gut-wrenching moment I thought they were referring to Mama, rather than the demise of one of their staff), they were putting someone new on the case. They made it sound like a police investigation.

I shouted (you must have heard me, my bird), 'Dog at a bone! Dog at a bone! But you'll not make a meal out of me!' I was at the kitchen table, had opened a can of hot dogs for our lunch of sausage and olive salad, and was in the process of slicing the pink dogs when I saw a worm wriggling out of the can. It plopped on to the table. I picked it up, held the squirming worm between finger and thumb. I dropped it back into the can which, I saw to my horror, was alive with worms. I pinched myself. Closed my eyes. Opened my eyes expecting now to see the can empty. But the worms remained, were writhing in a tangled mass, some crawling up the side of the can. Surely they had not been there when I tipped the dogs into the bowl for slicing? But I had not checked. How had they survived in a closed can? I decided I would return the can and the worms to the grocer's. I would make a complaint. I would even write to the health authorities informing them that Mama had eaten several. Or maybe not. I must not give them the slightest reason for interfering. The dogs looked edible enough. I washed them and continued slicing. Then the telephone rang. Marcia. Another intrusion, her voice piercing the delicate membrane of our new-found intimacy. There had not been, until now, a soul to disturb us.

She was, she said, still caught up with her sick sister. Then she asked whether she might speak with you. Was Ulva well? Oh, yes, I said, Ulva's very well. I said you were helping me sort some things out at Boxwood. I almost said 'after Mama' or 'Mama's things', but I was quite sure, my bird, you had not mentioned anything to Marcia about Mama's demise.

I called you downstairs. As I set the black receiver on the table, its shiny black length provoked a close-up detailed picture of Marcia's protuberance. You held the receiver to your chest, seemed to hesitate, gave me a brief smile. 'Thank you,' you said. I was being dismissed, of course. I left you to Marcia, returned to the kitchen though staying near the open door, but I could not catch what you were saying.

We ate the dogs and salad. I had checked and double-checked for wrigglers. After you'd lit your cigarette, casually, you told me you wouldn't be home that night. You were going to see Marcia in London. There was no explanation. Lips tight, arms folded, legs crossed, eyes avoiding. Clammed up, tight to your rock. Oh, that I could have slipped in a finger, prised you off, revealed your vulnerable flesh. Were you frightened I might peck at you like a guillemot?

Marcia. Really? Marcia had mentioned nothing to me. Not Marcia, then. But who? Your friend? A nugget of anxiety within. A worm in the apple.

When were you leaving?

Some time later in the afternoon.

I see.

When, an hour or so later, I went up to see whether you had time for a cake and a drink before you left, I found you in Mama's room. You did not hear me enter and evidently I had startled you. You were kneeling on the floor beside a drawer which you had pulled from one of the bureaux. It contained bottles of pills, boxes and jars of lotions and creams and numerous packets of throat pastilles. (Had I brought the

Throaties with me when I came back to Boxwood?) There was an envelope in your lap containing postcards, I think, and a photograph. You were also holding a photograph. As soon as I saw who was in it, my hairs rose. She was sitting beside Mama. Mama's arm tight around her. A clinch. Secure. You could not have prised those two apart, not with the meanest of wills. (Though, of course, you could always try.)

'I was just tidying,' you said, clearly disturbed, cheeks quite pink. 'This must be your sister, Erskine. She looks, looked, so much like Nora.'

'Similar colouring, yes,' I said. Nothing would induce me to look again.

'It must have been awful for you, losing her.'

'Awful. Terrible.'

A silence. I knew you were going to ask me again what happened. The question was there, splitting the air between us. A guillotine. What was I going to tell you? That she fell over the cliff?

'She was run over. She was playing out in the lanes. It was a bus – no, a coach,' I went on, 'full of holidaymakers. A winter tour. The roads were very bad. Black ice.'

Oh, black, my friends, black as a crow.

'It wasn't the driver's fault,' I said, 'it wasn't anyone's fault. Fortunate, really, that she was killed outright.'

(Outright. Whenever I see road-kill – a fox stretched beside the kerb, a squirrel splattered dead centre, a bear cub – I always imagine it was outright.)

'She was only young?'

'Just four years old. Mama blamed herself.'

(Once I started, how easily it flowed! I surprised myself.)

'She looks a lovely child.'

Looked.

'Yes, lovely.'

'I'm sorry. I shouldn't have.'

No, you should not have. I drew in my breath. Closed my eyes. I was sure that what I had just spotted had not been there before. Like a little orange devil sitting atop a bag of rags. Did it move? When I opened my eyes again, I saw you look round, though of course you saw nothing.

You left with a small overnight bag around five o'clock. You appeared edgy, checking your watch. I ascertained that you would be returning in time for supper the following day. I remembered to mention the letter from the health authorities. I suggested you should assume ignorance if anyone approached you about Mama. Give my regards to Marcia, I said, as I watched you walking away down the drive. You had apparently decided against taking the van, had arranged for a taxi to meet you up at the corner of the lane. Why not at the house? It was a new taxi firm, you told me, the driver was not familiar with the house. How much of an imbecile did you take me for, my bird? I shut the front door, feeling bereft. And uneasy. I returned to Mama's room. The rag was there but must have slithered to the floor. A scarf. An orange chiffon scarf, that was all! I folded it as small as possible and stuffed it into my trouser pocket.

What next? Supper. A supermarket Cuisine-for-One coq au vin.

I prepared for a long and lonely night.

Dreams in the night, strange as any. I did not think I could ever sleep. Minutes after switching off the light, I was up and going to your room. Why? To feel close to you? I sat on your bed for a time, then began to pick over your paltry possessions. Nothing of value, bits and pieces, tat: a metallic silver plastic box of supermarket cosmetics, a green cardboard box containing your decorations – bangles, beads, feathers. In the wardrobe, your clothes – well worn, cuffs frayed, a button missing here and there, chain-store labels.

Nothing I had not already seen. I fingered the long dark blue coat, noticed that part of the hem was down, considered whether I ought to stitch it. You required a little maintenance, my bird. A delightful prospect – me, your mother hen, fussing and titivating her baby bird. Just as Leodora clucked over me. 'Well groomed' was her favourite phrase. Every so often, she would have one of her 'maintenance nights' – hems checked, buttons sewn, shoes and belts polished. She kept her wardrobe in tip-top condition. She had a walk-in dressing-area, mirrored, sweet smelling, a bowl of rose pot-pourri beneath the film-star bulb-framed mirror. 'Appearance is all, Erskine,' she might say; 'Down at heel, down at soul', 'The outside reveals the inside' (I think she said this). I liked to watch her during these grooming sessions. She acquired, in my eyes, a girlish, coquettish quality – the adrenalin-fuelled chorus girl preparing for the big show! Yet, afterwards, I would often find myself before my own mirror, studying, with weighty heart, the discrepancy between the tastefully dressed figure and what lay beneath. How was I to value myself – a fraud, a freak?

You did not appear to value yourself, my bird. But could I inspire you? Might I take you in hand? I admit to a sense of the proprietorial – your, dare I say, mentor, keeper. But I did not own you. I knew nothing of you. Nothing in your room which revealed you – no books, papers, documents, journal.

I returned to my bed deflated. Having looked and discovered nothing only made you appear more mysterious. As I tried to settle to sleep, I realised I ought to have asked you for Marcia's number. I could have checked that you had arrived safely. Indeed, checked that you really were staying with Marcia.

My bird, I missed you. Alone, in the dark and silence, the questions and uncertainties – your occasional disappearances, this 'friend' of yours, your probing about Ursula – all these unanswered whys and wherefores now led me to convince myself you were up to something. My fears had adjusted to fact.

I woke early in the morning with the dream still clear. We were in a fairground – all the rides in motion but only us two there. We were on a Ferris wheel sharing a seat. You were frightened you would slip off the seat. I had my arm around you. The wheel was turning, faster and faster, began to spin a web around us. We both grew wings – yours like a fly's, mine thick-feathered, black. We were naked. The wheel had spun a cocoon and I was outside it. I was dangling the cocoon from a thread over the side of the cliff top. The water below was boiling, red. Then a guillemot swooped down, snatched you away in its beak. And then *she* appeared. In the sky, far away. Leodora, dressed like a fairy-tale godmother waving a wand – a long, thick wand. Her face was scaly and cracked. She had caught the thread to which you were attached and was pulling you towards her, and the thread turned blue-grey and knotty like an umbilical cord. I was reaching for you. You were so pale inside the transparent cocoon, pale and bloodless, and as I reached she speared me with the wand.

After breakfast, I considered a walk along the cliff path. But I would have to deal with Mr Pencil first. A peculiar-looking fellow, one who made me uneasy. I decided to have a go at working the tip into a point rather than producing the standard 'helmet'. But for the life of me I could not locate my sandpapers. While trying to remember exactly when I had them last, I realised I was carving the head in precise anatomical detail. A tiny eye had appeared in the centre. A difficult task – he was such a small fellow! Like a dog's extended phallus, but misshapen, a cock of the devil. As I paused to flex my fingers, the bugger moved, writhed before my eyes, then came slithering towards me! 'Be still.

Hellfire and damnation to you!' I cried. As if obeying, it reverted to the original monsieur, though I was loath now to touch the thing. He, it, disgusted me. It was the prick of an undernourished, malformed lout, an inbred lowlife. And then, while I was thinking all this, the thing laughed at me! This weasel stood upright, hands on hips, head thrust back, pointing and laughing. I felt not guilt this time, but anger. Why could I not simply burn the fellow? But I could not, of course. He would have to be boxed, contained. I fetched the block of lignum vitae – oh that Hackthrew's had sent me a large piece of sycamore! For how could I successfully complete with two different woods? I focused hard on a design for the box. But for the life of me I could not bring the wood of life to life.

To my surprise, I realised I had missed lunch. It was a quarter past three, which left only a few hours before the shops closed. I would have to move sharpish if I were to prepare the welcome home I intended. On the way to the village, I decided on rump steak and a bottle of Bull's Blood (on account of your pale dream body still in my mind perhaps?). Fortunately, I saw no one I knew, although I spotted Dr Foster's car in the distance. I purchased the steak, two bottles of Blood, together with a box of new potatoes, some mangetouts, Jerusalem artichokes and a bag of lychees for dessert.

On the way back, I took the cliff path and sat on my ledge for a while, allowing myself two lychees. (Such a moreish delicacy; I could have had the lot! The flesh so smooth under the shell, a crime to break it, yet a suggestion of shape in its contours, as though still forming. I think of a foetus, Lord knows why.) I put the stones in my pocket. They were too beautiful to throw. Such a calm sea below. Too calm? Resuming my journey, I found a shoe on the path, a man's brogue but small – size four and a half. I threw it over the edge.

Approaching Boxwood, I could not recall whether I had locked the workroom door. What if you were to return and walked in to discover Mr Pencil? Realising I was not wearing my keys, I quickened my steps.

I was ready a good hour before you were due. Eight o'clock, you said. I had treated myself to a long oily bath, had dressed up – bottle-green waistcoat and matching green silk dicky. I put a hot-water bottle in your bed, then removed it, thinking you might not like the idea of me being in your room. (I was feeling a little guilty about having pried). I put the bottle back in your bed. I was anxious, my bird, like a fraught mother awaiting the return of a child, or a lover at the point where anticipation downturns into disappointment. But you were coming back. You were. I waited at the front window, ears pricked, snout raised. I saw nothing but the sway of the trees, the tricks of light.

Then – at last! A figure coming slowly down the drive. But a figure I knew and could not believe I was seeing. A spectre from the past. Something about the set of the shoulders, hunched through carrying bags and parcels tucked under her arms . . .

I should have gone out to meet you, offered to carry your things. Halfway down the drive, you stopped, looked up at the house. I moved behind the curtain. You continued. Heavy trudging steps. You were returning for the truth, were you not, at last, at all costs.

'Ulva.'

'Erskine.'

I leant to kiss your cheek, but you moved away. And then, as if sensing my surprise at this avoidance, even coldness, you smiled, warmly, moved as if to touch my arm. I noticed then the case you were carrying – like a small briefcase, similar to those I use for my more fragile tools. It did not belong to you, I later discovered. There was, I saw, a tiny gold key attached to the handle. (What was it you two needed to keep under lock and key?)

'How is Marcia?'

You seemed confused, your words stilted.

'Oh – Marcia – yes. Very well. She sends her regards. Her sister's a little better. Marcia's off someplace else for a few days. I don't know where exactly.'

More presents. Marcia's friend owned a delicatessen apparently. (I should have recognised the wrapping, I know every deli in the area.) While you sorted yourself out upstairs, I opened the treats. A huge jar of pickled walnuts which I set on a shelf. It looked like something that might have sat on a laboratory shelf, a medical curiosity, or that a medieval quack or sorcerer might have stored amongst ingredients for potions. Like the brains of small creatures in formaldehyde. Pathetic, and macabre – a quality that might attract the colder eye of fascination and curiosity, an unclinically trained eye that might linger a little too lasciviously on the intricacies of what dissection reveals. I decided we would keep the walnuts as a rainy-day treat.

You had also brought morels. Two. Just enough. Now that was a delight. The morel is, in my opinion, the most supremely flavoured of all edible fungi. And most difficult to find. However, they would not have complemented the steak. I knew my mushrooms. They too would keep, would be used to add to (or indeed to disguise) the flavour of some future dish. Flowers, too, a bunch of carnations – though past their best – for Mama's grave. Gifts indeed!

You came downstairs revived, had applied a touch of frosted pink lipstick. We ate in silence for a while. You appeared ravenous, my bird, and gulped down your first glass of Bull's Blood. You asked about Mama.

'You must miss Nora. You were obviously very close.' Your voice, high, clipped, caught my attention.

'Grew closer,' I said, 'since my return to Boxwood. I hoped to make up for the years we had lost.'

'Lost?'

You were, of course, unaware that for thirty years Mama and I had had no contact. 'And I was not an easy child,' I almost told you, but I did not feel inclined, at that point, to elaborate. I refilled your glass, and then you told me about your mother. A picture of you now, my Ulva, when you set down your knife and fork, sat back, eyes lowered. You seemed suddenly diminished.

'At least you knew your mother. I never had the chance.'

You looked up. Your face was drawn down now with sadness.

'I was adopted. Before I could know her. I was a baby. Lydia, a distant cousin of my mother's, adopted me.'

I was disarmed by this . . . disclosure. You had been an unknown, almost unknowable. I was struck by the ridiculous notion that you had read my mind!

'I see. I'm sorry to hear that. I mean, she was ill, your mother? She could not look after you?'

'No. Perhaps she was just not meant to be a mother.'

'And your father?'

You simply shook your head.

'Lydia cared for you? She loved you?'

My voice had reduced to a whisper. Eggshells. Oh, careful, Erskine, careful how you tread. But loved you? Because I, I loved you, my bird. I almost told you.

'In her way. Lydia was, is, an artist. Lydia loves everyone. She told me once that her paintings were her real babies.'

You were gnawing at your lip. I feared you might cry. I felt awkward. But there was more to come.

'You are in contact with your mother? You hear from her?'

'Cards, presents, sometimes.' And then you looked right at me. 'Not any more.'

Were you challenging me? Was it an accusation?

You took a deep breath, but whatever it was you were about to share, what you eventually revealed, remained unsaid.

I was about to enquire whether you knew where your mother was, whether you wanted to see her, when you continued.

'I didn't want to see her. I was frightened. Am frightened. I don't know. That she wouldn't be who I'd imagined her to be. My mother, Erskine, still my mother. I wanted her to be so many good things.'

On the table, your tight fists unfurled like petals.

Oh, my bird, what I was thinking then and did not say is that people are never who you think they are. But are people who they think they are, or as we see them?

Silence. Our connection was lost.

We ate the lychees and what remained of the cheese with walnuts. While pouring brandies, I endeavoured to push a little farther, hoping to discover just how unattached you were. My questions pointed, of course, in the direction of the mysterious young man. Apart from Lydia, you said, you had no other family. A few friends scattered here and there.

'And my mother,' you added, with an odd defiance.

By this time you had kicked off your shoes, were nesting in an armchair. At home, my bird. Attached to me? I was filled with a growing delight, savouring the moment. And then came the request.

'I'd like to invite someone to dinner, Erskine. This week-end. Would you mind?'

You were looking down into your glass.

'Ah – yes – why, of course.'

The words came tumbling. A swerve in direction. So unexpected, my bird.

Someone. Someone. Someone.

'Your friend?'

'Yes.'

'Ah.'

The brandy glass cracked in your hand. Like a bone breaking. Blood bubbled between your fingers. I washed and dressed the wound. You needed to sleep, you said. As you went up the stairs, I asked you to let me know what I might cook. Did your friend have any favourite dishes? On the stairs, you were at such an angle that the shadows highlighted the two dark crescents under your eyes, giving you the sad and hopeless look of a pierrot.

I sat in the kitchen with a large nightcap, the box of morels on the table. Dark flesh, shrivelled tight. Old man's testicles. An icy hand clutched within.

Later, passing your closed door, I saw your light go out. I stopped, listened. I sensed you were on the other side, listening too. I went on to my room and, just as I entered, heard what appeared to be the sound of heavy furniture being dragged across the floor.

—Erskine? Oh, Erskine? I saw you on the cliff path that day. When you threw the shoe, I mean. Did you see me – perched on a rock, face in a cloud, angel in the blue? It wasn't a man's brogue, now, was it? A casual shoe – a training shoe, just like she wore that day. Or was it a child's summer sandal? Or a gumshoe's shoe! Think evidence. Think past crimes. Now you're thinking. I know, I know, I taunt. But what a confusion there was in your mind. Ulva, Leodora, Leodora, Ulva. Do I have to spell it out? Leodora and her play-man, Ulva and her young man friend. Seeing Ulva return that evening carrying her bags, you remembered how Leodora would return similarly laden after her so-called shopping trips. Once you asked her why she had not taken a taxi. But they – they – *had* taken a taxi and it had dropped her off around the corner. Always so careful to cover their tracks. What subterfuge! What deception! Memories, Erskine. You had lived it all before and here it was returning. Oh, that you could have wiped your slate clean! Now, Erskine, Chapter Thirteen – unlucky for all.

Let the show begin, dear boy.

Ladeez and gentlemen, I give you – Mr Truman Frankly!

13

First Supper

Melon balls and ginger to start, followed by pork with prunes. For dessert, plum clafoutis – and a summer pudding inspired by the vivid display of soft fruits and berries outside the greengrocer's.

While buying provisions, I popped into Farquhar's for sandpapers. (Mr Pencil would not be whittled away. Be crafty, then – rub him into dust. It was worth a try.) Henry John Farquhar was under the impression I had ordered wood varnish. There was a boxful put by in the storeroom. Two dozen tins. I assured him I already had a stock of varnish. Then he asked about Mama. She's very poorly, I said. Difficult to talk, I said. He pressed me further but I cut him short. I would have to avoid Farquhar's for a while.

Mr Frankly, you should have seen Boxwood's kitchen that afternoon! Busy, busy! Steamy. Alive with bustle and clatter. I think of the kitchen of the Halcyon. I even sported a chef's hat and striped butcher's apron. Activity was the only antidote. I was driven by anxiety. I was afraid of evidence, of the precise degree of intimacy between my bird and our guest. I topped and tailed and chopped. Scraped and peeled. I rubbed salt into flesh.

It seemed the kitchen staff had the day off. You did appear briefly, my bird, to enquire (half-heartedly) whether I needed any help. You had things to do, you said. What things? I noticed that your eyes were puffy.

Early evening, preparations completed and only the vegetables to steam, I was edgy. I took a stroll through the garden, spotted bladder campion, sea campion, dog rose, the pink-tinted flowers of wild blackberries, spotted medick, mezereon, spurge laurel, devil's trumpet, monkshood, deadly nightshade, hemlock. The carnations on Mama's grave had perked up. She was evidently good nourishment.

I took care over my ablutions. I would present myself as a fitting contender if it killed me! I even located some aftershave – 'Pour L'Homme', one of Leodora's last gifts. I selected my most elegant outfit – navy suit, lemon silk shirt, burgundy waistcoat and rose-madder dicky. According to Leodora, it rendered me a prince. (We had been invited to a theatre opening, though Leodora had to bow out at the last minute. The outfit was bought around the time of abundant gifts – clothing, cuff links, toiletries – arriving by courier and exquisitely wrapped, always a card enclosed with love and apologies that she could not be with me.) Final check in the mirror – a prince, on the outside, at least.

Then what a shock when, having poured myself a Scotch, I called up for you to join me and in the shadows of the landing it was her! All dolled up for dinner and dancing at the Halcyon! My bird, what dark motive led you to wear one of Mama's old dresses?

'You don't mind, Erskine? I found it in one of the boxes in the attic.'

As you came down stairs, slowly, queenly, again – that bright defiance in your eyes.

'No. Yes. I cannot recall Mama wearing it. It must be years old.'

But I might have minded, my bird. And it might have been cruel of you.

The dress was elegant. It suited you. Perfectly. The nap of the mink-brown velvet had worn in places, like the coat of a wild, hard-lived beast. The long sleeves finished in a point which extended over your hands, like the stretched jaws of two snakes as you held the tumbler of Scotch, adding to your overall animal look. You were wearing more than your usual hint of make-up. Your lipstick was fresh blood. Your mouth a new wound. And, most striking, or disconcerting: the low and, more noticeable, gaping unfilled area of your *décolletage* – the effect recalling the skin of a dead fox I had seen in the fields, the innards eaten out but the skin, save for the point of entry at the stomach, entire. Like a discarded fur wrap. You did not have Mama's bosom, nor Leodora's.

Oh, but, that evening, how like Leodora you were! Was it that regal poise (on account of those high heels, perhaps)? Was it the tiny flicks of eyeliner giving your eyes a feline vixen quality?

You asked whether I had found a pendant. A heart. You had lost a heart from your necklace. No. I hadn't. And a necklace would have complemented the dress, would have detracted from the disturbing expanse of skin. I willed the lacuna to be still.

We drank two glasses of Scotch. I pondered the reason for your apparent edginess. Were you worried that our guest might not come? Were you concerned I might not like him? Something was cooking – and not the pork and prunes – I knew it.

Eight o'clock. One minute past. *Voilà!*

I took my time answering the bell, deliberately delaying the moment of opening the front door.

'It's an honour to meet you, sir, at last.'

At last?

On my doorstep, the young man in the café. Indeed. But I felt we had already met, that I was already acquainted with the thin-fingered hand extending in greeting.

'Erskine, this is Truman, Truman Frankly.'

More than a small relief to see before me a figure so removed from the hero of film and fable, of myth and legend, I had imagined. For this hand I took briefly in mine was small (small-cocked, then?) and almost feminine, the fingers of a seamstress, a pianist, fingers clutched tight around mathematical theory, fingers intent on picking the bones of truth. Even behind the thick-lensed glasses, the eyes were as small as a rat's, continually narrowing, giving that characteristic look of the often surprisingly highly intelligent. A clever, persistent mind, then, behind those confused focusing eyes. In the hunched shoulders, the beaky snout, there was a touch of the Frankie Deuce, of the health visitor. But the sibilance nagged – 'Mr Flessing'. Fless-ing. We had met. I knew you. But when had our paths crossed?

I poured more aperitifs. I watched. So far, no evidence of physical closeness. (I had already pictured you naked together in a summer field, upon silk sheets, on an animal-skin rug before an open fire. Ulva and a black shape, tailed and horned, grotesquely endowed. The black hairy phallus pushed right up you, my bird, until it protruded from your mouth like a swollen tongue.)

I had decided you two would sit opposite each other. I needed to observe your eye contact. I needed to know the precise nature of your relationship. I had to know whether you posed a threat, Mr Frankly. When it came down to it, however unprepossessing you appeared (and Lordy knows what was hiding beneath your trousers!), I started with a handicap.

The meal did not get off to a good start. You were allergic to melon, Mr Frankly. (And all that fiddling about with my baller!) I remembered there was some pâté in the fridge.

I assumed an air of nonchalance while we feasted, bounced my questions offhandedly here, there. What do you do, Mr Frankly? Where are you staying? Are you down here on business? I apologised for my cross-questioning, but we had so few guests at Boxwood, I said, it was easy to forget just how nosy one should be. My friend, you gave little away. You told me you were doing some research, that you were staying near by. Research? (I saw the charged look between you.) But you avoided answering with skill, returned a very hard ball indeed.

'So sorry to hear about your mother, Mr Flessing.'

You sat, arms folded, Frankly. Such a tight-wrapped creature.

Then you turned to me, my bird.

'I have told Truman about your wish to keep the matter private, Erskine.'

Really? So I could trust you, then.

'Yes,' I said, 'the village grows a long and tortuous vine. Gossip. Chinese whispers. I avoid all that myself.'

Mr Frankly, did you notice, when you said you knew what it was like to lose a parent, that all went quiet. I looked at you, my Ulva. You were staring ahead. I noticed your bandaged hand gripping your wineglass. I waited for the crack. Another bone. I remembered then, you had also lost your mother.

'In a way,' I said, 'in losing a parent, one has the chance to be reborn. Until you are truly alone, you are not fully fledged. Did you know that many species abandon their young soon after they are born?'

'But we are not animals, Mr Flessing.'

'No, Mr Frankly, Truman, no we are not.'

We had almost finished the first course. The meat had been on the tough side, as unyielding as the company. In an attempt to loosen your lids, I was overgenerous with the wine. But what tightly sealed vessels you were. Shell creatures. I thought of the limpet, *Diodora apertuna*, clinging to the slippery rock, peeping through its keyhole. I thought of *Nucella lapillus*, the common dog whelk, the one that releases porporra – I mean purpurin, a poisonous purple dye.

'Where did you two meet?'

'A party,' one of you said.

'Through a friend,' said the other.

'And will you be staying in the area long, Truman?'

'Perhaps. It depends.'

On what exactly? Just what did it depend on, young sir?

The desserts were a hit. Two helpings of plum clafoutis and summer pudding for our guest.

You, young sir, had a penchant for fruit puddings, for fresh berries. How fortunate.

Coffee and brandy to conclude, in one of the more cosy sitting rooms, where I had prepared a fire, where I had imagined your two young bodies entwined, wax pale, passion moist. Ah – but not too close to the flames, my bird. We did not want those wings to melt.

'You returned to Boxwood two and half years ago, Mr Flessing? It is an impressive house.'

'Erskine, Mr Frankly. Erskine. Please.'

Was it a good sign that she had told you about me? Was I to be flattered? You were after something, Frankly. I could smell it.

'Not any more.'

'Oh?'

And I would not give you any more. I was on the alert. Something about that 'Flessing'. Like an itch one cannot get at. But I knew you, Mr Truman Frankly, sir. I knew who you were.

Returning from replenishing the coffee pot, I was aware of the ragged-edged silence, as if the conversation had been abruptly torn when I entered. A fresh, still-singing wound.

'Truman has to go now, Erskine.'

And you did touch him then, my Ulva, or rather – and a more intimate gesture this – gripped the cuff of his jacket.

'I must thank you for your hospitality, Mr . . . Erskine. Until the next time.'

Ah, the next time.

As you were leaving, I thought I caught you whisper to Ulva: 'Will you be all right?'

There was no parting kiss.

I slept, eventually. Between my shoulder blades, an unreachable, persistent itch.

There was no post-mortem. You spent the whole of the following day in your room, my bird, only emerging – a will-o'-the-wisp – to make a midday sandwich which you ate in one of the sitting rooms. And the phone call. To Frankly, I was sure. I watched you through the crack in the kitchen door. Your face serious, tense. Your skin was unusually pale – or was it because of your hair, even darker now. Not blond at all. Red. Like old dried blood. Cola mahogany. Or was it Goncalo Alves?

My day was spent sanding Mr Pencil. Or trying to. He kept slipping from my hands. I thought of attempting the box. But the lignum vitae remained dead. Just a simple box! My sketch pad stayed blank. I could not even picture a design. Now this was a first. An unboxed monsieur was unthinkable. Strangely, now, an absence of guilt, though looming terror. I could neither complete the sycamore monsieur nor begin the box. I was in limbo! This could not be. I began to panic. My throat was tight. I could not swallow. I had to get some air. My cliff top.

Walking along the cliff path, I made a connection. My troubles with the wood might be linked to the appearance of our guest. Three was a crowd. Things were out of my hands. Mr Pencil was Truman Frankly! A spanner in the works. I sat on my ledge. Below, a full tide. I leant against the rock. Things had been so tickety-boo. I realised I had, through anxiety about meeting your friend, been fuelled by adrenalin, planning the meal and so on. Now, uncertainty. When would I be seeing Mr Frankly again? Would I be? How often? How long was he staying in the area? How long were you staying, my bird? Just then, a guillemot circled, alighted on a nearby rock, watched me out of the corner of its eye. A vicious gust ruffled its feathers, lifted its wings. But the bird stuck firm. The rock was beginning to chill my bones. I wrapped my arms tightly around me. I looked down to see that the tide was retreating, the tips of the rocks just pricking its surface. And it was then that I allowed it to seep into consciousness. I had known all along. The itch was easily located. The hunched shoulders, thin bony fingers, the letters, the phone calls – that 'Mr Flessing'. *Defier of Definition – who was the real Erskine Flesching?* To write the story of my life, Mr Frankly? What were you really after?

Strange, how anger can often still the soul, can calm the violent beating of the heart, reduce it to that point of near-death when the blood stops flowing, begins to cool, to chill, like the last sounding of a note on the edge of silence.

Play along, Erskine. Catch them off guard. A game of wait-and-see.

The guillemot spread its wings, took flight. But up there in the blue, its eyes were on me.

I took the long route back. Why had you not brought up the matter of wanting to write my biography? You had not revealed your identity. You had made no mention of previous contact. Something was cooking. I would have to be on my guard.

Just then, turning into the lane, two figures in the distance, embracing. Henry John Farquhar and Signora Pergolesi! And his lily-white paws all over her rump. And her still in mourning! Lordy Lord. But at this stage, nothing could surprise me.

I returned to find the front lawn of Boxwood looking like the back yard of Hackthrew's. A large quantity – a couple of hundred planks at least – had obviously been misdelivered.

They appeared to be oak floorboards. On the hall table I found the delivery note. The wood was from Farquhar's, not Hackthrew's. I called out to you, my bird, then found your note telling me you had gone out and probably would not be back for supper.

I phoned Farquhar's but the assistant told me Mr Farquhar was out. Yes, I had seen him. I decided then not to tell them about the oak. Their fault, their problem. I might even help myself to a sample. I mentioned the varnish Mr Farquhar had erroneously ordered. Was Mr Farquhar out of sorts? According to the assistant, there had been a number of such instances of late. Love, of course. Mr Farquhar and Maria Francesca. Love has much to answer for. I spent the next hour or so loading the oak into one of the sheds. From some demolished church perhaps. Worn smooth by the constant tread of the faithful. When I had finished, I sat atop a stack and drank a Scotch. Like the guillemot on the rock, watching, waiting.

3 September. A small chapel in the grounds of Boxwood. Not too ambitious a project. Return the wood to its original use. I put in an order at Hackthrew's for timber. It will be a modest construction. Simple, puritan. Room enough for a couple of witnesses, a small altar, a representative from the church. Oh, and a bride and groom.

Frankly, was it during that first supper when the subject of losing parents was raised that you told me your father had committed suicide? Something about a broken heart? Unable to live without his love? No matter. But around that time, an undated entry, a divertissement. I had become a little bored waiting for your next move. Here, listen—

A play within a play within a play, as it were. His last

work, never performed, of course, for it was never fin-
ished. A brief synopsis: young playwright meets mature
woman. They fall in love. But mature woman already
has a love interest. Though love interest disabled in some
way (?).

   NB: *Love interest = human curio (?)*

   Female only interested in what she can get out of it.
GETS LOVE INTEREST – THE WOUNDED SOUL
– OUT OF THE WAY.

   Mature woman and playwright live happily ever
after . . .

Should I finish it for you?

14

An Identity Crisis – Beginning of
the End – Last Night

Waiting. But not for long, Frankly. For after that initial meeting, you were a frequent visitor to Boxwood. As concerned about Ulva's safety, I now realise, as you were intent on getting answers. What did you think I might do to her? Did you not question your own safety? The hours you spent up in her room! Me, old Tom, at the keyhole, but no hanky-panky from what I could see. I let you come and go for a week or two, Frankly. Even provided refreshments. Hotel Boxwood, indeed! And no questions asked – at least, not until the evening I told you I knew who you were.

Then, later – what Ulva had to tell me! Even now, I can hardly believe it.

But first, the night you moved in. Listen, you could not have accused me of not cooperating. I made it easy for you. Gave you the room directly opposite Ulva's. Left the door wide open – and in you hopped!

What a change in you, my Ulva, that day, helping out with the laundry, making lunch, offering to go shopping, to help prepare supper – spaghetti and meatballs à la Pergolesi. (I had planned shepherd's pie but in the village, apparently, you had overheard the widow Maria Francesca passing on her recipe to the butcher's wife.)

My bird, you returned from the village scented with the sea, fresh, salted, and bright eyed, pink cheeked. You were wearing a long black dress in cheesecloth and a flimsy white over-shirt which fluttered as you busied yourself about the kitchen. You were a little heavy handed, banging dishes and utensils – it suggested a forced show of industry, though it was probably a desire to show willing, or was it nervousness perhaps? You were never domestically at ease.

Us two, in the kitchen. Easy to forget you existed, Frankly. I was mesmerised. She was alive that evening. She even made a joke – 'What goes up and down and . . .'? I forget. But it made us laugh. We were so happy—

—Not happy, Erskine. You were bemused, admit it. It was a ploy, this helping-hand malarkey. You know, don't you, than on the way to the village Ulva telephoned Frankly. 'Keeping him sweet,' she said.

You're going to have to tell him, Ulva.

I will, Truman, tonight I will.

Just be careful. He's suspicious. He knows we're on to him.

Don't worry, I'll be fine. Wrapped round my little finger.

You realised, Erskine, didn't you? Your fears now veered in an altogether different direction. No attraction between these two. Their connection was altogether darker.

What else could I do? If I did not let Frankly stay at Boxwood, I would risk losing Ulva. At the back of my mind – how to be rid of him?

—Admit it, Erskine, Ulva's fate was also in your hands. She was not the innocent she had you believe. Remember, she stole from you. More than you realised – ornaments, trinkets, things of Mama's, books, even money. All stashed away at Marcia's. And it was her intention to come between Mama and you. Such confusion in her mind – she loved Leodora, yet she hated her. And she was desperate to know the truth in order to put the turmoil to rest,

and get on with her life. A motherless child. Should you
have felt sorry for her? Not her fault that the past turned
her bad.

I thought you were happy, my bird. You were making the
mince balls, rolling the raw flesh between your palms – ah,
the lacuna! And the downy hair on your arms, raised as
though inviting touch. How I resisted the urge to stroke
them. To get near you. To the small hollow at your nape,
perfect for the tip of my tongue. You were wearing your hair
high, a cockscomb of Goncalo Alves (or was it Coataquiana?),
though blond-tipped, that shivered as you moved, giving
you a frivolous quality, an aura of 'devil-may-care'. But
camouflage, my bird, for beneath was a newly guarded self.
So long since you had looked at me. I was beginning to miss
that elusive bluey-green, greeny-blue, of your eyes. I thought
at first Frankly had got to you. But it wasn't only Frankly.
Mama had sown the first bad seeds. Mama had told you
about Ursula. And you got to thinking, if I was capable of
that . . .

In the kitchen, I pictured the cat toying with some small
furry thing between its paws.

You had your back to me. You would not look round—

'Erskine, it's really good of you to let me stay, but—'

But? You weren't going to leave?

'But I just wondered, seeing this is such a big place and
there are so many empty rooms—'

'Yes?'

'There's been some mix-up. Truman's landlady has double-
booked. Could he stay here? Just for a while. Do you mind?
Until he finds somewhere else.'

my, oh my, said the spider to the fly

She was taken aback, Frankly, that I should so readily

agree. Such a pretty confusion on her face – relief, disbelief. Immediately after supper (meatballs had never tasted so good), she prepared your room. Within twenty-four hours, Mr Frankly, you had joined us at Boxwood.

For a day or two I spent much of my time in my workroom struggling with a design for Mr Pencil's box. He seemed to me now such a worm of a fellow. Then there was the oak insisting I give it some thought.

I kept out of your way, my friends. It was not difficult. It seemed I had almost ceased to exist for you. You barely acknowledged me, save for the quick thin crescent of a smile, a brief nod in passing.

But I watched, I listened. Late one afternoon – pitter-patter, the clickety-tap of birds hopping along across a tin roof. Up in the attic, you two, midgety maggots worming through Boxwood's brain. What was it you were seeking, my friends? You only had to ask.

I only had to ask. I waited a couple more days until I could contain it no longer.

As you had taken to eating your evening meal in one of the local public houses, I decided I would have to lure my Hansel and Gretel with tempting treats – veal, mangetouts, baby turnips, new potatoes, lemon-snow eggs, walnut cheese, a box of chocolate-covered walnuts.

I suggested you might appreciate a little home cooking – no trouble, my pleasure, delighted, a little company for Erskine would be welcome, blah-blah. (See old Erskine, at his beseeching best!)

It was a meal tainted by the air of conspiracy, my friends. A bitter taste. Three of us sat around the table, candlelit but bereft of romance. What could we talk about? The food, weather, Marcia – your research, Mr Frankly? But at this last you clammed up. My woodwork? Oh yes, I said, my woodwork keeps me busy. I was thinking of writing a book on wood, I said, woodwork. I surprised myself, my friends. Could this be my next project? *A Novice's Guide to the Pleasures of Woodwork*. Then – horrors – there, beside my cutlery, a knife for my heart – Mr Pencil! I closed my eyes, looked again. Another aberration.

I brought in coffee, handed round the box of chocolate walnuts, had decided the time was ripe, when you introduced the subject yourself, Frankly.

'Do you have any recordings of you singing, Mr Flessing?'

'Yes,' Ulva said.

But I had never shown you, had never played any for you, was, indeed, unaware of there being any of my recordings in Boxwood.

Your face, then, bright with candle-flame, and guilt.

Mama? Mama had recordings of Cercatore? What had Mama told you? What else had she told you? I was thrown off track. And I did not like being pre-empted. I went over to the mantelpiece, stood beside the framed photograph of Cercatore which I had previously set dead centre. I took up the pose, chin raised, one hand on hip. I cleared the throat, took a deep breath, filled my large lungs. Ahem! And I gave you the opening notes of a song, one we all knew, the words having lingered long in our hearts.

'*Defier of Definition: Who is the Great Cercatore?* Tell me, Mr Frankly, Mr Truman Frankly, sir, tell me, what is it exactly you want from me?'

But it was not you, Frankly, who gave me the answer. Ulva. Ah, the look in those greeny-blue eyes!

'Erskine,' you said, barely a whisper. 'Erskine, Leodora was my mother.'

Leodora. Your mother. Your truth.

'Erskine, what happened to my mother?'

But I loved you. How could I tell you the truth?'

My friends, what can I say? You could not imagine the effect of your revelation – a leeching, a curettage. I could barely understand what you were saying—

all we want to know is what happened to Leodora

she could not just have disappeared

you were living together, Mr Flessing, you must have had some idea

Was I on trial? You told me, Mr Frankly, that some time after Leodora disappeared, your father – her play-man – committed suicide. Yes, I had seen the newspapers. The police had been on to him for months. Your father was an unstable character. There had been a previous incident, apparently. He had been accused of beating up a former girlfriend and remorse had led to a suicide attempt. A year after Leodora went, your father was found with empty bottles of pills and vodka (or was it brandy?), clutching the unfinished manuscript of a play – *The Eunuch and the Unicorn*.

'What happened to my mother, Erskine? Please.'

Your baby-Leodora hand, my Ulva, gripping Frankly's paw, tight, tight. Let go of him. Let go of it all. But you needed something. And I needed time to think.

'I have no idea what happened to Leodora after she left me.'

Entirely the truth. One could only guess. The secrets of the sea are deep.

'Simply, she left. I was devastated. A man pared to the marrow. Forgive me, but I . . . still hard to speak of it . . .'

I was reeling, gripped the mantelpiece. Such a pro! Such a thesp!

'But you must have had some idea, Erskine.'

'Tomorrow,' I said, 'we'll talk tomorrow.'

I excused myself. Went up to my bedroom. A short while after, you both followed.

You were to spend your last night together, in Ulva's room.

I did not even bother to undress. I paced. Leodora – your mother! The words flew madly about my mind like trapped birds. What could I tell you? In the early hours, I went out to the garden, kneeled beside Mama's grave. I leant, put my mouth close to the ground. I told Mama, I said, 'They'll not get me. Things inside your Erskine's head they'll never know.' The dead carnations shook. The ground swelled, undulated. Mama had stirred; was she reaching out to comfort me? Not even at the Mansion House had I felt so alone. Then I looked up at the house. Your light was on and then I caught flickering torchlight through the ground-floor windows.

My friends, it was a terrible, terrible act – an invasion.

My friends, you should not have broken into my private collection room. What did you expect? Her body? Ah, your face, my Ulva, when I caught you. Shock, embarrassment! Dripping with it. My scooped-out heart in your hands.

'Welcome,' I said, 'to the messieurs. At the last count, two hundred and eleven, two hundred and eleven messieurs, not including the sycamore and a bull's-eye of boxes – one hundred and eighty! You have opened many of the boxes, I see, discovered that each monsieur has a matching box, that each monsieur and corresponding box are unique in design, type of wood, dimension. You will note that many of the messieurs – take Mr Ebony, for example – are neither life size nor anatomically precise, although some, such as the American ash, a creamy-white, skin-coloured wood, a wood used for tool handles, pool cues, cricket stumps and baseball bats, could pass as the real thing. One such as this sweet chestnut, an unmarked protuberance, a mere testicular nuance about the base spheres – those with the simplest design are often the hardest to achieve. My current project, Mr Pencil, is proving a devilish fellow and one I cannot—'

Your face crumpled, my bird, like tissue in my hand. You were shaking. I thought you were about to burst into tears. But you were laughing! Laughing at me!

'I'm sorry, so sorry,' you spluttered.

You were holding the foot-long ekki in one hand, the exquisite keruing in the other. Both messieurs had taken an age and I resented the fact that you had taken them from their boxes. Do not touch! Do not touch!

'Put my ekki back, if you please. And my keruing belinbing.'

You were uncontrollable. Frankly was smirking.

'She laughed at you. Didn't she, Erskine? Leodora. Remember – what I saw in the bathroom. She laughed. And that's what drove you to—'

I left you. I returned to my room. Of course, you were quite wrong, my Ulva. But I wept. You had hurt me more than you could ever know.

I prayed for divine intervention. Act of God. A tempest. A hurricane lifting Boxwood to the heavens. A lightning strike bringing Boxwood to the ground. Just then, a trickle of plaster dust on my forehead. Was the old hound on my side after all?

My bird, when you came to me a little before dawn, I believed it was a vision, that you might slip under the covers, snuggle up. You appeared to float across the floor. Then I saw you, Frankly, in the doorway, on guard. For a moment I thought you had a gun.

'Erskine? Erskine?'

Bird at my bedside, bedraggled bird. In your hands, a journal – *my* journal, *the* journal. You had found it. You were holding it out like an accusation.

'If you don't tell me what happened to Leodora, we will take the journal to the police.'

But why should the police be interested in my journal?

'Nora told me she had found your journal and hidden it but she could not remember where. Nora read it, Erskine, read all about your confession.'

'Confession?'

'About the health visitor. You killed the health visitor. It's all in here . . .'

And then you read, my bird—

'Twenty-fifth April. So easy. Wonder it did not come to me before. An opportunity presented itself. Sky grey, ungiving, a promise of nothing. Not too many people about. One or two down on the beach with their beasts. Keep out of the way, that's for sure. A sudden and delightful image of the den of lions – a haunch, a torso, indeed the entire victim (injured already, of course) tossed into the pit and then the scrum of beasts, like the first day of the sales! The gnashing and gnawing, the licking of lips. Every scrap devoured. What a clean-up! A chance meeting. On the cliff top. I had no idea she'd be there. I watched her for some time, nibbling at a chocolate bar as though she wanted it to last for ever. But it wasn't going to last for ever now, was it? Sitting right at the edge. No other soul but me. She did not even turn when I was right up close behind her . . .'

It did not happen, of course. I mean, I did not kill the health visitor. I had only thought about killing her, I told you, had only imagined it. But I did not kill her. Fantasy. Wishful thinking. You said you could not believe I could do anything so terrible. And that pleased old Erskine, my bird. You were sitting on the bed, looking straight at me. But if I had done it, you said, if I was capable of killing the health visitor, then I was capable of killing Leodora.

Do you not think people can change? I said. Are we to remain the same person our whole lives?

'Tell her, Flessing.' You, Frankly, in the doorway. Frankly, if I'd had a gun . . .

I said you could have your story. My life. It was all in the journals. I would give you the journals. Every word. But wait, I said, I had something to show you.

The truth, my friends.

I went up to the bathroom. I locked the door. And so, Erskine, I said, what lies beneath the glass? I lifted the full-length mirror from the wall and removed the panel behind it. I took out the large box. I selected the key from my sporran, unlocked the box, selected the five journals entitled *The Leodora Years*.

Coming down the stairs, I could see you two in the kitchen. He was kneeling beside you. Your hands covered your face. Oh, not for the world did I want to hurt you, my bird. You must believe that.

I set the journals at your feet. You will find in here, I said, all the truth you need. How much I loved her, your mother.

I imagine none of us slept through what remained of that night. In the morning, standing outside your bedroom door, I heard you two whispering and you weeping, my bird. I breakfasted alone then set out for the village to buy the necessary ingredients for that evening's meal. It would, I knew, be our last meal together.

It had crossed my mind to call in to see Dr Foster for some tablets. I would tell him I was having difficulty sleeping. Then it occurred to me he would most likely question me about Mama. And I did not feel ready for that.

I had decided on a roast – a juicy side of beef – but spotting a tray of sweetbreads in the butcher's window, I quickly revised plans. Sweetbreads with cream and brandy. And a wild mushroom soup to start – flavoured with morel.

For dessert, fresh berry flan. Wild berries. Your favourite, Mr Frankly. I knew exactly where to find them. But a stone's throw from my kitchen! What a feast we should have! (Oh, I remembered there were tablets in the bureau drawer – barbiturates, four, two apiece, just enough to blunt the edge. I am not a cruel man.)

By the way, a titbit for you. I was crossing over the lane to the field where I knew I would find the mushrooms when outside the artist woman's cottage I saw the hound again. It was looking right at me, motionless, poised, stately. I stopped dead. Felt the familiar lurch in the guts, my heart a frenzied creature. Should I make a run for it? I glanced about for a suitable tree to climb, my calves tingling, already feeling the jaws in the flesh.

And then – ha! I laughed out loud. The beast was stone. Cold dead stone. A statue! Had the old dog met its fate, then? Gone to ground? Was this a memorial? I was still chuckling to myself as I climbed the stile into the mush-room field.

The meal, though elaborate in presentation, would not require lengthy preparation. (I had cut corners with a ready-made flan and quick-set gel. I did not want to be sidetracked by fiddlesome details. I would need all my focus on the desired outcome.) Hours to kill, then, before I set to in the kitchen.

I intended to pass a couple of hours with the oak floor-boards. The next and final project which had begun to clarify on the way home. A Grande Finale. The only conclusion. A task requiring courage and resolve. (But look – here, now – I am almost done! Such is the anaesthetising effect of memory on present activity.) Boxwood had a mortuary silence. But I saw your beaded bag on the hall table. You were upstairs, no doubt, still engrossed in the journals. To the wood, then.

I went out to the shed where I had stored the oak. The size of the finished boxes dictated that I would do better to make them in the shed. Then I realised they would be too heavy to lift when completed. I returned to my workroom, rearranged my desk and workbench and so forth, then sorted out what I required. (By the way, in the process I mislaid Mr Pencil – and still no sign. Think of him trapped beneath a plank or machine tool, broken, barely alive, in absolute and eternal agony!) The oak needed little preparation (like our meal!), just cutting, assembly, a little finishing. I had set out my table saw then decided in favour of my as yet untouched tenon saw, pristine in its sealed plastic cover, teeth as sharp as a young beast's. I wanted this project to be as 'hands-on' as possible.

At one point, you came to see me, my Ulva. Puffy eyed and whey faced. You wanted to discuss what you had read of my journals so far. There were, it seemed, discrepancies, omissions. There was no mention, you said, of Truman's father, the playwright. I assured you we would talk over dinner. All would be revealed. I said I was preparing a special meal. A peace offering. In honour of our friendship. My bird, I needed you to know that my intentions were good.

A lure, my friends. I could not let you run. Not now.

I watched you return to your room. Back to Frankly. Thinking, if only we could be done with Frankly. If only we could return to how it had been.

Another hour in my workroom. I had sorted the wood. Fifteen planks for your two boxes, twenty for mine.

On my way to wash and change, I noticed small piles of pinky-brown plaster dust along the corridor. I looked up, shocked to find large cracks in the ceiling. Don't give up on us just yet, old dog, I thought. Not when I am so near to completion.

I decided on a purple silk shirt and my purple velvet dicky. The occasion required a certain sartorial elegance. A final performance. Last night. I replaced the full-length mirror on the wall and surveyed a pleasing, yes, even handsome, devil!

In the kitchen, I opened a bottle of claret. I flexed my fingers like a pianist about to perform. And I began.

I picked over the mushrooms. (I must confess to being a mycophile. A pity, I think, that it is only the cup and stalk we see. In my view, we leave hidden in the earth the most interesting part, in shape at least. For how curiously testicular is the bulb – the mycelium, the hyphae – like small hairy balls!) Within an hour, the soup was made, the sweetbreads were glistening in their sauce and the berry flan complete. I had poured a liberal amount of cherry liqueur over the flan base. Such an aesthetically pleasing dish – berryful! – intense and velvety black contrasting with the blood red. It resembled one of those imitation, almost too-too-perfect delicacies on a confectioner's display shelf. I filled a bowl with rich yellow-crusted clotted cream. Feast fit for a king! For a prince. For a princess.

I was a little disappointed to find that you had not dressed for dinner, my friends. Though you had more pressing matters to consider, understandably. I opened a second bottle of wine. I could not think of a suitable toast. To the future? To absent friends?

To us, I said, raising my glass, to us.

The morel worked a treat. A master of disguise! Both of you had second helpings. I had been cautious with the soup bowls. Mine, although also of white china, had a distinguishing scalloped edge. Of course, I had no room for dessert myself. Not even a mouthful.

We ate. We talked. Although you will recall little of our conversation. I dodged, skirted, waffled, blah-blahed – your minds rapidly becoming too dulled to realise. You had read most of the journals, you said, but you could find nothing. No mention, even, of Leodora's leaving.

'One day she's there, the next not, Erskine. Isn't she?'

'Isn't she what, dear Ulva?'

'There. Not there.'

Oh dear. Oh good.

'A confession, my friends' (ears just pricking to attention!), 'a confession' (and it was the truth, my friends). 'I simply could not accept she had left me. I could not even bear to think of it.'

'But even something, what if something, something terrible, even it had happened, Erskine. I would like to know this, that. I must draw a line. Want to lay her ghost to rest.'

You wanted to read in the journals that I had done something awful to her, didn't you? What did you hope to find? That I had hacked her to bits and thrown the pieces into some canal? You asked me then, Mr Frankly, whether I knew how much your father loved Leodora.

Oh yes, Mr Truman Frankly, sir, I knew.

Three helpings of wild berry flan for you, Frankly. More than enough!

Towards the end, you were both slurring your words so badly I could hardly make sense of either of you. You said you felt dizzy, my bird. I said we ought to sit somewhere more comfortable for coffee. I led you, one at a time, to my workroom. You were clutching your stomachs. I helped you to the floor, where you sat propped up against the desk, you, Frankly, retching into the waste bin, Ulva moaning.

Then I turned off the light, closed the door. And I locked it behind me.

(Undated) *I knew it was to be our last supper, but I could not bring myself to dwell on this. I focused on the selecting and buying of provisions, the planning and preparation. I hoped with all my heart you would understand even a little of what I was trying to tell you, that I had, at last, resigned myself to the truth. You did not . . . you had never loved me. At least, not in the way I had imagined. At least, not in the way I loved you. I could not, after all, give you all that you required. I was not complete. Our love could never be complete. But this does not take away the fact that you have betrayed me. You gave with one hand and took with the other. Should I be gracious? Should I simply let you walk away? Yet the feeling persists that somewhere, somehow, you will always be here in some form or another. I cannot lay you to rest. I look at you and I see her and I see her betrayal. Is it her hand that has delivered this punishment? I could not let you shut me in the dark again. How could you hate me that much? Have I hurt you? What did I do? Raise a glass this evening to the future. Look at me for the last time. Reach out your hand. Though it is not mine you will take. Did you not know that it was you who made me, gave me shape, gave me a place, gave me definition? Now you have gone. Who am I? How can I be? All those I have loved I have lost. Nothing but black, limbo. I twist and turn within my Mama's womb. I can never become. Eat, eat and taste the rich dark flavour of death.*

> *I could never imagine my world without you*
> *I could never imagine without you my love*
> *I could never continue without all your love*
> *I roll and shift within my own skin*

Oops—

My angels, it seems your haloes have slipped.

Erskine's Box

—Erskine, Erskine . . . The Great Cercatore? Leodora? Tell. Come on. I'm all ears. Tell. And Ursula. And all the rest. All ears. Bated breath, ahhhhhhhhhhhhhh—

15

The Great Cercatore, Leodora, et al.

Leodora was always very abrupt with those fillies who had managed to sneak to my dressing-room door. 'Mr Cercatore will not be signing autographs this evening. Recordings and signed photographs may be purchased from the foyer.' She was soon to employ a bodyguard. No thug, but a surprisingly slight, though wiry and nimble, bald-headed young man who had trained with the SAS.

His name was M, as in 'em'. He spoke little, usually no or yes. He never looked you directly in the eye but rather at the floor, one hand stuck in a trouser pocket, the other hanging at his side, the fingers clasped as though he were passing a back-hander. He was no weakling, let me tell you, had a distinctly sinister presence, an intimidating air. I likened him to a black hole. His ability to fend off attackers contained in something small but dense inside him. M was even slighter than he appeared, as I discovered, inadvertently, in the artists' men's room during the interval in a performance of *Billy Budd*. He could not have known I was there. He had a rendezvous later that evening with one of the fillies from whom he protected me, I gathered, and was having a wash and change – 'tarting meself up for me doll', as he later explained. He had removed his clothes and underneath was bandaged. Like an Egyptian mummy. I watched through the crack in the cubicle door as he undid a fastening at the shoulder and began unwrapping the bandage. I was reminded of that (terrifying for me) scene in *The Invisible Man*. I shut my eyes. When I dared to look, expecting nothing, I saw flesh, evidence of muscle, bone. (An even smaller 'M', then – lower case!) When I came out of the toilet cubicle, M, or em, explained it was bullet-proof wrapping. 'It is bullet-proof wrapping, Mr Cercatore.' That and his reference to tarting for dolls was the most he ever spoke. One day, M disappeared. Vanished into the air.

So. Leodora became my agent. A sudden thought – first me, then her play-man. Was Leodora perhaps always looking for the child she had given away? Would it hurt, have hurt, you to know that she mothered me? For she found me, a little boy caught in limbo, in the relentless state of never becoming. Perhaps, after all, she was better at playing the mother. She found me, possessed me. She would let no one take me. The minute she realised they were tempting me with offers, she shut me away. It was only a matter of a few performances before the offers came trickling in. Oh, I must tell you about my first radio recording. It did not go out live, so I was able to listen to it later. We had discussed me singing my Oberon from *A Midsummer Night's Dream*. But Leodora did not consider the part of King of the Fairies the most suitable vehicle through which to introduce me to a wider and possibly more vicious public. 'There are those, Erskine,' she said, 'who would jump at the chance of getting their teeth into you.' She finally decided on 'Caro sposa' from *Rinaldo*. I remember standing – on pins! – next to the radio. I was far too jittery to make myself comfortable. At one point, I actually put out my hand, reached out as though to physically recapture the Voice.

Leodora had described the peculiar quality of the Voice as disembodied. 'As if, Erskine, it comes not from you, but elsewhere, outside.' She said I had an extraordinary range. As if the Voice had come from the heavens, she said.

My friends, I was but a shell – and the Voice glistening, pulsating flesh.

But I did not enjoy hearing myself sing. All the pleasure was in the act of execution.

The radio broadcast of 'Caro sposa' and a few other arias made the arts pages of three national newspapers. You would have thought the reaction would have delighted Leodora. Yet, as she read the reviews, I noticed a narrowing of her eyes, her mouth contorting as the teeth gnawed the inside of her cheek.

'They loved you, Erskine,' she said, 'they really do love you.'

She became preoccupied, did not seem to delight in my success as I had imagined she would.

I received a little fan mail, mostly from women, the letters ranging from the sweet message in a flowered notelet to the outright lustful. One woman told me that for the last twenty years she had been frigid until she heard me sing. 'You have', the lady wrote, 'awakened feelings and responses I believed were but withered and dried petals.' Another communication simply bore the word 'orgasmic' followed by five hundred exclamation marks. I kept all the letters in a shoebox. One day, Leodora came in while I was taking a bath and she stood before me, stiff and starchy, the box under one arm, her red varnished talons pawing it so hard I could see marks. She was holding it so tightly the cardboard buckled.

'I do not think, Erskine, it is terribly good for you to read these. You have such purity of voice, I am concerned about the effects.'

That was the last I knew of fan mail.

Around this time, I was contacted by two opera companies. It would entail travelling, touring, signing contracts. What did she advise I do?

'Nothing,' she said. 'I am going to build your own theatre, Erskine. Let them come to us.'

And so Angel House was built in the grounds of Elysium

Manor. It sounded far grander than it really was. Elysium Manor was a sad, forgotten place. Even Boxwood retains evidence, albeit dark and gloomy, of former glory, is, at least, inhabited. Elysium Manor was but an exoskeleton. Just bones, old dry bones. A building that might collapse under a hearty puff. A withered thumb, an unfleshed heel. And Leodora preferred to be at the full-blooded, blood-bursting, pumping heart of things. I was, I recall, quite taken with the delightful folly in the grounds of the manor. It appeared to be a round summer house, the door apparently on the farthest side. From a distance, the structure appeared to have an interior, a furnished depth. One could see right through to the windows on the other side. But walking round, one discovered that the windows were merely boxes filled with fake objects but cleverly placed so as to give the impression of an interior; the 'opposite-window effect' was produced by a small cut-out in the wall.

Leodora decided she would sell off some land to raise finances for the building of Angel House. Planning permission was not a problem. She had contacts. And it would not be on a large scale. Seating was eventually enough for, at most, a hundred people. A private audience of Leodora's choosing. Her cronies, mainly. Even the orchestra were friends. Not many have received such a gift, a guarantee – always somewhere to perform and someone to perform to.

Yes, there was some form of a contract. Quite artful, the way she presented it to me, after Angel House was completed, the day of its official opening in fact, a second after I had cut the purple ribbon. Snip, snip! Angel House was mine. But I could perform nowhere else. How could I be other than grateful? At that precise point, I would have done anything for Leodora. But angels, like butterflies become less beautiful once trapped.

Angels and monsters, my friends, monsters and angels.

I did not have my eyes open. I was looking through pink-tinged glass. Leodora loved me, you see. I mean, I believed she really did.

It took little more than a year to build and decorate Angel House. Leodora had engaged the expertise of a selection of internationally renowned craftsmen – stonemasons, glaziers, and so forth. The building was baroque influenced – giant fluted Corinthian pilasters framed the front, the keystones were carved not into grotesque masks but cherubs, and above the entrance grew a pair of spread golden wings. Only the highest-quality materials were used. The colour scheme was gold and purple. Purple velvet drapes, purple-and-gold Persian carpets, gilt-and-velvet Louis XIV chairs. On the stage there was a piano and a raised platform to one side for a modest musical ensemble. The three walls of the theatre bore fake fluted columns and the ceiling was painted midnight blue and convincingly patterned with stars. Along the two side walls was a series of breathtakingly vivid stained-glass windows depicting scenes from Greek myths, and below these what Leodora referred to as her 'angel piccies' – Botticelli's *Mystic Nativity*, Francesco Botticini's and Matteo di Giovanni's *The Assumption of the Virgin*, Lorenzo Costa's *The Adoration of the Shepherds with Angels*, and so on – as though she had rummaged around art's lucky dip and come up with any winged creature she could lay her hands on. She became obsessed – even the gargoyles sported haloes. On the walls of the Ladies cloakroom hung various representations of Gabriel's Annunciation to Mary, while in the Gents you could find Saint Michael slaying Satan. In particular, Bartolomé Bermejo's Devil, a nightmarish combination of armour, snake, dragon's wing, vulture's claw and four – four! – sets of pirhana-like teeth disturbing enough to have me relieving myself in the Ladies, and to intensify the nightmares of the mauling. Towards the end, I set to wondering whether the Saint Michael was not some cruel joke. I could not help but suspect an element of mockery, so fantastic are the demons in these paintings, almost cartoonish, laughable. Then who did not titter at the marble copy in the foyer of Praxiteles' (or what is believed to be by the hands of Praxiteles) statue of the god Hermes with the young Dionysus. I could find no connection, neither to angel or song – it had to be something to do with the Greek idealisation (and idolisation) of the body; that is, the body beautiful. Or not. And there I had it: the inherent private irony regarding my own suffering of which Leodora had full knowledge, then the double irony (no, not the pair of almost delicious testicles – figs, could you not taste, feel them! – but the missing member Snapped off like Jack Frost's pinkie!) A damaged monsieur, and reference scarcely veiled. Oh, Leodora, how many laughs did you share with your cronies at my expense?

Angel House was a heady mix of the mythological, the ecclesiastical, and the theatrical. And I, the Great Cercatore, was both puppet and saint. Leodora suited to a T the ring-master's top hat and tails, cracking the snaky black whip with relish. During the building of Angel House, I did not perform. (There was a query in one of the music journals – 'Has the Great Cercatore flown?') My days, at Leodora's insistence, were spent practising. To begin with, in her apartment, where I wandered uneasily, unhappily, from room to room. I could not feel free there. The place seemed to suck the Voice until I often felt depleted. Several neighbours complained. Then Leodora found me a small soundproofed studio not too far away, unused and owned by a friend of a friend. I have to admit, I consider it one of the best times. The Voice, pushed into such cramped conditions, was forced to expand, and the room to expand, so that tiny space became wide, long, cathedral high.

A small bare room, white walls, a piano, one chair. But

an intimate cell. Leodora also found a pianist. A Mr Snape. A bent shrivelled old man, blind, partially deaf, all hands. He used to keep his hands raised before him when not playing, the gnarled, unnaturally long fingers flexing and curling as though at invisible keys, giving the impression they were the last parts of him alive, keeping him rooted in life. The first time Mr Snape heard me, he raised his head, as though the sound were was located high above him.

In the whole time, he spoke to me once and apropos nothing. Had I not heard him speaking to Leodora, I might have thought him also mute. We were coming to the end of a practice session for a new opera by one of Leodora's composer friends. Something loosely based on *Love's Labours Lost*. A rather sombre, depressing opera, I thought. After I had finished the penultimate aria, fingers poised over the keys, Mr Snape said: 'It is a rare and singular thing. It has colour and shape and substance. It pours. It flows. A river in the sky, this voice. Given to you from another world. Such a rare, rare thing.'

My throat was indeed fleshed with velvet, with mink, suede, silver and gold. My soul flowed through it. And my soul was continually replenished by this sound given to me: breathtakingly beautiful, almost unreal, yet natural – how could this be? But there is evidence of such beauty all about us: like the colour and patterns of certain tropical fish, the printed perfection of a passion flower, the intricately packed jewels of pomegranate seeds, patterns in certain breeds (I mean species!) of wood – cross-section of mbembakofi, tangential mbembakofi, cross-section zebrano, tangential zebrano, radial zebrano, cross-section tampar hantu, radial tampar . . . and so on. To clutch at such beauty, however, to trap it, destroys it.

Angel House was a work of art. But, my friends, you cannot

cage an angel. You should not. To cage an angel is to invite silent and eternal darkness.

They must have thought me an innocent fool. But I am no fool. Neither am I innocent.

He was there, you know, for the opening of Angel House. Among Leodora's crowds of cronies. Like cardboard cut-outs she'd prettily arranged. They all clapped and cheered at a snap of her fingers. Bravo! Bravo! went her two-faced marionettes. Bravo! Bravo! Luring the animal into the trap. She had tied the doors with ribbon. She handed me a pair of scissors and a gold key. She stayed right by me, urging me to cut, edging me in through the doors. Like an animal nudging its prey into the trap. Once inside, I do believe, I was never meant to get out.

There was a cake elaborately decorated with raised icing in the shape of musical notes painted in confectioner's silver. On top of the cake stood a plastic angel. There was a tiny lever on its back which, when flicked, set the angel singing excerpts from the great operas.

I often imagined Leodora turned to stone. Even in her petrified state, she would retain the poise of a lioness, the head with its curling mane. A sitting-dog pose, the arms placed firmly in front, paws rooted in the ground, yet ready to pounce. A proud, immutable statue guarding the entrance to a stately home. Lifelike, yet as if the craftsman had abandoned his creation too soon, leaving the eyes unfinished, embryonic, where his finer tools might have, in scoring a little deeper, breathed sadness or, better, forgiveness – yes, an unspoken plea to be forgiven – into the cold stone.

Except that usually there are two statues guarding entrances – a pair.

Tired, my friends. So very tired. Have been working since dawn on this last box, the largest. I am a bulky fellow, after all.

So. The truth. Leodora. What you have been waiting so long to hear.

My final performance. The opera of all operas—

Swansong of a castrato:

Act I: Suspicion

Act II: Evidence

Act III: (What shall I call my final act? Retribution? The Ball in My Court?)

Act I – Leodora and her Play-man. Affair of the Heart tucked beneath the wing of 'Mature Female Mentor Leads Young Talent to Success'! Ah, but who was following their tracks, casting dark shadows on their dark deeds – Erskine Flesching, gumshoe extraordinaire! Eat your heart out, Frankie Deuce!

I followed the pair, one day, all the way to some seedy guest house in the North. Leeds. What a kitschy venue! Vase of plastic flowers in the window. (There was a fairy on a stick in the vase too, like a Christmas tree fairy – or was it a madonna?) A brief glance through the window revealed imitation tongue-and-groove panelling decorated with horse brasses – and there was a clock like a rayed sun above an electric coal fire. In one corner, a hostess trolley bearing a rainbow of liqueurs. Simply not Leodora's style at all. Oh yes, also on the window ledge a framed card stating: 'A Good Deed Means a Good Heart'. (Or was it 'Makes'? Makes a Good Heart?)

Imagine their faces seeing Erskine peering in like the little match girl!

Leodora had done her best to ensure I was out of the way, had suggested a particularly demanding piece for the next soirée at Angel House – the final aria of the new *Billy*

Budd opera. Solo for the soul, where the angelic, saintly, almost otherwordly Billy, confronting death, sings from the crow's-nest of the HMS *Indomitable*, as though already ascending to the heavens. Leodora had organised a number of sessions for me with Mr Snape. She was unaware I had overheard her making arrangements for the trip to Leeds with her play-man. What schemers! On two previous occasions, he had come to the flat on the pretext of discussing the script for his latest play, yet the manuscript had remained unopened on the coffee table.

Oh, I could tell you about the light in her eyes, the meaningful glances, the simmering passion – they could barely keep their hands . . . I shall not. I cannot. Will not relive . . .

I had cancelled the session with Mr Snape. Bought a ticket for the Leeds train, and a disguise – a cream mac and a trilby, spectacles, and a moustache from a theatrical supplier's. I carried a briefcase. I watched them board the train and sat in a compartment in the next carriage, my nose stuck in a library copy of *Emil and the Detectives*. Arriving in Leeds, I followed: to a café for tea and cakes, to a department store, the menswear section, where she bought her play-man two jackets, four shirts and a pair of fountain-pen cuff links; next a Greek restaurant, finally the cinema – Italian subtitles – where I left them, just managing to catch the last train home.

A long weekend, Leodora had said. Working on some youth theatre project. No, even then, months before I witnessed the precise nature of their so-called work, I had my suspicions. Leodora Ableyart and her play-man – betrayal. I do not have to spell it out for you.

But she slipped up, my friends. Leodora made a boob in taking her Erskine for granted. She misread my affection as naivety. I had been once bitten. I would not be gooseberry again!

There was a concert at Angel House. Leodora had been

away for another long weekend and had left a message on the answerphone to inform me she would be there. I had booked a table at our favourite restaurant, Mamie's, for after the show. We had spent little time together of late. Minutes before the concert was due to start, I peered through the gap in the curtains to see Leodora's seat still empty. The jewel was missing from the front of the crown. But I knew where I might find it, should I care to look.

The evening began with several undemanding pieces – Purcell, Handel, Bach, arias by Riccardo Broschi (composed originally, by the way, for his brother Farinelli, the great castrato). But I could not give it my all. I began to feel, not the bird taking flight, ascending, soaring, as I usually experienced, but a force within which was reining me in, attempting to ground me. I was beginning to feel anxious about the Merlin aria, the *pièce de résistance* which had been written for me, 'La mort d' amour' from Mervin Berlin's new and as yet unperformed opera *The Predictions of Merlin*, where Merlin confirms Guinevere's love for Lancelot:

> I saw the coupling, like wild wood beasts,
> I saw the plunging sword, and Guinevere
> the hilt, the stone. Blame this Lord of Death,
> Good King, for it is he, not your Fair Queen,
> who all betrays.

I had barely begun when the Voice faltered. I was aware of the audience shifting in their seats. I could hear the music in my head, but I could not produce the sounds I wanted to make. My throat was closing. And then I experienced the terrifying impotence of the nightmare's silent scream. I drew air into my lungs, felt it pushing inside me, as if everything inside was compressing, so I was but a hollow skin, my body a tube, a vacuum from which nothing emerged.

The musicians gradually stopped playing, the notes trickling into silence. I closed my eyes, bowed to my confused audience. Whispers. Muttering. Why doesn't he sing? What's wrong?

'Ladies and gentlemen, you must forgive me. I am not well.'

I left the stage.

People followed, calling after me. Was I ill? Should they call a doctor? I ran out of Angel House, down the long drive and into the country road. I knew there was a phone box minutes away. I ran. I phoned for a taxi. The taxi took me to the station. But I had no money. There was a woman in a café. Well dressed. Could she lend me some money? I gave her my address. An hour later I was outside the flat, Leodora's flat. They were in there, I knew.

Very quietly, so as not to disturb what I feared I would find inside, I let myself in.

They were on the leather sofa. Two naked bodies. Like snakes. Curling, coiling round one another. Through the lace curtain I watched, with a cold unblinking eye.

I booked into a hotel for the night. Each time I closed my eyes, I saw them, naked, writhing, the phallus, the full-seeded, bursting, ripe balls, heard Leodora's gasps of pleasure.

My throat was tight, raw. I must have slept. I woke head throbbing, my throat on fire. I lay in bed until the maids knocked, wanting to clean the room.

I could barely walk, let alone summon the energy for a confrontation. Had they still been in the flat when I returned, I would have feigned ignorance. All I wanted was to crawl into my bed.

There was a note on the bedside table. She apologised for missing the concert, knowing how much it meant to me, et cetera. She was going away for a couple of weeks. Rehearsals for some play. Be in touch. Et cetera, et cetera.

Was it a death, or a rebirth? I am still not sure. I got up only to visit the bathroom and for water and a little bread. I lost all sense of time. A beast had got its fangs in my throat. I felt its weight as it pounced on my chest, felt the wiry fur, the tight-packed muscle. Ripping my flesh, ripping open my throat. I was a rabbit in its jaws, its jaws working side to side. I smelt its stinking breath. One time, I was looking down at myself from above, could see the cavernous gash in my throat and, low down my body, the white sheets turning red. I saw the Voice, too, one night. It was dark – and in the dark a white-hot pulsing ball, hovering before me, circling, moving away, slowly dulling to red, dark red, black. I saw Cercatore too, beating his wings against golden bars. I saw Mama. I heard Mama calling, calling from far away, but not for me. Ursula. Ursula. Where was Ursula? Then I saw her, crouched on top of the wardrobe, evil goblin, huge head, thick, stubby limbs. She scrambled to her feet, stood hands on hips, rocking back and forth, laughing, laughing. I thought one time Leodora had returned. But it was her voice, just her voice on the machine. 'Back soon, Erskine. Soon, my love.'

As the Voice weakened, it seemed as if I was losing myself, and whatever made me what I was, my essence, soul, my very 'self', was rapidly seeping away. I was emptying. I would become a vessel of thin glass. For the Voice *was* me, defined me. I was held within its sound, its shape and resonance and echo. The Voice was all my joy and all my pain. Delirious, I saw it leaving me, a wisp of smoke, a cirrus thread, the shirt-tail of a departing ghost. It was a gutting, an exsanguination. All that I was, all that remained of me, taken in a slow extraction.

By the time Leodora returned, I was a husk, emptied, consumed. A shell abandoned even by the music of the sea.

We did the round of specialists – antibiotics, tests, acupuncture, herbal remedies, throat massage – laryngeal tension was mentioned. (I learnt much about the anatomical workings of the throat. You may have seen Leonardo's drawings. They may also have reminded you of the flaps and pouches of female genitalia. Indeed, the ribbed trachea bears more than a passing resemblance to the phallus. And, a pleasing detail for you, my bird – there is a fleshy extension of the soft palate which hangs above the throat. It is called the Uvula.)

I became stronger. They could find nothing wrong. But I still could not sing.

Oh, briefly, I think, Leodora experienced a little guilt. I saw it as she was folding the sheet I had thrown over the leather sofa, folding it over and over into one neat, easily packed-away square.

Why her? Why be rid of Leodora and not her play-man? You may well have asked. I have asked myself. Because he meant nothing to me. And because one must always look to the source, surely, always the source of the pain. And then destroy it.

They put a padlock on the door of Angel House. All concerts cancelled until further notice. Until my last, my very last song.

Intermezzo

Leodora had a face-lift – did I mention? 'Just a little nip and tuck, Erskine, dear.' She was unaware of my feelings on the matter. My horror of the knife. It was, I remember, around the time she met your father, Frankly. She convalesced in some exclusive health and beauty club. I visited her only the one time. She was wrapped like a mummy. I had little sympathy. Despite all she appeared, she was, I think, insecure. Hence the attraction for the youthful play-man. Her dressing table and bathroom cupboard were like the cosmetics department of Delderfield's. Here, an inventory for you:

Anti-ageing creams, thick cream for night, thin cream for day, creams for day wrinkles, creams for night wrinkles, creams to seal the moisture in, creams to stop the moisture getting out, anti-sun creams, under-eye creams, over-eye creams, creams for brightening the eyes, creams for soothing the eyes to sleep, throat creams, creams for knees, elbows, mouth, anti-cellulite creams, creams for fading liver spots, thread veins and general blemishes, creams for youthful skin, creams of fruit, sea salt and placenta, hand cream, body cream, creams for nooks and crannies, creams for greasy skin, for dry skin, creams for wind and rain, for storm and tempest, creams to take the shine away, creams to put it back again, creams for laughter lines, for crow's-feet . . .

Ice creams, anyone?

I had arranged the concert for the eve of Leodora's birthday. I had been practising all hours, whenever Leodora was away on one of her now all too frequent trips.

Months later, the Voice returned – yes, though never again to reach those giddying heights, those dark velvet depths. Suddenly, one morning, the conviction on waking that when I opened my mouth I would sing. The strangest sensation, as though I were reaching out to the hand of a long-lost friend, a friend I could not see through the thick mist separating us, but whose presence I felt. I took a breath, one small breath, and I took the hand. As I held it, I felt fingers pressing mine. A connection. I rose from bed, slowly, stood, reaching out with both arms now, raised my head, and I sang, I sang, I sang.

The song of my heart, my friends, the music of my soul.

By the time Leodora had returned from her travels, the Voice and I were properly united. Though it did not shine with its former full clear light, it was enough to convince my audience that Cercatore was back.

I made all the arrangements for my final concert myself. Every last detail, right down to ordering a diamante-studded white silk gown for Leodora and a limousine to take her to Angel House. My lioness had no idea of my plans. She had often pressed me as to when I would return to the stage. But I resisted. Not yet. Not yet, my love.

It was to be a one-man show, apart from Mr Snape on the piano. With a little persuasion (he was not adverse to a good malt, I discovered), he arranged the music. Simple, but apt, a loosely linked theme – eternal love, betrayal. I had written the words myself. A purely musical event unadorned by theatrics. Neither costume nor scenery. Simply Cercatore, the Voice, alone on stage, spotlit.

Picture, if you can, Cercatore beneath the one light, the whole of Angel House in darkness—

> I could never imagine my world without you
> I could never continue without all your love
> I cannot forgive you this pain that I suffer ...

The performance of my life, my friends. That night, the pure, white, holy essence of me. Cercatore. And, amidst all those eyes upon me, all those hearts beating for me, I saw only one, heard but one – Leodora's eyes, heart.

I took several encores. The stage was a carpet of red roses. After the last encore, I bade Leodora join me on the stage. She was, poor love, moved to tears, two tracks of mascara marking her cheeks. I told them all, right there on the stage, after the applause had ceased and the house lights came on. I told them I owed everything to Leodora. It was Leodora who should take credit for my success. I wanted them to know, you see, how much I loved her.

Somehow, we managed to pull ourselves from the throng. Although I had been quite gregarious, and not my usual reticent self at the after-show gathering. I had to ensure that all those assembled that evening would be in no doubt as to the depth of my affection for Leodora Ableyart. (Your father, by the way, Frankly, had not been invited.)

On the way home, in the limousine, Leodora took my hand, and we sat in silence on the long drive back through the countryside. It wasn't until we were under the bright lights of the city, when I could see her face, that I realised she looked troubled.

'I just want you to know, Erskine,' she said, 'I am grateful to you. For this evening. For everything.'

I believe there was a shadow of sadness in her eyes.

Later, holding each other in bed, I put it to her that seeing it was her birthday, we might take the following day off. We had both been working so hard and had seen precious little of each other. She took a little persuading, I might add. My bird, Leodora – your mother – was the sort of stoic workaholic who allowed herself only Christmas Day free from her commitments. She told me she had meetings, engagements, phone calls – yes, I could imagine, the play-man was a demanding fellow. For me, Leodora, then do it for me. I told her we could go to the coast. Just her and me. And the sea.

The next morning, we rose early. I packed a small picnic hamper – hard-boiled eggs, foil twists of salt, pâté, mini-balls of Edam, crusty rolls, fresh figs and bananas, a fist of ripe bananas.

I had suggested to Leodora she wear casual clothes and shoes. We might, I said, go walking along the cliffs. Something dark, I said, which wouldn't show the dirt. Navy or, better, grey. Grey. To blend in. Camouflage. Casual was a somewhat alien concept to Leodora. Her style fell, or should I say stepped boldly, into the category of 'over-dressed'. Think plural, think large, bold, brassy, big. Three strings of pearls. Gold buttons. She had a gold tooth, by the way.

At breakfast she appeared in grey slacks, navy polo neck, and dark grey jacket. And training shoes, which she had apparently purchased on one of her trips to the North. She said they were for the gym. (I misheard at first. 'Jim who?' I said. You could hardly blame me. I was on tenterhooks owing to concern over proper execution of my mission.) She had pulled her mane back into a neat ponytail. A hint of frosted pink lipstick. Nothing like her usual self. More honest, in a way. Leodora, without her mask, was an altogether more vulnerable animal.

The sky was clear. The forecast good. On the train (a first-class apartment which we had all to ourselves), travelling through the countryside, I almost forgot the purpose of our expedition.

It was while journeying through rolling hills, crops swaying in the breeze, through the landscape of carefree lovers, it was then that Leodora brought her play-man into the conversation. Such monstrous talent, such energy, and yet, Erskine, so vulnerable. (Oh, really?) What was it she said? Glass. He had the properties of glass, she said – fiery, molten, able to flow, to be teased, to be wrought, and yet, once cold, fragile, transparent. (Was that what she said? Or do I embellish? Whatever, it was the cold, fragile play-man I preferred.)

If I recall correctly, she mentioned there had been a previous suicide attempt. In fact, two. Wrists slashed the first time and for his next trick pills and vodka. So, the desire or inclination to self-destruct had been seeded long before I came into the picture. (Frankly, I will never accept responsibility for his death.) She lingered a little too long on the pills and vodka part but (and quite innocently, I believe) the idea that he had been within minutes of death had obviously affected her and because of this I was somewhat deflated. Had she been wittingly attempting to provoke my jealousy, I would have experienced a less affecting sense of rejection. I changed the subject.

Or rather, the weather did it for us. By the time we reached the coast, the sky was grey. Although, as we parked the car, I realised this might be in our favour. A case of inclement weather clearing the decks. It worked. No one about. Only a couple and a dog, a big black hound, in the distance, walking in the opposite direction.

A light drizzle made for a slippery walk along the cliff path. And a mist now, rising from the sea, which probably obscured us from the view of anyone who may have been down on the beach. Leodora was off at such a pace I had to frequently remind her to 'watch how you go, my dear'. She had rather large feet, did I mention? Manly. Not a bit like Mama's. Or yours, my bird. She was chatting away excitedly about her forthcoming commitments. Another tour of provincial theatres, presenting the Young Playwright of the Year award (no prizes for guessing who was in the running). All of which I considered a trifle unconvincing. A case of 'the lady doth protest far, far too much'. So we wouldn't be seeing a lot of each other in the near future, she said. I told her, in all honesty, I would miss her.

I chose a spot overlooking a horseshoe formation of rock to eat our picnic, at a point where the cliffs split into a ravine. Leodora, unfazed by heights, was most relaxed, munching happily on our feast, her large feet dangling over the edge. I knew that down below the sea churned and pounded. Because of the formation of the rock and the angle of the tide, even if the water was relatively calm elsewhere, down below us it continually raged.

Leodora. Those eyes. Greeny blue. I will never forget. Indefinable. Neither blue nor green. But which? Which colour? You could spend a lifetime looking and still never define them. Just like your eyes, my bird.

The last time I saw them, they expressed such utter, utter disbelief. But why? Why? they said.

But wait! A point of possible contention. The car. We took the train to the coast, did we not? So what is all this business with the car? It was a hire car Leodora collected in the town. That was it. Just after breakfast she arranged a hire car. But no. Too easily traceable. Not a hire car, then. We caught a coach. That's right. Now I remember. See? Memory does play tricks.

I could not believe how effortless it was. One minute here, the next – oops! Now you see her, now you don't. Like a trinket falling from a necklace. A heart slipping from a chain.

It was drizzling hard. She was shivering. She said she wanted to walk. I could see no one. She practically invited me to it. Stood right at the edge. Her back to me. Did not see my hand move out towards her. Tip of a finger, that's all it took. But she turned as she went over the edge. And her eyes – oh, such confusion, supplication. No, I will never forget.

Listen, my friends, there is a spot not far from here, a ravine in the cliffs you could jump across. But the fall is deep, sheer, and however calm the sea is, it's always a maelstrom down there. And whatever falls in never returns.

It was an end. That is all.

September. Plans for Boxwood have taken a dramatic turn – the place is to be demolished. It is falling down around us. So, the old dog finally lies down to rest. Listen, listen, closer now – deep, deep within – listen to the last beats of its old dried heart—

pa . . . pa . . . pum

pa . . . pum

pa-a-a . . . pum

The walls crumble, the roof is caving in. Us? We. Us two. Together, at last.

Ulva and I . . .

Everyone I have ever loved, I have lost.

16

Heartwood

—Erskine? Oh, Erskine? Not quite an end. See those two fallen angels – their truth is not your truth. One box remains empty. Now, answer – who is Erskine Flesching?

Boy Erskine, on the cliff top, his hand reaching out, finger poised to push, Ursula right at the edge of the cliff. Why, Erskine? Why?

Mama knew, didn't she? Which is why you had to kill her. Yes, she had read the journal entry about killing the health visitor, but she did not need her suspicions confirmed. She knew what you were capable of – not what you wished to do, but what you had done.

One night you were tucking Mama into bed and, as you leant to kiss her cheek, she whispered: 'Ursula. I know. I know what you did, Erskine.'

Be honest. It was not so much that you were afraid Mama would tell, or might already have told Ulva (and how could Ulva love a murderer?). No, it was then that you realised your relationship with Mama had been a sham, that Mama's love for you was lost with Ursula all those years ago. And that, that, you could not bear.

So. Over several days you put wood varnish in Mama's tea, disguising it with sugar and brandy. A relatively quick end. Sleeping tablets in her final cup meant she did not suffer through those last hours. Just before she slipped away, remember? Her hand crawling towards you, slow, a dying crab. Gripped your arm with unnerving strength. Her face was set, a face prepared for death, with last pride, composed, the jaw tilted. Her lips moving—

Mama? Mama? You put your ear to her mouth.

'Sing. Sing, Erskine.'

And it came back to you then. Not the voice of Cercatore, but yours, your voice, Erskine.

'Can I sing you the Angel Song, Mama? You remember, at night, how you used to lie beside me in bed and sing me to sleep.'

> Oh as you lay sleeping gently
> feel the beating of my wings
> take my hand in slumber let me
> lift you up and we shall sing . . .

Her eyes opened. Jewels in the mask.

'Ursula,' she whispered, 'your sister. I have always known.'

Erskine, Mama had known all along how much you hated your sister. Remember the piano, Erskine? They were always playing together on the piano. Once, there had been room enough for just you and Mama on the stool. But your place had been taken on the purple velvet.

'Time for your sister to have a turn, Erskine.' And Mama would pull you away, her face closed up so you knew it was useless to protest. But Ursula could not even play 'Chopsticks'! Couldn't Mama hear how terrible it sounded? How could she bear that plonkety-plonk? How could Mama smile and kiss those fat, shiny little-girl cheeks? Stroke those red curls?

'Oh, that's lovely, Ursula. Aren't you Mama's clever girl?'

You would put your hands over your ears, sing loud and hard to drown out the sounds, then Mama, still with her arm around the piggy body, not even looking at you, would tell you in that knife-sharp voice to go away.

'Shoo, Erskine! Leave us alone.'

Sometimes, when it was just you and Ursula, Ursula would

climb up on to the piano stool, crying, 'Lid! Lid!' She'd push the heavy lid up all by herself. She must have had some strength because you could barely manage it yourself. Mama used to tell you off if she caught you doing it. If you weren't careful, Mama said, the lid would come crashing down on your fingers. Once, Ursula forced up the lid so hard the surface chipped. But Mama never said a word.

Mama was out in the garden – you remember, Erskine? There was Ursula, standing on the stool, thumping the keys hard, hard. You were trying to read and you kept shouting at her to stop but she would not stop. Like clanking steel in your head. Like boulders crashing into the sea. On and on. And Ursula was shouting at the top of her voice. Her face red. Such a defiant face. Staring at you, daring you to try to stop her. As if she knew how much you hated it. Hated her. As if she knew, yes, how much Mama loved her, loved her more than you. Stop, Ursula, stop! But she kept on banging the keys with those porky little fingers. You put your book down. You went over to the piano.

All it took, one push with the tip, the very tip of your finger. And – BANG! – down it came.

You ran upstairs.

Silence when the lid came down. Silence at first. Her mouth open wide. But no sound. You were at the top of the stairs. She must have held her breath that long. Then you saw her come running out into the hallway, hands held up just like Mr Snape. Her mouth wide open. A dark red 'O'. And then it came—

'Aaaaaaaaargh . . . Aaaaaaaargh.' Then, 'Mama! Mama! Mama!'

You still cannot believe what Mama did. Or the way she did it.

You were upstairs in your room, lying on your bed. Mama came marching in. She took hold of your hand, pulled you from the bed, dragged your downstairs. Mama's lips pressed tight. Would not look at you. Pushed you into the cupboard. Under the stairs. The bolt was drawn across. Like a muffled gunshot. Dark. Oh, dark. Didn't know how long you were in there. You must have fallen asleep, were woken by the sound of the opening bolt. Oh, dark, dark in the cupboard.

When you dared to come out, it was night. Ursula and Mama were in bed.

Oh, yes. Dark. Pitch in the cupboard. But I was warmed and comforted by a quiet sense of victory.

How pretty. Such a satisfyingly neat, symmetrical image. When they raised the piano lid, they would find ten neatly chopped – severed – still-pink fingers. Splayed. Like ten baby phalluses decorating the keys.

 —But Mama had locked you in the cupboard under the stairs before, Erskine, hadn't she?

After Ursula was born, Mama started putting me in the cupboard again. Imagine, little boy Erskine, huddled, all alone, hearing Mama's pacing back and forth upstairs. Mama at her wits' end. What was she to do with me? Bad boy, Erskine. Why are you always hurting your sister, Erskine?

But the first time. After Father went. Went away for ever.

Pushed me into the black hole. Hard-faced creature gripping my wrist so tight I feared my bones would crack. Not my Mama. She was the hook-nosed hag with her bundle of sticks and poison, the ice giantess with icicle fingers and a frozen heart, the black-cloaked queen with mirrors in her eyes. Bad boy, Erskine.

Earlier that day, we had been down to the beach. It was late autumn and cold. So very cold that my ears ached deep and the tips of my fingers burned. Mama should have known it was going to be cold. She'd always make sure I was wrapped up warm. My hat and my gloves. But this time she'd forgotten. She had been forgetting a lot of things. Like when it was the housekeeper's day off and there was no food in the house. Four in the afternoon and Mama still in her bedroom. Whenever I knocked, she told me to go away and play. I found a packet of jelly and some dried fruit in the pantry. Days when I'd come downstairs in the morning to find her sitting by the window still wearing yesterday's clothes. Didn't answer when I asked for my breakfast. And sometimes, she was happy. But an intense and secretive happiness she seemed to covet, to withdraw as soon as it was expressed, as though her smiles and laughter were not to be shared. Times then when she was simply elsewhere, a shape, an outline I could not interpret, more than a stranger. Just as she was that day on the beach.

From the low rocks at the foot of the cliffs, I watched her walking along the water's edge. She was looking down into the shallows, arms limp. She did not notice, nor seem to care, that the water was coming up over her boots. I called out to her to come and see what I had found. She took ages crossing the beach, as if she had no interest. It wasn't a nest, she said, just a pile of seaweed. And they weren't eggs, they were stones. Six smooth pebbles. My eggs. We walked up the cliff path, and at the top she told me she needed to rest. I found a ledge where we could sit. She was huddled against the rock, shivering, staring out to sea, her mass of red hair a crazy halo in the wind. Once or twice she warned me not to go too near the edge. But I took no heed, sat at the edge, my eggs nestled in my jumper. I told her I wished it were summer. I told her I wished we were at the Halcyon. I asked whether we could go again. But she did not answer. Then she said: 'I miss your father, Erskine. I wish he was still with us. Don't you? Don't you miss your father, Erskine?'

I think she was trying not to cry. She put her hands over her face.

'Father's never coming back, is he?' I said. 'He won't be coming back now, Mama. Will he?'

She took her hands from her face. Why was I looking at her like that? she said. Why was I talking in such a way?

I turned away, looked at the sea. I was cold. But I was happy. She could not see I was smiling. I put my hands into my jumper, fetched out one of the stones. I let it drop over the edge. I watched it disappear into the white-laced surface of the water.

Splash. Gone. So quick.

I dropped another stone. And another.

Such easy disposal brings unexpected satisfaction.

I don't know why Mama did it. What had I done wrong? Had she decided on the long walk back home? She did not explain. Grabbed my wrist. Marched me to the cupboard. Pushed me inside. Locked the door. When you're locked up in the dark, it could be brilliant sunshine out there, there could be singing, dancing, a party, all sorts of wonderful things going on outside; there could be kindness, gentleness, forgiveness. But when you're locked up in the dark, whether it was for something you did or did not do, all you see is black, all you know is the badness.

Father gone for ever.

The summer house.

Tell them about the summer house.

Heartwood II

For what it is worth I have just watched one of my more violent shark films – *The Great White. Carcharodon carcharias.* (Arias – ha!) Yes. They move in with such swift, ineluctable intent. Yet how gracefully they move, changing direction with their fins, like birds dipping their wings. There are about four hundred species of shark, but new species are continually being discovered. And of all known species, only four attack human beings with any frequency – bull sharks, tiger sharks, oceanic whitetips, and great whites. As an eminent sociobiologist said, it is not simple fear; we are spellbound by our predators, we make stories, fables, we are fascinated, because it is our fascination which keeps us prepared, and to be prepared is part of our survival. We love that which pursues us, which is intent on our annihilation.

My friends, a little white lie regarding my interest in wood. You recall, I told you it began while at the Mansion House with Joe? Not so, my friends. But why tell you now? Perhaps I have hardened – Pinocchio Man! – for I no longer feel either guilt or remorse. And Mama is no longer with us.

My special relationship with wood began a couple of years prior to Mama sending me away to the Mansion House. Somewhere in this house, though precisely where I do not know, is another box (not another box, I hear you cry!), an amateur attempt at construction (I was but seven years old, after all) – mismatched edges, lid askew, the hinge an aesthetic boob (it was all I could find; father was no handyman, after all). A box, approximately thirteen by thirteen of Afrormosia or devil's tree (similar to African teak and possibly a rogue, a replacement plank in the wall of the summer house, for it was one of the few planks that did not match the majority).

After the 'peep show' – remember, I told you I had witnessed something in the summer house in the grounds of Boxwood? – after the activity had ceased and I could see the two bodies one atop the other, could hear his grunts, her soft moans, I realised that to replace the plank in the wall would be too risky. They would surely find me out, would know I had been watching them. So I took the plank back to my room and hid it in the bottom drawer of the tallboy. By 'hid' I mean put it out of sight. For though I could not bring myself to throw it away – I could so easily have pushed it into a bush or lost it among the junk in one of the sheds – I did not wish to see it. The wood had life. How can I describe it? In my hands I felt it, a vibrancy, a just perceptible pulsing. Why did I not throw it out? But it had potency – power over me.

One morning, I woke with the image clear in my head – a box. And I heard a voice, which I believed, in my innocence, was the voice of an angel – 'Make a box, Erskine.' Why a box? My reasoning went thus – I knew I could never get that scene inside the summer house out of my head. It provoked such intense and disturbing feelings, set up such an ugly mass of emotions – anger, guilt and, yes, excitement. I would make a box. To contain the feelings. Then shut the lid. By using the very wood which had, as it were, revealed, I would be able to negate those feelings.

Ah! I hear you exclaim. Erskine Flesching – psychotherapist extraordinaire! But I swear to you, my friends, all this was quite clear to me at the time. So, I made my box (sawing a finger in the process – here, see, the scar remains) and I kept nothing inside it, except those feelings—

. . . he was at her like a dog – two locked together – Father bare arsed – balls a-jangling – diddly-dangling – Mama moaning as if it hurt and I could not – no, I would not – see the fire in her eyes, the lust-wide mouth – down on the floor of the summer house – I could almost touch them – if I reached through the gap in the wood – oh, and this desire to pull Father right off her and wanting to stay there and watch and growing hot myself and excited and guilty . . .

Like larvae bodies of Pompeii, father, Mama, when I left them. As if I'd left them for dead. I hated him.

Time for another tool inventory, I think.

MEASURING AND MARKING
Aluminium rule (2), carpenter's Square (1), combination
square, (1), mitre square (2), spirit level (3)

SAWS
Rip-saw, coping Saw . . . coping Saw . . . coping saw . . .

and so on

17

Closure

I have just been down to the village. A most welcome breath of fresh air. Stale, in here. Already tainted. The beginnings of decay. Invasive. Like the scent of newly bloomed hyacinths. Sweet still, not yet sickly, nauseating.

I had to pop into Farquhar's for hinges. Butt, drill or soss hinges? I eventually decided on soss. Although a complex, sophisticated hinge requiring routed recesses, they are invisible when closed. It is important. The neatest end.

'And how is that dear mother of yours, Flesching?' Henry F. said. The waxwork mien melted into a smile – what big teeth he has! 'You must both come round for supper one evening. Maria Francesca makes a mean zabaglione.'

What a turn-up! Henry J. Farquhar and Signora Pergolesi a public item!

I told him Mama was in good spirits, thank you, that she had gone to stay with Aunt Frieda. (It crossed my mind that maybe I should pay a visit myself, go down to see Cousin Chester too. What is left of him, that is.) Oh, and on the subject of happy couples – last night, the most beautiful dream. Sylvia and me – getting married in the grounds of the Mansion House, in the Gethsemane family chapel. Mrs Bainlait and Mr Gelert-Bones were there, canoodling! Sylvia was a vision – cream silk and lace wedding dress, six-foot lace train. She held a bouquet of wild orchids. A thousand white doves were released into the air – and you, you were among them, my bird, white, pure.

I bought provisions – globe artichokes (four – all for me!), passion fruit, fresh figs, avocados, mince for meatballs, more sweetbreads, fresh figs (as I said), cucumbers and bananas. Then, on the way back, who should I bump into? Marcia! She is back at the cottage. (Good news – the vegetable deliveries will resume.) Apparently, her sister has made a full recovery. She enquired after you, my bird, and I told her you had gone away with your friend for a while – a working holiday on an orchid farm. (Do they exist?) She said there were some things of mine and Mama's at the cottage – books, ornaments, clothes. I'm sure your mother did not mean for me to have them, she said with a look of knowing and pity. She knew Mama was somewhat forgetful, she said.

Oh no, Marcia, I thought, no, she is not. Was not.

Oh yes, the concert for the Golden Years Rest Home is definitely on.

'You are going to sing for us, Erskine, aren't you?'

Am I?

I told her I would be in touch.

I took the coast path back home. I walked along the cliff to my ledge. I sat. There are places – havens – which find their way inside you, which are as much of you as you of them. Leaning back against my rock. Like settling into a shape, my shape. Sea, sky, birds. Below, above, around. Erskine contained.

I was thinking of Marcia's cottage, another, former, haven. I was thinking I might visit Marcia one last time. Saw myself, boy Erskine, playing dominoes with Marcia. I liked to set them standing in a long line, then I'd tip the first with my finger and down they all came, one upon the other.

Mama did not want me. Not after Ursula. Not after Ursula went. Marcia liked me to visit. I wanted to be Marcia's lost child. I almost was. Must have been what brought Mama and Marcia together. Marcia had kept the child's room exactly as it was – toys, clothes, books. A little boy, of course. My age.

Her tragedy. A fall. Sitting on the three-legged milking stool, the fire hotting my cheeks, toasting crumpets on a long fork. I was aware of Marcia watching me – a Marcia softened, made silent and wistful by memory. Eyes dry, but I knew she was crying inside. Almost believing in resurrection. But I was not her child. She knew I never could be. And Marcia was not my Mama. I'm sorry, Erskine, I'm a bit busy. Not today, Erskine. My visits stopped.

No, I decided not to go to Marcia's cottage. Some things are better left as memory.

Ah, my Ulva, I was hurting, tight with jealousy seeing you in Marcia's arms that day. Like seeing Mama and Ursula. And so I made of you a pair of coupling females. I saw Marcia's thick black phallus but only in my mind, for you had gone there for comfort, for tenderness, all that which I craved.

Now, where was I?

Here, fitting soss hinges. It cannot be rushed. Bear with me, my friends.

I have brought in the journals. Too many to take with me in the box, but I shall keep them beside us. I had intended to speak a little of my journals over our last supper. There was no chance. I have to admit I was not expecting the poison to work so rapidly. And you two had so many questions left unanswered.

You would have wanted to know why the journals had been written – I mean, as fiction, not truth. Listen, my friends, we are the very last to whom we tell the truth. There is no factual reportage. There is a world of difference between what we believe and what is. Belief is enough. Desires adjust to facts. Each eye sees its own rainbow. Erskine Flesching was a negation. I needed to be someone.

I might have asked you if you really intended to write the biography, Mr Frankly. But it was a ploy, of course. I knew that. Although I could have played along at the beginning.

Sent you the journals in answer to your letter and have been done with it. But I simply wanted to be left alone – to at last 'be'. With Mama.

I could have asked you, my Ulva – who are you really? I could have spent a lifetime finding out. (It occurs to me now, my bird, that I have not properly brought you alive. I was loath to. For the more I attempted to revive you, the more you reminded me of Leodora, though I did not want to admit it.)

Another 'by the way' for you. Possibly my last. While poking about upstairs for my purple velvet dicky (I can only go out, as it were, in the purple velvet), I came across my cache box. I have amassed quite a collection. Amongst other bits and pieces – a glove, a false eyelash, the pen of an up-and-coming playwright, a bus driver's identity badge, a pair of thick-lensed (glass cracked) black-rimmed spectacles, a curl of red hair, a canary-yellow feather. I shall put your heart into it, the pretty little trinket I found. I will keep the box with me, the way Egyptians equipped their dead with treasured possessions – like that quaint custom of putting the drinking bowl, the ball and the blanket into the grave with the dog. Oh, and the photograph of Cercatore shall go in – the only image I have left. There is another photograph slipped behind him.

See? Look, look now, before I close the last lid. Me. Me. Sitting on the cliff top, among the guillemots. Look, young Erskine, there he is.

I am a man in parenthesis.

I am closing the last lid.

Fermez – fermez les guillemets—

Author's Note

The castrati were an operatic phenomenon of the seventeenth and eighteenth centuries. Boys, usually between eight to ten years of age, underwent an operation known as orchidectomy (removal of the testicles). The effect was to halt the development of the voice; the larynx, instead of descending, remained in the same position, producing an unbroken voice, somewhere between that of a child and a woman. The boys were first anaesthetised with drinks containing opium, or put into a comatose state by the application of extreme pressure on the carotid arteries, thus cutting off circulation. They were plunged into a milk bath to soften the genitals, then the testicles were removed (with a knife). The operation could cause haemorrhaging, or infection, could even be lethal, and some boys lost their voices altogether. The physical changes in these castrated males were dramatic. There was, of course, no Adam's apple, and the lack of testosterone meant the female hormones were overactivated, which led to breast development and a tendency to obesity. Overactivity of the growth hormone, because the action of the pituitary gland was not counterbalanced by testosterone, meant they were taller than average. There was little or no body hair, but usually a thickening of hair on the head. The sexual organ was small, but a level of sexual relations could be enjoyed.

The castrati were usually from humble beginnings. Parents were enticed by the promise of a glittering career for their son and the resulting financial rewards. Although famous castrati such as Crescentini, Vittori, Cavali and Farinelli achieved the status of our present-day pop stars, castration itself did not guarantee success. Training at such special establishments as the Neapolitan Conservatories was long and arduous, involving hours of daily practice in breathing and vocal technique for many, many years. But even this was no guarantee of a lucrative career.

The castration was usually veiled in secrecy and lies. Excuses such as a riding accident, a kick to the groin, or a mauling by an animal were often given, and there is documentation which suggests that many castrati were unclear as to the origin of their fate. For how could a parent justify such extreme and irreversible mutilation of their child's body? A mutilation which not only interfered with the physical development of their son, but with his very sense of self?

That the castrati escaped definition, were not man, woman or child (yet possessed qualities of all), was part of their attraction. Their sexual ambiguity and disturbing androgynous beauty had a profound effect on women. Perhaps their voices had such power and emotional intensity because they had no other means of fulfilment. Surely, there must have been bitterness against those who had taken from them? Many castrati suffered depression throughout their lives and many never knew exactly how or why they had been castrated at such a tender age. They had, after all, been deprived of normal relationships, of progeny, of their maleness, of their very identity.

If they had not been able to express their emotions through their voice, who knows what such suppression may have led them to? Who knows what darkness lay in their souls?

Of course, whatever darkness there was, the seeds may have been planted long, long before the physical castration.

Bibliography

Young Explorer's Guide to the Seashore
Haute Cuisine
Young Biologist's Journey through the Body
Idiot's Guide to Ornithology
The Tinderbox and Other Stories
Beginner's Guide to the Opera
John Henry Farquhar's Book of Tools
National Geography, May 1957–June 1963
Sharks, Sharks and More Sharks
Who Was Cavali? – Life and Loves of the Great Castrato
   (with illustrations)

All books borrowed, with kind permission, from the
Gethsemane family library

One Moment Later

Three of us, on the beach, Mama in her purple dress, the wind coming off the sea, whipping it up and making it billow and pulse – she had the look of some giant squid. The long skirt pulsing and puffing up as if she were moving through the deep. A tentacle reached out to a fish, a small bright orange fish. And me, in the shadows, one of those darting, hiding, transparent creatures in the rock pools.

Looking up at the cliffs now, I see the birds on the ledges, hundreds of them, all nestling together, hear their calling – 'plee-o, plee-o'.

I start to climb and she follows behind me. I can hear Mama calling out: 'Look after her, Erskine. It's too high. It's dangerous up there. She might fall.'

Mama is coming up the cliff path now. She will meet us at the top.

At the top, now, on the ledge, the smooth stone, back against the rock and waiting for Mama. Ursula is standing right at the edge and for one moment, just long enough, the ice melts and I slip through the crack into the space between Ursula and Mama.

She's calling at the birds, Ursula, flapping her arms. And I move now, slowly, slowly, and reach out my hand, reaching out and almost touching the frill of her orange bather.

Someone behind me. Mama. Mama coming along the path. She calls out and I turn. And now I see the cold dead eye of the box camera.

The guillemots circle around me.

'I'm here, Mama, Erskine.'
Here I am.

Letter from Lenora Flesching to Charles Gethsemane

Boxwood
1 April

My dear Charles,

Forgive me for writing to you. I know that ten years ago when we last met (can it really be ten years?), the agreement was that we should never again have contact, but I do not know who else I can turn to.

I fear I must come straight to the point. There is no easy way of putting this. Charles, it is as if Erskine has become a stranger to me. A dangerous stranger. It is such a terrible thing for a mother to have to admit about her own son, but I have to say that I am almost afraid of him. And I am afraid of what he might do to Ursula. The way he looks at her, with such venom in his eyes. And the way he looks at me. I have not told anyone of this until now, but I am sure, indeed I know, that Erskine is capable of bad things. Once, although I was not there to witness it, and I so much wanted to believe it was an accident, he let the piano lid fall on little Ursula's hands. Fortunately there were no broken bones, but she was so tiny, her hands, her little fingers, so tiny. Charles, she must have suffered so much pain. And there have been other things. He seems to hate her so much. Why? Why? I have tried so very hard to be fair. But I think the hatred was there, inside him, even before Ursula was born. When I was pregnant, we had taken a picnic up to the cliff path and I was lying on the grass and Erskine ran at me and jumped hard, hard, with his full weight on my stomach. As

305

if he was trying to get rid of the baby before it was born. And I have other suspicions in my head I don't wish to think about, but I cannot stop these thoughts. About John's death. I still cannot believe he took his own life. I know he was unsettled because of his father's business going under, and he was drinking more than usual, but I would swear he had no wish to take his own life, to leave us. When he came back home that last time, after sorting out his father's company in America, I really thought, at last, he and I could live peacefully together. I thought the three of us – me, John, Erskine – could live as a family. John swore he would never leave us again. He told me he loved me. And he seemed so happy, so content. And then, when he knew I was expecting a baby, he was overjoyed – truly. I do not think I shall ever get over seeing his body down on the rocks. I thought he had finally managed to stop drinking. The autopsy revealed a high level of alcohol in his blood. He must have lost his footing up on the cliffs, gone over the edge.

Forgive me, Charles, I don't know why I am telling you all this. I just feel so low, so afraid. The other day Erskine told me, in a fit of rage, that he hated me, that I was not his mother. He said he was adopted. I tried telling myself this is what children often say, simply a stage in growing up. Cross my heart, I have kept to my promise. Erskine has no knowledge – and never will he know – that you are his father.

Now, my request. A plea from the heart. I know you are away on business for much of the time, but Charles, do you think it would be possible for Erskine to come and stay at the Mansion House for a while? Just for a few months? I feel it would benefit Ursula too. She is becoming nervous and there have been terrible nightmares. Just so that we may have a little reprieve? I was wondering if Mrs Bainlait was still with you? Could she keep an eye on Erskine? Of course, I would pay. Perhaps a tutor could be arranged and I could tell Erskine it was for study purposes.

Oh dear. This seems quite wrong. But I really am worried. For Ursula, about what Erskine might do. I apologise for not expressing myself very well – but I am not myself at all. I am sorry. I do not know what else to say. Other than I will understand and will never hold it against you, Charles, if you feel unable to help. You will always have a special place in my heart.

Yours,

Lenora

PS. There is good in Erskine – the good that is in you is in him somewhere. He is not, essentially, a bad person.

Postscript

If I confessed to killing my father, would it mean I am bad?
It could mean I loved my mother too much. Or not enough?
Sometimes, it is easier to confess to what we have not done,
in order to escape the confession of our one true sin.

My heart, believe me, is essentially good.

JULIAN BRANSTON

The Eternal Quest

In seventeenth-century Valladolid, Spain's new capital, Miguel Cervantes is busy writing his comic masterpiece, *Don Quixote*. Issued in instalments, it is fast making him the most popular author in the country when a series of blows strikes: Cervantes discovers that Don Quixote is more than a figment of his imagination; a jealous rival concocts a scheme to thwart Cervantes's success; and he is smitten by a beautiful, influential – but unavailable – widow.

This sparkling tale of crazed knights, thwarted love and literary rivalry is set against the background of a mighty empire suffering from a century of reckless wars and with a ruling hierarchy stultified by patronage and ritual. Peopled with an engagingly idiosyncratic cast that ranges from a Machiavellian duke to a misanthropic poacher, it is imbued with the spirit, verve and humour of the great novel to which it pays playful tribute.

'[A] lively pastiche that includes fine Cervantian comic stereotypes, feisty, foul-mouthed Iberian babes, and a vivid portrait of 17th-century Spain . . . Branston has taken Cervantes's playfulness to a new level'
Guardian

'There is much here to enjoy . . . [his] love of Cervantes shines through this affectionate homage.'
Sunday Telegraph

'An inventive, beautifully written piece of literary fiction.'
Good Book Guide

SCEPTRE

MIRANDA HEARN

A Life Everlasting

In 1784, at the age of thirty-six, James Mallen is murdered on the banks of the Thames. His restless spirit lives on, searching for Augusta Corney, the woman who in life enthralled him and who now holds the key to his death. Yet she constantly dances out of reach, while around him gather other spirits, like Queen Caroline, still bewailing her ill-treatment by the King, and his young friend Franny Bright, still keeping an eye out for him.

Woven into the tale of Mallen's quest is the parallel narrative of his life: of his rise through London's middle classes as a physician-midwife, his marriage, and his fateful encounter with Augusta Corney. Together they form a captivating narrative, as vivid in its depiction of the real world of 18th and 19th century London as of the disembodied passions of the dead, as irreverently humorous as it is achingly sad.

'I was taken with it from the opening page. Her eighteenth century seems totally convincing to me . . . I found it fascinating to see how she built up a vision of a world beyond this which was both sinister and full of pathos, and I admire the indirection and subtlety of her writing. She has a beautiful and distinctive style, and I think I should read with pleasure anything she wrote.'
Hilary Mantel

'Hearn's writing is characterful, witty and wise, and she does a great thing in making history seem tangible and dense, a sea in which all of time mixes.'
Victoria Lane, *Daily Telegraph*

SCEPTRE